Peter Lovesey began his writing career with *Wobble to Death* in 1970, introducing Sergeant Cribb, the Victorian detective, who went on to feature in seven more books and two television series. Lovesey's novels and short stories have won him awards all over the world, including both the Gold and Silver Daggers of the Crime Writers' Association, of which he was Chairman in 1991–2. In 2000 he joined the elite list of recipients of the Cartier Diamond Dagger Award. He lives in Chichester.

By the same author

WOBBLE TO DEATH
THE DETECTIVE WORE SILK DRAWERS
ABRACADAVER
MAD HATTER'S HOLIDAY
INVITATION TO A DYNAMITE PARTY
A CASE OF SPIRITS
SWING, SWING TOGETHER
WAXWORK
THE FALSE INSPECTOR DEW
KEYSTONE
ROUGH CIDER
BERTIE AND THE TINMAN
ON THE EDGE
BERTIE AND THE SEVEN BODIES
BERTIE AND THE CRIME OF PASSION
THE LAST DETECTIVE
DIAMOND SOLITAIRE
THE SUMMONS
BLOODHOUNDS
UPON A DARK NIGHT
THE VAULT
THE REAPER
DIAMOND DUST
THE CIRCLE

Short stories

BUTCHERS AND OTHER STORIES OF CRIME
THE CRIME OF MISS OYSTER BROWN AND OTHER STORIES
DO NOT EXCEED THE STATED DOSE
THE SEDGEMOOR STRANGLER AND OTHER STORIES OF CRIME

The House Sitter

Peter Lovesey

TIME WARNER
BOOKS

TIME WARNER BOOKS

First published in Great Britain in 2003 by Little, Brown

This edition published by Time Warner Paperbacks in 2004
Reprinted 2004
Reprinted by Time Warner Books in 2005 (twice), 2006

A CIP catalogue record for this book
is available from the British Library.

ISBN-13: 978-0-7515-3458-0
ISBN-10: 0-7515-3458-7

Typeset in New Baskerville by
Palimpsest Book Production Limited,
Polmont, Stirlingshire
Printed and bound in Great Britain by
Mackays of Chatham plc, Chatham, Kent

Time Warner Books
An imprint of
Time Warner Book Group UK
Brettenham House
Lancaster Place
London WC2E 7EN

www.twbg.co.uk

To Tom and Marie O'Day and all the others in the
Malice Domestic family

After lunch Georgina Dallymore, the Assistant Chief Constable at Bath, took an hour off work and drove out to the cattery at Monkton Combe. She'd decided to board Sultan while she was away on holiday. She needed to be sure it was a place where he would be treated kindly. He wouldn't get the devoted attention he got at home, but he was entitled to some comfort, and she was willing to pay. She'd brought along the framed photo she kept on her desk, just to make clear how special he was.

She expected a better response than she got.

'He's a long-hair, then,' Mrs O'Leary, the cattery owner, noted without a word about his good looks. 'He'll need grooming.'

'Every morning.'

'Getting down to basics . . .'

'Yes?'

'Getting down to basics, has he been done?'

Georgina frowned. Even an officer of her rank didn't always catch on immediately. 'I don't follow you.'

Mrs O'Leary gave a wink, raised two fingers and mimed the action of scissors. 'I won't have rampant males making nuisances of themselves in Purradise.'

This was the moment Georgina decided there was no way Sultan would be happy in Purradise. 'He was neutered as a kitten, if that's what you mean.'

'I should have known, looking at the picture. He's too

dopey-looking for a stud. Is he up to date with his injections?'

'Fully.'

'Any problems I should know about? Parasites?'

'I don't think I need take up any more of your time,' Georgina said, putting the photo away. 'I've several other addresses to visit.'

'Please yourself. You won't find one better than this.'

'I'll make up my own mind, thank you.'

'Where are you off to, anyway?'

'That's really no concern of yours.'

'I'm not asking which catteries you're trying. I'm talking about your holiday.'

Georgina couldn't resist telling Mrs O'Leary. 'Egypt. The Nile cruise, as a matter of fact.'

'Not bad. I thought you police were underpaid.'

'It's my first overseas trip in ten years.'

'They treated their cats like gods, the Ancient Egyptians. They were more important than people. Did you know that?'

'Yes, and I applaud it. Good afternoon.' Georgina turned and walked with dignity towards her car.

'Stuck-up cow,' Mrs O'Leary said. 'You'll end up paying through the nose for some house sitter who runs up enormous phone bills and burns holes in your carpet.'

But she wasn't heard.

1

If you were planning a murder and wanted a place to carry it out, a beach would do nicely.

Think about it. People lie about on towels with no more protection than a coating of sunscreen. For weapons, there are stones of all weights and sizes, pieces of driftwood, rope and cable. When it comes to disposing of the body, you're laughing. If a hole in the sand doesn't suit, then with a bit more effort you can cover the victim with stones. After the deed is done, the tide comes in and washes everything clean. Your footprints, fingerprints, traces of DNA, all disappear. Scenes of crime officers, eat your hearts out.

Every half-decent weekend in summer, the shoreline at Wightview Sands on the Sussex coast is lined with glistening (and breathing) bodies. This stretch of beach is estate-owned and spared from the usual seaside line-up of amusement arcades and food outlets. The sand is clean and there is plenty of it, in sections tidily divided by wooden groynes. Lifeguards keep watch from a raised platform. There are no cliffs, no hidden rocks, no sharks.

This Sunday morning in June, the Smith family, Mike, Olga and their five-year-old daughter, Haley, arrived shortly before eleven after an uncomfortable drive from Crawley, paid their dues at the gate, and got a first sight of the hundreds of parked cars on either side of the narrow road that runs beside the beach.

'Should have started earlier,' Mike said. The heat had really got to him.

'We'll have plenty of time to enjoy ourselves,' Olga said.

'If we can park this thing.'

They cruised around for a bit before slotting into a space on the left, sixty yards past the beach café. Outside the car, the breeze off the sea helped revive them. They took their towels and beachbags from the boot. Mike suggested a coffee, but young Haley wanted to get on the beach right away and Olga agreed. 'Let's pick our spot first.'

Picking the spot was important. They didn't want to sit too close to the lads with shaven heads and tattoos who had several six-packs of lager lined up beside them. Or the howling baby. Or the couple enjoying what looked like a bout of foreplay. They found a space between three teenage girls on sunloungers and a bronzed family of five who were speaking French. Mike unfolded the chairs while Olga helped Haley out of her clothes. The child wanted to run down to the sea with her bucket and spade. The tide was well out.

'Remember where we are,' Olga told her. 'Just to the right of the lifeguards. Look for the flags.'

'You're fussing,' Mike said.

'Stay where we can see you. Don't go in the water without us.'

'Lighten up, Olg,' Mike said. 'This is a day out. We're supposed to relax.'

Haley ran off.

'If I don't get my fix of coffee soon, I'll die.' Mike went in the other direction.

Olga sat forward in her chair and watched every step Haley took. Whatever Mike said, she didn't fuss for fussing's sake. She knew how easily things could go wrong because she'd worked as a nurse in an A & E department before she got married. The beach was new territory. Until the child had been to the water and found her way back at least once, it was impossible to relax.

Briefly Olga's line of sight was blocked by a woman doing exactly what Olga and Mike were doing a few minutes before, choosing the best place to sit down. She was hesitating, taking a good look around her. Olga couldn't see past her. The woman took a few steps down the beach, spread a large blue towel on the sand, unfurled a windbreak and pushed the posts into the sand to screen herself on three sides. To Olga's relief, she could now pick out the tiny figure of Haley again, jumping in the shallows.

The woman took time to get settled. She took off her headband and shook her hair loose. It was copper-coloured and looked natural, too; right for the pale, freckled skin. She was some years older than the giggly girls on sunloungers. Around thirty, Olga reckoned, watching her delve in her beachbag and take out a tube of sunscreen and a pair of sunglasses. Finally she sank out of sight behind the windbreak.

Sunscreen was indispensable today, unless you wanted to suffer later. The light was so clear you could see the green fields of the Isle of Wight ten miles across the Solent.

Mike returned with his hands full. 'Where's the kid? I got her an ice cream.'

Olga pointed Haley out. 'You'd better take it down to her.'

'My coffee's going to get cold.'

She laughed. 'Should have thought of that when you bought the ice. All right. Give it to me.' Her own coffee was just as certain as his to lose its heat, and she was not one of those submissive women, but she didn't want another argument to ruin the day so she took the ice cream down the beach, threading a route through the

5

sunbathers, feeling cool drips on her hand and trying not to sprinkle them on other people's warm, exposed flesh. Grateful to reach the damp sand where no one was lying, she kicked off her flip-flops and enjoyed the sensation of the firm surface against the soles of her feet. She felt like a child again.

Haley had found two other girls about her own age and was helping them dig a canal. She didn't want the ice cream, or, more likely, didn't want to eat it in front of her new-found friends.

'Shall I eat it for you?' Olga offered.

Haley nodded.

'You remember where we are? Near the lifeguards. The flags. Remember?'

Another nod.

Olga turned and made her way back more slowly, licking the sides of the ice cream. The beach looked entirely different from this direction. The people, too, when you saw them feet first. She was surprised at where she'd left the flip-flops, much further to the right than she thought. She set a course for the flags above the life-guard post, beginning to doubt if Haley would have the sense to do the same. Before spotting Mike, she passed the woman with the copper hair, now down to a white two-piece and spreading sunscreen on her middle. Their eyes met briefly. She had a nice smile.

'She all right?' Mike asked, propping himself on an elbow.

'She's with some other girls, digging in the sand. Can you see?'

'What's she wearing?'

Typical Mike, she thought. 'Navy and white.'

'Right. I can see.' He lay back on the sand and closed his eyes.

Typical Mike.

Olga lifted the lid off her less-than-hot coffee, still watching her child. Bits of conversation were going on all around. A beach may be restful, but it's not quiet.

'I didn't fancy him,' one of the teenagers was saying. 'He's scary.'

'What do you mean – "scary"? Just 'cos he didn't have nothing to say to you. That's not scary.'

'His eyes are. The way he looked at me, like he was stripping off my clothes.'

'You wish!'

The giggles broke out again.

Just ahead, a man in a black T-shirt crossed Olga's line of vision. She could see his top half above the windbreak. He was talking to the copper-haired woman. From the tone of the conversation, they knew each other and he was laying on the charm and not getting the response he was trying for. To Olga's eye, he wasn't an out-and-out no-no. In fact, he was rather good-looking, broad-shouldered, with black, curly hair and the cast of face she thought of as rugged – that is to say, strong-featured, with a confident personality defined by the creases a man in his thirties begins to acquire. He was saying something about coincidence. His voice was more audible than hers. 'How does it go? Of all the gin-joints in all the towns in all the world . . . For that read "beaches". What are you doing here?' She made some reply (probably 'What does it look as if I'm doing?') and he said, 'OK, that was pretty dumb. It's a nice surprise, that's all. Can I get you an ice cream or something? Cold drink?' Obviously not, because he then said, 'Later, then? You don't mind if I join you for a bit?' Then: 'Fair enough. Suit yourself. If that's how you feel, I'll leave you to it. I just thought – oh, what the fuck!' And he moved off, the smile gone, and didn't look back.

Olga glanced towards Mike to see if he'd been listening. His eyes were still closed.

In another twenty minutes the tide was going out amazingly fast across the flats, transforming the scene. Haley hadn't moved, but she was no longer at the place where the waves broke. She was at the edge of a broad, shallow pool of still water. A bar of sand had surfaced further out, and the waves were lapping at the far side. A child could easily become disorientated. The other girls were no longer with her.

'I think I'll go and talk to her,' Olga said.

Mike murmured something about fussing.

She made the journey down the beach again, marvelling at the huge expanse now opened up. Men on skateboards were skimming along the wet sand, powered by kites as big as mattresses. A game of beach cricket was under way.

Haley looked up this time and waved.

After admiring the excavations in the sand, Olga asked if she was ready for some lunch. Hand in hand they started back. 'I like it here,' Haley said.

'Isn't it great? But it's lunchtime. Now let's see if we can find our way back to Daddy.'

'There.' The child pointed in precisely the right direction. Kids have more sense than adults think.

'Race you, then,' Enjoying the sight of her loose-limbed, agile child, she let Haley dash ahead and then jogged after her to make it seem like pursuit, until the risk of tripping over a sunbather forced her to slow to a walk. Already Haley had reached Mike and given him a shock by throwing herself on his back. Laughing, Olga picked her way through the maze of legs, towels and beachbags. The copper-haired woman, comfortable behind her windbreak, looked over her sunglasses, smiled again and spoke. 'You're a poor second.'

'Pathetic is a better word.'

'Wish I had her energy.'

'Me, too.'

Olga flopped down beside Mike and reached for the lunch bag.

Mike revived with some food inside him and actually began a conversation. 'Amazing, really, all this free entertainment. Years ago, people would queue up and buy tickets to see a tattooed man. One walked by just now with hardly a patch of plain skin left on him. No one paid him any attention.'

'I wouldn't call that entertainment.'

'Then there are the topless girls.'

'I haven't noticed any,' Olga said.

'Over there, on the inflatable sunbeds.'

She took a quick glance. 'Girls? They look middle-aged to me. Trust you to spot them.'

'I was talking about the way things have changed. Your dad and mine would have paid good money to watch a strip show.'

'Not mine.'

'Don't you believe it. He was no saint, your old man. I could tell you things he said to me after a few beers.'

Olga said, 'Let's talk about something else. When are we going for a swim?'

'Not now, for Christ's sake. It's miles out.'

Unexpectedly, Haley asked, 'Can I bury you, Daddy?'

'What?'

'I want to bury you in the sand.'

'No chance.'

'Please. The girls I was playing with buried their daddy and it was really funny. All you could see was his head.'

'No, thanks.'

'You can bury me, then.'

'I'm not going to bury anyone.'

'*Please.*'

'Later, maybe.'

Haley sighed and went down the beach to look for her new friends. Olga, reassured that the child wouldn't get lost, opened a paperback. Mike lit a cigarette and took a leisurely look around him to see if there was more entertainment on view.

The afternoon passed agreeably, more agreeably for Olga when the topless women turned on their fronts.

'A bit creepy, I thought, the kid wanting to bury me,' Mike said after a long silence.

'There's nothing creepy about it. It's something children like to do. It's comical, seeing someone's head above the sand and nothing else, specially if it's their own dad.'

'If you say so.'

'Well, you've got to have a sense of humour.'

'There's enough death on a beach without having your own child wanting to bury you.'

'I don't know what you're on about.'

'You only have to take a walk along the shoreline. You'll see fish half eaten by gulls, bits of crabs, smashed shells. Nothing is growing. It's a desert, just stones and sand.'

'Cheerful!'

'You asked.'

Olga may have slept for a while after that. She felt a prod in her back and seemed to snap out of a dream of some sort. The paperback lay closed beside her.

'Time to face it,' Mike said. 'The tide's turned.'

Olga heaved herself onto her elbows and saw what he meant. That big expanse of sand had disappeared. 'Oh, my God. Where's—'

'She's OK. Over to the right.'

Haley and the others were playing with a frisbee.

'We must tell her if we go for a swim. I don't want her coming back and finding us gone.'

'We'll do it, then.'

On the way down, Olga interrupted the frisbee-throwing to tell Haley they wouldn't be long. The child was so involved in the game that the words hardly registered.

The conditions were ideal. The waves had reached the stretch of beach that shelved, so getting in was a quick process, and the water coming in over the warm sand wasn't so cold as she expected. After the first plunge, the two of them held hands and jumped the waves and it was by far the best part of the day. Once when a large wave swept them inwards, Mike lifted her and carried her back to the deeper water. There, they embraced and kissed. The tensions rolled off them like the beads of water.

They stayed in longer than they realised. The people closest to the incoming tide were gathering their belongings and moving higher up.

'Where's Haley?'

Mike didn't answer. He took a few quick steps higher up and looked around.

'Mike, can you see her?'

He said with his irritating, offhand manner, 'She'll be somewhere around.'

'I can't see the girls she was with. Oh, God. Mike, where is she?'

'She won't be far away.'

'We've got to find her.'

'You told her we were going for a swim. She saw us.'

'But she isn't here.'

He began to take it seriously. 'If she's lost, someone will have taken her up to the lifeguards. I'll check with them. You ask the people who were sitting near us.'

She dashed back to their spot. No sign of Haley. The woman with copper hair was lying on her side as if she'd been asleep for hours, so Olga spoke to the teenagers.

'No, I'd have noticed,' one of them said. 'She hasn't

been back since you ate your sandwiches. Pretty little kid with dark hair in bunches, isn't she?'

'You're sure you haven't seen her?'

'We've been here all the time. She went the wrong way, I expect. Not surprising, is it, with all these people?'

Olga asked the French family. They seemed to understand what she was saying and let her know with shrugs and shakes of the head that they hadn't seen Haley either. She looked up to where the lifeguards had their post, a raised deck with a wide view of the beach. Mike was returning, looking about him anxiously.

She felt the pounding of her heart.

'They're going to help us find her,' he said when he reached her. 'It happens all the time, they told me. All these sections between the groynes look the same. They say she's probably come up the beach and wandered into the wrong bit.'

'Mike, I don't see how. I told her several times to look for the flags.'

'Maybe there's another flag further along.'

'She'll be panicking by now.'

'Yes, but it's up to us not to panic, right?'

Easy to say.

'You stay here. This is the place she'll come back to. One of us must be here,' he said. 'I'll check the next section.'

She remained standing, so as to be more obvious when Haley came back – if she came back. Appalling fears had gripped her. A beach was an ideal hunting ground for some paedophile. Her Haley, her child, could already be inside a car being driven away.

'She'll be all right,' one of the teenagers said. 'Little kids are always getting lost on beaches. It happened to me once.'

Olga didn't answer. She was shivering, more from shock

12

than cold. Supposedly a non-believer, she started saying and repeating, 'Please God, help us find her,' out there on the beach. All around her, people continued with their beach activities, unaware of her desperation.

Mike came quickly around the edge of the groyne shaking his head. He wasn't close enough to be heard, but it was obvious there was nothing to report. The worry lines were etched deep. He pointed as he ran, to let Olga know he would search the section on the other side. She folded her arms across her front. Her teeth were chattering.

'Why don't you cover up your shoulders?' one of the teenagers suggested. 'There's a wicked breeze since the tide turned.' She got up and brought a towel to Olga. 'Try not to worry, love,' she said, wrapping it around her and sounding twice her age. 'Someone will bring her back.'

Olga couldn't speak. She wanted to be doing something active towards finding Haley, organising search parties, alerting the police. Instead, she had to stand here, gripped by fear and guilt. How selfish and irresponsible she had been to go for that bathe and stay so long in the sea. She'd put Haley completely out of her mind while she and Mike enjoyed that stupid romp in the waves.

'Isn't that your little girl?'

'What?' She snapped out of her stupor.

The teenage girl who had brought her the towel was still beside her. 'With the man in the red shorts on the bit above the beach.'

'Oh, my God!' Haley, for sure. She was holding the hand of a strange man, the pair of them standing quite still. Olga screamed Haley's name and started running up the beach towards them. 'She's mine! That's my child! Haley!'

Haley shouted, 'Mummy!' and waved her free hand.

The other was still gripped by the man, a shaven-headed, muscled figure in tight-fitting red shorts that reached to his knees. He didn't attempt to leave.

Continuing to shriek, 'He's got my child! That's my child!' Olga scrambled up the steep bank of pebbles, nightmarishly slipping back with each step, yet oblivious of the pain to her bare feet.

As soon as she was close enough she shouted, 'What are you doing with my child?'

He called something back. It sounded like, 'Easy, lady.'

'Let go of her!'

She stumbled the last steps towards them and heard him say, 'I just found her. I'm the lifeguard.'

She had to play over in her brain what he had said because it was so clear in her mind that he was evil, a child-snatcher.

But when she reached the stone embankment above the pebbles, the man released Haley, who flung herself at her mother with arms outstretched.

'Oh, Mummy – I was lost.'

'What happened? Are you all right, darling?'

'This man found me.'

He said, 'Did you hear me, Mrs? I'm the lifeguard. She was in our hut. One of her friends went there for first aid.'

'One of those girls I was playing with was hit in the face by the frisbee,' Haley said. 'It wasn't me that threw it. Her eye was hurt, so we all went up to get some help. She's all right now. Her mummy came and took her and her sister away. I was left. I couldn't see you anywhere.'

Olga felt tears streaming from her eyes. She apologised to the lifeguard and thanked him all in the same sentence. Haley was still in her arms, gripping her possessively. She'd had a big fright. Olga carried her back to their spot on the beach. Mike hadn't returned, but the people around smiled and asked if Haley was all right.

Olga explained what had happened. She looked in the picnic bag and found a can of drink for Haley. 'We'll be leaving as soon as Daddy gets back,' she said. 'The tide's coming in, anyway.'

People were packing up all around them. The French family dismantled their windbreak and folded their towels. The teenagers said goodbye and carried the loungers back to the store. Of those around them, only the copper-haired woman appeared intent on staying until the tide forced her to move. It was practically at her heels.

'Where's Daddy?'

'He went looking for you. He'll be back soon.'

'We'll have to get up soon, or we'll get wet.'

'I know. We can give him a few minutes more. We might have to meet him at the car.'

'Is he cross with me?'

'I'm sure he isn't. We'll tell him what happened.'

Olga used the time to fold the towels and fill the bags.

Presently Haley asked, 'Why isn't that lady packing up? Her feet must be getting wet.'

The child was right. The woman hadn't made any attempt to move yet.

Olga couldn't see her properly. The windbreak was around her head and shoulders. Probably if Olga hadn't already made such an exhibition of herself she would have popped her head over the canvas and said, You'd better move now, sweetie, or you'll get a wave over you any minute. The experience with Haley had temporarily taken away her confidence.

A little further along, the lager lads with their empties heaped in front of them were watching with obvious amusement the progress of the tide towards the woman's outstretched feet.

Olga looked round for Mike, and there he was at last, striding towards them.

'Brilliant! She came back, then. Are you OK, Hale?'

Haley nodded.

Mike kissed her forehead. 'Thank God for that.'

Olga started to explain what had happened, but was interrupted by Haley.

'Mummy, don't you think we ought to wake the lady up? She's going to drown.'

'What are you saying?' Full of her own drama, she'd shut everything else out of her mind. Now she saw what Haley was on about. 'God, yes. Mike, you'd better go to her. She's out to the world. I don't know what's the matter with her.'

He said, 'It's none of our business, love.'

'There's something wrong.'

With a sigh that vented all the day's frustration, he stepped the few paces down the beach to where the water was already lapping right around the windbreak. He bent towards the woman. Abruptly he straightened up. 'Bloody hell – she's dead.'

2

'Isn't this a job for the police?' Mike Smith said.

The lifeguard gave him the look he used for people who drift out to sea in inflatables. 'By the time they get here, sport, she'll be three feet underwater.'

'Have you called them?'

'Sure.'

Three of the lads who had been drinking lager came over to see what was happening and got asked to help move the body. One walked away, saying he wasn't touching a dead person, but the others stayed, and so did Mike. Ankle deep, they lifted the corpse and carried it up the shingle and past the lifeguard post to the turf above the beach, watched by a sizeable, silent crowd. The lifeguard asked them to lay the body down for a moment. Evidently he didn't want it in his hut. He went inside and came out with a key and opened a nearby beach hut.

'We'll take her in there.'

Once the dead woman was deposited on the floor of the narrow wooden building, the lager lads walked away, and Mike started to go with them, but the lifeguard said, 'Hold on, mate. You can't leave. You found the body.'

'What do you mean, "found the body"? I was on the beach like everyone else. Anyone could see she wasn't moving when the tide came in.'

'The police'll want to talk to you.'

'I've got nothing to say to them,' Mike said. 'I don't

17

know who she is. We just happened to be sitting behind her.'

'Was she with anyone?'

'Not that I noticed. Look, my wife and kid are waiting in the car. We've got a long drive home.'

'The police should be along shortly.'

'I'll tell my wife, then.'

'You're coming back?'

'Sure.'

Mike marched to the car park, got in the car and started the engine.

'Is that it?' Olga asked.

'Yup.'

'We don't have to talk to the police?'

'We've had enough hassle for one day. We're leaving.' He put the car in gear and drove across the turf to the road leading to the exit.

He had to make way for a police car coming at speed with siren sounding and blue light flashing. It stopped a short distance ahead, opposite the lifeguards' hut, and two policemen got out.

'Are you sure this is right?' Olga asked.

'We can't tell them anything. We know bugger all. We don't know who she was or why she snuffed it. All they'll do is keep us here for hours asking idiot questions.'

Inside five minutes they were in a long line of traffic heading away from the coast.

Police officers Shanahan and Vigne stood in shirt-sleeve order outside the open door of the beach hut where the woman's body lay. They hadn't gone right in. The lifeguard offered them each a can of Sprite and they accepted. Somehow it made a morbid duty more tolerable.

'Are we one hundred per cent certain she's dead?' PC Shanahan asked. He seemed to be in charge, young as he appeared with his innocent blue eyes and smooth skin.

'You've only got to look at her,' the lifeguard said.

This they were in no hurry to do. In the doorway they could see the undersides of her feet, bluish-white and wrinkled by the water. That was enough for now.

'It's not up to us. A doctor has to certify she's dead.' Shanahan turned to PC Vigne, who looked at least five years his senior. 'Haven't you sent for the police surgeon, lamebrain?'

Vigne used his personal radio.

'What happened to her things?' Shanahan asked.

'Things?'

'Bag? Clothes?'

'Couldn't tell you. We just lifted her up and brought her here.'

'She must have had some things with her.'

'She was lying on a blue towel. I can tell you that.'

'There you go, then. Handbag?'

'Didn't notice one.'

'We'd better go and search. We won't know who she is until we find her bag.'

The lifeguard said, 'How do you know she had one?'

'Keys, purse, money. Where did she keep them?'

'A pocket?'

'Was she wearing something with pockets?'

The lifeguard shook his head. 'Two-piece swimsuit.'

'So let's look for a bag. Where exactly was she lying?'

They closed and padlocked the door of the hut and stepped at a businesslike pace along the path above the beach. The waves were rattling the pebbles and the exact spot where the woman had been found was two feet underwater already. Most people had quit the stretch of beach, except for an elderly couple just above the water-line in deckchairs. Shanahan asked if they had noticed anyone pick up a beachbag or anything else belonging to the person who was taken from the water. The woman said she must have been asleep. The old man was obviously gaga.

'Is that the towel?'

'Where?'

Shanahan pointed. He had spotted something blue shifting in the foam at the margin of the tide. 'Would you mind?' he asked the lifeguard. 'We're not dressed for the water.'

So the towel was recovered, a large, plain bath towel. A search of the bank of shingle above the sea produced nothing else. There should have been a windbreak, the lifeguard announced. When they'd first seen the woman, a windbreak had been set up around her. Someone must have seen it abandoned and decided it was worth acquiring. 'They'll take anything that isn't nailed down.'

'They can keep it as far as I'm concerned,' said Shanahan. 'We're looking for a bag.'

'That'll be gone, too. Something I've noticed about beaches,' the lifeguard said from the rich store of his experience. 'None of the usual rules apply. People find stuff and think it's fair game to take it if no one is around. Well, we've all heard of beachcombing. The bastards pick up things they wouldn't dream of keeping if they found them in a street.'

'Great,' Shanahan said. 'To sum up, we're supposed to identify this woman from one blue towel and the costume she was wearing.'

The lifeguard was more upbeat. 'At the end of the day you'll find her car standing all alone in the car park. That's your best bet. Most people come by car. This beach isn't the sort you walk to.'

'Unless someone nicked the car as well.'

'Or she was driven here by a friend,' said Vigne. A few years in the police and you expect no favours from fate.

They radioed back to say they were unable to identify the dead woman and some of her property was missing. They were ordered to remain at the scene and wait for the doctor.

So they sat in the sun on the canvas seats outside the hut, with the wind off the sea tugging at their shirts.

'What age is she, this woman?' Shanahan asked.

'Don't know. Thirties?'

'As young as that? Makes you think, someone dying like that.'

'Heart, I suppose.'

'Do you reckon?'

'Is sunstroke fatal?'

'Couldn't tell you.'

'My money's on heart. Could happen to anyone.'

Vigne said, 'There's something I heard of called sudden death syndrome.'

'Come again, lamebrain.'

'Sudden death syndrome. You can be perfectly fit and go to bed one night and never wake up.'

'I've heard of that,' the lifeguard said.

'But she wasn't in bed,' Shanahan said. 'She was stretched out on the beach.'

'There are worse places to die than a beach on a nice afternoon.'

'That's priceless,' Shanahan said, 'coming from a lifeguard. You should write that on a board and fix it to your hut.'

A dark-haired woman in a suit and carrying a bag stopped in front of the three of them reclining in the sun, and said, 'Nice work, if you can get it.' This was Dr Keithly, the police surgeon.

They all stood up.

'You've got a corpse for me, I was told.'

'In that beach hut,' Shanahan said.

The lifeguard added, 'A woman.'

'She came to you feeling ill?'

'No.' He explained how the body was found. 'Do you want me to open up, doc?'

'Well, I hate to spoil the fun, but . . . please.'

Presently Dr Keithly stood in the entrance to the hut beside the feet of the deceased. 'I could do with some light in here.'

'I'll fetch a torch.'

'That will help.'

Torch in hand, she stepped around the outstretched legs. She was silent for some time, crouching beside the body.

Shanahan stood in the doorway, watching until the examination was complete. It seemed to take an age. 'What's the verdict, doc? Definitely dead?'

'We can agree on that.' Dr Keithly stood up and stepped out, removing her plastic gloves. She sounded less friendly now. 'Did you take a proper look at her?'

'We were waiting for you.'

She turned to the lifeguard. 'But you recovered the body.'

'With a bit of help.'

'You got a good look at her, then. Didn't you notice anything unusual about her appearance?'

'Such as?'

'The mark around her neck.'

'What mark?'

'I'd say it was made by a ligature. She seems to have been strangled.'

'Christ almighty!' the lifeguard said.

'Come and see for yourselves.'

This had to be faced. All three men squeezed into the hut and watched as the doctor pointed the torch at the neck of the dead woman, lifting the reddish hair. A broad line extended right around the throat.

'Is that definite?' asked Shanahan. 'Couldn't it have been made by some kind of necklace?'

'Unlikely. If you look here,' said Dr Keithly, pointing to the nape of the neck. 'See the crossover? And there's some scratching on this side where she tried to tug the ligature away from her throat.'

'Christ. Didn't you notice this when you were carrying her?' Shanahan said accusingly to the lifeguard.

'Don't turn on me, sport. I wasn't looking at her neck. There was nothing tied around it.'

Shanahan sounded increasingly panicky. He could foresee awkward questions from CID. 'How could this have happened on a beach in front of hundreds of people? Wouldn't she have screamed?'

'Not if it was quick and unexpected,' the doctor said. 'She might have made some choking sounds, but I doubt if she'd have been heard. What surprises me is that no one saw the killer actually doing it.'

'She was behind a windbreak.'

'Even so.'

'She was probably stretched out, sunbathing. It would have been done close to the ground, by someone kneeling beside her.'

Vigne said, 'Hadn't we better report this? It's out of our hands if it's murder.'

'Hey, that's right,' Shanahan said, much relieved. 'You're not so thick as you look.'

3

Two hours were left before sunset. The local CID had arrived in force and sealed off the stretch of beach where the body was found, but they need not have bothered. Most visitors had left at high tide when only a small strip of pebbles remained and the breeze had turned cooler. Away from the beach, several barbecues were under way on the turf of the car park, sending subversive aromas towards the police vans where the search squads and SOCOs waited for the tide to turn.

Henrietta Mallin, the Senior Investigating Officer, was already calling this case a bummer. A beach washed clean by the tide couldn't be less promising as a crime scene. There was no prospect of collecting DNA evidence. The body itself had been well drenched by the waves before it was lifted from the water.

The SIO was known to everyone as Hen, and superficially the name suited her. She was small, chirpy, alert, with widely set brown eyes that checked everything. But it was unwise to stretch the comparison. This Hen didn't fuss, or subscribe to a pecking order. Though shorter than anyone in Bognor Regis CID, she gave ground to nobody. She'd learned how to survive in a male-dominated job. Fifteen years back, when she'd joined the police in Dagenham, she'd been given more than her share of the jobs everyone dreaded, just to see how this pipsqueak female rookie would cope. A couple of times when attending on corpses undiscovered for weeks she'd thrown up. She'd wept and had recurrent nightmares over a child abuse case. But she'd always reported for the next shift. Strength of mind got her through – helped by finding that many of the male recruits were going through the same traumas. She'd persevered, survived a bad beating-up at a drugs bust, and gained respect and steady promotion without aping male attitudes. There was only one male habit she'd acquired. She smoked thin, wicked-smelling cigars, handling them between thumb and fore-finger and flicking off the ash with her smallest finger. She used a perfume by Ralph Lauren called Romance. It said much for Romance that it could triumph over cigar fumes.

'You boys got here when?' she said to the uniformed officers who had answered the shout.

'Four forty-two,' PC Shanahan said.

'So how was the water?'

'The water, ma'am?'

She brought her hands together under her chin and mimed the breaststroke. 'Didn't you go in?'

Shanahan frowned. He wasn't equal to this, and neither was his companion, Vigne. Hen didn't need to pull rank. She was streets ahead on personality alone.

She explained. 'You reported suspicious injuries at five twenty. Forty minutes, give or take. What were you *doing*, my lovely?'

Shanahan went over the sequence of events: the call to the doctor, the search of the beach and the doctor's arrival and discovery of the ligature marks. He didn't mention the cans of Sprite and the spot of sunbathing while they waited for the doctor.

'Am I missing something here?' Hen said. 'You didn't notice she was strangled until the doctor pointed it out?'

'The body was inside the hut, ma'am.'

'Didn't you go in?'

'It was dark in there.'

'Is that a problem for you, constable?'

He reddened. 'I mean I wouldn't have been able to see much.'

'There was a torch.'

'The lifeguard didn't produce it until the doctor arrived.'

'Did you ask him for one?'

'No, ma'am.'

'Do you carry one in your car?'

An embarrassed nod.

'Heavy-duty rubber job?' she said, nodding her head. 'They come in useful for subduing prisoners, don't they? But there is a secondary use. Did you look at the body at all?'

'We checked she was dead, ma'am.'

'Without actually noticing why?'

Shanahan lowered his eyes and said nothing. Vigne, by contrast, looked upwards as if he was watching for the first star to appear.

Hen Mallin turned her back on them and spoke instead to one of her CID team. 'How many cars are left, Charlie?'

'In the car park, guv?'

With her cigar she gestured towards Shanahan. 'I thought *he* was half-baked.'

'About twenty.'

'When does it close?'

'Eight thirty.'

She checked her watch. 'Get your boys busy, then. Find out who the cars belong to, and get a PNC check on every one that isn't spoken for. The victim's motor is our best hope. I'm tempted to say our only hope. Have you spoken to the guy on the gate?'

'He didn't come on duty until two. He's got no memory

of the victim, guv. They just lean out of the kiosk and take the money. Thousands of drivers pass through.'

'Was anyone else directing the cars?'

'No. There are acres of land, as you see. People park where they want.'

She went through the motions of organising a line of searchers to scour the taped-off section of beach, now that the tide was on the ebb. Around high-water line they began picking up an extraordinary collection of discarded material: bottletops and ringpulls, cans, lollysticks, carrier bags, plastic cups, an odd shoe, hairgrips, scrunchies and empty cigarette lighters. Everything was bagged up and labelled. She watched with no expectation. There was no telling if a single item had belonged to the victim.

'Did anyone check the swimsuit?'

'What for, guv?'

'Labels. Is it a designer job, or did she get it down the market? Might tell us something about this unfortunate woman. We know sweet Fanny Adams up to now.'

'The towel she was lying on is top quality, pure Egyptian cotton, really fluffy when it's dry,' the one other woman on the team, DS Stella Gregson, said.

'There speaks a pampered lady.'

'I wish,' Stella said. She was twenty-six and lived alone in a bedsit in a high-rise block in Bognor.

'Never mind, Stell. Some day your prince will come. Meanwhile come up to the hut and give me your take on the swimsuit.'

Stella had a complex role in the CID squad, part apologist for her boss, part minder, and quite often the butt of her wit. She'd learned to take it with good humour. Her calm presence was a big asset at times like this. Together they crunched up the steep bank of pebbles.

'We can assume she was murdered some time in the

27

afternoon,' Hen said, as much to herself as Stella. 'I asked the lifeguard if there was any stiffening of the muscles when they carried the body up the beach, and he didn't notice any. As a rough estimate, rigor mortis sets in after three hours or so. In warm conditions it works faster. I'd like the opinion of the pathologist – when he finally gets here – but . . .'

'She was strangled here?' Stella said in disbelief, turning to give her boss a hand up the last of the steep ascent.

'That's the supposition.'

'On a public beach?'

'I know,' Hen said. She paused to draw a breath at the top of the bank. The smoking wasn't kind to her lungs. 'My first reaction was the same as yours, Stell, but I'm changing my mind. We can assume she was lying down, enjoying the sun, like most people are on a beach, and she had a windbreak around her head and shoulders, as the lifeguard stated. That means the killer was screened on three sides. He could choose his moment when no one was coming up the beach towards them.'

'Not easy,' Stella was bold enough to point out. 'On a beach as crowded as that, people are going back and forth all the time, for a swim, or just to look at the water. And some of the sunbathers are stretched out with nothing else to do except watching others.'

'You can't see much through a windbreak. He could strangle her without anyone realising what he was up to. She'd be relaxed, maybe lying on her side with her eyes shut. Even asleep. If they arrived together, he's already in position beside her. If not, he flops down as if he's going to sunbathe with her. They're lying on sand, so she wouldn't hear him arrive. When he thinks no one is watching, he pulls the ligature over her head and tightens it before she knows what's happening. If

28

anyone did get a look, they could easily think they were snogging. Any sound she makes will be muffled, and a beach is a place where no one gets excited if a woman screams.'

'Even so.'

'Don't you buy it, Stell?'

Stella gave a shrug that meant she was dubious, but couldn't supply a more plausible theory. 'There must have been people really close. They're stretched out in their thousands on a gorgeous day like today.'

'But they wouldn't expect to be witnesses to a murder. Not on a south coast beach on a Sunday afternoon.'

They found the lifeguard sitting outside his hut. His duties had ended two hours ago, but he'd been told to wait, and at this end of the day he was looking less macho than a young man of his occupation should, with goose-pimpled legs and a tan steadily turning as blue as his tattooed biceps. He had his arms crossed over his chest and was massaging the backs of them.

Hen asked him his name. It was Emerson. He was Australian. Almost certainly didn't have a work permit, which may have accounted for his guarded manner.

'You were here keeping watch, Mr Emerson,' she said to him, making it sound like dereliction of duty. 'Didn't you see what happened?'

'Sorry.'

'You lads have little else to do all day except study the women. Didn't you notice this one?'

'She was some way off.'

'But you don't sit on your backside all day. You're responsible for the whole beach, aren't you?'

'That's true in theory, but—'

'You didn't notice her?'

'There were a couple of thousand people here, easy.'

'Have you seen her before, on other days?'

A shake of the head.

'Do you remember *anyone* who was on the stretch where she was found?'

'The guy who told us about her.'

'This was when?'

'Getting on for high tide. Around four thirty.'

'Describe him. What age?'

'About thirty.'

'Go on.'

'Tall and thin, with short brown hair. Skin going red. Do you want his name?'

Hen said with more approval, 'You got his name?'

'Smith.'

A sigh and an ironic, 'Oh, thanks.'

'But he has a kid called Haley.'

An interested tilt of the head. 'How do you know this?'

'Earlier in the afternoon she was lost. Smith came up here and reported it. I told him kids often get lost and I'd spread the word. He told me where they were sitting and I said he should try the beach café, where the ices are sold. Kids stand in line for a long time there and sometimes the parents get worried. But I found the kid myself, looking lost, only a short way from here.'

'Waiting for an ice cream?'

'No. She'd come to our hut with some friends for first aid and then got separated from them.'

'Was she hurt?'

He shook his head. 'It was one of the other kids who needed the first aid. Hit in the face with a frisbee. Haley was OK. I handed her back to her mother.'

'The mother?' Hen said, interested. 'You met her mother as well?'

'Right.'

'Smith's wife?'

'I guess. The kid called her Mummy for sure. A bottle

30

blonde, short, a bit overweight. Red two-piece. She was in tears when I turned up with Haley.'

'So you saw exactly where these people were on the beach?'

'I didn't go right over. The mother ran up when she saw me with the kid.'

'The woman who was murdered must have been some-where near them.'

'If you say so. It was really crowded.'

'Where was Haley's father at this time?'

'Don't know. Still searching, I guess.'

'And he was definitely the same man who told you about the dead woman?'

'That's for sure.'

'Did he give his first name?'

'No. He just said his missing child was called Haley Smith, aged five, and he described her.'

'Did he have an accent?'

'Accent?'

'Where was he from? Round here?'

'Couldn't say. You poms all sound the same to me. He wasn't foreign, far as I could tell.'

'So Haley was returned to her mother?'

'That's what I said.'

'Then Mr Smith comes back and tells you he's found a dead woman?'

'That was a good half-hour after. I went back with him to look and it was true. The tide was already washing over her.'

'How was she lying?'

'Face down, stretched out. You could easily think she was asleep.'

'I understand she was behind a windbreak.'

'That's right.'

'Did you see any other property? A bag?'

'Only the towel she was lying on. I got some lads to help us move her.'

'Did Smith help?'

'He joined in, sure. We got her up here and into the beach hut.'

'How did you know she was dead? Did you feel for a pulse?'

'No need.'

She said with a sharp note of criticism, 'You've had first-aid training, I take it? You know you should always check?'

'She'd gone. Anyone could tell she'd gone.'

'That simply isn't good enough for someone in your job. You know why I'm asking, Sunny Jim? If you'd felt for the pressure point on her neck you would have noticed the ligature mark.'

The lifeguard didn't answer.

'So you dumped her in the hut and put in a nine-nine-nine call. Why didn't you ask Smith to stick around after the body was brought up here? You must have known we'd want to speak to him.'

'I did. I asked him.' Relieved to be in the right again, he responded with more animation. 'I said, "The police'll want to talk to you." Those were my actual words. He said he had nothing to tell the police. His wife and kid were waiting and he had a long drive home. I asked him a second time to hold on for a bit, and he said he needed to see his wife and tell her what was going on. He promised to come back, but he never did.'

'They hardly ever do,' Hen said, making it sound like a comment on the fickle tendencies of mankind as a whole. With a knowing glance at her companion, she turned away.

Before the two of them stepped inside the beach hut, Stella said, 'Guv, do you really think you should smoke in here?'

Hen looked at the half-spent cigar as if it was a foreign object. 'Do you object?'

'The pathologist might.'

She stubbed it out on a stone wall.

Inside, she directed the torch beam up and down the corpse. 'Any observations?'

'Would you point it at the head, guv?' Stella knelt and studied the line of the ligature, gently lifting some of the long red hair. 'The crossover is at the back here. Looks as if he took her from behind. Difficult to say what he used. Not wire. The mark is too indefinite. Would you hold it steady?' She bent closer and peered at the bruising. 'There's no obvious weave that I can see, so I doubt if it was rope. Leather, maybe, or some fabric?'

'Let's ask the pathologist,' Hen said. 'I thought you were going to tell me how she rates in the fashion stakes.'

So Stella fingered the hair, looking at the layers. 'It isn't a cheap haircut.'

'Is any these days?'

'All right. She went to a good stylist.'

'The manicure looks expensive, too.'

'Obviously she took care of herself.'

'The swimsuit?'

'Wasn't from the market, as you put it. See the logo on the side of the shorts? She won't have got much change out of two hundred for this.'

'A classy lady, then? No jewellery, I notice.'

'No ring mark either.'

'Does that mean anything these days?'

'Just that she doesn't habitually wear a ring. Did they find any sunglasses?'

'No.'

'I would have expected sunglasses. Designer sunglasses.'

'Dropped on the beach, maybe. We can look through

the stuff the fingertip search produced. Thanks, Stell. What kind of car does a woman like this tend to own? A dinky little sports job?'

'Maybe – for the beach. Or if she's in work, as I guess she could be, a Merc or a BMW would fit.'

'Let's see what the car park trawl has left us with.'

Outside, Emerson the lifeguard asked if he was needed any more.

Hen Mallin, half his size, took out a fresh cigar and made him wait, coming to a decision. 'What time is it?'

'Past eight. I'm supposed to be meeting someone at eight.'

'You're meeting one of my officers and making a statement.' She flicked her lighter and touched the flame to the cigar. 'Then you'll be free to go.'

Soon enough there wouldn't be much daylight left. The sky over the sea already had an indigo look to it. In the car park, a few of the search team dropped kebab skewers and tried to look busy when Hen and Stella approached.

'Eight thirty. Car park closed. So what are we left with?' Hen asked the sergeant in charge of this part of the investigation. 'How many unclaimed vehicles?'

'Four, ma'am. Two Mitsubishis, a Peugeot and a Range Rover.'

Hen muttered to Stella, 'I know what your money's on.' To the sergeant, she said, 'Did you check with the PNC?'

'Yes, guv.'

'And?'

'Two have women owners. That's one of the Mitsubishis and the Range Rover.'

'How did I guess? Tell me who owns the four-by-four.'

The sergeant read from his notes. 'Shiena Wilkinson, 37 Pine Tree Avenue, Petersfield. Had the vehicle from new, two years ago.'

'Mrs, Miss or Ms?'

'Dr.'

'Is she, indeed? And the Mitsubishi owner?'

'A Ms Claudia Cameron, Waterside Cottage, near Boxgrove. She bought it secondhand last January.'

'And the others are registered to men?'

The sergeant told him the second Mitsubishi was owned by a Portsmouth man called West, and the Peugeot belonged to a Londoner called Patel.

'It doesn't prevent a woman from driving them,' Hen said. 'However, let's start with the obvious.'

Dr Shiena Wilkinson's Range Rover was parked near the entrance gate in front of the windsurfing club premises, a black vehicle in mint condition. Hen walked around it, checked the tax disc, and saw that it had been issued in Petersfield in April. Forced to stand on tiptoe for a sight of the interior, she looked through the side windows. On the front passenger seat was a pack of mansize Kleenex. A paperback of Jane Austen's *Emma* was on the back seat.

'I need to get inside.'

'We'll have to break in unless you're willing to wait, guv,' the sergeant said.

'As you must have discovered, my darling, there are women who will, and women who won't. I belong to the second group.'

A jemmy did the job, at some cost to the side window. Hen put on gloves and overshoes, stepped in, tried the seat and said, 'She's longer in the leg than I am, but that doesn't tell us much.' In the glove compartment she found a roll of peppermints, a bottle of cologne and a small bag of silver coins, presumably for parking machines. Right at the back was a doctor's prescription pad. 'Some people would kill for one of these.' Attached to the door on the driver's side were a couple of tickets for the Waitrose car park in Petersfield, dated a week before.

Dr Wilkinson's medical bag was out of sight in the

storage space at the rear. It held a stethoscope, blood-pressure gauge, speculum, syringe, sterile pads and dressings, tweezers and scissors. Nothing so useful as an address book or diary.

'Order a transporter, Stella. I want this vehicle examined by forensics.'

'Will you be wanting to look at the others, ma'am?' the sergeant asked.

'Hole in one, sergeant.'

The Mitsubishi owned by the Boxgrove woman was some distance away, near the beach café and close to the last remaining barbecue. This owner was not so tidy as Dr Wilkinson. The floor was littered with used tissues and parking tickets. A pair of shoes. Sweet wrappings. The tax disc was a month out of date.

'Do you want this one opened, ma'am?'

'Please.'

The jemmy came into play again, but not for long. From behind them came a scream of, 'What the bloody hell are you doing to my car?' and a woman came running from the barbecue.

'I thought you told me the owner wasn't around,' Hen muttered to the sergeant.

'You bastards! You've smashed my bloody window and the paint on the door is chipped,' Ms Claudia Cameron protested. She was wearing a white wrap made of towelling and candy-striped sandals. Her spiky blond hair looked like the result of poking a wet finger into a live socket.

'Hold on, love,' Hen said as if she was speaking to a child. 'Didn't you see us checking this vehicle?'

'Yes, but I thought you might go away. I'm only a few days over on my tax. It doesn't give you the right to smash your way in . . . does it?'

'You're Claudia Cameron?'

'How do you know that?'

'You'll be compensated, Ms Cameron.'

'That isn't good enough.' Now that she had a legitimate grievance, she was going to get some mileage out of it. 'Just who's in charge here?'

'Speak to the sergeant, OK? He'll need your address and so on.'

She was part of the action and obviously didn't want to be sidelined. 'This is about the dead woman they found, isn't it? Did you think my car belonged to her, or what?'

'Did you see her yourself?'

'No, but everyone is talking about it, poor soul.'

'So how much do you know, Ms Cameron? Did anyone say anything at all to you that might help us find out who she was?'

'Not really.'

'"Everyone is talking about it",' Hen repeated to Stella in a good imitation of Claudia Cameron's voice as they walked away, 'but what did everyone see? Diddly-squat. What's the betting Dr Wilkinson is cooking sausages at the same barbecue and will presently notice her beautiful Range Rover being hoisted onto the transporter and come running over?'

'Don't even think about it, guv.'

'Actually, I'd welcome it.'

'Why?'

'I wouldn't mind seeing a doctor.'

'Aren't you well?'

'It's in my head. I've got this feeling the whole world is against me, and when that happens all I want to do is shut myself in my car and listen to my Agatha Christie tapes.'

Stella laughed.

4

Hen had chosen to direct operations from her own
police station at Bognor rather than park a mobile
incident room beside the beach at Wightview Sands. The
crime scene wasn't likely to yield any more evidence than
they'd picked up in that first search. Two high tides had
already rearranged the sand and stones. The Range Rover
was no longer where it had been found. It had been transported to the vehicle forensic unit.

'We have a possible victim, playmates – and I stress that
word "possible",' she told her team, assembled for the
first formal briefing. Small as she was, there was no
disputing her authority. 'She is Dr Shiena Wilkinson, from
Petersfield, whose Range Rover was found in the car park
close to the scene last evening.'

'Don't we have a positive ID yet, guv?' one of the team
asked.

'Later this morning, I hope. One of the other doctors
is going to the mortuary.'

'A photo?' Stella Gregson said.

'Not yet.'

'There ought to be one in her house.'

'And the lads doing the search have been told to look
out for it.'

'Sometimes they have the doctors' pictures on view in
a medical practice.'

'Not in this case.' Stella was right to pick up on these

points, but Hen wanted to get on. 'The car is Dr Wilkinson's. That's for sure. All the others have been accounted for. She's thirty-two and a GP, one of five who practise from a health centre in the town. She is unmarried and lives alone in Pine Tree Avenue, a newish development of detached houses overlooking that golf course that you can see from the Chichester Road to the south. She wasn't on call over the weekend. She'd arranged to take three days off, Saturday to Monday. Likes going to the beach, apparently. But before we all get too excited about Dr Wilkinson, let's get back to what we know for certain.'

She took a drag at her cigar and pointed with it to the poster-size colour photo of the face displayed on the board behind her. The woman's wide-open eyes had the glaze of death and the mouth gaped. 'Our victim has copper-coloured hair. All that was found with her was the two-piece swimsuit she was wearing. The towel was recovered from the water not long after. We were told she was partly hidden by a windbreak, but it was missing when our patrol arrived. Going by the quality of the towel and swimsuit, she wasn't short of cash. She had a nice haircut and well-kept nails. No jewellery.'

'Do you think the motive was theft?' George Flint asked. George was the pushy sergeant who wanted Stella's job.

'It has to be considered. But you don't need to commit murder to nick a handbag from a beach. People take amazing risks with their property every time they go for a bathe. If you want to steal a bag all you have to do is watch and wait.'

'I know that, guv.'

'She may not even have had a bag with her,' Hen pointed out.

'So where did she keep her car key?'

'A pocket.'

'In a swimsuit?'

'They can have pockets.'

'Ah, yes.'

'Actually, this one didn't,' Hen admitted.

'So where were her clothes? In the car?'

'We found no clothes in the car, and no bag either.'

'Then the killer walked off with her clothes, or her bag, or both. We're dealing with theft here.'

Hen tilted her head sharply. 'You don't give up, do you? OK – probably she did have a bag. But theft may not be the real motive. The killer may have taken the bag to make identification more difficult. I don't see the link between strangulation and stealing handbags.'

'What's left if we rule out theft?'

'Wise up, George. Most killings are carried out by people in a close relationship with the victim. Family, lovers, ex-lovers.'

George Flint had hammered away at this theory for long enough. It was another voice that asked, 'Guv, do we know if she was alone on the beach?'

'We know nothing. The lifeguard claims he didn't see her alive. The witnesses all left before the patrol car arrived.'

'We'll have to put out an appeal, guv.'

'I'm coming to that.'

'What about this lifeguard? Is he a suspect? Can we believe everything he tells us?'

'He's an Australian named Emerson, and he's not comfortable. I dare say there are things he doesn't want us to know about how he got the job. But he was on duty. To have killed her, he'd have needed to leave his post for a while, and someone might have noticed.'

'There must be other lifeguards. I've seen more than one of them sitting up there. He could ask one of his mates to cover for him and take time out to kill her.'

'For what reason?'

'Who knows? He recognised her as someone who dumped him some time in the past?'

'Not much of a motive,' George Flint commented.

'We don't have *any* motive yet.'

Stella nudged the discussion in another direction. 'If the victim *is* this doctor, we could have another motive: the patient with a grudge.'

'That's good, Stell,' Hen said, forgetting her own insistence that they'd said enough about Dr Wilkinson. 'I like that. GPs deal with life and death issues every day. There are always people who feel they were denied the right treatment, or misdiagnosed.'

'Or refused the drugs they want.'

'Would you take that on, Stella? Go to the health centre and find out what you can.'

'You mean look at patients' records?'

Someone sitting near Stella murmured in a sing-song tone, 'Data Protection.'

'Talk to the receptionists, pick out the gossipy one and ask about the nutters and complainers they have to deal with,' Hen said. 'You'll get names. Then try the nurses and the cleaners and the caretaker. I don't have to tell you, Stella.'

'But you did.'

Smiles all round, Hen's included.

'Getting back to what happened on the beach, we need to find this guy who alerted the lifeguard. He was asked to remain at the scene, and didn't. We have a description of sorts. Tall and thin. Short brown hair. Around thirty years of age. Skin turning red, so presumably he wasn't a regular on the beach. And we have his name . . . Smith.'

She timed the pay-off like a stand-up comic and got the laugh she expected.

'He has a wife or partner, short, a bit overweight and with dyed blond hair. Also a five-year-old daughter called Haley.'

'Are we regarding him as a suspect?' a youngish DC asked.

'Because he left the scene, you mean?'

A sergeant across the room said dismissively, 'He called the lifeguard. We can rule him out.'

'Not yet, we can't,' Hen said. 'It's not unknown for the perpetrator to blow the whistle. Ask any fire investigator. In a high proportion of arson cases the informant is the guy who started the fire. They think it draws suspicion away from them.'

'Does that hold for murder as well?'

'I said it's not unknown, sunshine. Let's say Smith is our principal witness. I want to talk to all three members of that family and anyone else who was on that stretch of beach. I'm going on the local TV news tonight – by which time we should know for sure if Shiena Wilkinson is our victim.'

The Smiths lived on a housing estate in Crawley, close to Gatwick Airport where Mike was manager of a bookshop – the terminal bookshop, as he called it in his darker moods. As usual after the weekend mayhem, Monday had been chaotic, with the shop still cluttered with unsold Sunday papers, two staff off sick (hungover, Mike suspected), three mighty boxes of the latest Stephen King to find shelf-room for, a couple of publishers' reps wanting to show their wares, the phone forever ringing and a problem with one of the tills. He wasn't in a receptive frame of mind when he finally got home at six thirty.

For Olga, also, the day had been stressful. She worked on a checkout in the local Safeway, an early shift that freed her in time to collect Haley from school at three thirty. At lunchtime in the staffroom, she had seen the Sun's headline, 'STRANGLED ON THE BEACH', and was appalled to discover it referred to the dead woman at Wightview Sands.

'I've been waiting all afternoon to talk to you,' she said as soon as Mike came in. 'I tried calling the shop, but I couldn't get through.'

'Something up?' he said without much interest.

'This.' She held the paper up to her chest, watching for the headline to make its impact.

'You think I haven't seen that? We sell papers – remember?'

'It's the woman we found, Mike. It says Wightview Sands. They're appealing for witnesses.'

His offhand manner changed abruptly. 'You haven't phoned the police?'

'Not yet. I thought you'd like to speak to them.'

'Whatever for?'

She stared at him. 'I told you. They want to hear from witnesses.' She slapped the paper on the table in front of him.

'That isn't us. We didn't see anything.'

'I *spoke* to her, for God's sake. She was sitting right in front of us.'

'About what? What did you say?'

'I don't know. Something about Haley.'

'What?'

'Her high spirits, her energy, something like that.'

'That's all?'

'It was just a few friendly words.'

He tossed the paper across the room onto a chair. 'What use is a few friendly words? They want witnesses to a murder, not people making small talk. You'd be done for wasting their time.'

'That isn't true, Mike. It says they want anyone who

43

was there to come forward, however little they saw. We can tell them what time she arrived – soon after us – and that she didn't have anyone with her. No, hold on, there was that guy who tried to chat her up.'

'I didn't see anyone.'

'Black T-shirt. Tall, dark, with curly hair. This was before lunch. You were asleep. She wasn't amused, and he walked off, not too pleased. It didn't amount to anything, but . . .'

'If it didn't amount to anything, forget it.'

'They may want to know about him. She seemed to know him.'

'OK, she recognised someone. Big deal.'

'He didn't upset her, or anything. She was in a cheerful state of mind, or she wouldn't have spoken to me.'

'We know bugger all about her state of mind,' he said, troubled by her old-fashioned faith in the system. 'You can't read anything into a couple of words exchanged on a beach. Forget it. Other people may have seen something. We didn't. We're minor players. They don't want the likes of us wasting their precious time.'

'Do you think so?' The force of his words was starting to tell on Olga.

'I know it. Listen, do you want a police car outside the house and all our nosy neighbours having a field day? That's what's going to happen if you call them.'

'I don't care what the neighbours think. This poor woman was murdered.'

'Right. And what can we expect if we call the police? They'll tear us to shreds. They won't believe we sat on the beach all afternoon and saw sod all. The woman was murdered a few yards away from us. How come we didn't notice? We'll look a prize pair of idiots.'

Olga hesitated. She hadn't thought of this.

'And that's not all,' Mike hammered the point home.

'If the case ever goes to court, we'll be called as witnesses *for the defence.* Think about that for a moment. You and I will be the dimwits who failed to spot the killer. How do you fancy being cross-examined by the prosecution about your memories of that afternoon just to save some pervert from justice?'

'But if it's true that we didn't see anything—'

'They'll make a laughing stock of us. We'll be filmed going into the court and coming out of it. People will think we're on the killer's side. You know what I think?' he said, letting his voice sink to a lower, more reasonable note. 'I think she was killed while we were swimming.'

Olga was relieved. 'That's what I was thinking, too.'

'We could have been a million miles away. We saw nothing.'

'When we came back from our swim, and Haley was missing, I thought the woman was asleep,' Olga recalled, picturing the scene. 'She was very still. She could have been dead already.'

'Must have been.'

'I wouldn't put it quite so strongly as that. When Haley went missing, you went off to look for her and I was in no state to notice anything. The woman could have been strangled while I was standing there, looking along the beach. What a ghastly thought!'

'Unlikely.'

'And when the lifeguard brought her back, I ran up the beach towards them. It could have happened then.'

'Does it matter?' Mike said. 'The whole point is that we don't know because we saw nothing.'

'You were the first to find her dead.'

'Someone was going to find her. I'm keeping out of this, Olga. Our life is heavy enough. We can do without this.'

He'd talked her round. She was uneasy, but she didn't

45

want another argument. There had been too many in their marriage in recent days.

'What's she like – Dr Wilkinson?'

Stella had targeted the receptionist she reckoned would say most if encouraged, the smiling woman in her fifties with carefully made-up eyes that gleamed through dark-framed oval rims. Mrs Bassington would have you believe she ran the entire health centre without interference from doctors, nurses or her fellow receptionists. She had shown Stella straight into Shiena Wilkinson's consulting room, a stark place with little in it suggestive of the doctor's personality except a Vermeer print on the wall behind the desk. There was a box of tissues on the desk. No family photos.

'What's she like?' Mrs Bassington repeated. 'A sweet doctor, very popular with the patients.'

'I meant in appearance.'

'Oh. Rather pretty in an intelligent way, if you under-stand me. She's slim and about your height. Lovely hair with a reddish tinge to it. Natural, I'm sure. You can tell, can't you?'

'Reddish?'

'Chestnut, I'd call it.'

Would chestnut pass for copper, the description everyone seemed to agree on? Stella wondered. She thought of copper as more red than brown. She was too experienced to put words in the witness's mouth. 'What length?'

'That I couldn't tell you. She always wears it up, fastened across the back with a large wooden clasp like a geisha. It could be quite long. I've never seen it loose.'

'You knew she was off duty at the weekend?'

'Naturally I knew. The doctors' schedules are my responsibility. Her next surgery was this afternoon.'

'And did she say how she planned to spend the weekend?'

'Not to me personally, but she goes to the beach to relax sometimes. She's mentioned it in the past.'

'When did she join the team of doctors here?'

'It must be two years now. Her first GP appointment. We were overstretched at the time. Normally I'd ease a new doctor in, specially a first-timer, but she was given a full list straight away and she coped brilliantly. You see, Dr Masood had died suddenly and Shiena had to step into his shoes. We unloaded a few of his patients to the other doctors, but basically she took over his list.'

'Dr Masood? He was here before she came?'

'Yes.'

'And died suddenly?'

'Killed in a motorway accident. A great shock to us all. You don't really believe Shiena is this woman who was strangled, do you?'

'We don't know yet,' Stella said. 'We found her car abandoned. That's all.'

'It would be too awful – another doctor dying.'

'What can you tell me about her personal life?' Stella asked, leaving aside the possible implications of another dead doctor. 'Is there a family?'

'Not here, for sure. I think they lived abroad. She used to talk about Canada. Her people are over there if they're anywhere.'

'Any men in her life?'

'Apart from two or three hundred patients? I couldn't tell you. She isn't very forthcoming about her life outside this place.'

'Let's talk about patients, then. I'm sure she must have had a few difficult characters on her books.'

'What do you mean by difficult?' For a moment it seemed Stella had miscalculated and was about to be lectured on patient confidentiality.

'Unstable personalities.'

Mrs Bassington spread her hands and laughed. 'They're two a penny in Petersfield. It's that sort of town.'

'Anyone with a grudge against her?'

'All the doctors have complainers, if that's what you mean. People who think they're not getting the treatment they deserve, or the miracle cure they read about in some magazine.'

'Try and think, please. Someone angry enough to be a threat to Dr Wilkinson.'

'A man?'

'I'm asking you, Mrs Bassington.'

After a significant pause, she said, 'Is this strictly between you and me? I wouldn't want him knowing I gave you his name.'

'He won't find out.'

She took off her glasses and polished them with one of Dr Wilkinson's tissues. 'There's a certain man I could mention – a very unpleasant person who treated his wife appallingly, beating her up a number of times. Dr Wilkinson saw the injuries after the latest episode and got her into a women's refuge in Godalming. The wife is so scared of him she won't report him to the police. He's very angry with Dr Wilkinson for interfering in his marriage, as he puts it. He's not her patient, but he was here twice last week demanding to see her.'

'As recently as that?'

'The second time he marched into her room when she was seeing another patient. She called for help and we had to fetch two of the male doctors to evict him.'

'What's his name?'

'Littlewood. Rex Littlewood. People in the town know him well. It's the drink. He gets very abusive.'

'Did you see him yourself when he came in?'

'The first time, yes. No appointment. He came in last

Monday morning and told me he wanted to speak to Dr Wilkinson. He isn't even registered here. He's not the sort of man who'd go to a lady doctor. I could see straight away that he was out to make trouble. I told him she was fully booked – which she was – and suggested he tried later in the week. Usually people like him don't bother again if you can put them off. I can be very firm with difficult men. He *did* leave, but unfortunately he returned on Wednesday, when I wasn't here, stormed in past reception and into Dr Wilkinson's surgery, with the result I mentioned.'

'I'll need his address. Does he have a car?'

'If he does, it shouldn't be allowed. Each time I've seen him, he was smelling of drink.'

'Is the wife all right? Has anyone phoned the hostel?'

The blood drained from Mrs Bassington's face. 'Oh my God! You don't think he's killed her as well?'

'We should check. Where exactly is this refuge?'

Outside in her car, Stella asked for a PNC check on Rex Littlewood's form. He had two convictions for being drunk in a public place, but none for vehicle offences. Nothing, either, for assault or violence. This didn't mean he was a model husband; just that his wife hadn't reported him.

Stella was wary. It would be all too easy to cast Littlewood as Dr Wilkinson's killer, then find he was thirty miles away at the time.

She drove to Godalming and found the refuge north of the town, a derelict mansion someone had rented for a peppercorn. The rotten window frames were barely holding the glass. There were broken tiles on the ground by the front door. But someone answered the knock and it was a relief to hear that Ann Littlewood was alive and still in residence.

The mental picture Stella had built up couldn't have been more wrong. The battered wife was a huge woman with arms like a wrestler's. She was sitting on a bench in the overgrown garden, trying ineptly to shell peas. An entire pod's worth shot out of her hands when Stella approached. Perhaps someone had tipped her off that the police were here.

'I only want to ask about your husband.'

Ann Littlewood didn't look up. 'Don't want to talk about him.'

Stella picked some of the peas off the ground and dropped them in the colander. 'Can I help with these?'

After serious thought, Mrs Littlewood made room on the bench by shifting her substantial haunches from the centre to one end. Stella sat beside her and scooped up a handful of pods.

'This isn't to do with the way he treated you. It's about something else.'

'What's he supposed to have done now?'

'We're not sure. Does he have a car?'

'A Ford Fiesta. It's taxed.'

'Does he use it much?'

'Can't afford to. Didn't they tell you we're on the social?'

'Does he ever drive down to Wightview Sands at the weekend?'

'All that way? What for?'

'The beach?'

'You're joking. He's never been near the place. He hates the sea. He's always in the Blacksmith's Arms at the end of our road or sleeping it off in the churchyard. What would he want with the beach?'

A burgeoning scenario withered and died. Stella had almost persuaded herself that Littlewood had driven to the beach with a few six-packs and chanced upon his enemy Shiena Wilkinson sunbathing close by. She preferred it to the notion that he'd followed her there in the car.

She tried a different tack. 'Has Dr Wilkinson been to visit you here?'

'Why should she? I'm all right. It's just bruises and stuff. You've only got to touch me and I bruise.'

'So you haven't heard from her?'

'She's busy, isn't she? Got people who are really ill to look after.'

Between them, they finished shelling the peas.

'I'll be given a load of spuds to peel now,' Ann Littlewood said as Stella left her. 'This is no holiday.'

All the signs were that she would discharge herself and return to her violent husband in a matter of days.

Hen Mallin called St Richard's hospital at eleven thirty and asked if Dr Mears, a colleague of Shiena Wilkinson, had been in as arranged to identify the body recovered from Wightview Sands. He had not. A call to the health centre revealed why. At eleven fifteen in the Waitrose supermarket one of the doctor's patients had collapsed with chest pains. Dr Mears was at the hospital, in attendance at an intensive care ward, not the mortuary. The living had priority over the dead.

Hen seriously thought about having twenty minutes with her Agatha Christie tapes. It was that or another cigar. This case was an obstacle course. She *had* to be certain that the body was Dr Wilkinson's. Stella had reported back with news of a violent character who had created a scene in the surgery the week before. Really they should interview this man as early as possible. Yet all she could do at present was chain-smoke.

She got through two more deciding how to pitch the TV appeal. She wanted her message to reach the Smiths, the family who had reported the dead woman on the beach. It was a tough decision whether to name them and their child, Haley. Normally you kept children out of it, but this name pinpointed them and might prompt friends and neighbours into asking if they were the Smith family in the news. On balance, she thought she would go for it. The Smiths might not even have heard about the strangling. Some people sailed through life without ever reading the papers or looking at television news.

She would also ask for other witnesses. Plenty of the public had been on that stretch of beach when the body was found. The sight of four men lifting a lifeless woman from the water must have created some interest. And who were those four men? Smith, for sure, the lifeguard for another, and two others. How much had they seen?

By the time she went in front of the cameras she would expect to know if the dead woman was Dr Wilkinson. If the information was right that the doctor's nearest relatives lived in Canada, she'd make sure the police over there were requested to break the news to the family. Then she could go public and show a photo of the victim on TV – no reason not to – and ask for help in tracking her movements up to the moment of her murder. They'd need a bank of phones to handle all the calls coming in.

Now it was a case of drafting the text for her short slot in the regional news. Maybe thirty seconds. Every word had to count.

Satisfied at last with what she would say, she went for a late lunch in the station canteen. Half the murder squad was down there drinking coffee. She couldn't blame them.

Hen enjoyed her food. Light lunches were out. She had a theory that in this job she could never be certain where the next meal would come from, so she stoked up with carbohydrates like a marathon runner packing energy before the race. Steak and kidney pie and chips today, followed by apple tart and custard. She claimed she could go for hours after a lunch like that, though she wouldn't turn down a good supper.

At two thirty-eight, a call came in from a car park attendant at Wightview Sands. Hen was back in the incident room to take it.

'Yes?'

The speaker was self-important, typical of a certain kind of minor official, and he obviously had difficulty accepting a woman as chief investigating officer. 'Am I speaking to the person responsible for the murder?'

'Not literally. He's the one I'm trying to catch. If you want the person heading the enquiry, that's me.'

'The senior detective?'

'Right. Have you something to tell me?'

'I'm speaking from the car park at Wightview Sands.'

'I've been told that.'

'Are you sure you're in charge?'

'Look, do you have something to tell me, squire, or not? We're very busy here.'

'I'm not personally involved,' he said. 'If that's what you're thinking, you're wrong. I wasn't even on duty when the woman was found.'

'So what's this about?'

'Actually a lady here would like a word with you.'

What a relief. 'Put her on, then.'

The new voice was easier on the ear, low-pitched for a woman, well in control. 'I understand you've taken possession of my Range Rover. My name is Shiena Wilkinson. How do I get it back, please?'

5

Hen Mallin's television appeal needed some rapid script changes now. So it was Stella who drove out to Wightview Sands and met Dr Wilkinson. Not an easy assignment.

The first thing she noticed was the hair. Mrs Bassington, the health centre receptionist, had been right. It was emphatically more chestnut than copper. Thick, long, and worn loose, as if to make clear Shiena Wilkinson was off duty. She was in T-shirt and close-fitting denim shorts, with a figure that . . . well, maybe she looked more like a GP in her work clothes.

They spoke in the windsurfers' club, close to where the Range Rover had been parked. The car park attendant who had spoken to Hen on the phone lingered as if he might have something to contribute, but he was a new face. Another man had been on duty when the body was found. From the looks he was giving the young doctor it was obvious what this fellow's agenda was. He was around thirty, with thick, slicked-back hair and a stupid grin. Stella asked him if he shouldn't be back in his kiosk.

'It's on automatic,' he said. 'We put it on automatic when things are quiet. People put in their money and the gate goes up. I can get you ladies a coffee if you want.'

'Thanks, but no,' Stella said. 'Unless . . .' She gave Dr Wilkinson an enquiring look and was grateful for a shake of the head.

The car park man still hovered. 'I expect you thought Dr Wilkinson was the victim, being the owner of the Range Rover.'

Stella gave him a look she reserved for really pathetic cases. 'I'm asking you to leave us now, Mr, em . . .'

'Garth,' he said. 'My name's Garth.'

When the two women were alone, Shiena Wilkinson said, 'I understand you took my car away because you thought it belonged to that unfortunate woman who was found dead. Well, I need it back – urgently.'

'Understood.'

'It contains things essential to my work. I'm a doctor.'

'And I'm a detective, so I know you are.' Stella smiled to ease the tension. 'You'll get your things back directly. But as for the car, you'll need to hire another for the next day or two. We had to look inside. We'll put the damage right, of course.'

'*Damage?*'

'We broke a window.'

'I thought you had bunches of keys for a job like that.'

'We couldn't wait. We had a body, obviously murdered. We needed to identify her quickly.'

'Point taken,' Dr Wilkinson said in a more accepting tone.

'What made you leave it here?'

'That's personal. I was going to collect it today. Hairy moment for me when it wasn't here.'

'Do you mind telling me?'

She sighed. 'I met a friend on the beach yesterday and spent the night with him in Brighton. He took me there in his car. It's as simple as that. He offered to bring me back today to collect mine and he did.'

Stella drove the young doctor to the motor vehicle forensic unit to collect her medical bag and other things. On the way, Shiena Wilkinson talked about the man she'd met. He was Greg, a college friend she hadn't seen for a couple of years, though they'd phoned each other. It seemed he regularly came to the beach to surf. He'd produced a bottle of cooled Chablis from an ice box he had in his car, and it had been like revisiting her student days because she'd got (in her own words) 'rather mellow as the day wore on'. At the end of the afternoon Greg persuaded her she was in no state to drive (women being more susceptible to alcohol than men – at which Stella rolled her eyes, and Dr Wilkinson said, 'Yes, but more to the point, I'd drunk two-thirds of the bottle') and suggested it would be safe to leave the Range Rover overnight. If there was a problem, he'd say he was a member of the windsurfers' club and square it with the car park man.'

'Was he worth it?' Stella asked.

'Are they ever?'

Stella asked which section of the beach the couple had been on. It was too much to hope they had witnessed something.

'Close to where I parked my car, almost opposite the club.'

Too far off.

'Did you hear about the body being found?'

'At the time? No.'

'News travels fast. I thought maybe people along the beach knew what was going on.'

'If I'd known, I'd have offered to help. It's something you do, in my job. What time was she found?'

'What time did you leave?'

'Quite early. Around four, I think.'

Wrong woman, wrong place, wrong time of day.

After she'd been on TV, Hen Mallin returned to the incident room and told her team they weren't just to sit around and wait for witnesses to get in touch. 'What about the other cars left there on Sunday evening? There were three, apart from the Range Rover. One belonged to Claudia, the Boxgrove blonde. That leaves two.'

Sergeant Mason, the man who had contacted the Police National Computer, said, 'Another Mitsubishi and a Peugeot, both registered to men.'

'I remember. I suppose they're not still there, by any chance?'

'Both gone, guv.'

'Did you keep a note of the numbers?'

Mason sighed and shook his head.

'Or the owners' addresses?'

'Sorry. I thought when we fixed on the Range Rover . . .'

'But I did, and I checked with the PNC,' the keeno, George Flint, said with unconcealed self-congratulation. He produced a notebook. 'The Mitsu was registered to a guy by the name of Thomas West, 219 Victory Road, Portsmouth, and the Peugeot is down to a Londoner, Deepak Patel, 88 Melrose Avenue, Putney.'

'Nice work, George.'

He beamed.

'Follow it up, would you?' she told him in the same affable tone. 'See if there's any link with a missing woman.'

From looking like a golden retriever being stroked on the head, he changed to a snarling pit bull. 'You mean go there?'

'In a word, yes. Take DC Walters.' Walters was the newest officer on the team, so green that he still thought speed was what you did on the motorway and H was a sign for a hospital.

Flint's face said it all. What a way to reward initiative.

Stella said to the boss, 'Speaking of missing persons, I

looked at the MPI. You know how it is, guv. Thousands of names.'

'Yes, but we're only interested in the ones reported in the past twenty-four hours.'

'It could take another week before our victim gets on the index. We're talking about a missing adult here, not a kid.'

'Fair point. Keep checking each day. Do we have the list of all the objects picked up on the beach?'

'That's in hand.'

'Meaning, no, we don't.'

'It's a long list, guv.'

'Get it on my screen by six tonight. And, speaking of tonight, does anyone have a problem working overtime?'

No one did, apparently.

In spite of all the overtime, nothing startling emerged in the next twenty-four hours. The television appeal brought in over seventy calls from people who believed they had seen the victim on the beach on Sunday. As Hen remarked to Stella, 'I'm beginning to wonder if there was anyone on that bloody beach who *wasn't* female with copper-coloured hair and a white two-piece swimsuit.'

The team were kept busy taking statements and the computer files mounted up, but no one was under any illusion that a breakthrough was imminent.

George Flint visited Portsmouth and London and spoke to the owners of the Mitsubishi and the Peugeot. Each had good explanations for leaving their vehicles in the car park overnight. The Mitsubishi had run out of fuel and its owner had got a lift back to Portsmouth from a friend who vouched for him. He'd returned with a can of petrol the next day. The Peugeot owner had gone for a sea trip along the coast to Worthing with some friends in a motorised inflatable and returned too late to collect his car. No women were involved in either case.

The inventory of items found on the beach gave no obvious clue. A pair of Ray-Ban sunglasses with a broken side-piece could have belonged to the victim, but how could you tell without DNA or fingerprint evidence?

'Why does anyone choose to strangle a woman on a crowded beach in broad daylight?' Hen asked Stella. 'I don't buy theft as the motive. I really don't.'

'We don't know what she had with her,' Stella said. 'Maybe she was carrying a large amount of money.'

'On a beach? No, Stella, there's something else at work here.'

'Crime of passion?'

'Explain.'

'A man she's dumped gets so angry that he kills her.'

'What – follows her to the beach?'

'Or they drive there together to talk about their relationship, and she tells him it's over, there's a new man in her life. He turns ballistic and strangles her. Then he picks up her bag and returns to the car park and drives off. If they came together and he left alone it explains why we didn't find her car at the end of the day.'

'That part I like. The rest, not so much. The strangling was done from behind, remember, and with a ligature. I doubt if the killer grabbed her by the throat in a fit of rage and squeezed the life out of her. He took her by stealth.'

Stella didn't see any problem with that. 'So they had their row and she told him to get lost and turned her back on him because she didn't want to argue any more.'

'What did he use?'

'Use?'

'For a ligature.'

'I don't know. Anything that came to hand. There are pieces of rope on a beach. Or cable.'

Hen said, 'It's more likely he brought the ligature with him.'

'Meaning it was premeditated?'

'Yes.'

A fresh thought dawned on Stella. 'Well, what if she was wearing some kind of pendant on a thin leather cord? He grabbed it from behind and twisted it.'

'Better. You might persuade me this time.'

'You know the kind of thing I mean?' Stella said, her eyes beginning to shine at the idea.

'I do. Something out of one of those Third World shops, with a wood carving or a piece of hammered copper.'

'Exactly! You see, guv, I still think it's more likely this was a spur-of-the-moment thing. If it were planned, it wouldn't have happened where it did. He'd have taken her somewhere remote.'

'You're making a couple of assumptions here. First, the killer is a man. All right, the odds are on a man. Second, that he drove her there. *She* could have done the driving. Or even a third person. Until we get a genuine witness, all this is speculation. The people we've got to find are the Smiths, the couple who first raised the alarm. Why haven't they come forward?'

The post-mortem was conducted the following morning by James Speight, a forensic pathologist of long experience, with Hen Mallin in attendance, along with Stella Gregson, two SOCOs and two police photographers, one using a video recorder. Formal identification (that this was the body discovered on the beach) was provided by PC Shanahan, one of the two who had been called to the scene first. He left the autopsy room before the painstaking process of examining the body externally got under way.

Hen had to be patient in this situation. Dr Speight gave minute attention to the marks around the corpse's neck, having the body turned by stages and asking repeatedly for photographs. An outsider might have supposed the photographers were running the show, so frequently did the pathologist and his assistant step away for pictures to be taken. After three-quarters of an hour the body was still in the white two-piece swimsuit she had been wearing at the scene. The external findings would probably be more crucial than the dissection in this case. It was helpful to be told that there were no injection marks, nothing to indicate that the woman had been a drug user.

Dr Speight pointed out that the ligature had left a horizontal line, apart from the crossover at the nape. There was some bruising in this area, probably made by pressure of the killer's knuckles. He noted the two scratches above the ligature mark on the right side of the neck and said indications of this kind were not uncommon, where the victim had tried to pull the cord away from her.

'It's entirely consistent with strangulation by a ligature,' he said in that way pathologists have of stating the obvious. 'I can't see any pattern or weave in the mark, yet it's fairly broad, more than half a centimetre. Not so clear cut or deep as a wire or string. It could have been made by a piece of plastic cable or a band of leather or an extra thick shoelace. Certainly from behind. That's where the pressure was exerted.'

'These scratches,' Hen said. 'Is it likely she scratched her killer?'

'Possibly – but her fingernails are undamaged. I doubt if she put up much of a fight. Death was pretty quick, going by the absence of severe facial congestion and petechiae. There's no bleeding from the ears. It's not impossible she suffered a reflex cardiac arrest. We'll find out presently. And the sea appears to have washed away

61

any interesting residue under the nails. I've collected what I can, but it looks to me like sand.'

'Could she have screamed?'

'Before the ligature was applied, yes. Once it was in place, I doubt it.'

'So if he surprised her from behind, as it appears, and it was done under the cover of a windbreak, people nearby wouldn't have known?'

Dr Speight gave a shrug.

'They wouldn't have heard much, would they?' Hen pressed him.

'A guttural, choking sound, perhaps.'

'Like waves breaking on a beach?'

The doctor smiled. 'Romantic way of putting it.'

'But you see what I'm getting at?'

'And it's outside my remit.'

He continued with his task, removing the clothes and passing them to the SOCOs, and taking swabs and samples. Before proceeding, he gave some more observations. The relative absence of cyanosis, or facial coloration, suggested she had succumbed quickly, probably within fifteen seconds. There were no operation scars and no notable birthmarks or tattoos. She had the usual vaccination mark. Her ears were pierced. She still had all her teeth, with only three white fillings. Her copper-coloured hair was natural.

The next hour, the internal examination, might have appeared more proactive than the first, but mainly it confirmed the earlier observations, except that the unknown woman had definitely died of asphyxiation, not cardiac arrest. 'The strangling was efficient,' Dr Speight said without emotion.

The findings gave minimal assistance as to identity. She was about thirty to thirty-five and sexually experienced, but had not given birth.

'So what's new?' Hen muttered to Stella as they left the autopsy room. 'Don't know about you, but I need a smoke and a strong coffee.'

By three twenty each weekday, you couldn't get a parking space in Old Mill Road, where the junior school was. Parents massed outside the gates and waited for their offspring to emerge with the latest piece of handiwork made of eggboxes or yoghurt cartons. Haley Smith was always one of the last, and Olga was always waiting for her.

Today, unusually, the class teacher, Miss Medlicott, walked across the playground with Haley, hand in hand. For a moment it crossed Olga's mind that her child might be unwell, so she was relieved to see some colour in her face and a broad smile. Like many of the others, Haley was holding a sheet of paper.

'I've done a lovely picture, Mummy,' she called out, and waved it so energetically that it was in danger of tearing. 'Do you want to see?'

Olga nodded, at the same time searching Miss Medlicott's face for some clue as to why she was with Haley. 'Beautiful!' she said without really looking. Devoted as she was to her child, she knew she was no artist. Other children did work strikingly more colourful, confident and technically proficient than Haley's best efforts.

'It's the seaside.'

'Isn't it lovely?' Miss Medlicott said with a warm smile at Olga. She was a sweet young woman and the children adored her. 'I'd like a word, if you can spare a minute.'

'Of course.' Olga turned to Haley. 'Why don't you have a ride on the swing while I talk to Miss Medlicott?'

'I'll take care of your picture,' Miss Medlicott offered.

Haley ran across to the play area.

'Is there a problem?'

'Not really. At least, I don't think there is,' Miss Medlicott said. 'As you see, we were doing some art work this afternoon. I think this is one of her best efforts this term.' She held out the painting. There were several horizontal stripes in blue and yellow across the width of the paper. Some of Haley's characteristic stick figures were there, probably done with a marker pén.

'Is that the right way up?' Olga asked.

'Yes, I'm certain it is. The people are supposed to be lying down. They're sunbathers or swimmers, depending which bit of the picture they're drawn in, so Haley informed me. It's got its own logic. Her work usually has. She's a good observer.'

'That's nice to hear.'

'The reason I wanted to speak to you is that she insists one of these figures is a dead lady.'

Olga felt her flesh prickle.

'This one, I think,' Miss Medlicott said, with her finger on one of them, 'though they're all rather similar. I tried to persuade her that it couldn't be so – that she must have seen someone asleep who was lying very still. But she won't be budged. She's adamant that she saw a dead lady when you took her to the beach a few days ago. When would that have been?'

'Sunday,' Olga said. 'It was Sunday.'

'Yes. Obviously something made an impact. If certain of the children talked like this, I'd think nothing of it. The boys, in particular, have lurid imaginations. Dracula, dinosaurs, zombies, all the horrors you could name. But Haley isn't like that. She's in the real world, very practical, very truthful. That's why I'm just a bit concerned about this. It's real to her, and I think it troubles her.'

'Did she say anything else?'

'She said you were sitting just behind this woman, whoever she was.'

Olga wrestled with her loyalties. This young teacher was wholly sincere, concerned only with Haley's mental well-being. 'There was an incident,' she said. 'It was in the papers. Wightview Sands. A woman found dead. I expect Haley overheard us talking about it and linked it to someone she noticed lying near us.'

'Do you think so? That would explain it, then.'

'It may have been on the television as well. You can't always stop them seeing unpleasant things.'

'You'll talk to her, then?'

'I'll do my best. Thanks.' Ashamed of herself, she handed back the picture and went to collect Haley.

Miss Medlicott strolled back across the playground. The head teacher, Mrs Anderson, was at the school door. 'Was that the child's mother?'

'Yes. The mother is very sensible. She'll be supportive. She looked rather stressed herself, so I'm afraid I ducked telling her the most disturbing part of the child's story.'

'What was that?'

'Well, that her daddy was with this woman who died on the beach.'

6

Nine days after the body was found, Hen Mallin said to Stella, 'What is it with this case? Have we hit a brick wall, or what?'

With a touch of annoyance, Stella informed her boss that she had checked the Missing Persons Index regularly. 'Do you know how many we've followed up?'

'Don't take it personally. I'm not knocking your efforts, Stell. I'm trying to think of a reason why nobody misses this woman in all this time – a smart dame apparently not short of money, who doesn't come home, doesn't report for work, visit her friends or answer the phone.'

'Phones answer themselves.'

'Only for as long as you're satisfied talking to a machine.'

'There isn't much you can do about it.'

'Eventually you do. You ask yourself why the bloody thing is in answer mode all day and every day.'

'How long is it now?'

'Over a week. It looks more and more as if someone is covering up.'

'How, exactly?'

Hen spread her hands as if it were obvious. 'Making it appear she's away on holiday, or too ill to speak to her friends.'

'You're assuming he was the man in her life? The old truth that the vast majority of murders are domestic?'

'It looks that way. We accounted for all the cars in the beach car park, so how did she get to the beach?'

'Someone drove her.'

Hen agreed. 'That's got to be the best bet. They find a place on the beach and put up their windbreak and he waits for her to relax. She turns on her front to sunbathe. He chooses his moment to strangle her and then goes back to his car and drives off. Because he's regarded as the boyfriend, he's able to reassure her friends and work colleagues that she's still alive. He can keep that going for some time.'

'While we're going spare.'

'But there's always a point when the smokescreen isn't enough. People get suspicious.'

'If you're right,' Stella said, 'it's going to be simple when we reach that point because someone is going to say she's missing and point the finger at the same time.'

'We collar the guy.'

'Case solved,' Stella said with an ironic smile.

When the breakthrough came, on day twelve, it was not as either of them had foreseen. The MPI churned out a new batch of names and Stella found one that matched better than most, a thirty-two-year-old unmarried woman from the city of Bath. She was the right height and build and age and, crucially, her hair colour was described as 'auburn/copper'. No tattoos, scars or other identifying marks.

Hen Mallin was intrigued by the missing woman's profession. Emma Tysoe was listed as a 'psych. o.p.'.

'What's that when it's at home?'

'I guess it's shortened to fit the space. Psychiatric out-patient?'

'That's hardly a profession, guv.'

'What's your theory, then?'

Stella pressed some keys and switched to a glossary of abbreviations and found the answer: psychological offender profiler. 'She's not a patient. She's a shrink. I've seen them on TV telling us how to do our job.'

Stella's reaction was understandable. Television drama had eagerly embraced profiling as a fresh slant on the well-tried and ever-popular police series. *Cracker* had been Sherlock Holmes updated, an eccentric main character with amazing insights who would point unerringly to the truth the poor old plod couldn't see. The professionals never missed an episode, yet claimed it was a million miles from the real thing.

Hen was more positive. 'Profilers have their uses. The best of them are worth listening to. Check her out, Stella. Is there a photo? See if you can get one on screen.'

This took some organising with Bath police and when it appeared on the monitor it was in black and white and not the sharpest of images. It must have been taken in bright sunshine that picked out the features sharply but whitened the flatter areas of the brow and cheeks, giving no clue as to flesh tone. Wide, intelligent eyes, an even nose and full lips, a fraction apart, showing a glimpse of the teeth. A curved jawline above a long, narrow neck.

Even so, it convinced Hen. 'That's our lady. I'll put money on it.'

'All bets are off,' Stella said. 'I agree with you.'

'I feel I know her better looking at this than I did beside her body,' Hen said. 'There's a bright lady here.'

'It's the eyes, guv.'

'What *do* we know about her?'

'Her job.'

'Have we ever used her?'

'Not to my knowledge.'

'What was she doing on our patch, then?'

'Sunbathing. It's allowed.'

Hen merely nodded. 'There's a list of profilers approved by the NCF – the National Crime Faculty at Bramshill. Let's find out if she's on it and what they know about her. I'll take care of that. And you can get on to Bath police again. Presumably she lives or works there if they reported her missing.'

'Are you sure?' the young-sounding sergeant in Bath queried. 'She only went onto Missing Persons yesterday.'

'Would I call you if I didn't think this was a good match?' Stella said.

'It's so quick, though.'

'Not for us. We've had a body on our hands for twelve days. Can you send someone to look at it?'

'The next of kin, you mean? You'll have to be patient with me. I'm not fully up with it.'

'Why not? It's been on national television. Didn't I tell you she was murdered?'

'Yikes – you didn't.'

'So you'd better get up with it fast. Are you CID?'

'No, ma'am.'

'Why don't you get hold of someone who is and ask him to call me in the next ten minutes? I'm DS Gregson, at the incident room, Bognor police station.'

The name of Bognor never fails to kindle a smile. There is a story told of that staid old monarch, George V, that it was his favourite seaside place, and on his deathbed he was offered the incentive that if he got better he might care to visit Bognor, whereupon he uttered his last words, 'Bugger Bognor' – and expired. According to his biographer, they were not his last words at all. He spoke them in happier circumstances when told that thanks to his patronage Bognor was about to be accorded special status as Bognor Regis. It's still worthy of a smile.

'*Bognor?*' Detective Superintendent Peter Diamond repeated.

'But the body was found at Wightview Sands,' the sergeant who had taken the call informed him, then, listening to his own words and thinking how daft these places sounded, wished himself anywhere but in Diamond's office.

However, Diamond said without a trace of side, 'I know Wightview Sands. Big stretch of sand and a bloody long line of beach huts. And this is murder, you say?'

'They say, sir.'

'A Bath woman?'

'Emma Tysoe. A profiler.'

'A what?'

'Psychological offender profiler. She helps out in murder enquiries.'

'She's never helped me.'

The sergeant was tempted to say, Perhaps you didn't ask. Wisely, he kept it to himself. 'All I know is that she was reported missing by the university. She often goes away on cases connected with her work, but she always keeps in touch with the department. This time she didn't get in touch. After some days, they got concerned.'

'Where does she live?'

'A flat in Great Pulteney Street.'

'Posh address. There must be money in profiling, sergeant.'

'It's only a basement flat, sir.'

'Garden apartment,' Diamond said in the tone of an upmarket estate agent. 'No such thing as a basement flat in Great Pulteney Street. Why haven't I heard of this woman before?'

The sergeant sidestepped that one.

'How was she topped?' Diamond asked.

'Strangled. It's been in the papers.'

'It'll be all over them when they know what she did for a living. Strangled on a beach?'

'On a Sunday afternoon when everyone was down there.'

'Odd.'

'They don't have any witnesses either.'

'People are holding back, you mean? Someone must have seen it. This is weird. You've got me all of a quiver, sergeant.'

He sent a couple of young detectives to Great Pulteney Street to seal the missing woman's flat and talk to the neighbours. One of them was DC Ingeborg Smith, the sometime newshound, bright, blonde and eager to impress, recently enlisted to the CID after serving her two years in uniform. He asked Keith Halliwell, his trusty DI, to go up to the university and establish that Emma Tysoe was known to the Psychology Department.

Then he collected a coffee from the machine – with a steady hand for a man who was all of a quiver – and passed a thoughtful twenty minutes pondering why a profiler should have been strangled on a public beach on a Sunday afternoon. Finally he called Bognor and spoke to Stella Gregson. Enquiries into the background and movements of Emma Tysoe were well under way, he told her. He looked forward to full cooperation over this case, which he expected would require a joint approach. He would therefore accompany the identity witness to Bognor and use the opportunity to make himself known to the SIO.

'He sounds pushy,' Stella told Hen Mallin.

'Peter Diamond? I've heard of him, and he is. I've also heard that he pulls rabbits out of hats, so we'll see if his magic works for us. Don't look so doubtful, Stella. I've handled clever dicks like him before. When they stand up to take a bow, you pull away the chair.'

71

'I guess we can't avoid linking up with Bath.'

'We're not going to get much further unless we do. That's where Emma Tysoe lived, so that's where we look next.'

And Diamond duly arrived that afternoon, a big man of about fifty with a check shirt, red braces and his jacket slung over his shoulder. Going by looks alone, the beer belly, thrusting jaw and Churchillian mouth, he was pushiness personified. With him was a less intimidating individual, altogether smaller and more spry, a kind of tic-tic bird in tinted glasses.

'This is Dr Seton,' Diamond said. 'He's a professional colleague of Dr Tysoe, here to see if he can identify the body.'

Dr Seton's face lit up, suggesting he was relishing the prospect. 'But I have to make clear I'm not a doctor of medicine,' he said. 'I'm a behavioural psychologist.'

'No one in Dr Tysoe's family was available,' Diamond said, virtually admitting Dr Seton was second best. 'There's a sister, but she's in South Africa.'

'Good of you to come,' Hen said to Dr Seton.

'He was volunteered by the professor,' Diamond said. 'Shall we get on with it?' Considering Dr Seton had given up most of his day, this seemed unnecessarily brusque.

Hen started as she meant to go on with Diamond. She knew he must have quizzed Seton thoroughly on the journey down and could probably have summed up the salient facts in a couple of sentences. However, she intended to hear everything first hand. 'Before we do, I'd like a few words of my own with Dr Seton – that is, if you don't object.'

Diamond shrugged.

She swivelled her chair away from him and asked, 'So, Dr Seton, are you involved in Emma Tysoe's work as a profiler?'

'Absolutely not,' the man said, as if it was tainted. 'That's extracurricular.'

'Something she does independently?'

'I believe it arose out of her Ph.D research into the psychology of violence.'

'So you have some idea of what she does?'

'She acts as an adviser to the police.'

'Regularly?'

'Pretty often, yes. She has an arrangement with the university and takes time off when required.'

'Convenient.'

'Enviable,' Diamond said, winking at Hen.

'And was she currently working on a case?' Hen asked Dr Seton, ignoring Diamond.

'I presume so. We hadn't seen her for a while.'

'But you wouldn't happen to know the details?'

'No.'

'Did she keep it to herself, the offender profiling?'

'It doesn't interest me particularly. We all have different areas of interest.'

'So what's yours, Dr Seton?'

'Masturbation.'

For a full five seconds nothing was said. Diamond, who had spent the last two hours with the man and must have known what was coming, was gazing steadily out of the window at the trees in Hotham Park. Stella covered her mouth with her hand.

Dr Seton ended the silence himself. 'The subject was rather neglected until I started fifteen years ago. Surprisingly little was known of the psychology, yet it's a fascinating aspect of behavioural science and, let's face it, something we've all experienced.'

'Hands on,' Diamond said, but only for Stella's ears. Still with her hand over her mouth, she made a sound like a car braking.

Now he had started on his pet subject, Seton didn't want to stop. 'It was unfortunately branded as a sin by the religionists, so there's this burden of guilt that goes with it. Genesis 38. I can quote if you like.'

'I'll take your word for it,' Hen managed to say. 'Getting back to Emma Tysoe, do you share an office with her?'

'No. It was decided I should have my own room.'

Diamond murmured, 'I can't think why.'

Stella closed her eyes and went pink in the face.

Hen carried on resolutely, 'So do you know her well?'

'Not particularly. We meet in the staffroom on occasions.'

'Does she have any close friends in the department?'

'How would I know? I'm not sure why the professor picked me for this.'

Diamond said, 'Perhaps he thought you should get out more.'

Stella made the braking sound again.

Hen's glare at Diamond left the big man in no doubt that she'd had enough. 'All right. Let's go to the mortuary.'

Stella drove them to St Richard's, and not much was said on the way. Hen asked Dr Seton if Emma Tysoe gave lectures and was told all the staff were timetabled to lecture. Dr Tysoe normally did five hours a week and her topic was forensic psychiatry. When she was away on a case, colleagues would cover for her and usually tried to speak on something from their own field that related to the course. Nobody asked Seton what he found to talk about.

In the anteroom of the mortuary the formality of identification was got through quickly.

'That's her.'

'Dr Emma Tysoe?'

'Yes.'

Out in the sunshine, Hen lit up a cigar and said to Stella, 'We passed the outpatients' on the way in. Why don't you take Dr Seton there and buy him a cup of coffee? I need to check a couple of things with Mr Diamond.'

So Stella found herself reluctantly paired off with the masturbation expert, while Hen flashed a not-too-sympathetic smile and a promise of, 'We won't forget you.'

'The pay-off?' said Diamond to Hen, as they moved off.

'She was practically wetting herself laughing in my office,' she said. 'She had it coming.'

'She's with the right man, then.'

She didn't smile. Diamond would have to work hard to overcome that bad first impression.

'Anyway,' she said, 'I know a better place.'

'I hoped you might.'

These two strong individuals sat opposite each other at a table in the staff canteen like chess-players. They'd collected a pot of tea and Hen was determined not to be the one who poured. After Diamond had eaten a biscuit, slowly, he said, 'Do you take yours white?'

She nodded and reached for the milk. 'Are you going to pour?'

It seemed a fair distribution of the duties. 'OK, I'm sorry about Seton,' he had the grace to say. 'As you probably noticed, he's a one-subject man. I had two hours of it in the car.'

'Do you think the professor picked him specially?'

'I'm sure of it. And I'm sure everyone had a good laugh about it after we'd driven away.'

'You could have tipped me off.'

'But how? It's not the kind of thing you can whisper in a lady's ear.'

She weighed that. 'Probably not,' she conceded finally. Then: 'For pity's sake, how does he carry out this research?

Oh, never mind. I'll hear it all from Stella.'

'When I get back to Bath, I'll speak to the prof,' Diamond said, putting down the teapot. He hadn't done too well. Two pools of tea had spilt on the table. 'Don't you find metal pots always pour badly? The prof should be able to tell me more about the cases this woman was advising on. I'm assuming her death is in some way related to her job.'

'It has to be followed up,' Hen agreed, dropping a paper napkin over the spillage and wiping it.

'So what's been happening down here?' he asked. 'Do you have anything else under investigation?'

'Serious crimes? Nothing we'd need a profiler for, if that's what you're getting at.'

'Sleepers? We've all got sleepers.' He meant the unsolved crimes that stayed on file.

'A few of those, but none we're actively pursuing. Believe me, I didn't ask her to come and neither did anyone else I know.'

'Who are your neighbours? Hampshire police? Did anything happen in Portsmouth? Now *there*'s a place with a reputation. Naval base. All kinds of scams at the docks.'

'Portsmouth docks are more of a theme park these days,' she told him. 'I've spoken to them, and they haven't used her either.'

'She must have been down here for a reason.'

'Unless it was a holiday. People do go on holiday.'

'Dr Seton didn't seem to know about it.'

Hen said, 'Dr Seton seems to have narrow vision.'

He smiled. 'It's supposed to turn you blind, isn't it?'

Her real reason for setting up this tête-à-tête had to be faced. 'You'll report back to me on this?'

'Full consultation,' he said after a slight pause. 'It's a joint investigation.'

'It was initiated here,' Hen made clear. 'The incident room is at my nick. I'll take the decisions.'

He said, 'I wouldn't want to pull rank.'

'Then don't. It's a West Sussex murder.'

'She's a Bath and North-east Somerset woman. You may find the focus of the investigation is off-limits for you. Then you'll need my help.'

'Need it? I'm depending on it,' Hen said. 'Bath nick is my second home from now on.'

He grinned. Without getting heavy, they had reached an understanding. 'And you'll be welcome. So what's happening at this end?'

She told him about the TV appeal and the difficulty in finding a genuine witness. 'Plenty of people offered help, but not the ones we want most.'

'Who are they?'

'A family of three who were sitting close enough to notice her failing to move when the tide came in. The man fetched the lifeguard.'

'A responsible citizen, then?'

'But we've heard nothing from him since.'

'Do you have a description?'

'We have a name.'

'Good. What is it?'

She told him and he smiled. She told him about the daughter called Haley who had been lost for a short time.

'Haley is better than Smith,' he said. 'Not so many Haleys about. Have you tried the local schools?'

'No joy.'

'People drive miles to the seaside,' he said. 'They could be Londoners, or from anywhere. My way, even. Do you want me to take it on?'

She was guarded in her response. 'For the present, I'd rather you found out what you can about Emma Tysoe's life and work in Bath.' But it had not escaped her that he'd deferred to her. Maybe this man Diamond was more manageable than people said. 'Now that we have her name, it's going to open up more avenues.'

'As you wish,' he said. 'And let's get *our* names into the open. I'm going to call you Henrietta from now on.'

'Try it, and see what happens,' she told him with a sharp look. 'I'm Hen.'

'Fair enough. Is it time we rescued your colleague from the one-gun-salute man?'

'Stella? Not yet,' she said with a steely gleam in her eye. 'I think I'd like a second cup. How about you, Pete?'

Haley Smith's teacher, Miss Medlicott, was telling the class about their project for the afternoon. 'We're going to do measuring. Presently I'll ask some of you to come to the front and collect a metric rule. Not yet, Nigel! Then you'll work in pairs with the person sitting on your right. Anyone without a person sitting on his right put your hand up now.'

Without fuss, she made sure everyone had a partner.

'You'll also need a pencil and a large sheet of paper. One rule for each pair, one pencil and one piece of paper. Decide now who will collect the rule, and who comes for the pencil and paper. Quietly. Is everyone ready? Then we'll begin now.'

They carried out the instructions well. She explained that they would be measuring the length of their shoes, and showed them how to make two marks on the paper, and measure in centimetres. Most of the children understood and started making marks. She moved among them, assisting the slower learners.

After twenty minutes she said, 'Now we'll see what results we have.'

Not all of the kids had fully understood, so there were a few strange answers causing hilarity among those who had done the thing properly. Aidan, who was Haley's partner, reckoned the length of his shoe was eighty-four centimetres.

'I expect you used the wrong end of the rule,' Miss Medlicott said. 'What about you, Haley? What was your measurement?'

Haley held up the paper. She seemed to be hiding behind it.

'No, I'm asking you to tell me the length of your shoe in centimetres.'

Haley turned and whispered something to Aidan.

Aidan said, 'She says fifteen, miss.'

'Thank you, Aidan, but I'd like to hear it from Haley.'

Again Haley whispered to Aidan, who said, 'She can't, miss. Her daddy said she isn't to speak to you.'

After a moment, Miss Medlicott said, 'Very well. Who's next?'

She thought about asking Haley to remain behind to explain exactly what her father had said, but she decided the child was under enough pressure already. Something very wrong was happening in that family. She would have another word with the mother.

Diamond didn't mention to Hen Mallin that he intended visiting Wightview Sands beach before returning to Bath. She might have taken it as interference. He was going there, he persuaded himself, purely from altruism. To contribute as fully as possible to Hen's investigation, he needed to visualise the scene.

He didn't inform Dr Seton either, until they were most of the way down the road to Wightview Sands and Seton remarked, 'I don't remember coming this way.'

'We didn't. I thought you'd like to see where your colleague was found.'

'Not particularly.'

'Well, I do, and as I'm driving . . .' His stock of altruism was all used up.

This being towards the end of the afternoon, the oncoming lane was busy with cars leaving the beach, but the southward side was clear. At the car park entrance, they were asked for a pound.

'We're not here for the beach,' Diamond told the attendant. 'I'm a police officer, here about the murder.' He held his warrant card up to the cubicle.

'Bath and North-east Somerset?' the man said. 'I thought this was a Sussex investigation.' He had the look of a petty official, tight, thin mouth and ferrety eyes. Dark hair flattened to his skull.

Diamond gave him the benefit of the doubt. 'You're perfectly right. I have a kind of watching brief. You can help us, in fact. Where's the lifeguard hut?'

'Park near the beach café and you'll see it,' he said. 'Are they under suspicion, those lifeguards? They're Aussies, you know.'

'That's the bit of beach where the body was found, I was told.'

'So was I,' the man said. 'I was stuck in here issuing tickets, so I missed all the excitement.'

'You must have let the police cars through.'

'I meant I missed what was happening on the beach.'

'Do you happen to remember the woman who was killed?'

'Out of a thousand or more who came past me? I'm afraid not, my friend. No doubt I met the murderer as well, but don't ask me to pick him out.'

They drove through and parked where he'd told them. 'Want an ice cream?' he asked Dr Seton, as they were passing the serving hatch of the beach café.

'I haven't had such a thing for years,' Seton said

'Give in to it, then. It's allowed. Wicked, but not illegal,' he said, having his own private joke. 'If you don't want an old-fashioned ice cream there are plenty of things on sticks. Take a look at the diagram and pick one out.'

'I don't know, I'm sure.'

'Go for it, man. You look like a Classic Magnum fancier to me.'

'All right.'

When Diamond had paid for two Magnums and handed one over, he said, 'Looking at that board with all the different shapes and colours, I was thinking they'd make a nice research project for someone.'

Seton gave him a frown and said nothing.

They moved across the turf and sat on the stone wall above the pebbles. The tide was some way out, so Diamond was able to point to where the sand met the stones. 'That's approximately where she was found, I gather, in a white two-piece swimsuit. Don't suppose you ever saw her in a swimsuit, Dr Seton.'

'Certainly not.'

Diamond was the first to finish his Magnum. He said he'd go and have a word with the lifeguards. Unfortunately the two lads on duty hadn't been around on the day of the murder. 'You want to speak to the Aussies,' one of them said. 'They know all about it.'

He would have to leave the Aussies for another day. He crunched across the pebbles to Seton and said, 'Let's go. Mustn't keep you from your researches.'

Seton didn't smile. He was probably thinking Diamond was a suitable case for analysis.

7

Diamond got back to Bath just before seven and dropped Dr Seton outside his lodgings – where else but in Odd Down? He swore a few times to release the tension, lowered the windows for some fresh air, and then set off directly for the university campus at Claverton.

Tired from all the driving, which he knew he didn't do well, he found himself in the early evening snarl-up. Coming down Wellsway into the city in a slow-moving line of traffic he let his attention wander. Halfway down, they had erected one of those mechanical billboards with rotating strips that displayed three different ads. These had the same slogan, BECAUSE IT'S BRITISH METAL, but the pictures altered. He watched an image of Concorde being replaced by the Millennium Bridge – and then jammed his foot on the brake just in time to avoid running into the bus in front of him. Fortunately the driver behind him was more alert.

He was relieved to complete the drive without mishap.

The Department of Behavioural Psychology was quiet at this hour, though not deserted. A research student confirmed that Professor Chromik had been in earlier.

'Do you happen to know where he lives?'

The young man shook his head.

'It's important.'

'You might catch him at the end-of-semester bash later

tonight if he hasn't already pissed off to Spain, or some-where.'

'Where's it held?'

'The clubhouse at the Bath Golf Club.'

Dr Seton hadn't mentioned a staff party. Possibly his colleagues had decided not to tell him.

There was time to go home to Weston and shower. He called the nick to make sure he still had a job, as he put it to Keith Halliwell. Nothing more dramatic had happened in Bath than a middle-aged streaker running down Milsom Street. 'He didn't have a lot to show to the world,' Halliwell said. 'Nobody complained.'

'How did we get to hear about it, then?'

'A Japanese tourist tried to get a photo. The streaker grabbed the camera and carried on running and we had to decide whether to do him for theft. But you know how it is trying to nick a naked man. Not one of the foot patrols answered the shout, so he got away. The camera was recovered later behind a bush in Parade Gardens.'

Unwisely, Halliwell asked if the trip to Bognor had turned up anything.

'Which reminds me,' Diamond said. 'You went up to the university and spoke to the professor, right? Did he tell you about the tosser he unloaded on me for the day?'

'Not a word,' Halliwell said.

'Is that the truth?'

'Didn't you get on, guv?'

'Don't push me, Keith. I have a strong suspicion you were in on this.'

'In on what? I'm not following you at all.'

He seemed to be speaking sincerely, so Diamond moved on to other matters. 'What's this professor like? I'm going to meet him tonight.'

'He'll talk. Doesn't give much away, but I don't know

how much there is to tell. The dead woman was very brilliant, he said. She's on the list of approved offender profilers and the university seem to be under some obligation to let her go off and assist with investigations.'

'Pressure from the Home Office?'

'Could be. All their undergraduate students have to be found placements in their third year for job experience. Some of them go to the Crime Analysis Unit at the Yard.'

'Did he talk about the cases she's involved in?'

'He was guarded about that.'

'Let's see if I can catch him off guard tonight.'

He took that shower, and decided on the dress code for a university staff party at a golf club on a summer evening. Cream-coloured trousers, navy shirt and pale blue linen jacket. As a safeguard, he tucked a tie into an inner pocket. Golf clubs could be sniffy about open necks. The shirt was a favourite, made of a fabric that didn't crease. In the year since Steph had died, he'd scorched a couple of shirts trying to iron them.

It was after eight when he parked his old Cortina in a nice position outside the club, only for some member to point out that he was in the space reserved for the club captain. Tempted to riposte that the captain wasn't using it, he controlled himself and found another berth. As an extra gesture to conformity, he put on the tie, a sober-looking black one with a repeat design of silver handcuffs, some wag's bright idea for a birthday gift for a copper.

Inside, he located the psychology crowd in a private room upstairs. Plenty of beards and bow ties. Leather jackets seemed to be *de rigueur* for the men and black trouser suits for the women. Picking a glass of wine from a passing tray, he steered a course around the groups to where a dark-haired woman in a silvery creation with a plunge stood alone and conspicuous.

84

'You don't have the look of a trick cyclist,' he told her.

She said, 'Can I take that as a compliment?'

'Of course.'

'I'm Tara, the PA.'

'To the boss man, by any chance?'

'He's the only one of this lot who rates a PA. And who are you?'

'The unlucky cop who took Dr Seton to the seaside today.'

Tara gave the beginning of a smile, and no more. Like every good PA, she was discreet – which Diamond was not.

'After five hours in the car with that weirdo I deserve this drink,' he said, and told her his name. 'Which one is Professor Chromik?'

'Over on the right, with his back to us.'

'Frizzy black hair and half-glasses?'

'That's him. Did he invite you, then?'

'No, but I'm here to talk to him. You must have heard about Dr Emma Tysoe.'

Her features creased. 'It wasn't really Emma?'

'Seton identified her.'

She put her hand to her throat. 'None of us thought it was possible. She went missing, but . . . this!'

He was silent, giving her time to take it in.

'And here we are, enjoying ourselves,' she said. 'Did you come here specially to tell the professor?'

If the truth were told, he hadn't. He'd come to ask questions, not pass on the bad news. It hadn't occurred to him that someone had to tell them, and it was unlikely Seton would have got in touch already. However, it legitimised his presence here. 'I intend to break the news to him,' he said as if it had always been his painful duty. 'Have you any idea what she was doing down at Wightview Sands?'

She lifted her shoulders a fraction. 'Maybe she likes the seaside.'

'Was she on holiday?'

'Not officially. She had this arrangement to take time off to help the police with difficult cases. I expect you know about it. She told us she was on a case. But she usually lets us know where she is. She phones almost every day to check in.'

'But not this time.'

'That was why we got worried in the end. No one had heard from her for something like three weeks. I kept phoning the flat in Great Pulteney Street, but got no reply. I went round there myself one lunchtime and saw a heap of mail waiting for her.'

'Didn't *anyone* know what case she was on?'

'I assumed she'd told Professor Chromik, but it turned out she hadn't. He asked me if I'd heard from her.'

'Hush-hush, was it?'

'I couldn't say. I can't think why anyone would want to murder her, whatever she was working on. She was only an adviser.'

'What about her personal life? Was there a boyfriend?'

'She never mentioned one. She wasn't the chatty sort. A lovely person, but she didn't say much about her life outside the department. Mind, I don't blame her. They're a nosy lot. It goes with the subject.'

'Who were her special friends at work, then?'

'Nobody I noticed. She seemed to stay friendly with everyone.'

'Even the ones who had to fill in when she was away?'

'People grumbled a bit. They do when there's extra work being assigned. A few harsh words were spoken in the last few days.'

'About Emma skiving off, you mean?'

'Well, it could be taken that way, but they'll be regretting it now. It's not a reason for murdering anyone, is it?'

'Let's hope not.'

He drifted away from Tara and stood for a while watching the Behavioural Psychology Department socially interacting. It was not so different from a CID party, the high-flyers hovering around the boss while the subversives formed their own subgroups and the touchy-feely element played easy-to-get on the fringe.

In this heated atmosphere the tragic news circulated rapidly. You could see the stunned expressions as it passed around. The moment arrived when Professor Chromik was informed. Frowning and shaking his curly head, he disengaged himself from his colleagues and moved towards the door, perhaps to use a phone. Diamond stepped in fast.

'You've just heard about Dr Tysoe, I gather? I'm Peter Diamond, Bath CID.'

The professor's brown eyes were huge through his glasses. 'CID? It's true, then? Appalling. Do you mind stepping outside where it's more private?'

They found a quiet spot below a gilt-framed painting of a grey-bearded nineteenth-century golfer in plus-fours and cap.

'The whole thing is a mystery, and I'm hoping you can help,' Diamond said. 'We've no idea why she was at Wightview Sands, or who would have wished to murder her.'

'It's a mystery to me, too,' Chromik said. 'I'm devastated.'

'You must have known why she was away from your department.'

'She was a psychological offender profiler.'

'I know.'

'Well, this is your territory, not mine.'

Diamond recalled Halliwell's comment about the

professor not giving much away. 'She's employed in your department, isn't she? She has to let you know if she takes time off.'

'She did. She came to see me and said she'd been asked to advise on a case.'

'When was this?'

'Mid-June.'

'Can you be more precise?'

'The seventeenth.'

'. . . to advise on a case. Is that all she said?'

'It was confidential.'

'You mean she told you about the case and you're refusing to tell me? Confidentiality goes out of the window when someone is murdered.'

Chromik caught his breath in annoyance. 'That isn't what I said. She was not at liberty to speak to me about the matter. I can tell you nothing about it. That's why I said it's your territory.'

'You don't even know who contacted her?'

'No.'

'And you let her go off for God knows how long?'

'Emma was trustworthy. If she said it was necessary to take time off, I took her word for it. She promised to let me know as soon as she was able to return to her normal duties. That was the last I heard.'

He seemed to be speaking truthfully, but the story sounded wrong. Either Emma Tysoe had been tricked, or she'd put one across on the professor. If some senior detective wanted the help of a profiler, surely he wouldn't need to insist on secrecy?

'Are you certain she was honest?'

'What do you mean by that?'

'Is it possible she wasn't working on a case at all, and simply took time off for a few days by the sea?'

Chromik shook his head so forcefully that the black

curls quivered. 'Emma wouldn't do that. She valued her profiling work too much to put it at risk with a stupid deception.'

It was said in a way that made Diamond sound stupid for asking. Well, he didn't have a degree in psychology, but he wasn't intimidated by this academic.

'I'm trying to throw you a lifeline, professor. Your handling of this tragic episode is going to be questioned, not just by me, but by your superiors, I wouldn't wonder, and certainly by the press. It sounds as if you let this member of your staff run rings around you.'

'I resent that.'

'It's not my own opinion,' Diamond said, dredging deep for a word that would make an impact on this egghead. 'It's the perception. Do you know anything about her life outside the university?'

'In what way?'

'Relationships?'

'No idea.'

'Did you appoint her to the job?'

'I was on the appointments committee, yes. We were fortunate to get her. A first-class brain, without question one of the most brilliant psychologists of her generation.'

'So where did she come from?'

'She did her first degree in the north. Then she was at one of the London colleges for her Ph.D.'

'I meant her home town, not her college career.'

'I can't recall.'

'Any family?'

'I wouldn't know.'

'You don't even know where she was brought up?'

'I said I can't remember. We'll have details of her secondary education on file somewhere.'

'Is there anyone on the staff who knew her? Anyone she might have confided in?'

'You could speak to one of the women. Before you do I'd better break the news to them all.'

'I think they've heard by now.'

'That may be so, but something needs to be said. I'll make a brief announcement in there.'

'And I'll add my piece.'

Both men knew the object of this exercise was not really to break the news. By now, the entire room had heard it. Some formula had to be found to allow everyone to remain at the party without feeling guilty.

Back in the room, Chromik called his staff to order and said he had just been given some distressing news. One or two gasps of horror were provided as he imparted it. Without much subtlety, he went straight on to say he believed Emma would have wished the party to continue. There were general murmurs of assent.

Diamond stepped forward and introduced himself, admitting Dr Tysoe's death was a mystery and inviting anyone with information to speak to him. He said he wasn't only interested in the circumstances leading up to her murder, but wanted to find out more about her as a person.

As soon as he'd finished, a woman lecturer touched his arm. He was pleased. If one person comes forward, others generally follow.

'I can help with the background stuff. I'm Helen Sparks, and we shared an office.' She spoke with a South London accent. She was black, slim and tall and probably about the same age as Emma had been. Her eyes were lined in green.

He took her to a large leather sofa at the far end. 'Thanks. I appreciate this.'

'Like you said, I can talk about Emma as a person. I liked her a lot. She had style.'

'Are we talking fashion here?'

'Absolutely. For an academic, she was a neat dresser. She knew what was out there and made sure she wore it.'

'The latest, you mean?'

'No. The best. The top designer labels.'

'That must have used up most of her salary.'

'Emma wasn't short of money. I think her parents died a few years ago and left her comfortably off.'

'Did she have a lifestyle to go with it?'

'Depends what you mean. She was living at a good address in Great Pulteney Street. Drove a dream of a sports car that must have cost a bomb. But she wasn't one for partying or clubbing. I think she just loved the feeling that she was class. Shoes, hair, make-up, the works. Not showy. Elegant.'

'To attract?'

'I don't think attraction was in her scheme of things. Obviously men were interested, but she didn't encourage them. Certainly not in the workplace, anyway.'

'She preferred women?'

A shake of the head. 'If she did, I never got a hint of it. No, she had her own agenda to look a million dollars and that was it.' Helen Sparks laughed heartily. 'You've seen the rest of this lot. She was in a minority of one.'

'Two, I would think.'

She accepted the compliment with a shrug and a wry smile.

'Where was she from?'

'Liverpool, originally, but I don't think she had anyone left up there. Most of her travelling was to help the police.'

'So she talked about the work she did, the profiling?'

'Once or twice when she got back from a case she mentioned what it was about. There were some rapes in a Welsh town, and she put together a profile of the man that definitely helped them to make an arrest. She also helped with a horrid case in Yorkshire, of someone maiming farm animals. She said it became fairly obvious which village the man came from. They caught him in the act.'

'What about the case she was involved in this time? Did she say anything at all?'

Dr Sparks leaned back, frowning, trying to remember. 'One Thursday, she said she wouldn't be in for a few days, and if I had to cover for her, would I arrange to show the final-year students a film we have of juvenile offenders talking about their attitude to crime. I think I asked her where she was going this time and she said she wasn't allowed to speak about it. I said, "Big time, then?" and she said, "Huge, if it's true."'

'"Huge". She said that?'

'I'm sure of it.'

'"If it's true". I wonder what she meant by that.'

'I've no idea.'

'And that was all?'

'Yes, apart from some messages for students about assignments.'

'How was she when she told you this? Calm?'

'Yes, and kind of thoughtful, as if her mind was already on the job she had to do.'

'Is there anyone else she might have spoken to?'

'Professor Chromik, I suppose.'

'He says she didn't tell him anything,' Diamond said. He hesitated before asking, 'Is it just me, or does he treat everyone as if they crawled out from under a stone?'

She smiled faintly. 'It isn't just you.'

'Did Emma have enemies?'

'In the department? Not really. You couldn't dislike her.'

'Students?'

She drew back, surprised by the suggestion.

He said, 'She graded them, presumably. Her marking

might affect the class of degree they got, right?'

'It's not so simple as that. They're being assessed all the time by different people.'

'But one of them could hold a grudge against a member of staff if he felt he was being consistently under-valued?'

'Theoretically, but I don't think they'd resort to murder.'

Diamond disagreed, and explained why. 'Some students buckle under the pressure. Look at the suicide rate in universities.'

'That's another matter,' Helen Sparks said sharply. 'I wouldn't accept a link with murder, if that's what you're suggesting.'

'But if someone felt their problems were inflicted by one of the staff, the anger might be focused there, instead of internally.'

'Ho-hum.'

'What do you mean – ho-hum?'

'These are just assertions,' she said. 'You don't have any data base to support them.'

'There won't be data. Murder is an extreme act.'

'That's no reason to be suspicious of students.'

'Helen, I have to be suspicious of everyone.'

He asked her to introduce him to more of her colleagues, and he met three others on the staff. All professed to having been on good terms with the saintly Emma. It was obvious no one would admit to being on *bad* terms with her. Maybe he should have delayed the questions until they'd all had a few more drinks.

He left the party disappointed, feeling he'd not learned much from the stroppy professor and his uncritical staff.

'The key to this may well be the case she was working on,' he told the small team he'd assembled. They were

Keith Halliwell, his main support these days; John Leaman, the young sergeant he'd come to value in the case of the Frankenstein vault; and the rookie, Ingeborg Smith, chisel-sharp and chirpy. 'The word that was used about it was "huge". What I don't understand is the need for secrecy.'

'Maybe someone is knocking off members of MI6,' Leaman said, not entirely joking.

'Or the royals – and no one is being told,' Ingeborg said.

'The corgis?' Halliwell said.

'Had your fun?' Diamond said with a sniff. 'Anyone got any more suggestions? Whatever she was asked to do, we need to find out. As I understand it, profilers work with serial cases. There can't be that many under investigation. I want you to start ferreting, Keith.'

'Using HOLMES?'

Diamond gave him a glare.

'The computer, guv.'

'Fine. By all means.' In time, he'd remembered HOLMES was one of those acronyms he found so hard to take seriously: Home Office Large Major Enquiry System. In theory it collated information on similar serious crimes. Diamond's objection to HOLMES was that as soon as the computer came up with cases in different authorities, someone of Assistant Chief Constable rank was appointed to coordinate the efforts of the various SIOs. One more infliction. 'But ask around as well. Down in Bognor they claim there aren't any serial crimes under investigation.'

'If it's hush-hush . . .'

'Exactly.'

'Are they up to this – the Bognor lot?' Halliwell asked.

'I think so. Hen Mallin, the SIO, has a grasp of what's going on, and there's a bright young woman DS helping

94

her. They're having trouble finding genuine witnesses. That's the main problem.'

'From a crowded beach?' Ingeborg said in surprise.

'They put out a TV appeal and had plenty of uptake, but not one was any use. The only person they can definitely link to the case is the fellow who found the body, and he's done the disappearing act.'

'He has to be a suspect, then.'

'He is. Said his name was Smith.'

'That's suspicious in itself,' Leaman said.

Ingeborg's big eyes flashed fiercely. 'Thank you for that.'

Diamond said, 'Bognor police won't make much headway unless we turn up something definite on Emma Tysoe. I didn't get much from her workmates.'

'Colleagues,' Ingeborg murmured.

'You went to the home address?'

'Great Pulteney Street. There's a big pile of mail I brought back, most of it junk, of course. A couple of holiday postcards. A short letter from her sister in South Africa saying the husband went into hospital. Various bills.'

'Bank statements?'

'Yes. She has a current account with about fifteen hundred in credit, and two hundred grand on deposit.'

'A lady of means. Did you get into the flat?'

She nodded. 'Eventually. She has one of those code-operated locks on her front door. It's the garden flat, amazingly tidy. Living room, bedroom, study and bathroom. The main room is tastefully furnished in pale blue and yellow.'

'We don't need the colour schemes,' Diamond said. 'Did you find anything that would tell us what she was up to in recent weeks? Diary, calendar, phone pad?'

'We looked, of course. I got the impression she's organised. There's not much lying around.'

'In other words, you didn't find anything.'

He was confident Ingeborg had made a thorough search.

She said, 'There's an answerphone and I brought back the cassette. I've listened to it twice over, and I really believe there's nothing of interest on it.'

'Address book?'

'She must have taken it with her.'

'Computer, then?'

'There's one in the office, and she had a laptop as well, because we found the user's guide. I didn't attempt to look at the computer. I arranged for Clive to collect it.'

Clive was the whizzkid who handled all computer queries at the Bath nick. He would go through the files and extract anything of importance. Presumably Emma had written reports on previous cases. With luck, there might be e-mail correspondence about the new investigation.

'Is that it, then?' he asked Ingeborg.

'She drives a sports car, dark green.'

'Registration? Make? Have you checked with the PNC?'

The colour came to Ingeborg's cheeks. 'Bognor are onto it. They expect to trace it down there.'

'I don't mind who checks so long as we're informed. What else have you got?'

'She spends a lot on clothes. And she must be interested in golf. There was a photo of some golfer next to the computer, and it was inscribed to her. Do you play golf, guv?'

'If I did, I wouldn't be sitting here with you mob. It's the high-flyers' game, isn't it? I'd be wearing white gloves and taking the salute at Hendon.'

He summed up by handing out duties. Ingeborg was to get onto Clive for a speedy report on the contents of the computer. She would also make contact with the sister in South Africa. Leaman would set up a mini incident room. Halliwell would see what HOLMES could deliver on serial crimes in the coastal counties of Sussex and Hampshire.

Diamond himself would get onto the man at Bramshill who kept the list of profilers. Someone at the top knew what Emma Tysoe had been up to.

8

The National Police Staff College at Bramshill is in Hampshire, an easy run from Bath along the M4 to junction 11, but alien territory for Peter Diamond. His eyes glazed over at the name of the place. For years he'd ducked his head whenever anyone mentioned the Bramshill refresher course for senior officers. He pictured himself like Gulliver in Lilliput, supine and tied down by little men who talked another language. To find him driving there of his own free will was proof of his commitment to the Emma Tysoe murder case.

After reporting to an armed officer at the battlemented gatehouse, he was told to drive up to the house. Facing him at the end of the long, straight avenue was a building that made the word 'house' seem inadequate, for this was one of the stately homes of England, a Jacobean mansion with a south front that in its time had drawn gasps of awe from hardened policemen of all ranks. The brick facade rose three storeys, dominated by a huge semi-circular oriel window, mullioned and double-transomed, above a triple-bayed loggia. At each side were three tiers of pilasters. Vast side wings, also triple-bayed, projected on either end.

Mindful of his parking error at the golf club, he picked a bay well away from the main entrance and walked back, pausing only to buff his toecaps on the backs of his trousers. His appointment was with a civilian whose name on the phone had sounded like Hidden Camera. It turned out to be Haydn Cameron. But cameras hidden and visible are at Bramshill in plenty. This academy for top policemen is more secure than the average prison. Someone had watched him polish his shoes.

Inside, he gave his name and was directed to the National Crime Faculty. It sounds like a college for crooks, he thought. What names these desk detectives dream up. He stepped through the Great Hall, panelled from floor to ceiling, into a waiting area where, if he felt so inclined, he could leaf through the latest *Police Review*, or *The Times*. Nothing so subversive as the *Guardian*.

His spirits improved when a bright-eyed young woman with flame-coloured hair came in, asked him his name and invited him upstairs, that is, up the exquisitely carved stairs. On the way she told him that the staircase had been built in the reign of Charles II, adding with a bit of a giggle that it didn't belong to Bramshill. It had been plundered from some other mansion during the nineteenth century. He smiled at that. She was doing her best to put him at ease, and a pleasing thought crossed his mind. 'Your name isn't Heidi, by any chance?'

She looked puzzled and shook her head.

'I thought I might have misheard it,' he said. 'Heidi Cameron?'

'Sorry. No.'

'Or is Haydn one of these unisex names?'

She was highly amused. 'Now I know what you're on about, and you've got to be joking. I'm not going to interview you. I'm just the gofer here.'

Wishful thinking. He was shown into the office of an overweight, middle-aged man with a black eye-patch and hair tinted boot-polish brown. The charming gofer went. And closed the door on them.

'What's it like out there?' the real Haydn Cameron asked, as if he never left the office.

'Not so bad,' Diamond answered.

'Good journey?'

He tried an ice-breaker. 'The last part was the best.'

'Oh?'

'Following the young lady upstairs.'

It hadn't broken the ice here. 'I don't have a great deal of time, superintendent.' Cameron spoke Diamond's rank as if it was an insult. Probably was, in this place.

'Let's get to it, then.'

He got a sharp look for that. What did the man expect? Yes, sir, no, sir? He was just a civilian.

'We run regular courses on how to conduct murder enquiries for SIOs such as yourself. According to my records you haven't attended one.'

The old blood pressure rose several notches and this wasn't a good moment to have a coronary. Calm down and speak to the pompous prat in his own language, he told himself. 'No, I haven't found a window of opportunity yet.'

That was met with a glare. 'All the courses are over-subscribed,' Cameron said with pride.

'That could be why you haven't seen me, then.'

'You could go on the waiting list.'

There was a dangerous lack of contact here. Diamond tried not to curl his lip. 'The list that interests me is the approved list of offender profilers.'

'Oh?'

'I was told you deal with it. Each request for assistance goes through your office.'

Everyone in the police knew why the list was centrally controlled. After psychological offender profiling burst into the headlines in January 1988 following the conviction of John Duffy, the serial rapist and killer, forces up and down the country had turned to psychologists for help in tracking down serial offenders. Not all of the so-called experts were up to the challenge. A top-level decision had been made to oversee the use of profilers.

Personally, Diamond had never consulted a profiler. This wasn't from any prejudice, but simply because the cases he'd investigated weren't serial crimes in the usual sense of the term.

'But I understood from your call,' Cameron said, 'that this isn't a routine request.'

'Right,' Diamond responded. 'It's about the murder of one of the profilers on your list, Dr Emma Tysoe.'

'Which is why I made an exception and agreed to meet you. We're not unaware of the case.'

'Did you meet her personally?'

'Yes, several times,' Cameron said. 'Everyone we approve has been vetted.' He glanced at his notes. 'Dr Tysoe has been on the list since February 1999. She worked on five enquiries.'

'I heard she was good at it.'

'Exceptionally good.'

'Do you mind telling me how it works? When an SIO asks you to recommend someone, do you look at your list and choose a name?'

'It isn't just a matter of seeing who is available,' Cameron said acidly. 'The matching of the profiler to the case is far from simple. All kinds of criteria come into play.'

'Such as where they live?'

Not a good suggestion. Diamond got a basilisk stare from the seeing eye. 'That's of trifling importance. You really ought to do the course.'

This was not a comfortable interview. 'You mentioned all kinds of criteria,' Diamond prompted him.

Cameron braced himself with a wriggle of the shoulders and a tilt of the chin and started again. 'The term psychological offender profiler is a useful label, but I have to point out that it includes several different types of expert. There are currently twenty-six on my list – twenty-five now, unfortunately – and if you asked each of them to provide a job description you'd get twenty-five different answers. Some stress the statistical element and others the clinical. There are those who like to be detached about the whole business and those who involve themselves closely with the police team. Those who use strict scientific methodology and those who are more intuitive.'

'How did you class Emma Tysoe?'

'She was one of the latter.'

'Intuitive?'

Cameron sighed and rolled the eye. 'I thought you'd jump on that word. It gives the impression of guesswork.'

'I didn't take it that way.'

A better response, it seemed. A note of conciliation, if not approval, crept into the conversation. 'All right. She was a psychologist, as you know, not a psychiatrist, not medically trained. Her approach was more theoretical than hands-on. But it was based on a remarkable under-standing of the criminal mind. I've heard from officers who worked with her that she somehow immersed herself in the thinking of the offender and predicted what would happen next, and very often where, and when.'

'That's the intuitive part?'

'Yes, but only as a result of minute observation of all the data from the previous crimes. To give you an example, she assisted on a case of serial rape in North Wales. The attacks were spread over a long period, about six or seven years, and the local force were getting nowhere. Emma Tysoe was brought in, read the statements, visited the scenes, spoke to all of the victims, including several who were stalked but not attacked. By analysing the data – and interpreting the behaviour of the rapist – she decided he had spent most of his youth in custody or institutions and

lived with someone of his own sex who dominated him –
his elder brother, as it turned out. She said because of the
way he picked his victims it was clear he was actually in
awe of women. He would spend weeks or months stalking
them, but not in a threatening way, and only rarely
choosing to attack them.'

'More like a Peeping Tom?'

'Not at all.'

Another wrong note.

'He was on the lookout for certain women who
appeared even more submissive than he was. Dr Tysoe
produced her findings, estimated the perpetrator's age,
intelligence and the type of work he would do, and it led
them to a man they'd disregarded much earlier, a farm
worker. Broken home, fostering, youth custody, just as
she'd said. On his release he'd ended up living with the
bullying brother. He confessed straight away. That's only
one example.'

'So Emma got to be one of your star performers.'

The staring eye told Diamond he still hadn't clicked
with this mandarin. 'Please. This isn't show business. Her
name came up more frequently after that. Word travels
from one authority to another.'

'Do you, personally, deal with all the requests?'

'I'm not at liberty to say.'

'Her latest assignment?'

'That's confidential, also.'

He couldn't take much more of this evasion. 'I'm investigating a murder, Mr Cameron. I'm entitled to some
answers.'

'Correction. Bognor Police are handling the investigation, not you. Chief Inspector Mallin is the SIO.'
Cameron was well briefed.

'But the victim lived on my patch. In that sense it's a
joint enquiry.'

'Does she know you're here?'

'Hen Mallin? She will, if I manage to chip out any information at all.'

'In other words, you're doing this off your own bat,' Cameron said. 'That's the way you work, I'm told. Bull at a gate.'

Better a bull at a gate than a dog in a manger, Diamond thought, and wisely kept it to himself. Instead, he said with so much tact it was painful, 'You obviously have a high regard for Dr Tysoe's work as a profiler. Why not help us find her murderer?'

'By passing on classified information?'

'Sensitive, is it?'

'We run this service on the need-to-know principle. Our judgement is that you don't need to know.'

Great, he thought. More malpractice and corruption is perpetrated under the banner of the need-to-know principle than in the mafia. 'So I've come all this way for nothing.'

Cameron didn't answer. He looked at the ceiling with the air of a bored host waiting for the last guest to leave.

'If Hen Mallin came, would you do business with her?'

'We don't "do business".'

'Would you tell her any more than you've told me?'

'No – for the same reason.'

All this stonewalling had incensed Diamond. He couldn't pull his punches any longer. 'In the real world, Mr Cameron, I'd have you for obstructing a police officer in the course of his duty.'

'I'm sure you'd try, superintendent.'

'She was one of your experts. Don't you give a toss what happened to her?'

That touched a raw nerve. 'Of course we care, damn it! There's no evidence of a link between her murder and the case she was advising on.'

104

'The evidence isn't there because it hasn't been investigated.'

'The incidents are unrelated.'

'How can you be so sure? She was strangled for no apparent reason.'

'Have you enquired into her personal life?' Cameron asked in an unsubtle shifting of the ground.

'There isn't much to speak of.'

'Her work, then? The university?'

'We're looking at it, of course. The problem is that we have this black hole – the last ten days of her life when we don't know what she was doing, who she was meeting, where she was based, even. Her body turns up on a beach in Sussex. That's it. How can we conduct a murder enquiry without knowing any of these things?'

Cameron didn't move a muscle.

'You might as well tell me,' Diamond persisted. 'You've obviously been looking at my personal file, so you'll know I'm a stubborn cuss.'

'Anyone can see that.'

'Well, then?'

Cameron shook his head and sighed.

Sensing a small advantage, Diamond weighed in with another attempt. 'If I don't get answers from you today, I'll start rooting for them.'

No response.

'It's my job.'

And no response to that, either.

'How else can I find the truth? I'll beetle away until I get there. It could be far more damaging than finding out from you today.'

He seemed to have made some impact at last, because Cameron said, 'Sit there, will you? I have to speak to someone.' He got up and left the room.

Trying not to be overencouraged, Diamond amused

himself swaying back in the chair, looking for the gleam of a camera lens in the panelled walls. He was sure this interview would be kept for training purposes. How to deal with dickheads from the sticks.

Five minutes at least passed before Cameron returned and invited Diamond to go with him. He was out of that chair like a game-show volunteer. They entered the south-east wing, the business end of the house, by way of a magnificent drawing room with a marble chimneypiece and tapestries of classical scenes, and so into the library, a place of quite different proportions, which in the heyday of the house must have been the Long Gallery where the inmates and their guests promenaded. He was taken through a recessed, almost hidden door into a low-ceilinged office where a small man with a shock of white hair stood looking at a computer screen. Whatever was on the screen was more gripping than his visitors, because he didn't give them a glance.

Cameron stated Diamond's rank and name without any attempt at a two-way introduction. The need-to-know principle in action again. Obviously this was someone pretty high in the Bramshill pecking order. Diamond privately dubbed him the Big White Chief.

Closing the door after him, Cameron left the room, which was a relief.

Still without turning from the screen, the Big White Chief said, as if he were continuing the conversation in Cameron's office, 'This black hole of which you spoke, these missing days in Dr Tysoe's life.'

This came across as a definition of what was to be discussed, not a question, so Diamond said nothing.

It was the right thing to do. 'If I fill in some detail for you, you'll have to treat it as top secret.'

Progress at last. 'Understood.'

'You're not known for your discretion, Mr Diamond.'

'That's a matter of opinion.'

'No, it's a matter of record. What makes you think you can keep your mouth shut this time?'

'If you don't tell me what it's about, how can I answer that?'

The Big White Chief turned, unable any longer to resist a look at this visitor, and Diamond was glad to see he possessed two eyes and there was a spark of humanity, if not a twinkle, in each of them. He had a pencil-thin moustache of the sort military men, and few others, cultivate. 'There you go again, shooting off at the mouth. All right, you have a point. You may be a loose cannon, Diamond, but you hit the target more often than most. I'll take you on your own terms, and I may regret it. Let's hope not. The matter Emma Tysoe was engaged in is highly sensitive. If I tell you about it, you become one of a very small group who are privy to this knowledge.'

'I'm OK with that.'

'You may be OK with it, but is it safe with you?'

Diamond didn't dignify the question with a response.

'All right. Sit down.' The little man turned back to his computer, switched to a screensaver and swung his chair right round to face Diamond. He assessed him with a penetrating look, as if still reluctant to go on. 'You won't have heard about this. On June the fourteenth, a man was murdered in the grounds of his house – a rather fine house – in Sussex. Nothing was taken. There was a wallet in his pocket containing just over three hundred pounds and his credit cards. The house was open. It was hung with valuable paintings by Michael Ayrton, John Piper and others, and there are cabinets of fine china and pottery. Everything was left intact.'

'Except the owner.'

'Yes. He was shot through the head.'

'What with?'

'A bolt from a crossbow.'

'From a *what*?'

'Crossbow.'

Diamond took this in slowly. 'Different.'

'But effective.'

'It's a medieval weapon.'

'With modern refinements. They fit them with telescopic sights these days. Still used in sport for shooting at targets. And killing wild animals. Great power in the string, which isn't string at all, in fact. It's steel. But you don't have to be strong in the arm.'

'There can't be many around.'

'Actually, more than we ever imagined.'

'You'd still need to be an expert.'

'It's a surprisingly simple weapon to use.'

'Strange choice, though,' Diamond said. 'What kind of person uses a crossbow as a murder weapon?'

'This is where the profiler comes in.'

'Emma Tysoe?'

'Yes. She was consulted as soon as it was clear that an early arrest was unlikely. She was the obvious choice. Her reputation here was second to none.'

'And was she helpful?'

'We thought she could be. She seemed confident. But it all takes time. They don't like to be rushed.'

Diamond didn't need telling. The so-called scientists in the crime field seem to take a professional pride in delaying their results. Only the beleaguered policemen have any sense of urgency.

'So did she give you any opinion at all?'

'A few thoughts at the scene, though she stressed she didn't like giving off-the-cuff opinions. What she said was pretty obvious, really. The killer was methodical, unemotional and self-confident to the point of arrogance. He, or she – because a woman could use a crossbow just as

108

well as a man – had an agenda, and expected to carry it out.'

'What did she mean by that?'

'There's more. I'll tell you presently.'

Tiresome, but the promise was there, so Diamond didn't press him. 'You said the victim was in the grounds of his house. Was he alone?'

'Obviously not.'

'I mean was anyone there apart from the victim and the killer?'

'We know of no one else. It was a fine evening. He was sitting on a wooden seat watching the sunset. That's the presumption, anyway. He liked to do this.'

'Literally a sitting target.'

'Yes. Plenty of bushes within range as well.'

'When was he found?'

'The next morning, about eight. He had a manservant who lived out.'

'Who came under suspicion, no doubt?'

'Briefly. But he's in the clear. A good alibi. He was on a pub quiz team that night. They met early to drive to another village and spent the whole evening there.'

'His special subject didn't happen to be archery?'

The Big White Chief wasn't amused. 'If you'll allow me to continue, I'll give you the salient facts. The police arrived at eight twenty the next morning, and everything was done correctly. Jimmy Barneston, a young Sussex detective who has handled several big investigations, took charge. He was unable to find any obvious motive. The victim was a film and TV director, a highly successful one with a number of big successes to his name. Well, I'll stop talking about him in the abstract. It's Axel Summers.'

Diamond was no film buff, but he knew the name and he could picture the face. Summers had been at the top of his profession for over twenty years. He was well known for appearances on radio and television, a witty, confident speaker with a fund of stories about the film world. He was much in demand for chat shows.

'And they decided not to go public on this?'

'Not yet. I'll tell you why in a moment. Summers was in the middle of filming a major project for Channel Four, with a top American actor in the title role.'

'Which is . . . ?'

'*The Ancient Mariner.*'

'The poem?'

'Yes. You wouldn't think a poem could be turned into a feature-length film, but, as you probably know, the *Mariner* is a powerful story running to many verses and scenes. Summers decided it would cater very well to the current appetite for fantasy and myth and persuaded the backers to invest over fifteen million.'

'Is that big budget?'

'By UK standards, yes. There's a hefty financial input from industry. They get their corporate message on the credits and in the commercial breaks – that is, if the film isn't blown out of the water by this tragedy. Quite a lot is in the can already. Summers had just been away for five weeks shooting the sea sequences off the coast of Spain.'

'Nice work if you can get it.'

'Rather exhausting, actually. He'd told his office he was taking a complete break before the next phase, leaving them to deal with enquiries. He didn't want to be disturbed. Convenient for us, as it turned out. It wasn't necessary to announce his death immediately. Only a small number of people know of it.'

'Why are you suppressing it?'

'Do you know your Coleridge?'

'Do I look as if I know my Coleridge?'

'Inside the house on Summers' desk the murderer left

a sheet of paper with five words on it: "he stoppeth one of three".'

'"It is an ancient Mariner, and he stoppeth one of three",' Diamond chanted.

'So you do know it?'

'We did it at school. Heard it on disc. Ralph Richardson, I think. Some lines stay in the mind once you've heard them. I couldn't have told you who wrote it.'

'This was cut from a book and pasted on an ordinary A4 sheet of copying paper. Below were three names, cut from newspapers. The first was Axel Summers.'

'And the others?'

'Are equally well known.'

'A death list?'

'We have to presume so.'

'You could take it that way,' Diamond said. 'On the other hand, if you read the lines as Coleridge intended them you could take it to mean Summers was the chosen victim and the others won't be troubled.' Not very likely, he thought as he was speaking.

A nod, and no other response.

Diamond waited. 'So you're not going to tell me who they are?'

He was given a less than friendly stare. 'I'm telling you about Emma Tysoe's part in all this. As a matter of urgency the team investigating the murder wanted to know if the others were under serious threat – in other words, was this a serial murderer at work?'

'What was her answer?'

'After much thought and a couple of visits to the scene, yes. She said the killer was a type unknown in this country. By naming a list of potential victims he – and she was in no doubt that this was a man – was challenging the police, an act of pure conceit.'

111

'Psychotic?'

'"Emotionally disconnected" was the phrase she used. He was treating this as a chess game. He had planned it cold-bloodedly, and with the advantage of surprise was already several moves ahead in the game. It was probable that he'd drawn up his list in a way that best suited his plan. So we might be mistaken if we looked for motives, personal grudges against the people. Quite possibly there was no motive in the sense that you or I would understand it. The motive was the challenge of the game.'

'Chilling.'

'Yes, it shows a complete absence of humanity, the mentality of a psychopath. My word. Psychologists are wary of using it. But what she said made sense.'

'Did she get so far as to produce a profile?'

'Apart from what I've just told you, no. She was still absorbing the data. Profilers like to take their time, and there was plenty to take in – the reports from the scene, the forensics, the autopsy, all the follow-up stuff.'

'The strange choice of weapon.'

'Certainly.'

'That must limit the field. What sort of people learn to use crossbows?'

'I told you. It's not especially difficult. No doubt Dr Tysoe would have given us some guidance if she had lived.'

'Wasn't the SIO – this man Barneston – getting her advice?'

'That isn't the way she worked. She preferred to go away and make up her mind. When she was ready, she would come back with her recommendations. Barneston was running a full-scale murder investigation – still is – and she was on the fringe of it, really.'

'Was it her suggestion to keep the whole thing under wraps?'

'No, that was the SIO's decision, and I'm sure he's

right. We must protect the two other people the killer named on his list.'

'Are they going to be any safer if it isn't made public?'

'We're sure of it. This man, whoever he is, wants his crime sensationalised. He's picked people in the public domain as his targets. Imagine what the tabloids would make of it.'

'So have you slapped on a D-notice?'

'In effect. The local paper discovered something was afoot and we secured their cooperation. The nationals still don't know.'

'And the others on this death list?'

'Have been told, of course. They were offered round-the-clock protection, and they've taken it.'

'Quite a number are in on this, then?'

'Already more than we would wish.'

An ominous statement. 'One more is no big deal, then.'

'You don't need to know.'

Diamond knew as he spoke what the answer to his next question would be. 'So are you about to tell me the same thing your man Cameron was suggesting – that there's no link between the murders of Axel Summers and Emma Tysoe?'

The answer was laced with scorn. 'You can't compare them. This killer is focused, organised. A controller. Emma herself told us that. He's got his agenda and he'll stick to it. He's not going to put his master plan at risk by strangling her on a public beach. That's another MO altogether.'

'It's cool.'

'That may be, but it leaves far too much to chance. You're investigating an opportunist killing. This man doesn't work like that. He'd hate the idea of so many people around, so much outside his control.'

'Just now you said he wants it in the papers.'

'Ah, he's conceited, yes, a publicity seeker, but he'll carry out the killings – if his plan succeeds – in an environment he controls. A beach has too much potential for interference.'

Diamond doggedly refused to be steamrollered. 'It may be another move in the chess game. If this genius felt his master plan was threatened when Emma Tysoe was called in, wouldn't he do something about it?'

'But he didn't know she was involved.'

'How can you be sure? Certain people knew. The SIO and his team presumably. Yourselves. Her professor at the university.'

'He doesn't know the details of the case.'

'You keep this list of profilers. You said she was the obvious choice.'

'To ourselves, yes.'

'A cunning bastard like this is going to have heard of your list and know she's the number one choice.'

'Possibly,' he conceded.

'If the killer is as smart as you say he's going to have a line into the investigation.'

The Big White Chief was quick to say, 'So you think you should have a line in as well?'

'We're on the same side, aren't we?'

'I've told you more than I intended already, and I thought you'd have the experience to see that these killings are chalk and cheese.'

'I'd still like to have the full picture.'

'You've got it – apart from names, and they aren't germane to your enquiry. People's lives are threatened, Mr Diamond. I don't suppose you've ever worked with a burden like this, knowing that named individuals will die if you make a mistake. Show some sensitivity towards your fellow officers who carry that responsibility.'

Faced with an argument like that, he couldn't pursue

it. He shrugged and said, 'I can try.'

'If it's of any interest you can look at other enquiries she advised on. I don't mind giving you chapter and verse of those.'

Peter Diamond left Bramshill some time later with a sheaf of photocopied material that he slung onto the back seat of his car. He was unsatisfied and unconvinced.

9

D S Stella Gregson arrived in Crawley soon after ten and was driven to the school in Old Mill Road. She hesitated before knocking on the head teacher's door. Childhood conditioning never entirely leaves you. Even after the head had introduced them and left them to it, neither Stella nor Miss Medlicott sat in the chair behind the desk, or anywhere. They remained standing.

'I hope this isn't a waste of your time,' Miss Medlicott said. 'All I've got for you is secondhand.'

'You don't have to apologise,' Stella said. 'We're grateful for any information. This comes from a child in your class, I was told.'

'Haley Smith. She's acted strangely – perhaps nervously is a better word. She drew a picture of a visit to the beach and told me one of the figures on it was a dead lady. I tried to talk her out of it, but she wouldn't be budged, so I discussed it with the mother when she came to collect Haley. Mrs Smith seemed rather guarded when I spoke to her. The family were at Wightview Sands on the day that poor woman was found, she admitted that. She thought the child must have heard her talking about the incident with her husband and then assumed some sunbather had been the dead woman. But it was a strained conversation, I felt. And I didn't mention to her something else the child had told me – that her daddy had been with the lady.'

Stella felt goosebumps prickling her flesh. Suddenly this low-key enquiry took on a new significance. 'Haley said that?'

'Yes. And later in the week I had problems getting any response at all from the child. She was acting dumb, or so it seemed to me. One of the other children told me Haley's daddy had said she wasn't to speak to me. I tried to talk it over with Mrs Smith at the end of the day, but she was short with me and said it was obviously another misunderstanding, as if it was my fault. I've worried about it since, in case Haley did see something dreadful.'

'You did the right thing,' Stella said. 'May I speak to Haley?'

'You can try. You won't get much out of her.'

'Can I see her in the classroom?'

'That would be better than here.'

The children were on their morning break as Miss Medlicott escorted Stella along the covered walkway at the edge of the playground. Stella entered the classroom and the teacher went to find Haley.

The truth, simply stated, has to be used when questioning children. So when the small, dark-haired child was brought in with bowed head and sucking her thumb, Stella invited her to sit in her usual chair and sat beside her and said, 'Haley, my dear, I want to talk to you about what happened that day you spent with Mummy and Daddy at the seaside. I'm a policewoman, and you don't have to worry, because you're not in trouble. I think you can help me.'

The child's pale face, framed by the bunched hair, registered only apprehension. She was already shaking her head. Creases had formed around her little mouth.

'A poor lady was killed,' Stella continued, 'and it's my job to find out about it. We don't want anyone else being killed, do we? Did you see what happened?'

Haley looked up and there was eye contact. She shook her head, gazing steadily, and Stella had to believe her.

'That's good then. We can talk about other things. I was told you did a lovely painting of your day on the beach. May I see it?'

Haley showed she had a voice. 'Miss Medlicott's got it.'

'So I have. I'll fetch it,' the teacher said, going to the tall cupboard in the corner.

Stella said, 'Why don't you help Teacher find it?'

It was good for the child to move. She'd been going tense in the chair. In a moment she returned to Stella, the painting in her hands.

'My, that's a picture!' Stella said. 'Such colours. What a bright blue sea. That *is* the sea, across the middle?'

A nod.

'And this yellow part must be the sand. Is this you on the sand?'

Haley shook her head.

'Are you in the picture?'

She placed her finger on one of the figures.

'Of course, it has to be you. Is that a ball in your hand, or an extra large orange?'

'Frisbee.'

She hadn't clammed up completely. This had to be encouraging.

'So it is. Silly me. It's too big for a ball. Did you play with the frisbee on the beach?'

A nod. This was chipping at stone, but it had to be done.

'Who did you play with?'

'Don't know.'

'Some other children?'

Another nod.

'And while you were playing, where were Mummy and Daddy?'

The tiny forefinger pointed to two stick figures on the band of yellow, with circles for heads, a scribbled representation of hair and rake-like extensions on the arms for hands.

'So they are. But they seem to be lying down. Didn't they stand up to look for you when you were lost?'

'Don't know,' Haley said, with logic. If she was lost, she wouldn't have known what her parents were doing.

'I expect they got worried because they couldn't see you.'

The child felt for one of her bunches and sucked the end of it.

'So where were you?'

She was silent.

'Haley, no one is angry with you. I'm sure you can help me if you really try to remember what happened.'

Haley took her hand away from her mouth and pointed once more to the picture, to the figure of herself with the frisbee.

Stella said, 'That's you, of course. And these are children, too. You were playing with them, were you? That must have been a lot of fun.'

The comment disarmed the child and triggered the best response yet. 'A girl I was with got hit in the face by the frisbee and she was bleeding and crying and stuff, so we all went up to the hut where they've got bandages and things. Then the other girls went back to their mummy and I was lost, and the man found me and I went back to Mummy, and Daddy wasn't there.'

Stella did her best to recap. 'Who was the man who found you?'

'Him with a whistle and red shorts.'

'The lifeguard?'

'Mm.'

'Silly me. I understand now.'

Haley pointed again, to a horizontal figure immediately above the parents, half over the blue band representing the sea. 'That's the dead lady.'

'How did you know she was dead?'

'Daddy said so.'

'So Daddy came back?'

'I seed the lady lying on the beach and she wasn't moving and the sea was coming in and I thought she was asleep and Daddy went to look and said she was dead and got some men and carried her off the beach. It's not in the picture.' She'd answered almost in a single breath.

'So before this, Daddy must have been somewhere along the beach looking for you?'

'I 'spect so.'

'Did Daddy know this lady?'

'Don't know.'

'I believe you told Miss Medlicott he was with her.'

'Yes.'

'What did you mean by that?'

'He was with her. I told you.'

'Do you mean when he went to see what was the matter with her?'

She nodded.

'Daddy looked at the lady, did he? And got some help? Did you notice who helped?'

'Some men.'

'The lifeguard – with the red shorts?'

'I think so.'

'Did you remember the other men? What were they like?'

'Pictures on them.'

'Their shirts?'

'No.'

'On their bodies? You mean tattoos?'

'And earrings and no hair.'

120

'Young men? That's a help. You have got a good memory. Tell me, Haley, did you drive home after that?'

She nodded again.

'And did Daddy say anything about the lady?'

'He said we don't know who she is or why she snufted.'

'Snuffed it?'

'What's snufted?' the child asked.

'It's just a way of saying someone is dead. Did he say anything else?'

'About e-dot questions.'

'*E-dot?*' This was beyond Stella's powers of interpretation.

'They'll keep us here asking e-dot questions.'

'*Idiot* questions? Is that what he said?'

'I 'spect so.'

Stella thanked the little girl, and Miss Medlicott said she could go out to play again. She sprang up from the chair, then paused and said, 'Are you going to talk to my daddy?'

'Yes, but you don't have to worry. I'll tell him he can be proud of you. You're a clever girl, and helpful, too.'

After the child was gone, Stella said to Miss Medlicott, 'Am I going to talk to her daddy? You bet I am – and fast.'

For much of the journey home from Bramshill, Diamond carried on a mental dialogue, telling himself to cool it, and then finding he was simmering again. It's a blow to anyone's self-esteem to be denied the full facts when others have them. This was not just about pride. His freedom to investigate was at stake. He'd been told, in effect, to keep out. The Big White Chief had played the innocent-lives-are-at-stake card, and there was no way to trump it.

So the official line was that the murders of Emma Tysoe and Axel Summers were unrelated. Tell that to the marines, he thought. Emma had been at work on the Summers case when she was murdered. There was a link, and he would find it. He'd root out the truth in his own way and the Big White Chief, to put it politely, could take a running jump.

But he'd heard enough at Bramshill to know he was getting into something uniquely strange. No murderer he'd ever dealt with had used a crossbow, or quoted from an eighteenth-century poet, or named his victims in advance. If Emma Tysoe's observations were correct, and this was a killer playing a game, it was a sick way of being playful.

It would be interesting to see if the hot-shot sleuth from Sussex could make any sense of it.

Back in Bath late in the afternoon, he was pleased to find Sergeant Leaman had acted on the order to set up an incident room. The best he'd hoped for was a corner of the main open-plan area, but Leaman, good man, had found a first-floor office being used as a furniture store. He'd 'rehoused' the furniture (he didn't say where) and installed two computers and a phone. Keith Halliwell was already at work at a keyboard getting information from HOLMES.

Diamond asked if he'd come up with anything.

'It's given me all the unsolved cases of strangling in the past five years. More than I bargained for.'

'A popular pastime is it, strangling – like home decorating?'

'Do you mind, guv? I do a spot of DIY myself.'

'Don't I know it! We've all seen the bits of torn paper in your hair on Monday mornings.'

Halliwell, with half his attention on the screen, wasn't up to this. 'Bits of paper?'

'At one time I thought you were into polygamy.'

'Polygamy?' Halliwell was all at sea now.

'Confetti. While you're still spending time with HOLMES, see if there's any record of deaths by crossbow, will you?'

Halliwell swung round as if this was one send-up too many.

'I'm serious.'

He said with suspicion, 'Can I ask why?'

'No. Just do it. Is our computer geek about?'

'Clive? He's downstairs with Dr Tysoe's disks.'

Diamond found the whizzkid in front of a screen in his usual corner of the main office, fingertips going like shuttles.

'Any progress?'

'On the psychologist lady? Yes. I got in eventually. She had a firewall on her system.'

'Oh, yes?' Diamond said in a tone intended to conceal his total ignorance.

'A lockout device. You get three attempts to guess the password, and then the system locks down for the next hour.'

'So what was the password – "sesame"?'

Clive's fingers stopped. 'As a matter of fact—'

Diamond laughed. 'All this technology and it comes down to finding a password you can remember.'

'Her choice. Personally I'd have picked something more original.'

'Like the name of your cat.'

'Well . . .'

'Dog?'

'You're right about "sesame", Mr Diamond. It's always worth a try.'

'And has it helped us, breaking through the firewall?'

'I've done a printout. Thought you'd like to see it on paper rather than use the screen.'

'You know about me and computers, then?'

'It's common knowledge.'

'So what have you got?'

'See over there?' Clive pointed to a wall to his right stacked high with paper, reams of it. 'That's the contents of her hard disk. She was well organised.'

'All of that?'

'You wouldn't believe how much can be stored on a modern disk.'

'This could take months.'

'You could cut it by half if you learned to use a mouse.'

He didn't dignify that with a response. 'Did you read any of it?'

Clive shook his head. 'Not my kind of reading.'

'If I was looking for something in particular – case notes, for instance – is there any way I could find them quickly?'

'Depends. Is there a key word I can use to make a search?'

'Try Summers.'

The quick fingers rattled the keys, apparently without a satisfactory result. 'This could take longer. Give me an hour and I'll see what comes up.'

'And, by the way, Clive, this is under your hat, right? If you find something interesting I don't want it all over the world-wide web, or the Bath nick, come to that.'

'Stay cool, Mr D. My lips are sealed.'

Diamond returned to his office and called Hen Mallin. Liberally interpreting the need-to-know principle, he told her everything he'd learned at Bramshill. Senior detectives don't betray much emotion as a rule, but Hen spoke the name of Axel Summers as if he were a personal friend.

'You knew him?' Diamond queried.

'No more than you, sugar, but he's always on the box, isn't he? A bit old for me, but definitely dishy, I thought. Where did they say this happened?'

'A house in Sussex.'

'That's my manor. I haven't heard a whisper.'

'Shows how seriously they take it. Have you heard of Jimmy Barneston? He's in charge.'

'That makes sense. He's top of the heap, young, energetic, and gets results.'

'So I was told,' he said with a slight note of irony.

'Really,' Hen said. 'His clear-up rate is awesome.'

'Sounds like a vacuum cleaner. Where's he based?'

'Horsham, the last time I heard. Should I have a quiet word with him, do you think?'

'I wouldn't trouble him yet. He'll be trying to keep the cap on the bottle. Let's wait until we've got something to trade.'

She said, 'You're a wily old soul, aren't you? Good thinking.' After a pause, she added, 'You really believe she was killed by the man who did Summers, don't you? In spite of what you were told?'

'I wouldn't put it as strongly as that. But I'm not ruling it out just because Bramshill tells me to. One thing I've learned in this job, Hen, is that the people at the top have their own agenda, and it doesn't have much to do with what you and I are working on.'

'Speaking of which, I'd better let you know what's been happening here.' She told him about Stella Gregson's visit to the school and the interview with Haley Smith. 'We've now established that the father, Michael Smith, manages a bookshop at Gatwick Airport. Stella has gone to interview him.'

'Will she bring him in?'

'Depends what he says. She'll see him initially in the airport police office.'

'He'd better have a good story. Have you checked him on the PNC?'

'No previous. If we pull him in, do you want some of the action?'

'Try and keep me away. What about his wife?'

'Olga Smith. Done. I sent Stella to see her directly. Stella was all for racing off to Gatwick right away, but I wanted the woman's angle first.'

'Was it helpful?'

'It filled in some gaps. She's an ex-nurse who now works just round the corner from the school as one of the check-out staff at Safeway. Claims she was so taken up with Haley being lost that she scarcely registered what was going on with the dead woman. But she confirmed that her husband was the first to do anything about it. He saw that the woman was dead and alerted the lifeguard and helped carry the body to the hut. Afterwards they cleared off fast in their car.'

'Why?'

'They figured they wouldn't have anything useful to contribute. They hadn't seen anyone with the victim all day.'

'She'd been there all day?'

'Arrived soon after they did and set up her windbreak and lay behind it sunbathing.'

'Were they close to her?'

'Just a few yards. But there was a time in the afternoon when they went for a swim. And there was also a period when Haley went missing and they were both very taken up with searching for her. The husband went off to look and Olga Smith stood up to be visible. She says she was far too upset to have noticed whether the woman was alone, or if she was dead at that stage.'

'Makes sense.'

'Yes, Stella believed her, but got a strong impression that she's scared of her husband. He made the decision to quit the scene as soon as possible and he's insisted ever since that they can't help us in any way. She knew we were appealing for information. He seems to have put her under pressure to say nothing. And we know he ordered the child not to speak to her teacher.'

'He's got plenty to explain, then.'

'When we've picked him up, sunshine, I'll let you know.'

'What I didn't appreciate when I printed all the files is that some of them are encrypted,' Clive told Diamond when he checked with him after the hour he'd requested.

'You mean we can't read the stuff?'

He nodded. 'I guess she had reasons for keeping some of her case notes secure. The text is scrambled. It's put through a series of mathematical procedures called an algorithm and comes out looking like gobbledegook. If you go through all those sheets I printed out for you, you'll find some that make no sense at all. They'll be the encrypted files.'

'So how do you unscramble them?'

'Decrypt them. With blood, toil, tears and sweat. We need to know the key to access them.'

'Key?'

'Password, then.'

'Why not try "sesame" again?'

'You think I haven't? She wasn't messing about here. She really meant to stop anyone from breaking in. Most encryption systems use a secret key *and* a pass phrase. Some are asymmetric, meaning one key is used to encrypt the data and another to decrypt it. As I think I told you, she was obviously computer-literate.'

'Do we use any of these systems in the police?'

'Of course.'

'And are they listed somewhere? What I'm getting at, Clive, is that she could have been given the police software to use for her profiling notes.'

'I'll check it out. But even if I know the software, it

127

could still take me weeks to crack this.'

'Better make a start, then.' He rested a hand on Clive's shoulder and said as it began to droop, 'If it wasn't important, I wouldn't ask.'

Stella Gregson had only ever been through Gatwick Airport on holiday trips, but she found the right terminal and located the bookshop easily enough. Finding the manager was not so simple. He'd gone for a late lunch, the woman on the till told her, and he should be back soon.

Stella said she'd wait. She'd had no lunch, late or otherwise. She had a young male DC with her and she treated him to a toasted sandwich at the Costa shop, which offered a good view of the open-plan bookshop. People with time on their hands and flying on their minds were blankly staring at the shelves, occasionally picking something up, riffling the pages and replacing it.

After forty minutes Stella and her companion got off their coffee stools and started browsing through the magazines.

'Does Mr Smith carry a mobile?' she asked the woman on the till. 'We can't wait much longer.'

'He does, but I don't know the number.'

'Where does he eat, then? Somewhere in the terminal?'

The woman shrugged. 'This is only my second week.'

They asked at the shop next door, a place that retailed shirts and ties. The manager said he thought Smith went home to lunch. He lived nearby, in Crawley. 'Is he in trouble, then?' he added cheerfully.

'We just need to check something with him.'

'Police, are you?'

Stella's eyes widened.

'It's the way you walk.'

She called Hen Mallin to let her know they were about

to leave the airport and would call at the Smiths' house. Hen was talking on another line, so Stella left a message.

She nudged the DC in the back. He was looking at pink shirts. 'Leave it. We're on the move.'

The house was only ten minutes away, on the north side of Crawley. 'I don't know why,' Stella said to her young colleague as she drove out of the airport, 'but I've got a bad feeling about this.' The feeling got worse when they turned the corner at the end of the Smiths' street and an ambulance sped towards them, siren blaring, lights flashing. A police patrol car was parked outside one of the houses.

'That's the one.'

They drew up outside and went in through the open door.

'Who the fuck are you?' a sergeant in uniform asked.

Stella held her warrant card up to his face and said, 'So what the fuck is going on?'

He blinked. The words 'Bognor Regis CID' seemed to have that effect on people. 'It's a domestic. Some bastard beat his wife unconscious. She's on her way to hospital.'

'Is he in there?'

'No, he scarpered. She was in a right old state when she was found. We're trying to get the facts straight. The people's name, would you believe, is—'

'Smith.'

10

Very late the same afternoon, Diamond heard from Hen Mallin that Olga Smith had been attacked and was in hospital, and the husband, Michael Smith, was missing.

'I'll come at once,' he said.

'Hold your horses, squire,' she told him. 'She's in intensive care. She took at least one heavy blow to the head. She won't be talking to anyone until tomorrow at the earliest.'

'The husband did it, I suppose?'

'There's little doubt. His car was seen outside the house between two and three. A white Honda Civic. It was gone when she was found.'

'He'll be miles away, then.'

'Could be in another country. Working at the airport as he does, he'd know the likely standbys. Crawley police are checking the airport car parks.'

'Now you're depressing me. Who called the ambulance? The husband?'

'That's something I didn't ask.'

'It's got to be checked. What could have triggered this attack, Hen?'

A heavy sigh came down the line. 'You remember I told you about Stella Gregson visiting the school and speaking to the child? Immediately after, she went to see Olga Smith – at my suggestion.'

'You told me.'

'And the most likely sequence of events is that Olga phoned her husband at the airport after Stella's visit and he came straight home in a vile temper and knocked her senseless.'

'Why?'

'For blabbing to us. We know he wasn't willing to help us with the Tysoe murder.'

'But she didn't come to us.'

'Right.'

He thought for a moment. 'So if Stella hadn't spoken to Olga Smith . . .'

'Yes, and I take responsibility,' Hen stressed. 'We should have picked him up first. Mistake.'

'We all make them.'

'And Olga Smith is fighting for her life because of me.'

'Hold on,' he said, not liking the confessional tone. 'It was her decision to phone him – if that's what happened. She knows what he's like. If he's violent, she knew exactly what to expect, so don't take on that burden, Hen.'

'I still cocked up, Peter, and we both know it.'

He could tell there was no use in pursuing the point. 'What about young Haley? I hope she wasn't home when this was going on.'

'No, thank God. She has lunch at school. One of the neighbours is looking after her tonight.'

'Poor little kid. Mother in intensive care and father on the run.' Diamond had no difficulty empathising with children, even though he'd never been a parent. This man Smith couldn't have given much thought, if any, to his daughter. Callous behaviour would be characteristic of a serial killer, but it was too soon to build anything on that. Plenty of people who are not psychopaths treat their children with indifference. 'So what's being done to find him?'

'Crawley are handling the search and letting me

shadow the SIO. They've already held a press conference and issued a photo and announced that Smith is wanted for questioning. The main effort is being put into finding the Honda.'

'Are they doing enough?'

'No complaints.'

'Does he have form?'

'Apparently not – if Michael Smith is his real name.'

'How much have you told Crawley police about this guy's connection with the Emma Tysoe case?'

'They're aware of it. Obviously nothing was said to the press.'

'I'll come in the morning, then. Which hospital?'

'Crawley General.'

'Would around nine suit you? Main entrance?'

He went to the incident room to update those of his team who were still at work. And on his way back to Weston that evening he called at the library and borrowed a copy of *The Selected Poems of Samuel Taylor Coleridge.*

Evenings were hard for him. He no longer thought of the house as his home. He still grieved for Steph more than he would admit to anyone. When the place was silent, he would sometimes speak a few words to her as if she was in the room. If the phone rang, he would snatch it up in the expectation that through some miracle he'd hear her voice. When he was really unable to cope he went for long walks, and even that was no remedy because he'd find himself fantasising that he'd meet her in the street. Non-stop television seemed to be the only way to occupy his mind, except that it could trick him at any time with subversive images that brought pain. Whether reading *The Rime of the Ancient Mariner* would be a better distraction remained to be seen.

The next morning Hen Mallin sported a yachting cap

that gave her a maritime air, perfect for the esplanade at Bognor, but slightly frivolous for a visit to intensive care. She was waiting in the main entrance when Diamond arrived, his legs stiff and shaky from flogging up the motorway faster than he liked. An officer from Crawley, DI Bradley, was also waiting, but unfortunately for all of them the interview with Olga Smith would have to wait. 'There's a definite improvement,' the doctor told them. 'She's conscious now, but I can't have her subjected to the stress of questions when we're still looking for symptoms of more serious damage. Why don't you come back later this afternoon, say around four?'

Police work is like that.

Diamond asked about the extent of Olga Smith's injuries and was informed she'd taken a blow to the back of the skull, her right arm was fractured and there was extensive bruising.

'A single blow to the head?'

'Yes, and that could easily have killed her. The cranium is lacerated and there's a swelling under the scalp.'

'So she'll have concussion.'

'That's to be expected. It's highly likely she'll have no memory of the incident.'

'You haven't already asked her what happened?'

'I'm dealing with the injury, officer, not the cause of it.'

Thanks a bunch, doc, Diamond thought. He suggested a visit to see where the attack had happened. DI Bradley, the Crawley officer, looked at his watch.

'Is it far?' Diamond asked.

'It's not so much a question of how far it is—' Bradley started to say.

'It is to me. How far?'

So the hard-pressed DI Bradley drove ahead, and the house was only five minutes from the hospital. The Smiths lived in a semi on a recently built estate where coach-lamps and satellite dishes seemed to be standard fittings. Two laburnum saplings had been planted in the front and the lawn – like most of the others in the street – had the stripes of a recent mowing.

Bradley had a key and let them in. It seemed the Smiths had a taste for period furniture. A rosewood table and a pair of upholstered chairs stood in the hallway. The SOCOs had been through the previous afternoon, leaving a powdering of zinc over the hard surfaces.

'She was found in here,' Bradley said, pushing open a door.

This room was more typical of a young family, with fitted carpet, three-seat sofa and matching armchairs, a wall-unit with TV, sound system and a few books. The only period piece here was a mahogany dining table in the bay of the window, square, with built-in flaps to extend it. The surface had the same fine coating of white dust as the hall furniture.

'Where, exactly?'

'I thought that was obvious.' DI Bradley was making it clear this was all extremely tedious for him. He pointed to a bloodstain at the window end of the room, close to the table. It was the size of a beermat, but it blended with the carpet's busy brown and beige design. Diamond hadn't noticed it at a first glance.

'Was any weapon found?' he asked, knowing anything portable would have been taken for forensic testing.

Bradley shook his head. 'If he had any sense, he'll have taken it with him. Villains are wise to DNA these days.'

'I was thinking if there isn't a weapon she could have cracked her head on the corner of the table.' He stepped closer to the table and assessed its position in relation to the bloodstain.

'Theoretically possible, I suppose.' From his tone,

Bradley didn't think much of the suggestion.

'If this is where she was lying . . .'

'Are you saying it was an accident?' This was fast becoming a spat between Crawley and Bath.

'If she fell and hit her head, it wouldn't be the same as if he bashed her with a blunt instrument.'

Hen said with diplomacy, 'I don't suppose she tripped over the cat. The husband probably took a swing at her.'

'Maybe,' Diamond conceded without going so far as 'probably'.

'Anyway,' Hen added, 'forensics have obviously looked at the table. They'll find out if she cracked her head on it. Every contact leaves a—'

'Yes, we know,' Diamond cut her off. 'But were there signs of a fight?'

'Apart from a woman with her head bashed in and a broken arm?' Bradley said. 'What do you want? Teeth all over the room?'

Diamond could have erupted, but it was a fair point, forcefully made, and he kept quiet.

Like Bradley, Hen was in no doubt as to Michael Smith's guilt, and now she threw in more damning information. 'Yesterday you asked me who called the ambulance. It wasn't Smith. It was the woman next door, Mrs Mead.'

'How come?' Diamond said.

Hen invited Bradley to explain.

'What happened was that the Smiths' sprog—'

'Haley,' Diamond put in. He hated children being downgraded.

'Haley comes home from school on the school bus around three forty-five, can't get in, gets no answer when she knocks, so goes next door, knowing Mrs Mead has a spare key. Mrs Mead goes round and finds Olga Smith lying here and calls an ambulance.'

'Was it also Mrs Mead who noticed Michael Smith's

Honda parked outside between two and three?'

'Yes.'

'I'd like to meet this splendid woman.'

First, they looked into the other rooms. You learn a lot about the occupants of a house by seeing how they treat their surroundings. This seemed a lived-in home, with reassuring (or misleading) signs of family harmony. Holiday photos and postcards around the kitchen. A noticeboard with reminders pinned to it. Recipes cut from colour magazines. A sliced home-made cake under a perspex cover. Coffee mugs waiting to be washed. Haley's school blouse hanging up to dry. A wooden chest for her toys, with her name painted on it.

Diamond sifted through a batch of photos of the Smiths. The father had the same expression in all of them, with half-closed, ungenerous eyes and only the vestige of a smile. Olga Smith, a short, pretty blonde, projected a warmer personality. He picked out a head and shoulders shot of the pair of them in their garden and pocketed it.

Upstairs, the duvets were turned back to air, and clean clothes waited to be put away. The Smiths' bedroom didn't have the look of a battleground. They shared a kingsize bed. Each had a pile of books. He was reading Jeffrey Archer (but you can't condemn a man for that) and she Victoria Beckham's autobiography. His bedside drawer contained a bottle of massage oil and a gross-size box of condoms, with only a handful left; hers, a pack of tissues, a Miss Dior spray, a half-eaten bar of chocolate and a mini Cointreau.

One glance into Haley's room left them in no doubt that she was well treated. She had a vast collection of stuffed toys, a wigwam, a riding helmet, a computer, her own TV and three shelves of books.

The third bedroom had been converted into an office, with two filing cabinets and a computer. Diamond picked some letters off the desk. One was a bank statement.

'The argument wasn't over money by the look of things.' He showed it to Hen. It was a fourteen-day notice account. Michael L. Smith had a hundred and twenty thousand on deposit. 'Is that the kind of money a bookshop manager stacks away?'

'If it is, we're in the wrong job,' Hen said. 'Maybe he came into money.'

'Regularly, by the look of it. He makes two deposits in cash in August, one of fifteen hundred, the other of two grand. *Cash*, Hen.'

'A tax dodge?'

'Or some other scam.'

'Defrauding the shop?'

'On this scale? I doubt it. Anything so big would soon be picked up by the auditors.'

Agreeing to pursue the source of Mike Smith's cash deposits at an early opportunity, they went next door to call on Mrs Mead, a short, bright-eyed woman in her sixties with permed silver hair that matched the colour of a yapping Yorkshire terrier held against her chest. 'Let him sniff the back of your hand and he'll quieten down,' she told Diamond, and it worked. She insisted each of them went through this ritual. Then she put the dog down, said, 'Basket,' and it trotted off somewhere.

Pity you couldn't do that with people, Diamond thought. He'd be saying 'Basket' quite often.

Bradley introduced them and asked Mrs Mead to repeat her account of what had happened. She would make a useful witness, if needed in court. In precise, clear words, she described the day's events as she had seen them: the arrival of Mike Smith's car at two, or soon after, and the sight of him entering the house at a brisk step and leaving some fifty minutes later and driving off again. Haley had knocked about three forty-five saying her mummy hadn't met her from school and wasn't answering the door. 'Olga is a good little mother,' Mrs Mead went on. 'She collects the child at the school gate every day, so I was worried something was wrong. They gave me a front door key some time ago and I let myself in and to my amazement discovered her lying in the sitting room unconscious. I called an ambulance, and that was it, really. Haley stayed with me last night. An aunt came down from London this morning and collected her.'

'What sort of man is the husband?' Hen asked.

'A good neighbour. I've no complaints.'

'Good to his wife?'

'What are you implying, exactly?'

'You're obviously friendly with Olga Smith. Does he treat her well?'

'She's never complained to me about him.'

'And you've heard nothing?'

'Do you mean arguments?'

'Or anything else.'

'No violence, if that's what you mean. He has his moods, as most men do. A bit inconsiderate at times, unlike my Lionel, who was wonderful to me for over forty years, but he was an exceptional man. I find it hard to believe Mike struck her.'

Bradley said without much grace, 'You're the one who found her. You saw the state of her.'

But Diamond was quick to say, 'We don't know what happened yet. When you say "a bit inconsiderate", what do you mean?'

'Nothing so dreadful as hitting her. Small things I've noticed. For example, he doesn't ever help her with the shopping. She does it all, struggles back from the supermarket where she works laden down with bags. It wouldn't hurt him to pick it up in the car once in a while, would it? Those places are open well into the evening.'

'Doesn't she have the use of the car?'

'She doesn't drive, and that's a handicap these days, as I'm well aware because I never learned and it's too late now, but I'm not shopping for three.'

'Why doesn't she drive?'

'She confided to me once that she was banned. I didn't ask her for the details. We're on neighbourly terms, but not so close as that. There's a difference in our ages. I think she regards me as something of a mother figure, and you don't tell your mother all the mistakes you make.'

Hen asked if Olga Smith had spoken of a recent trip to Wightview Sands beach. She had not. Perhaps that, also, fell into the category of things you wouldn't tell Mother.

They left Mrs Mead. Diamond asked DI Bradley if he could recommend a pub for lunch, guessing, rightly, that the local man would be glad of a chance to say he was far too busy to idle away his time. So it was agreed that he would meet them again at four at the hospital, while they filled the unforgiving minute, or hour, or two, at the Boar's Head, south of the town, on the Worthing Road.

In his car, Diamond used his mobile – a toy he rarely played with – to check on the driving career of Mrs Olga Smith. When was she banned, and what was the offence? He was given an answer of sorts before he drove into the car park of the Boar's Head. The DVLC at Swansea had no record of Olga Smith.

He got out and ambled across to Hen. This time would not be wasted. They found a comfortable corner seat in a part of the main lounge no one else was using. Hen lit up a cigar while Diamond fetched beer for himself and dry white wine for the lady. Each felt able to relax in the other's company now that Bradley was gone, and they knew crucial things had to be debated.

'You seemed to be back-pedalling this morning,' Hen commented.

'In what way?'

'With DI Bradley, over what may or may not have happened to Olga Smith.'

'Inserting a note of caution, that's all. Just because Michael Smith is a dodgy character who doesn't welcome the idea of a chat with the Old Bill, we shouldn't jump to the conclusion that he bashed his wife.'

'If it was an accident and she fell and hit her head on the table, as you were suggesting, his behaviour is still suspicious. You don't leave your wife lying unconscious in a pool of blood.'

'No.' For a moment his eyes glazed over, his thoughts far away, to a park in Bath over a year ago.

'Did I say something?' Hen asked.

He took a sip of beer and forced himself to return to the here and now. 'What I was getting at – what I'm trying to say, Hen – is that when I looked at that bank statement with the large cash deposits I revised my thoughts about this man Smith. You find figures like that and you have to think this fellow is onto a scam.'

'Agreed. But how does that change anything?'

'It could be why he avoids us, why he didn't stick around at Wightview Sands to answer questions after the body was found. And why he did a runner yesterday after he heard the police had been to his house.'

'You're saying he may be in the clear? He didn't have anything to do with Emma Tysoe's murder?'

'I'm not ruling anything out at present. It's another way of interpreting his actions, that's all.'

'Take him out of the frame, and we don't have anyone,' she said with mock reproach. 'Is zees ze way you work, Monsieur Poirot? Me, I suspect everyone, including the cat.'

'And a couple of thousand others who were on that beach.'

'Them, too.'

'*Was* there a cat in the Tysoe house?' he asked.

'I didn't notice one.'

He grinned.

They looked at the menu. Diamond said he fancied the steak and Guinness pie with chips, and Hen surprised him by saying she'd join him. He hadn't yet heard her ship-of-the-desert theory of nutrition.

'The other thing about Smith,' he said, 'is that he's a family man. Not the most considerate of men, as Mrs Mead informed us, but a husband and a father, for all that. I find it difficult to cast a family man as the killer of Axel Summers.'

'You're sure the two killings are connected? The top brass at Bramshill didn't agree with you.'

'I'm not *sure* of anything, Hen. But I don't buy the theory that this killer is so rigid in his thinking that he wouldn't dispose of someone like Emma Tysoe who might have fingered him before he completed his quota of murders.'

'The method was different.'

'He had to be flexible. Strangulation was a suitable MO for the beach.'

'It's almost unknown.'

'What?'

'For a killer to use a different MO,' Hen pointed out. 'They find a method that suits them and stick to it.'

'This Ancient Mariner guy is out on his own,' he said in a way that blended disgust and respect. 'He's something else, Hen, totally callous. Self-centred. Committed. He kills to make some kind of point. He doesn't pick his victims because he hates them, but because they fit his plan.'

'But how would he have known Emma Tysoe was at work on the case? There was nothing in the papers. Even her workmates didn't know.'

'He'd expect a case like this to be referred to a profiler. He's read all the books on serial killers. You can bet he has. He'll know about the Home Office approved list. It's circulated. He'll have worked out which of the names were most likely to be consulted. Wouldn't be difficult to make a shortlist and find out who was currently off work doing some profiling.'

'Crafty.'

'He is.'

'I meant you, sport,' she said, 'thinking it out.'

'Thanks, but I'd prefer some other word. How about brilliant?'

'I could even run to that if you find me an ashtray.'

After he brought one to the table, she said, 'Peter, has it crossed your mind that when a profiler is murdered for being on a case, the police must be at risk as well?'

He played this down. 'Emma Tysoe was killed because she was clever – clever enough, given time, to finger the killer. He wouldn't expect the poor old plods to suss him out. Your ace detective Jimmy Barneston needn't miss any sleep over it.'

'What about you and me?'

He smiled. 'He's never heard of us.'

'I've been on TV appealing for information.'

'I wouldn't worry, Hen. That would just confirm his belief that we're up shit creek.'

'Oh, thanks!'

Their food arrived, pub-sized portions, and he looked at hers wondering where she could possibly stow it all. She was just a sparrow, the shortest officer he'd met in years, and she wasn't chunky, either. 'So what got you into this job?'

She rolled her eyes upwards. 'You want the story? I was looking for respect. Didn't get much in my family, being the youngest, with two older sisters and a brother. Wanted to prove I could hack it, and picked the toughest job I could think of. I was supposed to be five foot four, minimum, so I wore heels for the interview and put up my hair in a topknot. They had some fun at my expense, said the ballet school was up the street and stuff like that, but they liked my nerve and let me in. I was sent to Portsmouth Central first, and had to tough it out with the lads. If the sarge tells you to break up a fight in a pub on a Friday night, you don't argue. It's a funny thing how many of these bruisers turn out to be pussy cats when a woman shows up.'

'Respect.'

She laughed. 'No way. They're just embarrassed.'

'You get respect from your family now, I bet.'

'That's true. My big sisters phone me up and tell me their problems.'

'And you put in for CID and got it?'

'That was lucky timing on my part, just when they'd seen the need for more women. Some of the guys thought it was preferential treatment. Most of them want to get out of uniform, don't they? I didn't have any conscience. I'd put up with a lot to get where I was. And I've not done badly.'

'You've earned that respect.'

Hen grinned broadly. 'Oh yes?'

They might have gone on to discuss Diamond's in-and-out career, but they didn't. Instead, they talked strategy. Hen was still uneasy about Bramshill. 'They've put up the shutters – as they see it – on the Axel Summers murder, so we're right out of order trying to pin these two killings on the same guy.'

'I'm not worried,' Diamond said. 'Let's play it by the book. We're investigating the killing of Emma Tysoe and we've every right to find out what she was doing in the last month of her life. They can't stop us following up anything suspicious. We don't know where it will lead us, but if it takes us into forbidden territory we simply say we're doing our job.'

'Like finding out what's on her computer?'

'Exactly.'

'You're confident we can decrypt her hard disk?'

'I'm confident Clive can – given time.'

A surprise awaited them when they returned to the hospital. Instead of the saturnine DI Bradley in his leather jacket and jeans, a tall man in a grey three-piece greeted them outside the intensive care ward. He couldn't have been much over thirty, with dark, swept-back hair making him look as Italian as the cut of his suit, except that he was blue-eyed. Diamond's first thought was that this was a doctor with bad news, but Hen stepped forward and shook hands. 'For all that's wonderful! Jimmy the Priest! Peter, meet Jimmy Barneston.'

The man himself.

'The Priest?' Diamond queried, after he'd felt the firm handshake.

'He's always hearing confessions.'

'It's not down to me. It's the Sussex Inquisition. People like Hen Mallin,' Barneston told Diamond. He had an air of confidence it had taken Diamond twenty years to acquire. 'I decided to join you for this. We can be frank with each other, can't we?'

'Say no more.'

Diamond came under sharp scrutiny from the ice-blue eyes.

Barneston went on, 'Bramshill brought me up to speed on your investigation and they tell me you know about the case I'm on. Something of interest may be developing here, so I'd like to hear what Mrs Smith has to say.'

Which wasn't the Bramshill line at all. Jimmy Barneston shouldn't be underestimated.

'No problem,' Diamond said cheerfully. 'Let's see if they're ready for us.'

The sister asked them to keep the questioning to five minutes or less and showed them into the room where Olga Smith lay tubed up, with her head bandaged and cradled in a support. Only her eyes moved, and they were bloodshot. Her right arm was in plaster to above the elbow.

Diamond suggested to Hen, 'Why don't you ask the questions?'

Jimmy Barneston didn't object.

Hen stepped closer and said who the visitors were. 'Olga, we need to know how this happened. Can you remember?'

She mouthed the word 'no'. The voice came as a delayed reaction, and feebly.

'Do you have any recollection of anything at all about the day?'

She tried clearing her throat, and something hurt, because she winced. 'A little.'

'Do you recall Sergeant Gregson coming to the house?'

'Yes.'

'She told you she'd spoken to your little girl Haley, right?'

'Is Haley—'

Seeing the sudden concern in Olga's features, Hen said quickly, 'She's fine, perfectly OK. Your sister is looking after her.'

'Ah.' The muscles relaxed a little.

'We're interested in what happened after my sergeant, Stella Gregson, visited you. I expect you phoned your husband to tell him. Am I right?'

'Yes, I spoke to Mike.'

'Did he come home at once?'

'Yes.'

'You remember?'

'He was upset. Didn't think it was fair, asking Haley questions.'

'Upset. You mean angry?'

'Yes.'

'So what happened? You seem to have a memory of this. Did you talk at all?'

'Talked, yes. I told him what the policewoman said and what I'd said.'

'And then?'

'He told me he was going away.'

'Where to?'

'Didn't say. Business things.'

'Was that when he turned violent?'

'Violent?' Olga Smith repeated the word as if it was unknown to her.

'He hit you.'

'No.'

'You don't remember?'

'Mike didn't touch me.'

Hen exchanged a glance with Diamond. Was the episode erased from Olga's memory by the concussion?

'Are you sure of this?'

'He collected some things and left. I saw him drive off.'

Either Olga Smith was fantasising, or this challenged all their theories.

'You're certain?' Diamond broke into the dialogue. 'You watched him drive away? You were OK at that stage?'

'Yes.'

'Did he say where he was going?'

'No.'

'He just walked out? No fight? No violence?'

'I said.'

Out of the range of Olga Smith's restricted vision, Hen was exchanging disbelieving glances with Jimmy Barneston.

'So what happened next?' Diamond asked.

'Next?' The voice was faint again, as if she was drifting away.

'You were alone in the house, right?'

'That's right.'

'But you ended up here, in intensive care. You don't have any memory of being struck on the head? Or breaking your arm?'

She frowned, and a look of panic came into her eyes. Then they closed and her jaw slackened.

Hen said, 'I don't think we'll get much more.' And as if on cue the sister appeared and ushered them outside.

In the waiting area, Jimmy Barneston said, 'What did you make of that?'

'Weird,' Hen said.

'Can we put it down to confusion, or what?'

'She didn't sound confused. She was very definite. She didn't blame her husband at all.'

'Are we looking at someone else as the attacker, then? Someone who called at the house after the husband had driven away?'

'Hard to believe,' Hen said.

Diamond was unusually silent. A possible explanation was surfacing, but he needed to check something first. 'I'll be right back.' He left them and returned to the ward.

At his approach the sister stepped protectively forward. 'I'm sorry. I said no more questions. She's had all she can cope with.'

'It's you I want to speak to,' he said. 'When she came in, did you send for her medical records?'

'They're confidential.'

'Absolutely. But we're trying to establish whether she was attacked, whether the head injury was caused by someone else, or was accidental. I'm wondering if she's epileptic.'

'Is this relevant to your investigation?'

'Vital,' he said. 'It may well explain the injury, if she suffered a fit.'

'Epileptics don't very often injure themselves,' the sister said. 'They bite their tongues sometimes. This is an impacted blow to the head.'

'She was found beside a table. If her head hit the corner as she collapsed . . .'

'That's possible.' She hesitated, and glanced towards the room where Olga Smith was lying. Finally she sighed and said, 'Yes, if it helps, I can confirm that Mrs Smith has a history of epilepsy. That's one more reason why we're treating her as a special case.'

'Thank you.'

When he passed on the news to the others and they'd had time to absorb it, Hen said, 'Who would have thought it?'

Barneston said with a sidewards glance at Diamond that was not too admiring, 'He did, obviously.'

She told Diamond, 'You could be right about the husband as well. He may not even know his wife is injured.'

Barneston agreed. 'If she can be believed, she saw him drive off. She'll have had the epileptic fit after he left. Have you any idea why he came home at all?'

Diamond told him about the bank statement they'd found. 'If the cash deposits are dodgy, as we suspect, he could have panicked.'

'That's more than likely,' Barneston said. 'It's got to be followed up. And I'm even more doubtful that Michael Smith has anything to do with the killing of Emma Tysoe.'

148

He held out a hand to Diamond. 'Good luck with the investigation. You need it.'

After he'd gone, Hen asked Diamond, 'What do you make of him?'

'Young for a DCI.'

'They're getting younger all the time,' she said, grinning. 'Too brash for your liking? Plenty of people think so, but he gets results.'

'That's all right, then.'

'You're not going to commit yourself, are you?'

'Does he wear suits all the time?'

'Whenever I've seen him,' Hen said.

'He makes an impression.'

'But you're not going to say what sort?'

He smiled faintly and looked away. In his years in CID, he'd seen a few meteors rising high. They looked brilliant for a time, and then they fizzled out. A shooting star is just a small mass of matter made luminous by the earth's atmosphere. But maybe Jimmy Barneston had more substance to him. Time would tell.

Hen asked, 'Was that just a hunch?'

'What?'

'The epilepsy. What made you suspect Olga Smith might be epileptic?'

'The driving ban. At first, I took it to mean she'd been banned by the courts, but I checked with Swansea, and there's no record of her ever having had a licence. So it crossed my mind that the ban could be on medical grounds. No epileptic can get a licence.'

11

'Mr D?'

Diamond squeezed the mobile against his ear, as if more pressure would help. He'd heard the voice before, and it was friendly enough, yet he couldn't put a face to it. 'Yes?'

'Is this a good time?'

'A good time for what, my friend?'

'I mean, are you on your own?'

'I am.'

'I thought I ought to tell you I had some visitors this afternoon, two heavies from the CCU.'

The modern over-reliance on initials was enough to drive anyone down the paranoia road. 'You're losing me.'

'The Computer Crime Unit.'

The penny dropped – twice. This was Clive, the computer expert.

'What did they want?'

'They, em' – a long pause – 'they seized Dr Tysoe's hard disk.'

'What – the thing you're working on?' This was devastating. 'For crying out loud, Clive. Didn't you stop them?'

'I couldn't do that. They're part of SO6.'

This was one abbreviation he recognised. 'The Fraud Squad.'

'That's who they work for, but they handle any kind

of computer crime. They said they had authority, waved some piece of paper in front of me. It was no use arguing.'

The moguls at Bramshill were behind this, he guessed. If Jimmy Barneston were the instigator, he would have mentioned it, surely. 'We're down the pan, then. And I suppose you were still trying to crack the code?'

'It's a brute, Mr D. The geeks in the CCU can give themselves a headache now, can't they?'

'You didn't succeed, then?'

'Sorry. No.'

'I was banking on you, Clive.'

'I put some hours in, believe me. I could save those guys some time by telling them what doesn't work, but I guess they want to find out for themselves.'

Diamond said with a sigh, 'I'm whacked – flat out on the canvas with my eyes closed.'

Taking him at his word Clive made a silent count of five before asking, 'Do you want me to stop now?'

'What?'

'Should I give up?'

'But you have to, if they've got the disk.'

Clive said in the same calm tone, 'It's all right, Mr D. I can use the zip.'

'The what?'

'The zip disk. It's a back-up of everything on the hard disk. I wouldn't do a job like this without at least one back-up. I can carry on trying to decrypt those files if you want.'

With one bound . . .

Mightily relieved, Diamond asked, 'Do the Fraud Squad know you've got this copy?'

'They'd expect it. I'd have to be a complete nerd not to back up something as important as this.'

'Get back to it, then. Pull out all the stops, or whatever

you do with computers. You're still ahead, lad. You've done all this work already.'

'What do you mean – "ahead"? We're all on the same side, aren't we, Mr D?'

'Don't push me, Clive.'

He told Hen the news over a cup of tea made and served by the WRVS in the main waiting area of Crawley General Hospital. The next moves had to be discussed.

'I'm not surprised,' she said. 'Bramshill gave Dr Tysoe the job, so they're entitled to know what progress she made. The files could tell them.'

'I might be reading too much into this, but I thought it was a cynical move to stop us finding out stuff they want to keep secret.'

'Such as?'

'The names of the two other people this killer is out to get. She could have named them.'

'Let's hope she did. And let's hope your computer wizard delivers.' Hen gave an unexpected chuckle. 'It would be a hoot, wouldn't it, if this encrypted stuff turns out to be some other secret enterprise she was working on, like a thirty-something novel? Or erotic poetry?'

He winced. 'You're not helping my confidence.'

'Look on the bright side,' she said. 'A window into Emma Tysoe's thinking will be fascinating, whatever's there. Up to now I haven't felt I know her.'

'Me neither.'

'It could be a diary. We might get all the dirt on the Psychology Department.'

'Spare me that. I had five hours in the car with Dr Seton. I can only take so much.'

But he was forced to agree that Emma Tysoe's university colleagues had to be investigated further. And Hen promised to make another effort with the beach staff at

Bognor, the lifeguard and the car park attendants and café staff.

Hen was stubbing out her cigar prior to leaving when one of the tea ladies came over to the table and asked if they were from the police.

'At your service, ma'am,' Diamond said, uncertain what was coming next.

'Because we just took a phone call from Sister Thomas in intensive care. She said would you please go back directly?'

Diamond saw the flash of alarm in Hen's eyes. Tragedy had leapt into his mind as well. No words were exchanged. They got up from the table and moved fast to the exit.

The sister was waiting for them outside the intensive care unit.

'Thank God you're still here.'

'Bad news, sister?'

'We had a man here.'

'What?' Neither of them had anticipated this.

'Just a few minutes ago. He came to the desk insisting he was the patient's husband, and I think he was, because she seemed to recognise him. We were very alarmed, knowing the circumstances.'

'Couldn't you stop him?' Hen said.

'I tried. I told him visitors weren't allowed. He didn't get really close to her. There was a bit of a scuffle as he tried to go past me. He shouted her name from the door and then he left. I called Crawley police, and then I thought you might still be here, because I heard you say something about tea as you were leaving.'

'What's he like?' Diamond asked.

'Dark-haired, thirtyish. He could do with a shave.'

'He went which way?'

She pointed along the corridor. 'And he's in a rather crumpled black or grey striped suit.'

'Can he get to the car park that way?'

'Yes.'

Diamond started running.

The big man in quick motion was a danger to the public. In his rugby-playing days faint-hearted defenders had been known to step aside claiming they were sold a dummy when he charged at them. In a hospital corridor he was a potentially lethal force, dodging wheelchairs and trolleys and patients on crutches. Convincing himself this was for the greater good, and he was in control, he powered ahead, bursting through swing doors and around corners, trusting to God he wouldn't meet a freshly plastered leg-case being wheeled towards him like a scene out of a Charlie Chaplin classic.

By good fortune he made it to the main exit without mishap and dashed along a covered walkway towards what looked like one of the main car parks. Michael Smith had the use of a car, and it was likely he'd driven here after hearing that his wife was in intensive care.

Three hundred or more cars were parked in neat rows and others were in the aisles waiting for spaces. It was the time late in the afternoon when patients were leaving and visitors arriving. A few pedestrians were visible, but nobody remotely like the tall, mean-looking man Diamond knew he ought to recognise from the photo in his pocket.

He slowed to a walk and stopped altogether, catching his breath. The chase was over. The sister's estimate of a few minutes must have been unreliable. Or Smith had slipped out by some other route.

More cars were streaming in on the far side, through a gate system that seemed unable to prevent the congestion. Diamond watched the striped arm go up and down a couple of times before realising it could be his salvation. A pay system was in operation here. Each driver had to pay something at the automatic exit. So there was only one way out – and it was possible Smith hadn't got there yet.

Another dash, this time across the car park among slow-moving but still hazardous vehicles. Twice he had to swerve around a reversing car as if he was handing off a tackle. But it was worth the risk. At the exit was a queue of five or six waiting to pay, and the fourth in line was a white Honda Civic. Heart and lungs pounding, he approached the driver. Definitely the man in the photo. And the car couldn't move out of line.

Smith had his window down. One look at Diamond's warrant card said it all. He knew he was caught. Without any conviction he said, 'What's up?'

Diamond told him to switch off the engine and step out.

The questioning took place in a room normally used by the hospital almoner, with flowers on the desk and holiday posters on the walls – a distinct improvement on the average police interview room. This was a coup for Diamond and Hen. They would hand the prisoner over to Crawley police at the end of the day, but they had first crack at him.

Tired and scruffy, Smith now appeared not so mean, or guarded, as he had in the photographs. He'd evidently slept in the suit. But to his credit he seemed to have some concern about his wife's condition.

'Is she going to be all right?'

'They think so,' Hen said.

'She fell and cracked her head, didn't she? Do they know she's epileptic? You can never tell when a fit is going to happen.'

'She's going to be fine,' Diamond said. 'But you're under strong suspicion.'

'Of what?'

'Attacking her.'

His eyes stood out like cuckoo eggs. '*Me*, attack Olga? I wouldn't hurt her.'

'You were seen at the house yesterday afternoon. She was found there later when your daughter came home from school.'

'I'm not violent, I tell you.'

'You've got to tell us a whole lot more than that. Where were you last night?'

'Does it matter what I was doing? You're way off beam if you think I had anything to do with this.'

'Answer the question, Mr Smith.'

He sighed as if all this were too tedious to relate. 'I drove miles, and slept in the car. Salisbury Plain, I think. When I turned on the radio about midday I heard someone say Olga was injured and in Crawley General and they were looking for me. I drove here to try and see her.'

'Why were you on the run if you're innocent?'

'That's something else.'

'Come on. We're not arsing about here.'

'I panicked. That's all.'

'Why? What is there to panic about?'

'She told me on the phone the police had been to the house.'

'Is that so scary? What's the scam, Mr Smith? What have you been up to?'

He shook his head. Suddenly the eyes were more defiant than panic-stricken. It was obvious he wasn't going to roll over easily.

Diamond gave Hen an enquiring look, a slight lift of the eyebrows that said, in effect, shall we pursue this? Whatever racket Smith is in, banking large amounts of cash, there are more urgent matters to discuss before DI Bradley arrives.

Hen nodded. They had a good understanding already.

Diamond said, 'You know there's a lot of interest in the dead woman who was found on Wightview Sands beach?'

Smith stared back in alarm.

'We're in charge of that investigation.'

'You're not trying to swing that on me?'

'You're a key witness. You called the lifeguard, I understand.'

'Yes.'

'And then you quit the scene. And you haven't responded to any of the calls for help.'

'I couldn't tell you anything. I didn't want to get involved.'

'For the same reason you spent last night on the run?'

'Well, yes.' He held out his hands in appeal. 'But what do you expect from me? All I did was tell the lifeguard guy she was down there and helped him lift her off the beach and into a hut, and then I left.'

The next logical step was to remind him that he'd been requested to remain until the police arrived, but this wasn't a blame session. They needed cooperation.

'Now we've got you here, can you tell us anything else about the dead woman? Did you notice her before this?'

He took his time over the question. That day on the beach had been obscured by more vivid recent experiences. 'She was there most of the day. Arrived not long after we did, around eleven thirty, I suppose.'

'Alone?'

'Sure. There was no one with her.'

'Do you remember what she was carrying?' Hen asked.

'She had a windbreak with her, blue, I think. The first thing she did was put it up.'

'Any kind of bag?'

'I guess she must have had one, but I don't remember

any when we moved her. My wife is better at remembering stuff like that. Well, when she's OK she is.'

'Sunglasses?'

'For sure. And a towel. She had this towel that she spread on the sand to lie on.'

None of this added much to their knowledge, except that Emma Tysoe had arrived alone. The rest was familiar, its function mainly to assist Smith to visualise the scene. Now that the focus had moved away from Crawley, and he was less tense, he might contribute something of use.

Diamond took up the questions again. 'So she spread her towel quite near you?'

'Just in front. But we couldn't see her without standing up.'

'That was because the windbreak was in the way? But you'd have noticed if anyone joined her at any stage?'

'I guess I would have done. No, I don't remember anyone arriving. People going by, like they do on a beach, but no one actually joining her.' He shrugged, and he seemed to be genuinely trying to think of an explanation. 'Wait a bit. Olga said something about a guy who tried to chat the woman up, and she wasn't having any of it.'

'She did?' Diamond leaned forward eagerly. 'When was this?'

'Not long before lunch.'

'Did you see him?'

'No, I had my eyes closed. Well, I was probably sleeping, because I've got no memory of this.'

'How can you be sure of the time?'

'I'm going by what Olga said.'

'Did she describe this man?'

'Something about a black T-shirt. That's all I recall.'

'Come on. She must have noticed more than that.'

'I didn't ask. He didn't interest me.'

'He could be really important,' Hen said.

Smith obviously didn't think so. 'I wouldn't make too much of it if I were you. The woman was OK when he came by. And after.' He hesitated, dredging up another memory. 'Actually, Olga told me the woman spoke to her.'

Diamond's eyebrows shot up. 'They *spoke*?'

'Only something about Haley, friendly like. You know how people talk to you about your kids.'

Neither Diamond nor Hen had any such experience to draw on, but they could imagine.

'It would help if you could remember what was said.'

'It was Olga who spoke to her. I wasn't listening. She told me later. It was only some friendly piece of chat.'

'This was when – in the morning?'

'Before we had lunch. I'm just making the point that she was all right at that stage. It was some hours after that she was killed.'

'How do you know when she was killed?'

He reddened. 'It must have been the afternoon, mustn't it? A dead body wouldn't be lying there for hours with nobody noticing.'

'So when do you think the murder happened?'

'I've no idea, unless it was when Olga and I went for a swim.'

'What time was that?'

'Some while after the tide had turned, and was coming in. Towards four o'clock.'

'Do you remember looking at her when you got up for your swim?'

'Not particularly.'

'Not at all?'

'To be honest, there were some attractive women not far away on our left, showing off their assets.'

'Topless, you mean?'

'If you'd been there, you wouldn't have looked anywhere else, believe me.'

159

Hen rolled her eyes, and said nothing.

Diamond asked, 'How long were you away? Any idea?'

'For the swim? Half an hour to forty minutes. It was warmer than we expected, so we stayed in for some time. When we got out, the tide had covered a lot of the beach. It comes in fast. And that was when my wife panicked a bit – well, quite a lot – because we couldn't see where Haley, our little girl, had gone. We'd left her playing with some other kids, chucking a frisbee about. There was no sign of Haley or the other girls.'

'This was after four thirty?'

'Don't know for sure. I wasn't wearing a watch. I said I'd check with the lifeguards while my wife went back to our place on the beach. Someone had to be there in case Haley came back. So that's what we did. I went up to the platform where the lifeguards keep watch, not far away from where we'd been sitting all day. I told them my kid was missing and gave them a description and they promised to make a search. They suggested I looked for her by the ice-cream queue outside the café, because lost kids often find their way there. I tried there first and couldn't see her, so I went to look in the sections of beach either side of us. The groynes dividing it up are quite high in places.'

'You keep saying "they", as if there was more than one lifeguard,' Hen broke into his narrative.

'Right.'

'How many were there?'

'Two, when I spoke to them.'

'Because when the police arrived there was only one present. And I've only ever interviewed one, an Australian called Emerson.'

'There were definitely two when I first told them Haley was missing. A shaven-head one in red shorts and a tall, blond guy with a ponytail.'

160

'Were they both Australian?'

'I wouldn't know. I don't recall the blond guy saying anything. But you're right. He wasn't around later, when I reported finding the woman. I expect he'd gone off duty.'

'There should be two lifeguards on duty,' Diamond said. 'It's not a one-man job on a beach that size. Someone needs to be at the post all the time.'

'I'm going to follow this up,' Hen said. 'Tall, blond ponytail . . . anything else?'

'An earring, I think.'

'Just the one?'

'Yes. He was well tanned, as you'd expect, and built like an ox – well, an athlete, anyway. That's about all I remember. I was thinking about Haley at the time.'

'So it was Emerson who found her?' said Diamond, putting the story back on track.

'Must have been. You see, I was still flogging up and down the beach looking for her when she was brought back. Olga was there. It seems one of the other children got a nose bleed from a frisbee, or something, and all of them went up to the first-aid hut – which of course confused Haley when she was left alone up there.'

'You heard this from your wife?'

'Yes, when I got back.'

'Was that when you noticed the dead woman?'

Smith nodded. 'Haley drew our attention first. But we weren't the only people who noticed she wasn't moving. Some lads not far from us were having a good laugh about it, thinking she was asleep, I suppose, and about to get a drenching. Olga asked me to look and I went over and realised she was dead. Christ, that was a shock. I ran up to the lifeguard—'

'One lifeguard?' Hen queried.

'Only one at this point. Most people had left the beach

161

because the tide had come right in and it was the end of the afternoon anyway. The whole place was closing down. He was the Aussie. He came quickly enough. Asked those lads for some help to get her up the beach. A couple of them volunteered. And that's all there is.' He let out a long breath as if he'd been living through the crisis again.

'These lads, as you call them,' Diamond said. 'What age would they have been?'

'Late teens or early twenties.'

'You'd noticed them earlier?'

'Right at the start. They were on the beach when we arrived. I can recall saying to Olga that we wouldn't sit too close to them. They had their cans of lager with them. But as it turned out, they weren't rowdy or anything.'

'How many?'

'Four or five. I'm not sure.'

'None of them came forward when we asked for witnesses.'

'That's the young generation for you.'

'Neither did you.'

Smith gave an uneasy smile.

Hen asked, 'Did you notice anyone else sitting close enough to have seen what was happening?'

'There were three girls on sunloungers right next to us.'

'The topless ones?'

'No, these were just schoolkids, about fifteen, doing some serious sunbathing, but they'd packed up and gone by the time the body was found. The topless women were some way over to our left, about thirty yards off. You can forget them.'

'You obviously haven't,' Hen murmured.

'There was a French family on our right,' Smith went on. 'Mother, father and three small kids. I'm pretty certain they'd left as well.'

'That's one reason why people haven't come forward,' Diamond commented. 'They'd left the beach before the body was found, so didn't have the faintest idea they'd been sitting a few yards away from it.'

Hen asked, 'Did any of these people you've mentioned speak to the woman at any time during the day?'

'Apart from the bloke in the black T-shirt? Nobody I noticed.'

'Did she leave the beach at any stage?'

'No – unless it was while we were swimming.'

Diamond came in again. 'And after you helped carry the body up to the hut, you collected your things and left?'

'Right. We had to move anyway, because of the tide.'

Diamond glanced towards Hen. They'd covered everything except the real reason for Smith's avoidance of the police. He was a deeply worried man, almost certainly into something criminal for the first time in his life. But as a killer so cool that he'd strangled a woman within yards of his own wife and child, Michael Smith just didn't cut it.

12

Diamond's voicemail had been building up while he was in Sussex. He was not bothered. Much of it could be ignored now. And being out of the office has other advantages. He'd missed a meeting called by Georgina Dallymore, the Assistant Chief Constable, to discuss some desks and chairs that had mysteriously been dumped in the executive toilet upstairs. 'Couldn't have helped, anyway,' he said, as he called her to give his apologies.

Georgina said, 'Would you have any use for some extra desks?'

'Not really, ma'am.'

'I had to have them moved, and now they're cluttering the corridor. I'm worried about fire regulations.'

If that's all you have to worry about, he thought, it's not a bad old life on the top floor. 'Someone will have a use for them, ma'am.'

'I hope so. I'm going on holiday next week. When I come back, I don't want to find them still there.'

His interest quickened. Georgina off the premises was good news. 'Anywhere nice?'

'A Nile cruise.'

'Sounds wonderful. How long?'

'Ten days.'

He made a mental note.

Back to the voicemail. The one message that stood out

was from Clive: 'Mr D, I've got a result. Any time you want to go through those files, we're ready to roll.'

Clive's hours of work spoke of long nights on the internet. He never came in until after eleven. Today, it was twenty minutes after, and he looked spent before he'd started. Eventually the two got together with black coffees and doughnuts in a small office in the basement. While the computer was booting up, Diamond told the young man he'd done well. 'I just hope this is worth all the hours you put in.'

'It will be.'

'Hot stuff?'

Clive grinned. 'I haven't looked at all of it, but hot's the word, from what I saw.' He took something not much bigger than a cigarette lighter from his shirt pocket and attached it to a lead at the back of the computer tower.

'What's that?'

'A USB – portable storage device. I had to work on this at home, you see.'

'And that's all there is?' Diamond couldn't disguise his disappointment.

'Mr D, this little item is a hard drive. Five hundred and twelve megabytes. You could put the Bible and the complete works of Shakespeare on this and still have space.'

'So how much is there in reality?'

'Enough to keep you busy for the rest of the morning,' Clive told him as he worked the keys.

He explained that there had been three encrypted files on Emma Tysoe's hard disk, each allotted a number that he thought represented the date it was created. 1706 was the seventeenth of June. The next was the twenty-second. The last was the twenty-fifth.

'Two days before she was murdered,' Diamond said to

show he wasn't completely adrift. 'And we can now read it straight off the screen? Let's go. It starts on the seventeenth, you said?'

Clive had better ways of spending the rest of the morning than sitting beside Peter Diamond. He gave him a quick lesson with the mouse, showed him how to access the files and left him to it.

Magic.

The first lines of text were on the screen, and suddenly Diamond was right where he wanted to be, inside the mind of the murdered woman, getting that precious insight he'd been denied up to now. So direct was the contact, so vivid, it was almost too intimate to take in a sustained read.

Had this 8.30 a.m. call about another profiling job. Just when I was starting to coast, and think of holidays. Bramshill insists no one else but me will do, and won't give me any details except an address in Sussex. All very cloak and dagger. Just to cover my rear end, I'm going to keep this personal record of what happens and encrypt as I go along. I can't keep everything in my head.

I'm flattered in a way to get this assignment, kidding myself I'm indispensable, but it's a bloody nuisance too if I'm going to have to make up excuses for not going out with Ken. We're supposed to be eating at Popjoy's tomorrow night. Just my luck. Even if I get there it takes the pleasure out of a beautiful meal (not to mention the shag later) when you've looked at a mangled corpse the day before.

The upside is that I get out of the university for a bit. This end-of-semester time is when Chromik tries to think of jobs to keep people busy. I called the office and fixed it with Tara to take indefinite leave. More later.

I dressed for the country, smart casual, and drove to this house overlooking Bramber, a village tucked away below the South Downs in Sussex, and rather a dinky place. In fact there wasn't much to see – of the murder scene, I mean – except police photos. It all happened three days ago, so they'd already removed the corpse and finished their forensics. Victim was Axel Summers, that smooth old (fiftyish?) film director who can talk about anything. Saw him on Question Time a few weeks ago speaking up for the right to choose, and rather liked him. Someone didn't, obviously. He'd been hit through the head with a nine-inch arrow – a bolt, they call it – from a crossbow.

Archery isn't my kind of sport. I had no idea a crossbow packed such force. In the photos you could see the point sticking out of the other side of his head. They tell me when it was a weapon of war a crossbow bolt was made to penetrate armour. The power is in the bow part (or 'prod'), made of steel usually. The bowstring is pulled back to a catch, or 'cocked' (dear old Freud would have a field day with this jargon) with a lever or some winding mechanism far more powerful than you get with ordinary bows and arrows.

The reason they asked for a profiler is that the killer left a note – the usual paper and paste job – with a quote from The Rime of the Ancient Mariner, 'he stoppeth one of three', and two extra names. Is this a serial murderer declaring himself? they want to know. Strictly between you and me, Computer, one of the names is the glamour-boy golfer, Matthew Porter, and the other is gorgeous, pouting Anna Walpurgis, the one-time pop star.

'Get away!' said Diamond aloud. These were huge names. Already the decrypted files were yielding information he'd been denied. He took a gulp of coffee and scarcely noticed it was lukewarm.

Media people – and named. My first thought is that this killer must be some kind of attention-seeker. Egocentric, and either extremely stupid to announce his plan, or brilliant. I don't see much between. Summers has been filming a big-budget movie of The Ancient Mariner, that strange, long poem by Coleridge we did in the fifth year at school. The wording of the message was straight from the poem, and so was the weapon. The SIO (I'll come back to him, Computer!) reminded me that the Ancient Mariner in the poem uses a crossbow to kill the albatross. Coincidence? I don't think so. This is someone using murder as a melodramatic statement.

Does he have to be an insider, close enough to the victim to know what he was filming? Not necessarily. The Ancient Mariner project has been getting plenty of publicity. They brought over Patrick Devaney from Hollywood to play the main role, and he's a megastar in the movie world. The budget runs to millions. With some arm-twisting from the Arts Council they managed to get some of Britain's industrial giants to back it, companies like Superglass and British Metal. I said I couldn't imagine how a poem, a long one admittedly, can be spun out into a feature-length film. The SIO – a literate policeman! – tells me they could do a lot with the life aboard ship and the character of the Mariner even before the story gets under way. There's also a secondary plot involving the wedding guest the Mariner meets. And there are huge set-pieces ideal for all those special effects you expect in a movie these days.

God knows what happens now, because a lot of the film still has to be shot. Summers had finished directing the scenes with the star and was having a few days off. Up to now, they've put some kind of press embargo on the news of his murder, but it's bound to break soon.

The police have already warned the other two 'targets' and beefed up their security.

So what are my early thoughts? This could be a one-off murder. If the killer – the police team call him the Mariner – is an attention-seeker he may have thrown in a couple more juicy names just to see the effect. Somehow, I doubt it. I think he really means to get Porter and Walpurgis as well. This is an off-the-cuff reaction on my part, but I get the impression of a cold-blooded killer (unscientific terminology, but I'm doing my best to avoid the term psychopath) at work here, untroubled by conscience or emotion, figuring he's so far ahead of the game he can safely post his intentions. It's new in my experience, actually to name future victims. I can't remember anything like this.

And murdering Summers must have been a pushover for him. The level of security at the scene was nil. It's an isolated house built quite high up, well above the village, in a large, wooded garden with only a low iron railing around it. Summers was killed while seated outside on a bench that faced a gorgeous view to the west, watching the sunset and enjoying a g&t. Apparently this was his routine on fine evenings when he was home. If the Mariner knew of this, he had a good opportunity to choose his shooting position (do you shoot with a crossbow?). There was plenty of thick foliage only ten metres away, where the police say the killer probably stood or lay. No obvious footprints in soft earth, or fibres caught on the branches. He was ultra-careful to leave no trace except the bolt. They've carried out fingertip searches, but I'll be surprised if anything is found.

Motive? We'll see. At this stage it doesn't look like theft. Summers had valuable paintings and some cash in the house, and according to the housekeeper (a man I haven't yet met) everything is intact. Housekeeper, by the way, has an alibi for the evening of the murder. He knows of no feuds, no obvious enemies, though there's always bitching in the TV and film world. Actually Summers had the reputation of being a charming bloke, generous to others in the profession and always willing to help people out. There are no women in the frame. The police think he was probably gay by inclination, but sexually inactive. He put a lot of energy into his work.

What does the method tell us about the murderer? I'm relying on what I've been told here. The crossbow is an eccentric choice of weapon, as accurate and deadly as any gun, the only drawback being . . . the drawback. Unlike a handgun it takes time to load. However, there can't be all that many cross-bows in circulation, and I gather the dishy detective is pinning his hopes on finding where it was obtained. There are archery clubs all over the country, but they mostly use the longbow. There aren't more than a couple of hundred regular cross-bowmen, he's been told. But there's no official register of these things. You don't need a licence. Hunting using bows is against the law in this country, and that's that. They can shoot at targets if they want or, more rarely, for distance.

What interested me when we talked about crossbows is that anyone can learn to use them easily and quickly. You may not become a champion in a couple of hours, but you can learn enough to hit a target at thirty metres. There's no strain on the muscles, as there is with a longbow. The length of draw is fixed and the release is mechanical. The modern bows have tele-scopic sights. It's rather like shooting a rifle, except that there's no recoil. There's that disadvantage – and it was a major problem in ancient warfare – that it takes time to reload. But one shot should be enough.

I wouldn't mind DCI Jimmy Barneston showing me how to hold a crossbow. He's the SIO I've been itching to write about. Tall, a smart dresser, broad-shouldered, mid-thirties (I'd say), with amazing blue eyes like Peter O'Toole's. Long, elegant fingers. If he only knew what I was thinking when I looked at those fingers! I just know he'd be sensational in bed. Watch out, Ken. There's someone else for me to fantasise over now.

It's not just his good looks. He's got to be a crack hand to have been picked as SIO on this one. I like his confidence. Predictably, this hunky cop wanted an instant opinion and I had to tell him sweetly that certain things can't, and shouldn't, be rushed. I fed the poor lad a few first thoughts to keep him sweet, the idea that the killer was challenging the police and this could be a motive in itself. I warned him to expect surprises and gave him a bit of a look. I'm sure the blue eyes twinkled.

I drove back to Gt Pulteney St still thinking about it all. Didn't even bother to garage the car, I was so hyped up. I really want to make a contribution here. This, I feel strongly, has the hall-marks of a groundbreaking case, certain to be written up in the literature for years to come, and I don't want to put a foot wrong. There's huge pressure, with the lives of two named people at risk. True, the pressure isn't all on me. It's up to my new friend Jimmy to see that Porter and Walpurgis are given protection. There's a double bind here. They're public figures. If they're kept under wraps for long, they'll die a professional death anyway. In their lines of work they have to show them-selves, and the Mariner will be waiting.

He may not use a crossbow next time. He's obviously intel-ligent and capable of devising an even more ingenious method. Having killed once and got clean away from the scene, he'll be confident. With an inflated sense of his self-worth and a total lack of conscience, he'll throw himself into this challenge of his own making and try to show us up as incompetents. I'm scared, as well as excited. I fear thee, ancient mariner! Yes, Computer, I've found a copy of the poem, and I've read the whole thing again. It has more than enough scenes of horror in the text, without the added dimension this murder brings.

Too soon yet to start on a profile. I want to weigh up all the information I have. It's tempting to assume this is a serial killer before he carries out a second murder – and that may be a mistake. Am I dealing with a boaster or is he a committed killer? Obviously there's pressure on me to provide a profile before someone else is murdered.

So let's assume the Mariner intends to kill again. I can't duck the perennial question any longer: is this a psychopath? How I hate this word with all its colourful associations, suggesting, as it does, a biological propensity to kill, a pathogenic drive, when in reality there's no organic or psychotic explanation for such behaviour. All we can say for sure is that certain individuals who persistently commit violent crimes are able to function at two contradictory levels. They appear 'normal' with an ability to understand and participate in human relationships. Yet they have a detachment that allows them to carry out random acts of violence without pity or guilt. If the Mariner fitted this profile I would expect him to have a history, a trail of cruelty, broken hearts and suffering. They don't suddenly take to murder. It's part of a process that begins early. I keep saying him, and I ought to remind myself that a woman could fit this crime. Harder to imagine, but not impossible.

Then there's the other kind of serial killer, equally as chilling, acting not on impulse, but from a clear motive such as revenge, or ambition, or greed, probably deriving from some seminal incident in his life. He has an agenda and the killing of his victims is purposeful. He's not at all the same as the random killer who may claim to have a 'mission' to kill prostitutes, or gay men, or people of a certain racial group. He has made decisions to deprive certain individuals of life. He creates a role for himself in which he has the power to rectify what he sees as personal injustices.

I don't know yet where to place the Mariner.

This evening I cooled off in the bath and drank lager from the fridge and lolled around in my Japanese dressing gown listening to Berlioz and thinking. Just before ten the phone went and I jumped up and grabbed it. Only Ken, making sure I was still on for Popjoy's tomorrow. Couldn't get too excited about the prospect. I mean, I knew we had a booking already, and I suppose it showed in my voice. For him it's a very big deal. I could tell he was disappointed in me, but I told him I'd had a trying day and I'd be more like myself tomorrow night. He's getting clingy and I'm not sure I like that.

And now it's another day and I'm spending the morning at home with my books checking on the kinds of serial killers who

172

choose or need to communicate information about their crimes. I just want to see if it's an indicator. Jack the Ripper – if his letters are to be believed – must have been an early example of this type. 'You'll hear about Saucy Jack's work tomorrow. Double event this time.' Another was David Berkowitz, self-styled 'Son of Sam', who wrote to the police in 1976 claiming that he felt on a different wavelength to everybody else – 'programmed to kill'. About the same time in Wichita, Kansas, the so-called 'BTK Strangler' killed a family of four and followed it up with more murders of women. 'How many do I have to kill before I get my name in the paper or some national attention?' he demanded in a letter to a local television station. There's a sinister element of showmanship in each of these cases. Unwise to draw conclusions from so small a sample, especially as two of them were never identified.

I've been through all the data I have on serial killers and I've yet to find any who actually named their victims in advance. This must be arrogance without precedent. Can it mean, I keep asking myself, that the Mariner is really only a bluffer? I'd like to answer yes, only my gut feeling is that he's deadly serious. Many of these people I've been reading about were pathological liars, but their statements can't be dismissed when they amount to boasts. This man is too self-centred, too full of his own importance, to bluff about the one thing he's getting attention for. He has published his agenda and I fear he'll carry it out unless he is stopped in time.

The police are looking for links between the victim, Summers, and the 'targets', Porter and Walpurgis, in the hope that this will lead them to the killer. I wish them luck, but I fear they may be wasting their time. These are media people, never out of public attention. There will be parties two or more of them attended, charities they supported, journalists who interviewed each of them. What matters is their link to the Mariner, if any.

That was the sum of my thoughts this morning. After lunch I

washed my hair and turned my attention to what I would wear tonight. Finally chose the dark blue Kenzo trouser suit with the padded shoulders I bought last year in Oxford. Slightly formal – it is Popjoy's – and not too much of a come-on to Ken, who needs no encouragement. Oh dear, am I going cool on him?

The meal was the best part of the evening, a wonderful breast of pheasant as my main course and the most delicious crème brulée I've ever tasted to follow. You'd think that would have guaranteed the rest of the night would be a wow. Not so. Unfortunately, Ken picked a red Californian wine, Zinfandel, that always makes my head ache. I'm sure it was a good vintage, and expensive, but I wish he'd asked me first. He was doing his masterful bit, showing off to the waiter. In any restaurant they always give the wine list to the man and he takes it as a personal challenge to sound knowledgeable about what's on offer. Ken simply went ahead and ordered, murmuring something patronising about how I would enjoy this. Stupidly I drank a glass or two with the meal, not wanting to mess up the evening. My head started splitting before we got to the desserts. I was in no condition to talk about my day, as he suggested, and I didn't want to hear about his, either. He was really miffed when the waiter asked if we would take coffee and I said what I really wanted was a glass of still water with two Alka Seltzers. Yes, I embarrassed him horribly. He showed it by leaving a huge tip, far bigger than he can afford.

Then he proposed to walk me home – me in a pair of strappy high heels! – all the way from Sawclose, at least half a mile. He claimed it would be romantic. Stuff that, I told him, I want a taxi. Unfortunately the theatre crowd had just come out and we spent the next twenty minutes trying to beat other people to a cab. He isn't much good at that. Result: I wasn't in the mood for the shag he expected when we finally got back here. I'm going to draw a veil over what happened. Ugly things were said, entirely by me. If he'd called me a prickteaser or something

I might respect him more. He's so nice he's boring, but I can't expect him to understand that. He listens to me, praises me up, treats me like a princess, and that's OK – until the glitter wears off. Things went wrong in the restaurant and they weren't really anyone's fault, but it helped me to face facts. I happen to have a bigger-than-average appetite for sex and I needed a bloke and Ken came into my life at the right time and did the necessary in bed. And let's give him credit: I've known a lot worse. We had five or six good weeks. Now it's time to draw a line under them.

Basically, it's over. I said too many horrible things for us to kiss and make up – ever. And to be honest, I'm relieved.

Diamond used the mouse to close the file and sat back in the chair. He needed a short break from this outpouring. There is only so much you can take in at a session, especially when you are extracting crucial information. He found it demanding to switch mentally between two murders, trying to catch the implications for both. On one level it was a fascinating insight into Emma's analysis of the Summers case. Equally, it seemed to open the way to new lines of enquiry in her own murder. Ken, the lover on the skids, was a real discovery. Nobody in the psychology department had mentioned him. Not one of them he'd spoken to, Tara, Professor Chromik or Helen Sparks, seemed to have any knowledge of Ken's existence. She must have been very determined to keep the worlds of work and home separate.

Ken had to be traced – and soon. He would get Halliwell and the team onto it.

The Summers case, also, was opening up nicely. It was a definite advance to have the names of the two 'targets' Bramshill wanted to keep to themselves. They couldn't object. This was all legitimate stuff. The names had come up as a direct result of research into the beach strangling.

He had a right to know Emma's thoughts in the days leading up to her murder.

His own emotions were mixed. There was no denying that he felt some guilt at peeking into her private journal, tempered by the knowledge that she had locked away essential information there. Some of it would surely have been passed on to the police if she had lived long enough to assemble the profile. The other bits – the intimate stuff about Ken – might well have a bearing on her own murder. He had to go on reading. As a professional, Emma would understand the justification. That's what he told himself.

He reopened the file.

I got in touch with Jimmy Barneston today, wanting to follow up on a few matters. He's terribly busy, but came to the phone and listened to everything I said, and seemed genuinely grateful for my suggestions. The main thing I wanted to get across was that I now believe the Mariner really does intend to kill those two he named, and he'll be cunning and ruthless in carrying out his aim. The police should get them away, abroad if possible, and keep them under twenty-four-hour surveillance. And it's got to be kept up for months and years if necessary. Jimmy said he was confident of finding the bloke in a matter of days. He sounds convincing, too. I hope to God he's right.

He said I was welcome to sit in on one of their case conferences and I've agreed to drive down to Horsham tomorrow. I'll make another visit to Bramber in the afternoon without the murder squad in attendance. I'm probably kidding myself, but I feel I have a better chance of getting inside the mind of the killer if I stand where he did. I also plan to call on Axel Summers' housekeeper. He lives in the village.

Ken left a message on the answerphone, asking me to call back when I get a chance. He wants to start over, I suppose. I'm going to ignore him. Our fling is over. A clean break. He thinks I'll melt, but I won't. Now that it's done and dusted I can see there was never very much emotionally. I was keeping it going for the sex on tap, my personal demon, the tyranny of the hormones. Let's be honest, he was rather good at it, but not world class. There's better to be had. Let the quest begin!

Did some more reading today. This will not be easy, this case. You can't make too many inferences from a single crime. The horrible truth is that I need the Mariner to kill again before I can make an accurate assessment of his psychosis – if he has one. It's quite on the cards – I'd put money on it – that he has carried out crimes in the past, maybe even murders. But I can't access them unless the police pick up some piece of evidence that links him to their records. So I'm hamstrung.

What age might he be? It ought to be possible to posit a range. The trouble he took to pick out the crossbow suggests someone reasonably mature, calculating, rather than impulsive. Not a youth, I would say.

The choice of 'targets' is intriguing. They're all huge names, but apart from that they don't have much in common. Summers was creative and intelligent and over fifty. Porter is precocious, little more than a kid, certainly under twenty-one, famous for being young in a sport where older men dominate. Walpurgis is past thirty and very rich, still a celeb, but past her prime as a pop singer. Note: I must look at cases of celebrity slayers such as Mark David Chapman, the killer of John Lennon. What was his motivation?

This afternoon I took a walk to the top of the street and spent a couple of hours in Sydney Gardens wandering the paths and mulling over the case. I was crossing the Chinese Bridge over the canal when a jogger stopped to chat me up. Tall, thinnish, fair hair. Not a bad looker. Offered me a cigarette. I thought, What sort of jogger carries a pack of cigarettes in his tracksuit? Gave him a smile and said I didn't, and anyway I was waiting for someone. I am, in a way. But not a smoking jogger.

I notice Matthew Porter isn't competing in the big golf tour-nament at Sunningdale this week. I hope he's sensible enough to cooperate and lie low for as long as it takes. Wouldn't know about Anna Walpurgis. She's still a favourite of the tabloids. See-through dresses at film premieres. Married some million-aire twice her age and inherited a fortune when he died soon after. Then had a fling with a soap star. I can't imagine a ball of fire like her lying low – unless it's in someone's bed.

So off I drove to Sussex again for a day that was to surprise me. Lunched well at a quaint, low-beamed place in Arundel and called at the bookshop there and was delighted to find a copy of Hunting Humans, a Canadian study of multiple murder that has been on my want-list for some years.

Just as I hoped, no one was on duty at the Summers house in Bramber, so I let myself into the garden and tried to think myself into the Mariner's brain as he stalked his victim that fine evening. It's a safe bet that he drove there and parked some-where along one of the quiet lanes. Probably he'd risk leaving the car really close. He wouldn't want to be seen carrying the crossbow. A gunman in a country lane might not attract a second glance, but a crossbow is something else, awkward in shape, yet almost as long as a rifle.

I'm certain, looking at the scene, that he would have made a dummy run – maybe without the weapon – some previous evening, getting a sight of Summers sitting with his usual drink. If so, it would have been in the last couple of days after Summers finished filming the sea sequences. So the Mariner would have decided precisely where to set up. I know from Jimmy Barneston where the bolt appeared to have been fired from, a position fifteen yards or so away, behind a small rhodo-dendron bush. Actually tried it. Lay on my tummy and looked down an imaginary telescopic sight at the wooden seat where the body was found. The place is incredibly quiet, apart from birdsong. He must have been in place before Summers appeared with his g&t. And after the bolt was fired, he calmly entered the house and left his note.

It helped to confirm some earlier thoughts. Here is a killer who is painstaking, yet audacious. If he'd shot his quarry and quit the scene, we wouldn't have had a hope in hell of catching him. By choosing to leave a note, he issues a challenge, and takes a huge risk. He relishes the thrill of taking us on.

Aubrey Wood, the housekeeper, lives alone in a terraced cottage in the village. He was willing to talk when I explained who I was. Made me tea and brought out some home-made jam tarts that if they were from a shop would be way past their sell-by date. Poor man, I felt sorry for him. He's around fifty, slow of speech, and not yet over the shock. He had a nice little number working for Axel Summers, and now he's 'on the social'. There aren't many openings as a gentleman's gentleman in Bramber. He's not a countryman, so he'll probably return to London. I understand there's a modest legacy, a couple of thousand, coming his way.

He'd worked for Summers for nearly ten years, cooking and cleaning and doing jobs about the house. When Summers was away on film projects, he'd look after the place and sort the mail. He wasn't asked to travel. But he saw various friends of his boss when they came to the house. He never detected any bad vibes.

He said Summers had been planning this film for at least ten years and finally got the backing he needed about a year ago. He'd gone to infinite lengths to get the screenplay right, and the cast he wanted. It was over budget, but his films had a good record at the box office and no one was too concerned. He was very tired when he came home two days before he was killed. Prior to that he had been away filming in the Mediterranean for five weeks. He returned to Sussex knackered, but pleased that this phase of the project was complete. There was still a lot to be done, in particular the special effects sequences, bits now vivid in my brain like the skeleton ship with Death dicing with Life-in-Death, the souls of the crew whizzing upwards, the storms and calms and the water snakes. Summers was modifying things he'd mapped out in storyboard form. He'd been too busy to do any entertaining since his return. Hadn't even walked to the village for a paper, as he sometimes did when he was home.

On the evening of the killing, Wood served a light evening meal about six, loaded the dishwasher and left sharp at seven, on his bike. He noticed nothing unusual. No car parked in the lane and no strangers about. He left Summers in a good frame of mind, some crucial decisions about the film made. He was relaxed and looking forward to some late-night television programme. Wood met his friends at seven fifteen and was driven to Plumpton for the pub quiz they'd entered as the local team. I'm satisfied he's incapable of anything so callous as this killing.

After that, I had to get to the 4 p.m. case conference in Horsham and made it with not much to spare. Met in the incident room: the entire murder team and a couple of people from Bramshill. Jimmy Barneston chaired it. Watching him in action, I was more smitten than ever. He has a way of energising everyone, encouraging them to chip in and picking out the salient points. As expected, I was invited to contribute, but I made clear it was too soon to give them anything reliable, and I'd come to listen. They were OK with that.

Jimmy went through the various lines of enquiry. Sightings of cars around the village (inconclusive). Forensic reports on the fingertip search (little of interest). Crossbow manufacturers and retailers (more promising, although they don't all keep records of customers). The crossbow bolt was picked for the job, apparently, with a three-bladed head normally used for killing game. He spent some time going over Summers' career, pointing out that jealousies and hurts are common in show business. Even a man so popular and friendly must upset people when he makes decisions on casting and scripts. An embittered actor or writer might fit the profile of the killer. At the use of the 'p' word, heads turned to see if I had any comment. I looked steadily ahead and said nothing.

Two of Jimmy's senior people gave similar rundowns on Porter and Walpurgis. Was there some deeply wounded person who had been damaged by all three? Apart from possible attendance at a TV awards dinner in 2001, nothing to connect them had so far been discovered.

A question was asked about the security arrangements for Porter and Walpurgis. Jimmy answered that steps had been taken to safeguard each of them, but for obvious reasons he was not willing to comment any further. A long discussion about the practicality of keeping Summers' death out of the papers. Some kind of embargo could be enforced for a time, and the press would cooperate until word leaked out from some source – as it surely will.

It was after seven when the meeting ended. Jimmy asked if I'd like to eat before getting on the road. I took this to mean several of them would be going to some local pub and it seemed a good idea, because by the time I got back to Bath it would be getting late for a meal. Then would you believe it? He used his mobile and booked a table for two at a local Italian restaurant. Wow!

Mild panic. I'm in my denim jacket and designer jeans, still dusty at the knees from lying on the ground simulating the shooting. So I nip into the ladies and brush myself down and do some repair work on the face. Probably makes a bit of difference. Not as much as I would have liked.

Wasn't entirely sure if Jimmy fancied me or just thought I might give out some more about my thoughts on the case. In ten minutes we're in the window seat at Mario's looking at each other by candlelight, with Neapolitan love songs in the background. No, we weren't there to talk shop. Having established that we were both free of ties (he's divorced and has lived alone for two years), we spend the next hour getting to know each other the way you do on a first date. He's a graduate (business administration at Reading) and he shares quite a few of my tastes in music and film. Plays squash and goes to a gym.

We share a bottle of Orvieto – with none of that sexist nonsense over the ordering – and have chicken and pasta, and at the end he suggests coffee at his place. No heavy breathing or smouldering looks. Just a casual take-it-or-leave-it.

I answer just as casually that it might be sensible to get some caffeine into my system before I get on the road. So I find myself next in his gorgeous stone-built house beside the River Arun. Slate floors and expensive rugs. Real coffee, Belgian chocs and Mozart's flute and harp concerto, and I just know I won't be driving back to Bath that night. He takes me onto the terrace to see the view of the river and that's where we kiss.

Jimmy is a natural. Knows without asking what gets me going and goes for it with such a sense of sharing the excitement that I came very quickly still standing outside under the stars and before taking off any clothes. Talk about hitting the spot! It was obvious we both wanted more, so we moved inside to his bedroom and undressed each other and I set about enjoying him with a sense of freedom I never had with Ken or any other bloke. After several Himalayan-class peaks, we drift off to sleep some time after midnight, and that isn't the last of it. I wake up around four feeling the urge again and climb on him and ride him like a showjumper. A clear round. No faults.

Was it a one-night stand, or can it develop into something more permanent? The morning is when you find out, usually. Each of us played it cautiously over breakfast (toast and very black coffee), not wanting to seem possessive, and no commitment was made. But this man really is special, and I honestly think he finds me more adventurous (exciting?) than the average girl, so I'm hopeful of another invitation. It won't be

easy keeping a relationship fresh when we live a couple of
hours from each other, but we do have a good excuse to stop
over. This case requires close and frequent consultation!

Here, the file ended. Just as well, because Diamond was
at the point of spontaneous combustion. Jimmy
Barneston and Emma Tysoe! Barneston hadn't even
hinted at this when they'd talked about the case. He knew
the dead woman's private life was fundamental to the
investigation and he'd said bugger all. It wasn't as if he
needed to feel guilty. He wasn't having a fling with a
suspect, or a witness, or even one of his team. She was a
profiler, an extra. But once Emma had been murdered,
everything about her, and not least her love life, had to
be out in the open. Barneston had a duty to declare it.

'"Ride him like a showjumper",' he muttered to
himself. 'He's a dark horse, for sure.'

13

In the incident room he found Keith Halliwell and Ingeborg Smith looking at a website for the British Crossbow Society. Clearly it was no use any longer trying to keep the murder of Axel Summers to himself. Clive had talked. Those two had put him through the third degree. They were professional detectives and it was their job to root out information.

'Vicious weapon, isn't it?' he said, deadpan. 'I'd better bring you up to speed on the file I've just been reading – unless you've got your own copies already.'

Ingeborg reddened and Keith grinned sheepishly.

He gave them all the facts he knew about the murder of Summers, ending with a belated warning that Bramshill wanted to keep the lid on it. 'Emma Tysoe was involved in this case at the time of her death, so we have more than a passing interest in it, much as they'd like to insist we don't. But we still have a duty to keep it from the public – and that means anyone outside the team, right?' He made eye contact with each of them.

And each nodded.

'I know,' he said. 'You're about to tell me I should put a gag on Clive, and I thought I had. I'll speak to him again.' He took a glance at his watch. 'I haven't finished reading the files, and I'll give you a fuller rundown when I'm through, later in the day, if my head can stand it. Meanwhile there are two things you can do. Ingeborg.'

'Guv?'

'We got a false impression of Dr Emma Tysoe from her colleagues up at the university. She wasn't the shrinking violet they made her out to be. She had an above-average appetite for sex and a lover she dumped called Ken.'

'That's all we know about him?'

'It's pretty obvious he lives locally. Do some ferreting, will you?'

'Outside the university?'

'Outside the psychology department for sure. She kept her private life well hidden from that lot.'

'Wise.'

'Yes, if they'd known she was such a goer I'm sure someone would have wired her up and set up a research project. Anyway, Ken – whoever he is – has to be regarded as a suspect.'

'Because she dumped him?'

'Right. He took her for a meal at Popjoy's the evening after she was given this profiling job. There was some little spat over the way he ordered the wine, but I think the writing was already on the wall.'

'You mean she was dating another bloke?'

Diamond wasn't ready to go into that, not knowing how much tittle-tattle Clive had passed on. 'They fell out before she slept with anyone else. Ken had passed his sell-by date, it's clear from the file. I'm about to find out what happened next.'

Halliwell asked, 'Will anyone else get to read this steamy stuff?'

He couldn't suppress a touch of sarcasm. 'One way or another, I'm sure you will, Keith. Now, the other matter I want you to follow up is the whereabouts of her dark green sports car. She mentions in the file that she didn't put it in the garage one evening when she got back home.'

'In Great Pulteney Street?' Halliwell said. 'It doesn't have garages.'

'Right.'

'She rented one nearby?'

'That's my assumption. And I want to know if the car is still in there.'

'How can it be?' Ingeborg said. 'She'd have needed it to drive to Wightview Sands. She arrived there alone according to Michael Smith.'

'So where is it? They didn't find anything belonging to her in the beach car park. They accounted for every car left there at the end of that day. What make is it?'

Halliwell glanced towards Ingeborg, saw the startled look in her eyes, and attempted to cover up. 'As you recall, guv, Bognor were doing the index check.'

'And none of you thought to ask?' Diamond said. 'I give up! Even I know how to do a vehicle check. Get on that bloody PNC yourselves.'

Ingeborg recovered enough to say, 'I daresay one of her neighbours would know if she rented a garage nearby. Are there mews at the back of Great Pulteney Street? They're very big houses.'

'Both sides,' said Halliwell. 'You've got Pulteney Mews facing the Rec, and Henrietta Mews to the north.'

'Maybe a garage came with the flat. We can ask the landlord.'

'Do that,' Diamond said. 'If anyone wants me, I'll be in the basement, catching up on the next instalment.'

I'm keener than ever to make an accurate profile of the Mariner [Emma's second file began]. Let's confess an unprofessional thought to you, Computer: I'd love to amaze Jimmy with my findings. The problem is there's so little data to go on. I keep reminding myself this isn't a serial crime like others I've worked on. Not yet. As of today it's a single crime with the threat of more to come. Fortunately, the little we know is so exceptional that I'm beginning to firm up on certain assumptions:

(a) The killer is above average in intelligence, educated to a pretty high level. [The Coleridge quote]

(b) He's methodical and cool under stress. [The absence of any traces at the scene]

(c) He must have had some practice with the crossbow and knowledge of its firepower. [One bolt had to be enough]

(d) It's quite likely he has experience of stalking and killing animals – i.e., treats the killing of people as a logical extension of the rough shoot or the cull. [The effective use of cover]

(e) He has an exalted opinion of himself and his ability to outwit the police. [The naming of future victims]

(f) He may feel he is underrated, or cheated by some failure in his own career. [Choice of famous victims suggests he envies people in the limelight]

(g) He is well up with media gossip and may even have inside information. [He knew when Summers was back from the Med]

Not enough to be of use to the police, unfortunately. It's still too theoretical. He's little more than a concept, some way short of being an individual. What Jimmy needs from me are notes that will pin him down as an individual. Age, appearance, living arrangements, daily routine. Oh dear, I'm still a long way from that degree of detail.

The way forward must be to look more closely at the choices the killer has made. Why pick Axel Summers, by all accounts a charming, well-respected and talented man? What is it about the others that singles them out for slaughter? Is it only that they are so well known?

I definitely need to know more about Porter and Walpurgis.

How do they spend their time when they're not working? Do they own houses in the country, like Summers? What are their backgrounds, their interests, their politics (if any)?

A few minutes ago I phoned Jimmy. Glad to say he sounded pleased to hear from me. You can tell straight away when a man wants to back off (don't I know it, from past experience), and he doesn't. But this was strictly business: I was putting my case for a meeting with Matthew Porter. It caught Jimmy unprepared and at first he dug in his heels and said he couldn't risk it and anyway he didn't want Porter being troubled. This young man is under enough stress already, and so on. Gently steering him towards the worst possible outcome, I made the point that while Porter is alive we have the chance to question him about people he may have crossed and threats he may have received. If we'd had that opportunity with Axel Summers, we'd have a list of suspects.

He saw the sense in this. The police have put all their resources into investigating the murder and providing elaborate protection for Porter and Walpurgis. Nobody has sat down with either of them and gone through their recent history looking for possible enemies. So Jimmy took the point. He said he'd need to talk to the high-ups. He promised to get back to me.

(Later, in bed) Nothing yet from Jimmy, but I've had Ken on the mobile wanting to start over, giving me the hard sell about how he's missing me and his cat was sick yesterday and he almost pranged the car and he really loves me and can't face life without me. What a wimp. I know if I give him the slightest encouragement he'll be ten times as hard to get off my back. So I bit the bullet and told him I was seeing someone else – which gave him a seismic shock and showed him in his true colours. This guy who really loves me and can't face life without me called me a slag and a whore and lots of other disgusting names. I just said, 'Grow up,' and switched off. Closure – I hope. We'll see. I was very shaky, though, and poured myself a neat whisky – something I never normally do.

Keep thinking of things I should have said, like the cat isn't the only one who's sick.

I hope I sleep all right.

Better news. A message on the answerphone from Jimmy saying I should meet him in the coffee shop at Waterloo Station at 2.30 today. And I should erase the message after listening to it – real cloak-and-dagger stuff which was as good as saying he'd fixed the meeting with Matthew Porter. Brilliant.

I got to the station early and sat on one of those tall stools drinking an Americano. I'd put on the style for this, the dark red number with the split skirt. Black pashmina and matching tights. My Prada shoes. It's not every day you get to meet a top sports star. I got some looks.

Jimmy showed up dead on time in a gorgeous light grey suit I hadn't seen before. Purple shirt and matching tie with flecks of yellow. Cool. He kissed me on the cheek and steered me to the taxi rank. It was like being in a movie. I've never been at the sharp end of a crime investigation. In the cab, I sat close to Jimmy and slipped my hand under his arm and squeezed it. He smirked a little, but of course we were on a serious mission, so things didn't get any more intimate than that.

He told me we were going to a safe house. Special Branch have a number of addresses in London where they protect VIPs under threat of terrorism, or informers changing their identities. Jimmy phoned the house from the taxi to say our ETA. The cab stayed south of the river, through Kennington and Brixton, and ended up at the war memorial in Streatham High Road, where Jimmy tapped the glass and told the driver to put us down. Nobody takes a taxi to the front door of a safe house. We walked for ten minutes or so through the backstreets, me beginning to think I should have worn something less conspicuous, but no complaint from Jimmy.

The house is in as quiet a road as you're likely to find in London, old Victorian buildings with high chimneys and sash windows and tiny front gardens. I noticed a video camera quietly rotating under the eaves.

We didn't need to knock. The front door was opened by an unsmiling honcho in a tracksuit and we stepped inside without being frisked (disappointing) and were shown straight into a back room where Matthew Porter, a young man in a green polo shirt and white jeans, was sitting in an armchair watching the racing on TV. On the floor beside him was a heap of unopened letters. He turned his head briefly to give us a glance, but didn't get up or shift his feet from the coffee table in front of him, just pointed at the screen with the can of lager he had in his left hand. Never mind who we were, he was going to watch the finish of the race. A young man with attitude, I thought. So we stood tamely watching the horses race it out. The minder rolled his eyes as if to say he'd had plenty of this already, and then left the room.

The race result, when it came, didn't cause much excitement. Only a yawn – and even then Porter ignored us until Jimmy gave my name and explained my reason for wanting to meet him. This achieved some eye contact, no more.

Case-hardened by all those seminars with grouchy students, I wasn't going to take any of this personally, was I? I launched straight into my questions. Obviously, he'd been told about the murder and the note found at the scene, so I began by asking him if he'd ever met Axel Summers. He shrugged and continued to look bored, and I thought at first he was going to play dumb until I stopped and went away, but then he muttered something about always meeting people and not remembering them unless they were players. Trying another approach, I asked if he watched DVDs or videos and when he said there wasn't much else to do in hotels I told him he might well have watched one of Summers' films. This didn't excite him one bit. I wasn't doing too well.

I probed gently into his background, school, family and so on, and by degrees he loosened up. He was more comfortable talking about his start in golf. He must have done this many times in press interviews. His father, an amateur with a low handicap, had taught him to play when he was eleven. Their house backed onto a golf course in Broadstairs and he would practise shots at the nearest hole, the eleventh, early in the morning before anyone else was about. The club professional gave him lessons. At fourteen he was allowed to play a round with his father and made such an impression that the club rules were changed for him to become a member. A year later, he won the club championship. His progress since was phenomenal. He'd left school and turned professional at eighteen and started winning minor tournaments right away. Agents were keen to acquire him as a client and he soon had his own manager and sponsors and a regular caddie. His win in the British Open at the age of nineteen was what made him famous overnight. He told me all this in a deadpan delivery without conceit.

I asked if his parents still had a say in his career and he shook his head. They'd separated four years ago. His mother was now living in France with another man. His father was an 'alky'. He said he didn't want to talk about them. So who were the main people in his present life? His manager, Sid Macaulay, who looked after everything – his travel around the world, his interviews, his endorsements, even paid his tax. Girlfriends? He hadn't time, he said, adding – with a smirk – apart from one-night stands. He was travelling most of the year – normally.

He told me his main home was a manor house in Surrey and he owned another near St Andrews in Scotland. He would be getting his own Lear jet later in the year. He'd pay a pilot to fly it because he didn't have time to learn. His 'hobby' was watching television, especially scary films.

By now I was getting wiser about Matthew Porter. This looked like a case of arrested development. Golf had taken over his life before he had a chance to mature. All the decisions had been taken away from him. He did as he was told by the manager, lived in cocooned comfort and performed on the golf course when required. Sadly, it was stunting his personality. He couldn't relate to other people unless they talked to him about golf. He had no opinions, no conversation and no ambition now he'd got to the top in the one sphere he inhabited.

I asked if his manager knew where he was, and he said it was the manager who'd ordered him to come to this place for his own safety and given him the pile of fan mail to answer. (Jimmy told me later that Special Branch had told Macaulay there was a death threat that had to be taken seriously, but they hadn't given away any other details.) He didn't like it much, he confided, and he ought to be practising instead of sitting indoors.

Jimmy interrupted to say a move was planned to another safe house, away from London, with better facilities and maybe even the chance to get out and strike a ball from time to time.

It wasn't what Porter wanted to hear. He'd been told the security measures were temporary because the killer would be arrested in a matter of days. He swore, not at Jimmy or me, but his predicament. He said he'd rather go abroad and play some golf tournament in the Far East. He'd be safe there. Jimmy pointed out that these days you're not safe anywhere in the world from a determined assassin. Porter swore again and asked to speak to his manager. His phone had been taken away from him by the guards.

Jimmy stood firm, stressing that his team was following several promising leads and making progress. He told Porter in language he understood that this was a serial killer who had named him as the next victim, who almost certainly knew every detail of his daily routine, and definitely meant to carry out the threat.

At this, the protest melted. The interview got back on track, but not for long. I asked if he could think of any link with Anna Walpurgis. He'd heard of her, it was obvious. He pulled a face and said her music was crap. He liked Chill, 'stuff that takes away the stress', and she was the opposite of Chill, all hype and frenzy. I asked if he was talking about her singing or if he'd met her – which brought the strongest response so far. He thought I was suggesting he might have dated her. Just for the record, young Matthew Porter thinks of the celebrated Anna as 'that old boiler'. Let's hope no one has the bright idea of putting those two in a safe house together.

I switched back to golf. With so much money at stake, I said, was there any pressure to fix results? He gave me a filthy look and said he always played his best. What about when you played different tournaments from week to week with the same players, I pressed him? You're an outstanding player who will probably win most weeks. Isn't there any arrangement to make sure others get a look-in sometimes?

If nothing else, it animated him. He went purple protesting that he always played to win. He said he wasn't a cheat and I'd better shut my face (his verbal skills really coming into their own). To restore calm, I tried Jimmy's tactic and reminded him that somebody meant to kill him if they could. I said my job was to find out if the threat came from a complete stranger or somebody he'd upset. Only then could I begin to form a profile.

Unexpectedly, the last word made an impression. He stared at me open-mouthed and asked if I was a profiler and I confirmed it. I don't think Jimmy had used the term when he introduced me. Now it worked like a charm. He took his feet off the table and looked me up and down with real interest. I guessed what was coming next, and usually my heart sinks, but this time it was a plus. He pressed an unopened can of lager into my hand and asked if I did the same job as Fitz, in Cracker. All those hours of watching television in hotel rooms had turned him into a fan.

I didn't give my standard answer (terrific television, but a million miles from my experience of the job). I swallowed and said that basically, yes, we both did the same thing. There were differences in approach, but like Fitz I helped the police by giving them pointers towards the likely suspect. He grinned and said I was better-looking than Robbie Coltrane, but what was I like in a fight? A joke! I smiled back and said I could look after myself, but the job shouldn't really entail fighting. It wasn't even about being tough and shouting at people. The scriptwriters had to make it look like that to keep up the interest. I was sure Fitz did a lot of quiet thinking that wasn't shown because it wasn't visual.

Jimmy, thank God, kept quiet. He could easily have said Fitz wouldn't have lasted five minutes in any murder inquiry he'd led.

How I wished we could start over again. This pig of an interview would have been so much easier. In fact, we talked genially for twenty minutes more about his chances of meeting Robbie Coltrane and perhaps teaming up with him in a celebrity tournament. I promised to put in a word if I ever met the man. I've no idea if he's a golfer, but he's a Scot, so he could be.

When we left, Porter picked up a photo of himself from a stack on the table and signed it for me, first asking me my name and writing, 'To Emma the female Cracker, love Matt Porter.' As he was handing it to me he hung onto my wrist and leaned towards me for a kiss. Poor kid's feeling lonely, I thought, and turned my face to him and got my bottom groped at the same time. He lost my sympathy then.

All in all, the visit wasn't the success I'd hoped for. At least I'd met target number two and satisfied myself there was no obvious link with Axel Summers or Anna Walpurgis. One thing I do believe: he won't survive without police protection. I asked Jimmy how much longer they could expect to keep him in the safe house against his will. He said it was up to the manager. He thought Porter would do what he was told. He said they were losing money already. If he was released, it could give a whole new meaning to the sudden-death playoff. He'd been storing that one up, I reckon.

We walked back to Streatham High Road and Jimmy waved down a taxi. Much to my surprise, he asked the driver to take us to Crystal Palace. 'Something I've laid on,' he said mysteriously. 'It's a short drive from here.'

My imagination went into overdrive. Love in the afternoon? A luxurious hotel suite, with caviar and chilled champagne?

Dream on. He'd arranged for someone from the British Police Archers to demonstrate the crossbow. Once I was over the disappointment, it was truly amazing. The guy waiting for us near the dry ski-slope had brought two Swiss target bows for us to try. What I hadn't appreciated is that they are very like a rifle in appearance, with a wooden stock shaped to fit against your shoulder. You have a trigger and telescopic sight, and of course a groove along the centre of the stock to guide the bolt when it's released. The 'cross' part, making the shape of the bow, is the prod. I giggled a bit, always amused by funny words. He said it should never have been called a prod, but a rod. Someone made an inventory of King Henry VIII's armour, and when it was copied by some scribe who knew nothing about crossbows, he wrote 'Crossbowes, called prodds', and it got into all the standard works before anyone noticed the mistake. So they're stuck with it.

The power of these things was a revelation. The bowstring is made of steel cable, but the force of the pull, at least two hundred pounds, is in the prod. We were each given a padded glove to wear on our left hand, the one that supports the bow, because if that cable snapped you could sever your fingers. But first he simply demonstrated what happens when the bowstring is cocked and the bolt is in place and the trigger pulled. The snap of the cable was awesome. The bolt thudded into a target thirty metres away.

I felt goosebumps on the backs of my arms and legs. I was glad I hadn't seen Axel Summers' body.

195

We were each given a bow and shown how to zero the sights (i.e. adjust them to the target) and cock the string. Our instructor told us he preferred a kneeling position with the left elbow supported on the knee. So my assumption that the Mariner was belly-down may have been wrong. We tried the position, yours truly showing slightly more thigh than your average archer does.

I've fired a rifle before, and I'm certain the trigger was easier to pull than this one, even though the catch and trigger were well greased. Provided you hold the bow steady and squeeze the trigger evenly without shifting your aim, you should succeed. My bolt hit the target, though not the bull. Jimmy's was about the same. We had two more shots, and definitely improved. But I still think the Mariner must have put in plenty of practice.

My adrenalin level was pretty high after that. As we walked back across the park, I linked my arm through Jimmy's and asked what other surprises he had in store, and he knew exactly what was on my mind. But he said he had to get back to Horsham, and hadn't I heard him promise Matthew Porter quick progress? I said something really naff about how he could make even faster progress with me behind a bush, and I meant it at the time. Those hormones were in overdrive. I would have screwed him silly regardless of my posh clothes. But it wasn't to be. We hailed a taxi and he dropped me at Waterloo, saying he was looking forward to my report. He gave me a peck on the cheek.

Bloody men.

The second file ended there. Diamond closed it and switched off. He sat for a moment, taking it in, reflecting on what he'd learned, and not just about Emma Tysoe, but Matthew Porter and Jimmy Barneston as well. He'd taken to Emma with her Prada shoes and her overactive hormones. Reading the journal, it was difficult to accept that she was dead. It saddened him.

The glimpse of Porter, too, was valuable. Diamond wasn't a golfer and didn't follow the sport with any real interest, but everyone had heard of Magic Matt, the kid who rolled them in from anywhere on the green and made it look simple. The clip of him winning the Open with a twenty-five-foot putt at the eighteenth was shown over and over on television. Everything about the young man's demeanour on the golf course suggested he was mature beyond his years, possessed of an extraordinary physical and mental harmony. It was revealing to find that this didn't extend to his life outside the game. The routine of the safe house was going to be increasingly irksome to him.

As for that dark horse – stallion – Jimmy Barneston, mixing business with pleasure, Diamond thought he wouldn't care to be in his shoes when the Big White Chief at Bramshill decrypted the files and read them. But he'd modified his own opinion of Barneston. He could understand the man trying to keep his one-night stand with Emma off the agenda (maybe more than one night, if file number three was as frank as the first two). But since it was no longer a secret, he'd have to face some questions. It was important to know if Emma had communicated anything that might touch on her murder.

A voice interrupted his thoughts.

'Finished, Mr D?' It was Clive.

'You?' he said, swinging his chair around.

'Something the matter, boss?'

'I'm not best pleased with you any more. There was I, relying on you, thinking you were watertight, and you leaked like a hanging basket.'

'But Ingeborg is on your team, isn't she?'

Ingeborg. That young woman would go far.

'Doesn't mean I tell her everything. Haven't you ever heard of the need-to-know principle? Someone else might be put in a very embarrassing position by these files.'

'That DCI who got his leg over?'

'Heads could roll, Clive, and not just his.'

'You mean . . . ? Jesus, I'm sorry, I really am.'

'Sorry isn't enough.'

'Believe me, if there's anything I can do . . .'

Diamond let him squirm a moment longer. 'There could be something, as a matter of fact. Is it possible for me to press a couple of keys and send a copy of these red-hot files to someone I know?'

Clive's eyes widened. 'What – in this place?'

'No – another officer, in another county. A DCI Mallin, at Bognor Regis.'

Keith Halliwell had tracked down the registration details of Emma Tysoe's car. It was a 2000 Lotus Esprit.

'Not a bad motor,' Diamond said. 'And lecturers are always grouching about being underpaid.'

'We also found the garage she rents, in Pulteney Mews, just like Ingeborg suggested.'

'Surprise me, Keith. Was there anything in there?'

'Not even a bike, guv.'

'What colour was this motor? Dark green, am I right?'

'Yes.'

'Put out an all-units call on this. London and everywhere south and west. The thing must be somewhere. Where's Ingeborg?'

'She's up at Popjoy's, looking at their reservations book, trying to work out the name of the ex-boyfriend.'

'She'll be lucky. Restaurants usually make bookings with surnames alone.'

'Yes, but we know which evening it was, so we'll have the names of everyone who made a reservation. How many would you say – twenty maximum?'

Diamond raised a thumb in tribute. 'Good thinking, Keith. I must be blinkered.'

Halliwell smiled wryly.

'Couldn't think past the name of Ken,' Diamond explained. 'Pity she didn't once call him by his surname in the journal.'

'She wouldn't, would she?'

'She used full names for everyone else.'

'But she was sleeping with Ken.'

'No, she'd stopped sleeping with Ken. That's what makes him special.'

He returned to the basement to finish reading Emma Tysoe's files. The third was dated two days before her death. It turned out to be the shortest.

Can't get Jimmy Barneston out of my mind. I know he's working all hours on the case and I can't expect him to call me and make another date, but I keep wondering if he thinks of me as nothing more than an easy lay. It didn't seem like that at the time. OK, neither of us made a big emotional deal of it. We fancied each other and went to bed. But the sex was special (I ought to know) and I've never felt so good as I did lying beside him afterwards. I'd like to be cool and tell myself he was just another shag, but I can't. There's a whole lot more about Jimmy that I find attractive. I want more. I want a real relationship.

Computer, what can I do? Sit here biting my fingernails, or think of something positive? I could ask to meet Anna Walpurgis, I suppose, but even if it could be arranged I really doubt if she can tell me anything useful. I sense I'll get nothing more from her than I did from Matthew Porter. I'm thinking they were chosen because of their fame, to create more of a sensa-tion when they are killed. I say 'when' because in spite of all the security I feel strongly the Mariner knows what he's doing.

Hold on. I've just made a whopping assumption. OK, profiling is all about probabilities rather than certainties, but let's stand this one on its head. All along I've been reminding myself there may be nothing personal in the Mariner's selection of these people as targets. Could I be mistaken?

From a profiling perspective, I'm conditioned to expect the victims to be randomly picked. Serial killers – the true serial killers – have no personal involvement with the people they kill, no other motive than that they fit a pattern. That's why they're so difficult to catch. They choose a class of victim, like prostitutes, or schoolgirls, or young boys, or old women, and prey on them ruthlessly. I've taken it for granted that the Mariner fits the mould and has targeted the famous and successful. He gives the impression of being detached, cool, calculating, everything I expect.

But is he a true serial killer after all?

Maybe – just maybe – he does know them personally. I'VE GOT TO EXPLORE THIS. The fact that he has named his second and third 'victims' in advance is a departure. It adds another dimension to his agenda as the killer, and makes the whole process more difficult for him. Why take the risk? Is it because he wants to strike fear into these people's hearts? Is there a personal grudge behind all this?

If so, then Porter and Walpurgis are the key to this case.

I should insist on a meeting with Walpurgis. She may tell me some detail of real importance, maybe linked to what I already know about Summers, or Porter. She's the one I know least about, simply because bimbo popstars don't interest me at all. But I've looked her up on the internet, and there's plenty. She's better known for the clothes she wears than her talent. She can afford the best. She did very nicely out of the pop singing, first with the Fates, and then her solo career. She topped the charts in Britain and America in her best years and had a huge three-album contract with one of the record companies. And when the first album flopped they paid her off with about twenty million. Twenty million for not singing! She married one of the super-rich kings of industry and came into all his money when he fell off the perch not long after. In one of those lists of Britain's richest women she's in the top twenty and has the controlling interest in her old man's company, so she can't be a total airhead. Even so, I can't see her discussing poetry with Axel Summers, but let's not prejudge.

(Later) Jimmy isn't sure if he can fix an early meeting with Walpurgis. He says she's in a panicky state, close to a break-down, and finding the security hard to take. They think she shouldn't be disturbed in her present mental state. Ridiculous. I reminded him that I have a Ph.D in psychology, but it cut no ice. 'Maybe in a couple of days,' he said. I told him the profile can't progress until I've spoken to her. You have to get tough with Jimmy, as I discovered when I insisted on meeting Matt Porter (my pin-up). This time he didn't promise to get back to me, or anything.

I asked him if he'd spent any time with Walpurgis, and he said he had about forty minutes with her when they broke the news that she was on the Mariner's death-list, and he's visited her in the safe house a couple of times since. This man-eater has seen Jimmy more times than I have. Soon I'll be getting jealous.

I said if I couldn't get to see her myself, could I give him a list of questions to put to her? He agreed, so I jumped in with both feet and said it wasn't quite so simple as making a list. In view of her fragile mental state I'd need to brief him person-ally about the way it was done, and debrief him afterwards (I have no shame), and how was he fixed this weekend?

He sounded slightly ambushed, but that's it. Perfecto! He's agreed to see me tomorrow morning (Saturday), and I'm off (or on) for the weekend, I hope. The weather's going to be glorious. I shall pack my swimsuit, just in case I can tempt him out of the nick and down to the coast.

Wish me luck, Computer.

Diamond smiled at the last line, then shook his head and sighed, as if it had been addressed to him in person. Wish me luck as you wave me goodbye. Emma's luck had run out on Wightview Sands.

He closed down the computer and went upstairs.

14

Hen Mallin had read the files overnight. 'I learned a sight more than I expected,' she said on the phone next morning to Diamond. 'Almost enough to bring a blush to my innocent cheek. And I thought profiling was all about maps and diagrams.'

'Like so much else it comes down in the end to people making judgements about other people,' he said, in a rare reflective vein. 'Emma Tysoe had it right about one thing. We're all governed by our hormones.'

'Snap out of it, Pete. You're talking like an agony aunt.'

He laughed.

'So what's next?' Hen asked. 'Do you pull in this guy Ken and wrap it up fast? He looks bang to rights.'

'We're working on it.'

'Meaning you haven't nicked him yet?'

'Still trying to trace him.'

'He's right in the frame,' Hen said as if Diamond needed more convincing. 'The jilted lover, consumed by jealousy. It's one of the oldest motives around. I'm willing to bet he was the guy in the black T-shirt the Smiths saw.'

'Olga Smith saw,' he corrected her. 'The husband didn't see him.'

'So what? My money's on him.'

A bit sweeping, ma'am, Diamond thought. He liked accuracy, and he also liked to understand why things happened. 'If that was Ken, what took him all the way down to Wightview Sands?'

'Car, obviously. Emma gives him the elbow, but he won't go away. Guessing there's another guy in her life, he follows her to Horsham and sees her cosying up to Jimmy Barneston. While those two spend Saturday night together, the luckless Ken is sitting in his car thinking murderous thoughts. In the morning he trails her down to Wightview Sands and tries to talk her round. When his limited amount of charm doesn't succeed, he gets really mad and strangles her.'

'Maybe,' he said, leaving plenty of room for doubt.

'Give me a better scenario if you can.'

'I'm still thinking about yours. We don't know for certain if she spent another night with Barneston.'

'So are you going to ask Jimmy?'

'We'll have to, obviously. Indeed, if you'd prefer to have a word with him yourself . . .'

'Nice try, matey,' she said in a tone that was not impressed at all. She probably regretted airing her theory now.

'You know the bloke better than I do.' He gently turned the screw. 'You might get more out of him than me.'

She wasn't fully tuned in to the Diamond sense of humour. There was a stiff silence, broken eventually by Diamond. 'All right, let's see him together.'

'When do you suggest?' she said with a definite lift in the voice.

'ASAP. You're sure you don't object to me being there?'

'Object? You're a star. I'll buy you a pub lunch.'

'You're on.'

'And you say Bramshill have got their own copy of the files?'

'They commandeered them. It's just a question of how long they take to decrypt them. I'm hoping you and I get to Barneston first.'

'He won't like it one bit.'

'We're entitled,' Diamond emphasised. 'He's become a crucial witness.'

She sighed. 'OK, I'm convinced.'

'He could be a suspect, in fact.'

'Hold on, Peter. That's pushing it. He's a brother officer. He's one of us.'

His skittish mood suddenly altered. His stomach tightened. That argument had been tried on him in the worst weeks of his life, and it had proved to be false. 'He's got to be treated like anyone else.'

'What, for being the last bloke Emma was seen with?'

'We don't know what passed between them that last night. She had another night of passion in mind, but Jimmy could have gone cool on her.'

'Really?'

'It's not unknown.'

'She'd be devastated,' Hen said. 'That's an angle I hadn't considered. A falling out between those two. But surely it couldn't have ended in murder? Do you truly think that's a possibility?'

'I don't know enough about Barneston yet. It's all speculation until we speak to him, isn't it?'

'Let's do it, then.'

There was a danger of being carried away by Hen's get-up-and-go. 'Before we do, I'd really like to hear from Olga Smith, if she's recovered enough to talk.'

'About what she saw on the beach? Now that's a smart move. She's out of hospital. She's at home now. Her sister is looking after her.'

'Any news on the husband?' Diamond asked.

'He's facing charges of smuggling cigarettes.'

'Is that all?'

'Honey, this wasn't a few packets in his hand luggage. This was big-time smuggling, a profitable scam at the airport with some baggage handlers. They delivered them to his stockroom in cartons the size of tea chests, and he acted as a conduit to the criminal trade right across the south-east.'

'Which explains the large cash deposits?'

'And why he cut and ran when Stella Gregson called at the house. Customs and Excise have taken it over now. He'll go down for a spell.'

'And I reckon a few of those fags will have found their way into officers' pockets. Did he deal in cigars?'

Hen laughed. 'No such luck.'

They agreed to meet at midday at the Smiths' house in Crawley. Hen would call Olga Smith and arrange an interview. Later they would drive the short distance to Horsham and speak to Jimmy Barneston – and not by appointment.

Ingeborg was back in the incident room using a phone when Diamond looked in. He asked if she'd identified Ken.

She shook her head. 'I'm still checking the reservations at Popjoy's.'

'Do they ask their customers for phone numbers?'

'Yes. I'm running through the list right now. The thing is, they only write down the surnames.'

'Did you think about checking the credit card slips? You might pick up some initials there.'

'Oh.' She put down the phone. 'Good thinking, guv.'

When he told Ingeborg and Halliwell he could be contacted later if necessary at Horsham police station, knowing glances were exchanged. Not much escaped them. He was damned sure they knew about Jimmy Barneston's romp with Emma Tysoe.

On the drive through Wiltshire and across Salisbury Plain

he welcomed the chance to catch up mentally on the past twenty-four hours. Emma's lively love life had shifted the balance of the case. Earlier, he'd assumed her reputation as a top profiler had put her in the path of her killer. Now it seemed possible it was a crime of passion.

He hoped not. If this turned out to be no more than a matter of pulling in Ken – whoever he was – and charging him with the strangling on the beach, there would be no pretext for staying involved in the more fascinating case of the Mariner. He really wanted to pit himself against this arrogant killer. But as soon as someone else was charged with the murder of Emma, Jimmy Barneston could say, 'Hands off. The Mariner is my investigation.'

It was almost a temptation to hang fire for a bit. Pity he'd suggested the credit card slips to Ingeborg. She might have found the right name already.

A small, solemn girl with her hair in bunches tied with white ribbon came to the door.

'You must be Haley,' Hen said.

A nod.

'We've come to see Mummy, my darling. Can we come in?'

Olga Smith, pale and tight-lipped and wrapped in a black dressing gown made of towelling, was sitting in the living room they knew from their previous visit. Another woman sat at the table in the window bay, arms folded, making it clear she intended to remain. She had the watchful look of a solicitor.

Olga said, 'My sister Maud is here to support me.'

She could still have been a solicitor.

Hen said, 'Whatever you wish.'

So the sister remained. Haley had already nestled close to her mother on the sofa.

'This is not easy for any of us, Mrs Smith,' Diamond

opened up, 'and we're grateful to you for seeing us. You're looking much better than when we saw you last.'

She said, 'I've been advised not to discuss the trouble my husband is in.'

'That's fine by me. We're here on another matter entirely.'

'The woman at Wightview Sands?'

'Yes.'

'I don't mind talking about that. I wanted to say something when we first heard what happened, but Mike, my husband—'

The sister interrupted. 'Careful, Olga.'

Diamond said evenly, 'That's OK. We understand. Just tell us what you remember of that Sunday on the beach.'

'I'll do my best. We got there at about eleven, I think, and it was already crowded in the car park. We found a spot on that part of the beach near where the lifeguards have their lookout, and we hadn't been there long when she arrived and sat more or less in front of us.'

'On her own?'

'Yes.'

'Do you remember what she was carrying?'

'A blue towel and a windbreak for sure.'

'A bag?'

'Yes, some kind of beachbag, blue, like the towel, with a dolphin design, about the size of the average carrier bag, but not so deep.'

This was new, and possibly important. Olga Smith had made the journey worthwhile already.

'She was wearing a headband that she took off and put in the bag. I think she was in denim shorts and a top that she took off later. She spread out the towel on the sand and set up the windbreak. She took her sunglasses out of the bag and put them on. And she had a bottle of sunscreen. After that, she settled down behind the

208

windbreak and I couldn't actually see her. But later I went down the beach to take an ice cream to Haley, and when I returned I had a different view and the woman was sunbathing in a white two-piece.'

'She didn't speak?'

'Not that time. She smiled at me. And quite soon after that, a man came by and spoke to her. They seemed to know each other from what I overheard.'

'What did you overhear?'

Olga Smith blushed. 'I'm not nosy. You can't help picking up bits of conversation on a beach. He was being amusing, or trying to, trotting out that line from some old film about all the gin-joints in all the world.'

'"Of all the gin-joints in all the towns in all the world, she walks into mine."'

'That's it.'

'Humphrey Bogart in *Casablanca.*'

'Was it? Anyway, as a chat-up line, it didn't seem to work very well. I couldn't hear what she was saying, but I heard his side of the conversation. He offered to get an ice cream or a drink and she wasn't interested. Then he asked to join her and she obviously gave him a short answer because he said something like, "Suit yourself, then. I'll leave you to it." Then he swore and walked away.'

'What were the words?'

'The swearing?' She blushed again and glanced at her sister, who turned her head and looked out of the window.

'He said, "Oh, what the fuck."' She mouthed the final word, unseen by her small daughter.

'He was angry, then?'

'Annoyed, anyway. After he'd gone, he didn't look back.'

'This is really helpful,' Diamond told her. 'Can you remember what the man looked like?'

'I'd say he was around thirty. He had a black T-shirt and I think he was wearing jeans. His hair was black, quite curly. Latin looks, I think you'd call them.'

'Was he tall?'

'Not specially. About average, I think, with wide shoulders and narrow hips. He was nice-looking, a broad, strong face. I think he had sunglasses on, because I don't remember his eyes.'

'But you'd recognise him if you saw him again?'

'I expect so.'

'Your husband told us he didn't see this man. Why was that?'

'Mike was face down with his eyes closed.'

She'd sketched a pretty good word-picture. Diamond had his own mental image of the Smiths relaxing on the beach while this potentially fatal rebuff took place in front of them.

'Before I ask you about the rest of the afternoon, do you remember who else was sitting to either side of you?'

'A French family to our right. Parents and three small children. And to our left, three girls in their teens.'

Tourists and teenagers. He doubted if any of them would come forward as witnesses. 'You seemed to suggest just now that the woman spoke to you at some stage of the day.'

'Yes, it was when I went down to the sea to collect Haley. We were going to eat some sandwiches for lunch. Haley and I had a little race up the beach and I was some way behind. The woman said she wished she had such energy, or some such. That was all.'

'But she seemed relaxed?'

'I thought so. And I can't remember any more about her until later when we had a crisis of our own, with Haley going missing after Mike and I had been for a swim. I was asking people if they'd seen her, but the woman looked as if she'd been asleep for hours, so I didn't disturb her.'

'Definitely asleep?'

'Well, how can you tell? I didn't look closely to see if she was breathing, or anything.'

Hen asked a question. 'Who was it who found Haley?'

'The lifeguard. I saw him holding her hand and I thought for a moment he was abducting her.'

'Which lifeguard?'

'He was the only one I saw. No hair, or very little. Very muscular. Australian, by his accent.'

Hen nodded and murmured to Diamond, 'Emerson.'

Diamond resumed. 'So you got your child back, and she was the one who noticed that the tide had reached the woman?'

'Yes. We couldn't see all of her but her legs were poking out of the windbreak and it was obvious she wasn't moving. Mike went to look, and you know the rest.'

'He alerted the lifeguard?'

'They carried her – Mike and the lifeguard and a couple of young blokes – over the stones to one of the beach huts and put her in there. Then we left. That's all I can tell you, I think.'

He said in a mild, almost dismissive tone, in consideration to young Haley, 'Obviously you know she was strangled at some stage of the afternoon. You didn't notice anyone else with her?'

'Nobody. Didn't hear anything or see anything. It must have happened while we were swimming. That's all I can think.'

'So the last time you saw her alive was just before you had your lunch?'

'Yes, about one thirty, I think.'

He thanked her, and looked to Hen to see if she had anything to ask. She obviously hadn't. And it was no use

211

questioning the child, because she'd spent most of the day playing near the water's edge.

They drove to Horsham, Hen leading the way in her car. She hadn't forgotten her promise of a pub lunch and the Green Dragon was her choice. She picked her way to it unerringly, parked and strode inside while Diamond was still finding a place to put his car. Brisk and boisterous, it seemed the right setting for her. There were two main drinking areas, a large-screen TV and bar billiards.

'Fish and chips suit you?' she suggested when he reached her at the counter where the food was ordered. 'We've plenty of time. A little bird told me Jimmy is out of the office until three.'

So he found a table in the main eating area, known as the conservatory, and fetched the drinks, two half-pints of Tanglefoot. He usually drank cheap lager, but this seemed the kind of place where you raised your sights and went for a full-bodied beer. Tom Jones was coming over the sound system.

'It's not too loud, is it?' he remarked to Hen.

'I like it. But I'd forgotten they don't let you smoke in this area,' she said. 'Before you sit down, do you mind if we move to the patio?' She led him outside to a table with a plate of uneaten baked beans someone had also used as an ashtray. 'I always find my level eventually.'

'But will they find us with the lunch?' he said.

'No problem.' She took out her cigars and lit one. 'I told them I'd be with the Sean Connery lookalike.'

They talked for a while about films, or at least Hen did. He hadn't been to a cinema since Steph died. It seemed Bognor was a good place to catch the latest movie. English seaside towns usually had more than one cinema, she remarked. There were so many wet afternoons when there was nowhere else to go.

Then they talked shop again. 'Thanks for sending me Emma Tysoe's files,' she said. 'We're a lot wiser about all kinds of things.'

'Well, it's helpful to know the names on the Mariner's death list,' he said smoothly, as if Jimmy Barneston's amours were well down the scale. 'Bramshill had no intention of telling us.'

'Top names, too. Young Matt Porter is one of my pin-ups. I don't want him getting killed.'

'He'll be all right if he does as they say.'

'He sounded stroppy.'

'But his manager Macaulay makes the decisions, and he'll crack the whip. The woman sounds more at risk.'

'Anna Walpurgis? Do you think she'll quit the safe house?'

'It sounded as if she was causing problems.'

'And how,' Hen said. 'Jimmy will bring us up to date.' She paused before saying, 'How do you want to play this?'

'Straight bat. I've brought my copy of the files. I think we should let him have a read before we say a thing.'

'Good thinking. But then what?'

'We simply ask what happened next. We're entitled to know if he slept with her the night before she was murdered. And anything she said that might throw light on it. Did she tell him she was planning a day on the beach? Did she feel under threat from anyone at all?'

'And what were Jimmy's own movements that day? He's got to prove he has an alibi.'

'Are you going to tell him?' Diamond said.

She blew out smoke and flashed a big, beguiling smile. 'It would come better from you, sweetie.'

This time he didn't argue. All along, he'd expected to be eyeball to eyeball with Barneston. He was confident of Hen's support when the going got tough.

He said, 'There's another thing I'd like to find out from

213

JB, and it goes back to when Emma Tysoe was first brought in on the case. How many people knew? Bramshill were in on it, obviously. So was Jimmy. But who else?'

She stared at him for a moment. 'So you're still holding on to the possibility she could have been killed by the Mariner?'

'I haven't excluded it.' A bland admission. Deep down, he was more committed. From the beginning, everyone had told him the cases were unconnected, so his stubborn personality wanted to prove the opposite.

Their food arrived shortly after. Hen slid the vinegar towards him. 'I expect you're quite a connoisseur of fish and chips.'

'Living alone, you mean? Actually I'm a pizza specialist.'

'Do you cook for yourself at all?'

'Pizzas from the freezer. I sometimes open a tin of beans. I could be asking you these questions.'

'Me?' Hen said. 'The canteen at Bognor nick is second to none.' She leaned back in the seat as if her attention was taken by a group of young office workers celebrating someone's birthday. They all had paper hats. Then her eyes returned to Diamond and she took a long sip of beer before saying, 'I heard about your wife being murdered last year. I know you don't want sympathy. Just wanted to say – as a total outsider – you're bearing up better than I would.'

'Thanks. I've learnt a few tips about living alone,' he said, sidestepping the heart-to-heart he saw coming. 'One thing you can depend on absolutely. If you go to the bathroom, you just get settled and somebody will ring the doorbell. If you're able to get there in time it's a bloke selling oven gloves. If you don't make it, you find a card to say you missed the postman and you've got to go into town and collect a parcel.'

She smiled. 'Don't I know! And when you collect, it

isn't a parcel at all, but a letter from some plonker who forgot to put on a stamp.'

'Yes, and when you pay up and open the letter it's from the doctor to say you need a booster jab for anti-tetanus.'

'So what's the tip?'

'Don't use your own bathroom. Use the one at work.'

Hen shook her head. 'There's always someone in there.'

End of exchange, thanks be. He'd been told more than once not to bottle up the grief, but it wasn't in his nature to discuss it with anyone. The process had been drawn out over many months, still without closure. The shooting, the funeral, the investigation, the arrest, the trial and, yet to come, an appeal. The open wound remained and the pain didn't go away. Let no one underestimate the effect of murder on the surviving spouse.

The music had switched to 'Staying Alive'. They finished their food as fast as possible and left on foot for the police station, a ten-minute walk through the park that would do them good after fish and chips, Hen assured him.

He asked how the Wightview Sands end of the investigation had been going, and she told him she hadn't yet traced the second lifeguard, but she had a name and a mobile phone number – which had not helped, as they couldn't make contact with it. The assumption was that the phone needed recharging.

'What's his name?' Diamond asked.

'Laver.'

'Straight up?'

She frowned. 'What's wrong?'

'Just that the first lifeguard – the one we met – is called Emerson, or claimed to be. Laver and Emerson were two of the biggest names in Australian tennis in the sixties.

They won God knows how many Grand Slam titles between them. They played doubles together as well.'

'You think they were having us on?'

'Having someone on for sure. It could be about casual labour and work permits, rather than what happened on the beach that day. They'd have thought up more original identities if they knew it was a murder enquiry. Is Emerson still working there?'

'The last I heard, he was,' Hen answered. 'I'll follow this up.'

They reached the north end of Horsham Park, where the three main emergency services are sited. At the police station, they were asked to wait in an office, because DCI Barneston was still not back.

'What time is it?' Diamond asked the sergeant. 'He has a good lunch break.'

You could generally count on the lower ranks enjoying a poke at the high-ups, but this sergeant didn't rise to it. Was Barneston an example of that rare breed, a chief inspector popular with the lower ranks?

They had an upstairs room to themselves. It was typically barren of anything of interest. There were three plastic chairs and a table stained with tea. On the wall facing the door were two notices about foot-and-mouth regulations and a map of West Sussex.

'A bloody ashtray would help,' Hen said as she lit up.

Diamond was looking at the map. 'How far are we from Bognor, then?'

'About twenty-five. You take the A29.'

'And Wightview Sands?'

'Probably another ten miles on top. Why?'

'If Emma Tysoe was here with JB the night before she was murdered, she had a drive of thirty-five miles to Wightview Sands. From what I can see, Worthing or Brighton would have been nearer.'

'Or Bognor.'

'Or Bognor,' he echoed. 'But why Wightview Sands?'

'It's different, isn't it?' Hen said. 'All those places are seaside towns. Wightview is only a beach – well, there's a small village set back from the shore, and some posh houses. There's almost nothing along the front except one beach café and a long row of beach huts. You haven't got piers and pubs and amusement machines by the hundred. It's quiet.'

'Unspoilt.'

She wagged a finger. 'Hold your horses, squire. You won't get me to say Bognor is spoilt.'

'It sounds as if she went to Wightview because she knows the place. It was what she wanted. Somewhere to relax.'

'Presumably. Unless she'd agreed to meet someone.'

'Doesn't appear so. She arrived on the beach late morning, after the Smiths, put up her windbreak, lay on her towel and that's about all we know until she was found dead. We have about two thousand suspects.'

'A shortlist of four,' Hen said.

'Four? Let me try. The ex-lover, Ken. The two lifeguards under false names. And the Mariner.'

'Check.'

'But you left out Jimmy Barneston.'

She creased her features. 'You don't really rate him?'

'I want to hear his story. Where *is* the guy?'

Hen, unable to supply an answer, took the question as rhetorical. She was still brooding over the suspects. 'There are problems with each of them. We don't know how Ken or the Mariner knew she was on that beach on that particular morning.'

'But both are single-minded characters,' he said. 'They could have followed her. What about the guy in the black T-shirt who tried to chat her up and got nowhere? He could have been Ken. Apparently they recognised each other. She wouldn't have been too happy if he turned up unexpectedly. He got the brush-off, but he could have come back in the afternoon.'

'The two suspects we know for certain were on that beach are the two Australian guys,' Hen said, doggedly working through the possibilities, 'but we don't have a motive for them. There's no suggestion that this was part of a sexual assault.'

'Theft? Her beachbag was missing.'

'But we agreed it's dead simple to steal a bag on a beach. You don't have to strangle someone if you're only after cash and credit cards.'

He yawned, and checked the time again. 'True.'

'However, we haven't found her car yet.'

'Good point, Hen.' He snapped his fingers. 'Now that raises the stakes. A Lotus Esprit might be a prize worth having for a young guy living on a shoestring without a work permit. He steals the bag – her bag and no other – because it contains her car key. He's seen her park this beautiful car—'

'People have been killed for less.'

'A lot less. I rather like it, Hen. I'm not sure if I like it more than the Mariner, or Ken, or the man in the black T-shirt, but it's persuasive, very persuasive. There's only one problem with it.'

'Yes?'

'Any one of our other two thousand suspects could have done it.'

At this point the smoke alarm went off.

Order was restored after an embarrassing few minutes explaining to the safety officer that, as visitors, they hadn't taken note of the no-smoking signs all over the building. The only places you could light up were the canteen and the interview rooms, provided that the interviewee wished to smoke as well.

'You want to try patches,' Diamond told Hen when she took out her lighter again. They were standing outside the front entrance of the police station.

'You know where you can put your patches, chummy.'

The placid street life of Horsham continued in front of them while that cigar was reduced rather quickly to a tiny butt.

'It's bloody near four o'clock. I'll go inside and see if they can get a message to him,' Diamond said.

The desk sergeant had changed. This one didn't appear to know that they were waiting outside. Diamond had to identify himself.

The sergeant apologised. 'You're waiting for DCI Barneston, sir? He won't be coming back this afternoon. He's dealing with an incident.'

'What kind of incident?'

'I wasn't informed, sir – except that he's tied up for the rest of the day and probably tomorrow as well.'

'Well, I'm going to need his mobile number. I've come from Bath to see him, and another officer outside has come up from the coast.'

Not so simple. Getting Barneston's number was like trying to steal meat from a pride of lions. By sheer force of personality he eventually obtained it on the say-so of a CID inspector.

When he got through, he found Barneston incensed at being troubled. 'Who the fuck put you onto me? Didn't anyone tell you there's a fucking emergency here?'

Diamond gritted his teeth. 'We're coming to see you.'

'You're joking. I'm dealing with a crisis here.'

'So are we, and you'd better listen up, Jimmy, because it concerns you.'

'What are you on about?'

'Emma Tysoe came to see you the day before she was strangled.'

After a long hesitation, Barneston said, 'You know about that?'

'There's a whole lot more we know.'

Another pause. Then: 'I'm at Littlegreen Place, South Harting. That's near Petersfield. It's laughingly described as a safe house.'

15

Littlegreen Place was a large, brick-built house standing in chain-fenced grounds on the northern escarpment of the South Downs. There was no other building within sight. When Diamond drove up, with Hen Mallin seated beside him, the electric gates were open and three police minibuses, two patrol cars and a Skoda were parked on the drive

Someone with a tripod over his shoulder and a camera in his free hand came from the open front door, heading for the Skoda, and Diamond asked him if DCI Barneston was about. The man nodded towards the interior.

'Got your pictures already?' Diamond said, just to be civil to someone else in the pay of the government.

'Waste of time,' came the reply, and it set the tone for what was to come.

They went inside, through a sizeable entrance hall, in the direction of voices that turned out to be from the kitchen. Jimmy Barneston, looking like a football manager whose team has just been relegated, was slumped at the table, his head in his hands. Two others in plain clothes, holding mugs, were standing together watching a uniformed inspector speaking urgent orders into a mobile phone.

'Are you supposed to be here?' one of them asked.

Diamond identified himself and Hen and asked what was happening.

'You tell us.'

Hen said, 'Jimmy?'

Barneston raised his eyes, but that was the extent of it.

Diamond asked, 'Is someone going to let us in on this?'

Barneston gave a groan that was part threat, part protest, as if his sleep had been disturbed.

The inspector using the phone moved out of the kitchen into what was probably a laundry room.

Diamond put a hand on Barneston's shoulder. 'You cocked up, is that it?'

This got a response. He looked up and said with a heavy emphasis, 'Not me.'

'The people on duty?'

He nodded, all too ready to shift any blame. 'Two hours ago, a call was made to this place, a scheduled call, to the Special Branch officers supposed to be guarding, em, a person under threat.'

'Matthew Porter,' Hen said.

She wasn't supposed to know the name. Barneston took note with a twitch of the eyebrows. 'This was only a routine check. It's done at regular intervals. There was no response. They kept trying. Still nothing. So an RRV was sent here. They found the front gate wide open. The double doors at the front of the house were also open. No one was inside, except a police dog, shut in the garage. The bulk of the security system was disabled. Two armed officers vanished.'

'And Matthew Porter?'

'Yes. The Range Rover used by one of the officers is also missing. There's no sign of a struggle, nothing out of place.'

'Like the fucking *Mary Celeste*,' one of the others, obviously a romantic, summed it up.

'Video cameras?' Diamond enquired.

'All disabled from the control room upstairs. We're checking the cassettes in case anything was caught earlier.'

Barneston scraped his fingers through his thick black hair and then held his hand out, palm upwards. 'What can you do? This is the state-of-the-art safe house – allegedly. We moved him here from another address because it was more secure. The Mariner has found it and strolled in and out as if it was a public toilet. Someone's going to swing for this.'

'Are you certain this is the Mariner?' Hen asked.

'How could it be anyone else?'

'Matthew Porter didn't like being cooped up in Streatham. What if he didn't like it here and walked out? Wouldn't the guards go after him?'

Barneston glared at her. 'What do *you* know about Streatham?'

'We can talk about that at a calmer time.'

'Sod that. We've had a major balls-up in security and you people know too fucking much for my liking. Tell me now. It could be relevant.'

Hen flushed bright pink, and not because of the language. She shouldn't have mentioned Streatham at this stage.

Diamond felt the muscles tighten across his shoulders. Working as a double act had its drawbacks. This wasn't the moment he would have chosen, and there was no way now of putting it off. He let his eyes meet Barneston's. 'Emma Tysoe – whose death we are investigating – kept some files on computer.'

'I know about Tysoe's files,' Barneston said with impatience. 'They haven't been decrypted yet.' After a beat, he said lamely, 'Have they?'

Hen gave a nod. 'She kept a record of her visit to Streatham.'

'And much more besides,' Diamond couldn't resist adding.

'Oh, shit.'

'I have a copy with me, as decrypted by a lad in my nick.'

It wasn't Jimmy Barneston's day. While he was taking that in, Hen tried to divert him, 'Coming back to the present emergency, don't you think it possible Porter simply got brassed off with all the security and made a break for it?'

'No, I don't,' he said. 'Come and see this.' Whatever the incentive was, it got him to his feet. He led them out of the kitchen, across the hall and upstairs. He pushed open the first door on the landing. 'Porter's bedroom.'

The interior was in pretty good order, a bed with a quilt doubled back, a couple of books on the bedside table. On the pillow was a sheet of A4 paper with words in newsprint pasted to it.

'Don't touch it,' Barneston cautioned them.

Diamond took a step closer and bent over to read the message.

'"Three under par."'

'You know what that is?' Barneston said.

'A reference to golf, I suppose.'

'Three under par is an albatross. The albatross is the bird the Ancient Mariner killed. Now tell me the bastard wasn't here.'

They stood in silence, absorbing the force of the words and feeling a chilling contact with the mind of their author, as if they'd been touched by him. This gallows humour was at one with the note left when Summers was murdered. It dashed any hope that Porter would survive.

'Who are we dealing with here – Superman?' Hen said with awe. 'How the heck does he find out about this place? How does he get in and overcome two armed guards?'

'And a dog,' Barneston said. 'You tell me. No signs of

a break-in. No shooting. Nothing out of place.'

'Have you got road blocks in operation?' Diamond asked.

'Full-scale alert, but it could have happened four hours ago. The last check-in we logged was at noon.'

'Who are these Special Branch guys?'

'Good men, I've been told, one with ARV experience, the other a dog handler. Both of them Sergeant rank. They're not wet behind the ears.'

'And the building has been searched?'

'From top to bottom.'

They returned downstairs. In the kitchen, Barneston seemed to be getting a grip again. 'Was anything useful in those files?'

'Depends where you're coming from,' Diamond told him.

'Explain.'

'We've learned a lot more about our murder victim and the job she was on.'

'Do you think the Mariner strangled her?'

Diamond didn't answer directly. Why confide in a man who had just treated them like plods? 'He's capable of it. He doesn't lack anything in daring.'

'Because he feared she would finger him?'

'She was the top profiler.'

'Does she say anything in these files that will help me right now?' Barneston asked. 'Did she put together a profile I can use?'

'How do I know what's going to be helpful to you?' Diamond told him testily. 'Read it yourself. Is there a computer here?'

'Upstairs.' The man looked as if he would sink back into his lethargic gloom, and then he changed his mind. 'OK. There's sod all happening, so I might as well make use of the time. Where's the disk?'

Diamond took the tiny USB drive from his inside pocket and handed it across.

'This is it?'

'All of it.'

'Do you want to stick around in the meantime?'

Diamond didn't need to ask Hen. 'We're as keen as you are to find out what's been going on.'

They remained downstairs, leaving Barneston to read Emma's files in private. The officers in the kitchen said there was no progress yet in the hunt for the Range Rover. The Sussex police helicopter had been called into use and every car within a thirty-mile radius was on alert.

It can be frustrating standing about, waiting for news. Hen went outside for a smoke. Diamond got on the mobile to Ingeborg and asked how the hunt for Ken was progressing.

Even Ingeborg seemed to be lacking in zest this afternoon. 'Still trying, guv. I went through those credit card receipts.'

'No joy?'

'No Kens, anyway. Do you think he could have paid cash?'

'It's possible, I suppose. You'd be better off asking Popjoy's, not me. Have you talked to the neighbours?'

'The thing is,' she said, on a note immediately telling him this, too, had not helped, 'she had her own entrance, living, as she did, in the basement flat. The people upstairs didn't see very much of her and they don't have any memory of seeing her with anyone.'

'What about the people across the street?'

'You know how wide Great Pulteney Street is. They'd need binoculars. I've been across and asked, but no, it's another world.'

'You're going to have to track down everyone who dined at Popjoy's the evening they were there, and see how much they remember about the other guests. A description would be a start, even if we don't have his name. You've talked to the waiters, I hope? Did you ask them about that overgenerous tip she mentions? Surely one of the staff pocketed that and remembers where it came from.'

'I'll get onto that,' she promised. Apparently she'd been talking to the management, not the waiters.

He joined Hen outside. The area near the kitchen door had an overgrown look. This safe house had once been someone's home, and there were the remnants of a vegetable patch and an apple orchard, but garden maintenance wasn't high priority in Special Branch. Across a stretch of meadow that had once been a lawn, a line of officers searched the undergrowth near the fence. Somewhere overhead the helicopter buzzed.

'Are you all right for time?' he asked Hen.

'I'm seeing this through if it takes till midnight, matey.'

'He could be clean away.'

'With three hostages? I doubt it. What's his game, Peter?'

He gave a shrug and shook his head. 'Whatever it is, I'm certain it's just as he planned it.'

'That message upstairs doesn't give any grounds for hope.'

'No.'

'He brought it with him like a calling card, the bastard. It's bloody arrogance. I mean, we don't need telling he was here.'

He smiled faintly. 'Don't we? Didn't I hear you suggesting to Jimmy Barneston that Porter might have got pissed off with the place and made a break for it?'

She gave him a sharp look. 'At that stage I couldn't believe anyone was capable of penetrating the security. Now we know.'

She finished her smoke and they returned to the kitchen. One look at the others told them no news had come through. Diamond picked someone's *Daily Mail* off the table and looked for news of the rugby. Bath were slipping in the league.

There was still nothing to report to Barneston when he came downstairs and found them in the garden again. He had the look of a man in deep shock, thoughts whirling in his brain. He made a visible effort to focus on the immediate problem. 'He'll be clean away by now.'

'It doesn't look good,' Diamond agreed.

A short, nervy sigh. 'It bears out what she wrote in the files – he knows he can outwit the police.'

'She didn't put it quite like that, if I remember,' Hen said. 'It was something like "has an exalted belief he can outwit us". There's a difference. He'll get overconfident.'

'Breaking into this place will have done his confidence a power of good,' Barneston said gloomily. 'Mine is at rock bottom.'

'Shouldn't be,' she said. 'Come on, Jim lad, some of that stuff in the files was a massive boost to your self-esteem. A clever and attractive woman slavering over you – what more does a guy want?'

He didn't answer.

Diamond took a more head-on approach. 'We need to know if she spent the night with you, the last night of her life.'

Barneston confirmed it with a nod.

'At your house again?'

'What do you mean – again? It was only the second time.'

Diamond had never scored points for sensitivity. 'So she did what she planned, came to Horsham with a list of questions for Anna Walpurgis?'

228

'Yup.'

'For *you* to ask Walpurgis?'

'That's correct. Things are pretty fraught with Walpurgis. I didn't want to panic her. Emma came to my house and we went out for a meal and spent the night together.'

'Did she say anything to you about this man Ken she mentions in the files?'

'Not directly.'

'But . . . ?'

'She told me she'd been in another relationship that was finished. She didn't give a name.'

Hen said, 'Jimmy, you'll appreciate that he's under suspicion of murdering her. Can you remember anything she said about him that will help us to identify him?'

'No.'

'Did you get any impression of his age, or whether he lived near her, or what kind of job he did?'

'Nothing at all. She only mentioned him in passing, and I didn't probe. I'd rather not know who slept with her before I did.'

Diamond asked, 'How did she refer to him – as a boyfriend, or a long-term lover, or what?'

'I told you. She simply said, "I was in a relationship and it's over now."'

This wasn't helping overmuch. Diamond said, 'We know she dumped him. Do you think it's possible he could have found out about you?'

'I don't see how. I didn't visit her in Bath.'

'We're wondering if he followed her to Horsham and saw you together. Did you have a sense of anyone following you, or watching you?'

'No.'

'Was Emma relaxed?' Hen asked.

'I thought so. She seemed to be enjoying herself.' He

spread his hands in a gesture of openness. 'Listen, if there was anything I could think of to help you, I would. She was a sweet girl. I really enjoyed being with her. I can tell you, I freaked out when I heard what happened to her.'

This little tribute didn't melt Peter Diamond's heart. 'But you didn't come forward and say you spent the night with her. You didn't even tell us when we met you at the hospital.'

'Because it was a red herring. You could have wasted time questioning me when you should have been after her killer.'

'You just hoped we'd make an early arrest and leave you out of it?'

No answer. Diamond had hit the mark.

He said, 'Tell us about the morning of the day she was murdered. Did she talk about her plans?'

Barneston looked down at the ground, shifting a stone a short way with his well-polished right shoe. 'She did her best to persuade me to spend the day with her at the beach. Said she knew I was working flat out on the Mariner enquiry, but I'd function better for a few hours away from it. Six days shalt thou labour, and all that. It was Sunday morning, of course.' He paused and sighed. 'I was almost persuaded, too.'

'So what happened, exactly?'

He continued to poke at the stone with his toecap. 'I gave her breakfast in bed and told her to take her time getting up. When I left around nine, she was about to take a shower.'

'You left her alone in your house?'

'Sure. I trusted her.'

'Did she say anything about going to the beach alone?'

'Oh, yes. It was a beautiful day. She was going, with or without me.'

'She must have driven there,' Diamond said.

'Yes, her sports car was on my drive. And that's about all I can tell you.' He rubbed his hands together, ready to move on to other matters.

'There is something else,' Diamond said. 'Would you mind telling us how you actually spent the rest of the day?'

Barneston frowned, glared and then gave a hollow laugh. 'You're not asking me to account for my time?'

'You've got it in one, Jimmy.'

'You know what you can do.'

'Not until this is sorted,' Diamond said with a look as unrelenting as his voice. 'Did you go into work?'

Barneston hesitated for a long time, perhaps to show dissent. Diamond's eyes, unblinking, had never left his. Finally, he submitted. 'I went to the nick and worked on the case.'

'Until when?'

'I don't know. Late morning, early afternoon. I had a canteen lunch. Do you want to know if it was roast beef and two veg?'

'And then?'

'A stroll around the park.'

'Alone?'

Barneston's face reddened. 'I don't have to take these innuendoes. Who do you think you're questioning here?'

'Alone, then,' Diamond said. 'How about the rest of the afternoon, Jimmy?'

'Didn't you hear me? I've had enough of this crap.'

Hen put in gently, 'He's doing his job, Jimmy. He's got a duty to ask.'

Making every word sound like an infliction, Barneston said, 'I returned to my office for about an hour and finished the job I was on. Then I went home and looked at the cricket on TV. I guess it was about two thirty when I left the nick. No, I didn't make any phone calls, and

231

nobody knocked on my door, so if you want to fit me up it's perfectly feasible that I could have driven to Wightview Sands inside an hour, found Emma and strangled her.'

Hen said, 'Jimmy, calm down.'

He carried on in the same embittered flow: 'Of course, you have the minor problem of the motive – establishing how we fell out after a night together – but I guess that's not beyond your fertile imagination.'

'Probably not,' Diamond said evenly, 'but there is another problem. How would you drive two cars away from the scene? Hers hasn't been seen since the murder.'

Barneston was silent while he played this over in his mind. After a longish interval he saw the point. 'So you're not about to caution me?' It was an attempt to recoup, a feeble joke.

Diamond indulged him with a grin.

Above them, the helicopter crossed so low that they saw the trees bowing in the down-draught.

Hen said, 'Do you think they've spotted something?'

After the tension of the past few minutes it was a relief to go back inside the house and check developments. But nothing *had* developed. The Mariner had come and gone as he did in Bramber, leaving no clue except his newsprint taunt.

'How could he have conned his way in?' Diamond asked.

'God only knows,' Barneston said. 'The guards have an entry code that even I don't know. Anyone at the gate is under video surveillance from the control room upstairs.'

'Are you sure of the guards?'

'Special Branch is. One hundred per cent.'

'And the system is fully tested?'

'It's the best they have. We only moved him here three days ago. And, yes, it was tested, every item of equipment. Infrared sensors in every room, lasers, cameras, the lot.'

'Fine – so long as they're activated.'

'Well, yes, but you need to know the codes before you can tamper with anything.'

'Who knows the codes?'

'Only the guards – and if you want to know how many are involved in this operation, there are six men, all experienced, all armed with Glock 17s and Heckler and Koch machine guns. They rotate their duties, of course. And in addition there are four dog-handlers. At any one time, there are always two officers and a dog on the premises.'

'Did Matthew Porter approve of all this?' Hen asked.

'Sure. He was given more freedom than he had in the Streatham safe house. It's considerably bigger, with an outdoor heated pool and a games room. He was OK.'

'I mean, potentially he's the security risk, isn't he, even though it's all set up to protect him?'

'You mean if he wanted out? That could have been a risk in Streatham. Not here, I think.'

A personal radio gave off the sound of static and a voice came through clearly enough for everyone to hear. 'Oscar Bravo to Control, reporting a sighting from the chopper. A four by four, possibly Range Rover, stationary in Caseys Lane, reference six-eight-five-eight-zero-three. Repeat six-eight-five-eight-zero-three. Shall we investigate? Over.'

'Await instructions. Over.'

'Caseys Lane. Where?' Barneston demanded, already poring over the map on the kitchen table.

Hen found it. 'Less than a mile, I'd say.'

'Give me that,' Barneston said to the officer holding the radio. He touched the press-to-talk switch. 'We're on the way. Over and out.'

There was a stampede to the cars.

16

The map reference wasn't required. The helicopter marked the spot by hovering over it. The convoy of three police vehicles travelled at speed in emergency mode, blue lights flashing. When they got closer the sound of the rotors beating the air drowned out the sirens.

'One thing's certain,' Diamond said to Hen, some distance in the rear in a fourth car, his own. 'We're not going to surprise anyone.'

But it was wise to advertise their approach. The width of the lanes left no margin for the drivers. After a series of bends they passed a derelict cottage, its roof stripped of most of its tiles, foliage thrusting through the rafters. A short distance ahead was the gate to a field where sheep were grazing, indifferent to the activity. Beside an oak tree, a dark green Range Rover stood in front of the gate on turf, just off the lane. The helicopter pilot had done well to spot it under the tree's thick foliage. There was no movement at the windows.

Having pointed the way, the helicopter climbed higher, circled a couple of times and remained overhead in case someone made a dash to escape.

The convoy stopped about thirty metres short and two armed officers were detailed to make an approach. A few people got out and crouched behind the vehicles, but Diamond and Hen chose to wait in the comparative safety of the car. They still had a view of the two men moving cautiously ahead, stooping below the level of the hedge. The Range Rover looked unoccupied, but there was no telling what was below window level.

Hen muttered under her breath, 'I don't like to think what they'll find.'

Neither did Diamond, though he said nothing. The young man had been under Special Branch protection, and it had let him down. If the very worst had happened, any police officer who took his job seriously was going to feel regret, if not shame.

The two armed men in black coveralls and body armour separated, one taking a wide arc through the field on the far side of the Range Rover, while the other remained in the lane. After a series of short forward movements, one of them – the man in the lane – flattened himself to the ground and began a crocodile-like approach to the rear of the vehicle, using his knees and elbows for leverage, but still gripping his short-barrel machine gun. He was close enough to be below the sight range of the wing mirrors.

The afternoon sun caught every detail of the drama. It was getting hot inside the cars.

Progress was agonisingly slow. The man inched forward, and finally got right up to the rear bumper of the Range Rover. For about half a minute he did nothing, listening, no doubt, for a voice or a movement inside the vehicle. Then he raised himself into a crouching position and slowly stood high enough to look through the rear window. Abruptly he turned towards the others and gestured with both hands for them to approach.

'Go, go, go!'

The response was immediate. Everyone got out and started running towards the Range Rover, with Diamond and Hen well in the rear. Even the helicopter dipped its nose and zoomed lower.

The officer was shouting, 'They're on the floor. We've

got to get in.' He smashed the side window with the butt of his gun – which activated an alarm loud enough to shatter ear drums. He put his arm through, swung back the door and dipped inside.

In a moment he emerged with a body trussed with plasti-cuffs and leather belt. Others helped lift the man out and onto the grass, where they unbuckled the belt that pinioned his legs. He was breathing. He opened his eyes.

A second man was removed from the space behind the back seat. He, also, had been tied up and handcuffed, and he, also, was alive. Like his companion, he looked dazed and ill. The heat inside, with all windows closed, must have been appalling.

Neither of the rescued men was Matthew Porter.

Jimmy Barneston wasn't too concerned by the state of them. Quite rightly, he wanted information. Someone thoughtfully produced a bottle of water. Barneston snatched it, unscrewed the top and splashed most of the contents across the face of the nearest man.

'Somebody kill that fucking alarm!' Barneston yelled.

It took a few minutes to get under the Range Rover's bonnet and locate the mechanism. A uniformed inspector disabled it.

The men's groans could now be heard by everyone. The more animated of the two was still handcuffed and lying on his side. But at least he was conscious.

'Where's Porter?' Barneston asked. 'What happened to him?'

One question was a lot to cope with. Two was over-doing it. The man shook his head.

Barneston asked again, 'What happened? Come on, man, I need to know.'

The mouth was moving soundlessly, like a beached fish.

'I can't hear him,' Barneston said. 'Someone tell that chopper to get the hell out of here.'

Hen said, 'He's dehydrated. Give him a drink, for pity's sake.' She snatched up the plastic bottle and held it to the man's mouth.

He gulped at it.

They fetched another bottle for the second man. 'Can't we get them out of these cuffs?' Hen asked. 'The poor guys are in pain.'

One of the police gunmen unhitched cutters from his belt and snipped through the plasticuffs.

The man who seemed in slightly better shape sat up, and immediately vomited, throwing up all of the water he'd swallowed and more.

It definitely wasn't Jimmy Barneston's day. He'd taken some of it on his shoes.

The man seemed to be about to retch again. In fact, he was trying to speak a word that he eventually spluttered out.

'Gas?' Barneston said. 'Did you say gas? He used gas on you?'

A nod.

'What – CS?'

He shook his head, and the movement seemed to hurt him, because he winced and shut his eyes.

'Did he put it to your face, or what?'

Now he managed a few connected words. 'Took me from behind. I was coughing. Couldn't breathe. Don't remember any more.'

'So the gas knocked you out. This was inside the house?'

'Living room.'

'Did you see him?'

He shook his head and placed his hand, palm inwards, against his face, covering his mouth and nose.

Barneston was quick on the uptake. 'He was wearing a gas mask?'

'Yes.'

'Didn't you get any warning? Alarms?'

'Going to throw up again.'

This time, just in time, Barneston stepped aside.

When the man's head came up, Barneston said, 'What about Matt Porter? Was he in the room with you?'

'Another room.'

'So he would have been gassed as well. What happened then?'

'Don't know.'

'You don't have any memory of being driven here? You didn't see what happened?'

The man looked around him and asked, 'Where are we anyway?'

The question remained unanswered because Barneston had turned to the second guard and was trying to question him. But the gas had affected this one more seriously. He was talking gibberish.

This was a medical emergency. Up to now, Peter Diamond had thought of himself as an observer, but someone had to take some initiative here because there was no telling how seriously these men were affected. They'd been unconscious for some time. Heatstroke and even brain damage was a possibility. Barneston was entirely taken up with extracting any information he could, so Diamond told the nearest man with a mobile to call an ambulance.

When Barneston stood up, muttering in frustration at getting so little out of the guards, Diamond drew him aside and told him what he'd arranged. It was a courtesy. You don't muscle in on someone else's incident. But the message didn't seem to register. JB was extremely keyed up. He turned his back on Diamond and returned to the more coherent of the two men.

'This isn't getting anywhere,' Diamond confided to

Hen. 'It's up to Barneston to do something.'

'He's in shock,' she said. 'I've never seen him like this. If there's stuff he should be doing, you'd better tell him. You've got experience.'

In fact, this wasn't really about experience. Every incident brings its own unique problems, and the challenge is to stay cool and deal with them as well as resources allow. Considering Barneston was one of the generation who made 'cool' into a cardinal virtue, he wasn't shaping up at all.

So Diamond tapped him on the shoulder and discreetly suggested he ordered everyone off the grass and onto the lane.

'What's the problem?' Barneston asked. 'What's up now?'

At least there was communication this time.

'Crime scene procedure. You've dealt with the incident. Now it's a matter of preserving what you can of the scene.' For a man who had never been a slave to the rulebook this was rather rich, but Diamond was putting it in language the new generation of CID should understand. 'Particularly the treadmarks.'

'Oh, yeah?' Barneston said vaguely.

'Not the Range Rover's marks.'

'No?'

'The Mariner's. The Mariner had his car waiting here.'

'You think so?' Those blue eyes showed little understanding.

'You've got the picture, haven't you, Jimmy?' But it was obvious Barneston's brain hadn't made the jump, so Diamond laid out the facts as he saw them. 'Back at the house he gassed these blokes and Porter and trussed them up and put them in the Range Rover and drove here. He must have had a vehicle waiting, right? So he transferred Porter into his own motor and drove off, God knows where. The least we can do is find the treadmarks his tyres made.'

The last twenty minutes had been too frantic and traumatic for Barneston to give a thought to anything so basic as treadmarks, but he nodded his head sagely as if it had always been in his plans and ordered everyone off the turf and onto the hard surface of the lane. The ground was already marked with many footprints as well as the contents of the guard's stomach. Crime scene tape was fetched and used to seal off the area.

Hen said, 'That's better. Feel as if we're getting a grip, even if we aren't.'

'He's away,' Barneston said bleakly. 'He's hung us out to dry.'

'Snap out of it, Jimmy,' Diamond told him. 'Have you sent for the SOCOs yet? I'd get one of those sergeants onto it if I were you.'

'Good point.' He went over to arrange it.

When he came back, he was still in the same fateful frame of mind. 'We can check the motor inside and out and every inch of the field, but let's face it, we knew fuck all about this guy before this, and we're still up shit creek.'

That kind of talk didn't go down well with Diamond. 'Haven't you heard of DNA?'

'What use is that without a suspect? We don't know a thing about him.'

'We know several things,' Diamond said. 'He's extremely well informed on our security. Somehow he found out Porter was transferred here. He knew how to get in without activating the alarms or panicking the dog. He must have had some kind of training or inside information. He has access to gas, not CS, but something that knocks you out completely. He's well organised, very focused. He could have killed the guards, but he chose not to.'

'Christ, that's not bad,' Barneston said, the interest reviving in his eyes.

'Common sense,' Diamond said dismissively.

But Hen wasn't letting it pass so lightly. 'Uncommon good sense, more like, and a lot better sense than any of those berks at Bramshill ever talk. Isn't that right, Jimmy?'

Barneston appeared to agree, because he asked Diamond what he recommended next, and there wasn't a hint of irony in his voice.

'The Mariner's car is the thing to concentrate on,' the big man answered. 'Obviously it was parked in this lane for some time. There's a chance someone drove by and noticed it. A farmhand, maybe. These are quiet lanes, but people are moving farm machinery around a lot of the time. I'd order a house-to-house on all the inhabited places in the vicinity, asking (a), if they saw anyone along the lanes, or crossing the field – which I think is more likely – and (b), if they noticed a vehicle parked here, or being driven away.'

'I was thinking along those lines myself,' Barneston said.

'Great minds,' Hen said with a wink that only Diamond saw. 'And, of course, you'll have your SOCOs going over the house and the Range Rover and all of this area. We ought to get some of his DNA out of this.'

'We can hope.' He moved off to speak to one of his team.

Diamond turned to Hen and said, 'Any more of that and I'll buy you a damned great spoon.'

'Why?'

'Stirring it up between Barneston and me. "Uncommon good sense".'

'Quite the opposite, Pete. I was throwing him a life-line. Can't you see he's poleaxed, poor love? His whole world has blown up in his face. He's lost the man he was

241

supposed to be protecting. He's got a neurotic woman in another so-called safe house who is going to go bananas when she hears about this, and who wouldn't? He knows Bramshill will come down on him like a ton of bricks, and what's more they're going to decrypt those deeply embarrassing files any time. No wonder he's in such a state.'

He couldn't feel the same degree of sympathy. He said (and immediately regretted it), 'Why don't you give him a cuddle, then?'

'Sod off, mate. He badly needs advice from someone with sand in his boots and a few ideas in his head. If you want to stay involved in the hunt for the Mariner, ducky, this is your opportunity.'

'*Our* opportunity,' he said, recouping a little.

'That goes without saying,' Hen said. 'You'd better talk to him man to man.'

They remained there while the paramedics arrived and took the two SO12 guards away for treatment. They would be questioned again, but there was little prospect that they'd remember any more. Not long after, a team of three SOCOs drove up and pulled on their white protective overalls. Jimmy Barneston pointed out some potential treadmarks to the right of the Range Rover. The SOCOs looked at all the other marks they had to contend with and didn't seem overly impressed.

Barneston eventually came back to where Diamond and Hen were watching the action from behind the tapes. He was looking marginally more in control. 'All the farms and houses in the area are being visited.' He cleared his throat. 'There was something you said just now. You suggested this could be an inside job, seeing that the Mariner found out about Porter being moved here.'

Diamond lifted his shoulders a fraction. 'He must have got it from somewhere.'

'Or someone,' Hen added.

'You're right, and it's a bloody nightmare,' Barneston said, the anxiety returning to his features. 'I don't know who I can trust any more. I *think* I know my own squad, but you can never be totally sure. Bramshill are involved, and Special Branch. That's a lot of people. It only needs one.'

'If we had a suspicion, we'd let you know,' Diamond told him.

'The worst of it is that I've got someone else under protection. Well, you read the files, so you know who she is. The Mariner found his way to Porter, so what's to stop him finding Anna Walpurgis? She's more of a risk than Porter was.'

'Why is that?' Hen said, as if, like some High Court judge insulated from the real world, she'd never heard of the volatile pop star.

'Temperament,' he said. 'She's hyper. You'd think she was on something, but she hardly ever stops.'

'That would be a problem.'

Barneston looked about him to make sure no one else was close enough to overhear. 'You see, this story is going to break in the press any time. I can't keep the lid on much longer. I was able to hold things down with Axel Summers because he was known to be taking a complete break from his work. And Matt Porter could miss one tournament. But questions are being asked about them both.'

Diamond said, 'In that case, you'd better go public right away.'

'Jesus Christ!' Barneston flapped his hand as if swatting away a wasp.

'Face it, Jimmy. You just said the story is about to break. You don't want it leaking out by degrees. Take control. Call a press conference and tell all.'

243

He stood as if stunned, his eyes making tiny nervous movements.

Diamond hammered home the message, 'What's the value of secrecy? You can't rely on safe houses being safe for anyone any more. If Anna Walpurgis is locked away in the country somewhere like this, she's a sitting duck for the Mariner. He'll get to her, whatever hi-tech security you have protecting her. And he'll relish the challenge.'

'Yes, but what's the alternative? Let her swan around the country – or abroad – inviting a bullet? That's as good as handing her over to the bastard.'

'Not this guy. He's a planner. He works everything out, down to the last detail. We've seen two examples. The killing of Summers was a blueprint job. He must have done his research, learned his technique with the crossbow, picked his spot in the garden, prepared his sheet of paper with the quote from the poem and the names. Today was the next stage on, even more precision-planned than that. Agreed?'

'Tell me about it!'

'Right. And you may be sure he anticipated that you'd give these people the best protection possible. The classic safe house set-up. By some means or other – let's set that aside for the moment – he knew in advance that he could get inside the safe house and snatch Matthew Porter. Which he did. So isn't it a surefire bet that he has a plan drawn up for Miss Walpurgis?'

The worry-lines on Jimmy Barneston's forehead said it all.

Diamond warmed to his theme. 'Do you see what I'm driving at? Up to now, he's remained ahead of us because he knows we're an institution that works along predictable lines, as easy to see as a mail train coming up the line. Now, I haven't met Anna Walpurgis. I haven't had that pleasure.'

'Plenty have,' murmured Hen.

'OK, she's a lively lady, not the sort to sit at home every night with her knitting. That could work in her favour. She'll be safer from the Mariner in the arms of some admirer than she will being guarded by Special Branch in a safe house.'

'Happier, too,' Hen said.

Barneston was still under the cosh. 'It's too big a risk. Huge.'

'Not so huge as leaving her in a safe house,' Diamond said.

'Even if I believed you, it's not my decision. She's in the care of SO12. They call the shots.'

'Come off it, Jimmy. They're in disarray now. After this cock-up, you can seize the initiative. Tell them you've lost all confidence in their security – which is true.'

'I'm not sure if I want her on my plate.'

'She is already. When this is over, do you think SO12 are going to put up their hands and say it was their fault?'

Barneston looked away and let out a long, troubled breath. He knew Diamond was right; this was obvious in his expression. He'd carry the can if things went wrong. He'd be the plodding idiot who tried to remove these hapless people from the scene and played right into the Mariner's hands. He hunched his shoulders and looked down at his vomit-stained shoes. For a while he was silent, brooding over what had been said. Finally he came out with a kind of confession. 'I thought I could take this on and win. After what's happened today I'm not so sure. Listening to you, I think you've got a better handle on this case than I have. Your way of thinking is different.'

It was a huge admission. Hen said, to assist him, 'It's easier when you're not in close. We can see things you can't.'

He nodded. 'I was too close in every sense.'

'Honey, you couldn't avoid it,' Hen said. 'The Mariner named names, so you can't help meeting the people he targets. You got to know them. You feel responsible in a way we can't.'

'I like them,' he said. 'They have their downside, both of them, but they're real people, very different from each other, but brave, trying to deal with a death threat the best way they can. I won't say they're friends with me, but it's personal, and that's totally new to me as a detective.'

He didn't mention the killing of Emma Tysoe. He didn't need to; it was on all their minds. Emma *had* been his friend, more than just a friend, and she was dead. Maybe he blamed himself for turning down her invitation to spend the day on the beach with him.

Axel Summers was dead. No reason to feel any personal involvement there. But now he faced the strong possibility that Matthew Porter, the man he'd promised to keep under police protection, was dead. Anna Walpurgis remained alive. The responsibility was too much.

'Would you do me a favour?' he asked Diamond. 'Would you meet Anna Walpurgis and tell me if you still think I should give her a free rein?'

He couldn't say more clearly that he was floundering.

'Sure,' Diamond said, 'but not in a safe house, right? Get her out of there fast.'

'Where to?'

'Send her to me in Bath with an overnight bag. I'll see she comes to no harm.'

Hen's eyebrows pricked up sharply, but she said nothing.

'You really mean that?' Barneston said on a note at least an octave higher.

'Then you can get down to what you're good at – detective work.'

After Barneston had gone off to see if the SOCOs had

yet found a distinctive set of tyre marks, Hen asked Diamond, 'Do you think that's wise?'

'In what way wise?' he said. 'In terms of my career, definitely not. I'll have Special Branch as well as Bramshill wanting my head on a plate. In terms of my reputation, well, I've never had much of a reputation. But as a way of wrong-footing the Mariner, it's the best I can think of, and that's the priority now.'

'Entertaining Anna Walpurgis?'

'One thing could lead to another, Hen.'

'You're telling me! What about the trifling matter of the murder you and I are supposed to be investigating?'

'Remind me, would you?'

'Plonker.' She folded her arms. 'I hope you know what you're taking on, squire, because I'm completely foxed.'

It was time to stop being playful. 'We're about to pull in Ken, the boyfriend Emma Tysoe dumped just before she was murdered. My team are working on it. He's a local man, we believe, and it shouldn't be long. When we collar him, you'll be in on the questioning, I hope.'

'It's my case – remember? But what does this have to do with Anna Walpurgis?'

'Walpurgis is the bait.'

'For the Mariner?'

'Yes. He's going to have to adjust his master plan now. He expected her to be under Special Branch protection, probably moved from one safe house to another in the hope of confusing him. Instead, she's coming to Bath.'

Hen said, 'He'll find out, as sure as snakes crawl.'

'And follow her.'

'You don't have to look so happy at the prospect.'

He raised his forefinger. 'Right. But Bath is my patch. I know it better than he does. The odds have changed a bit. That's how we'll pinch him, Hen.'

She pondered that for a moment. 'It's bloody dangerous.'

'For Walpurgis, you mean? So what's new? She's under threat of death already.'

'But you're right about one thing,' she conceded. 'You're forcing the Mariner's hand. I've no idea how you'll cope with this crazy bimbo, but the show definitely moves to Bath, leaving Jimmy Barneston here in Sussex looking at tyre marks.'

17

Bath was travel-brochure bright as Diamond drove in from Weston the next morning. Innocent, even. Who would be so coarse as to think about crime in surroundings such as these? You couldn't imagine a mugger on the streets, let alone a serial killer. The tall trees in Queen Square were thick with gently stirring foliage at this time of year, softening the views across the green towards the corner house, number thirteen, where much of *Northanger Abbey* was written. 'My mother hankers after the Square dreadfully,' Jane Austen wrote in 1801. While Diamond was unlikely ever to hanker after Queen Square or any other, he did feel a flutter of unease about his plan to lure the Mariner to the city.

'Back to reality,' he called across to Keith Halliwell when they both happened to park at the same time behind the ugliest building in Bath, the Manvers Street police station. 'What's been happening?'

'Progress, guv.'

They went through the code-operated door and started upstairs towards the incident room.

'Come on, then,' Diamond said after giving Halliwell ample time to say more.

'I think Ingeborg would like to tell you herself. She worked her little butt off yesterday.'

'Keep me in suspense, then.'

Most of the team were already in there clustered

around John Leaman, who was telling a joke. At the sight of their burly superior, people sidled back to their desks.

'Did you want to give them the punchline, John?' Diamond offered.

'They can wait, guv.'

He looked to his right. 'Well, Ingeborg?'

The new face in CID glanced up and batted the long lashes. 'Hi, guv.'

Halliwell said quickly, 'Don't make a meal of it, Inge. I told him to expect something.'

'Oh.' She smiled. 'Well, I finally nailed Ken.'

'Tell me more.'

'His name is Bellman – Kenneth Bellman. He works for an IT firm based in Batheaston.'

'A nightie firm? Our suspect? What are we talking here – black lace, see-through, baby doll or plain old winceyette?'

'IT,' Halliwell said through the laughter. 'He's in information technology.'

'Pity. Not much glamour in that. As what?'

'A consultant,' Ingeborg said.

'I've met a few of them in my time, borrowing your watch to tell you what the time is.'

Ingeborg smiled. 'In the IT business it means anyone who isn't actually employed by the company, but does a job for them. An outside expert.' She stopped and gave him a wary look. 'You're going to say a window-cleaner, aren't you, guv? I know it.'

'OK, let's call an amnesty,' he said. 'How did you get onto him – through the credit card slips I suggested?'

'No. It turns out he paid cash. They had his name wrong in the reservations book. I spent ages trying to trace somebody with the name of Cableman. On the phone he must have told them K. Bellman.'

'Easy mistake.' He smiled. 'I can overlook it. Cableman

wouldn't be a bad name for a computer nerd, now I think about it. What else do we know?'

'He works for a city firm called Knowhow & Fix. Lives in digs in a house on Bathwick Hill, about halfway up on the left-hand side.'

'Bit of a climb. Does he have wheels?'

'I expect so. I couldn't tell you for sure.'

'But you know why I asked?'

'Yes, guv. The drive to Wightview Sands.'

He nodded. 'So have you spoken to him?'

Halliwell said, 'We thought you'd want first crack at him.'

'You thought right.' He showed an upturned thumb to Ingeborg. 'Nice work.'

She asked, 'Can I bring him in, guv?' – and couldn't conceal her eagerness.

She'd led with her chin, never a wise tactic with Diamond, but he restrained himself and shook his head. 'Not yet. I promised DCI Mallin, our colleague from Bognor, that I'd give her the chance to come in on this. More important than that, I want the SP on this guy before we see him. Keith, see what you can get without alerting him or his employers. Do it discreetly. I don't want him to know we're onto him.'

'Now, guv?'

'No time like the present.'

He called Hen and told her the news. She offered to come right away, so he explained about getting some background first, and she agreed it was right to do the job properly. Until this morning, Ken had been just a name, his only known achievement the bedding of Emma Tysoe.

'Probably tomorrow,' he said. 'I'll keep you posted.'

'I wish I could report some success at this end,' Hen went on to say. 'I was hoping my lot would have found Mr Laver by now, but he's vanished into thin air.'

'That figures. They called him Rocket, you know.'

'Who?'

'The tennis player.'

'Give over, Peter. And to make matters worse, Emerson has not been seen on the beach for a couple of days as well. I've got visions of chasing Aussies in camper vans all over Europe. Let's hope your Ken puts his hand up to the murder and saves me the trouble.'

If only it were so simple, Diamond thought. After he'd put the phone down, he said to Ingeborg, 'Do you know much about IT?'

'Not a lot, guv.'

'What did they say it stands for?'

'Information technology.'

'It was on the tip of my tongue. Supposed to be the answer to everything, isn't it? Taking over our lives?'

She said, 'Look around you, guv. We depend on it.'

Keeping his eyes resolutely off the hardware on every side, he said, 'I can't agree with that. They're tools, nothing more. We always had office machinery. Typewriters. Dictaphones.'

A voice behind him murmured, 'The abacus.'

'Did you say something, John?'

'Adding machines, guv.'

'Right. Just because they're all contained in one machine it doesn't mean we're slaves to it.'

'I said we depend on it,' Ingeborg stressed, returning him to the point she'd made. 'If this lot crashed, we'd be in trouble.'

'You're right about that,' he conceded, and added jovially, 'We might have to ask the Cableman to fix it. I wouldn't want his job. It must be tedious, staring at screens all day. Then they go home and watch TV.'

'Sometimes they don't leave home,' she said. 'They work from their own PC.'

'I'm not surprised Emma Tysoe found this fellow boring. What can he know about the real world, sitting in front of his screen? How does he make friends, meet women?'

'There are chatlines.'

'That's not meeting them.'

'I expect he makes an effort to get out. You'd have to.'

'We don't know, do we?' he said.

'I could chat up his colleagues if you like,' she offered. 'Face to face.'

'Not at this stage. We don't want him finding out we're interested. Let's keep the chatting up in reserve.' He didn't doubt Ingeborg's ability there. 'Why don't you check him on the PNC? See if he's got form.'

If she noted the irony of this suggestion, she had the good sense not to take it up with him.

Later in the morning he took a call from Jimmy Barneston. The shell-shocked Jimmy of yesterday sounded more in control. More deferential, too.

'I thought you'd like to know I slept on your advice and decided it made sense. I've called a press conference for this afternoon.'

'Good move. Take the initiative away from the killer.'

'I'm going to tell them just about everything except the third name on the Mariner's list. You know who I mean?' Clearly he didn't trust the phone, and he was probably right.

'I'm a detective. I can work it out,' Diamond said. 'Speaking of that person, have you told her about Porter – I mean a well-known sports personality – being snatched?'

'Not yet. Oh, fuck, I'll have to now, won't I? Don't want her hearing it first on the telly.'

'Have you moved her?'

'Er . . . yes. She's in another – em – place.'

'A *safe* place?' Diamond spoke the words in a tone of dread.

'I, em . . .' The voice trailed off.

Diamond waited, and then said, 'That's not a good idea, Jimmy. Have you told her about my offer?'

'Not yet. She doesn't know anything yet.'

'When you break the bad news about Porter being snatched you can tell her my offer is the good news.'

'All right.'

'You will mention it?'

'I'm still thinking it over.'

'Don't spend too long thinking. You could regret it. I guess there's nothing new on the Mariner? Did the house-to-house achieve anything?'

'No. And the treadmarks aren't sharp enough to help. Forensics are looking at them, but they told me not to expect much. They tested the steering wheel for DNA and they reckon he wore gloves. He's ultra-careful. We haven't even found what type of gas he used.'

'Are both of the guards recovering?'

'They were sent home last night. I've spoken to them. They added nothing to what we know already.'

'You may get some help from the public after the media get to work on it.'

'I won't hold my breath.' He asked how the search for Emma Tysoe's killer was going and Diamond gave him the news about Ken Bellman. They agreed to keep in touch.

After putting the phone down, Diamond was fidgety. He sat back in his chair and fiddled with a stapler, shooting at least a dozen across the desk. Certain things were starting to go his way, but plenty could still go wrong, and probably would. His team was up to the challenge of Ken Bellman. If the man was guilty they'd have him, the mug who lost in love and kicked back. But the Mariner was in a different bracket. No passion there. He was a class act, a cerebral killer, calculating every move. If he came to Bath, he wouldn't come blindly. He'd estimate the risks and minimise them. How would the likes of Keith and Ingeborg cope with a professional assassin?

Soon they had to be told. He had no hesitation pitting himself against a serial killer, but it was asking a lot of Ingeborg, little more than a rookie, and Keith, dependable as the days of the week, but not the brightest star in the firmament. John Leaman was quicker, but still inexperienced for a sergeant.

For a few indulgent moments he daydreamed about having Julie Hargreaves back on the team, Julie, the sidekick who'd taken one kick too many and asked for a transfer. She was an original thinker, as well as a check on his own lapses and excesses. He was still in touch, and she'd been a tower of strength after Steph was murdered. Still, she'd made her position clear about working with him ever again, and it was no use wanting the impossible. You play the cards you're dealt with.

Towards midday Ingeborg reported her findings on the PNC: no findings at all. Kenneth Bellman had led a blameless life apparently.

'Bellman, Bellman – why does the name seem familiar?' he said.

'*The Hunting of the Snark*?' she suggested.

'The what?'

'It's a poem by Lewis Carroll. A nonsense poem. The Bellman was the main character.'

He gave her a bemused look. 'No, it can't be that. You read poetry, do you, Ingeborg?'

'Sometimes.'

'Do you happen to know *The Rime of the Ancient Mariner*?'

'Bits, guv.'

'I don't mean know it by heart. Have you read it?' With pride in the performance he recited those first two lines: '"It is an ancient Mariner / And he stoppeth one of three."'

Innocent of the tightrope she was walking, Ingeborg completed the verse. '"By thy long grey beard and glittering eye / Now wherefore stopp'st thou me?"'

But her boss's reaction was positive. 'Hidden depths. Tell me, what was it about the albatross that made it such a big deal in the poem?'

'It's a bird of good omen, guv. Should have brought good luck to his ship, but he shot it.'

'With his crossbow. Then everything went pear-shaped?'

'Yes.'

'Right. I can understand that.' He sighed softly and shook his head. Some things he would never understand. 'It's a strange thing, Ingeborg. Since coming to Bath I've had to mug up so much English literature.'

'Yes?' She sensed he was unburdening himself of something she ought to know about.

'Famous writers keep cropping up. Jane Austen, Mary Shelley, and now Coleridge.'

'Are you doing an Open University degree, guv?' she innocently asked.

'Christ, no. Whatever put that idea in your head?'

Keith Halliwell was back by lunchtime and Diamond took him for a bite and a pint at Brown's, just up the street on the site of the old city police station in Orange Grove, an Italianate Palazzo-style building so much easier on the eye than their present place of work. 'So what do we know about Ken Bellman?' he asked, when they were settled in one of the squishy sofas upstairs.

'There's not a lot to report, guv,' Halliwell told him. 'He's been around for about six months. Gets his paper – the *Independent* – from a shop on Bathwick Hill, and also buys computer magazines and chocolate. He dresses casually in polo shirts and baggy trousers with lots of pockets.'

'Where's he from?'

'The north, I was told. He boasts a bit about the life up there being better than anywhere else.'

'Sounds like a Yorkshireman, all mouth and trousers. Why come south, if it's so much better up there? Anything else, Keith? Is he a driver?'

'Yes, he has an old BMW that he services himself.'

'Useful to know. Colour?'

'He's white.'

'The car, Keith, the car.'

'Oh, I didn't discover that. It's a series 3 model.'

'Description?'

'Thirtyish, about five nine, with a mop of dark hair.'

'You mean curly?' Diamond said, thinking of the man in the black T-shirt.

'It's what *they* mean, not me, guv,' Halliwell said, with reason on his side but at the risk of nettling his boss. 'And they said a mop.'

'You didn't catch a glimpse of him, I suppose?'

'He wasn't about.'

'He hasn't done a runner?'

'No. He was at the shop for his paper this morning, eight thirtyish. That's the routine.'

It was decision time. 'Wait for tomorrow and then bring him in late morning. I want to give DCI Mallin a chance to get here.'

'When you say "bring him in", do you mean by invitation?'

'Oh, yes. No coercion, Keith, unless he's really stroppy.

We need cooperation at this point, help with our enquiries, right?'

'Shall I ask Ingeborg to fetch him?'

'Why not? She's got to get experience. Pick some muscle to go with her, but let her do the talking. Tell them to be there early, keeping watch on his movements, the walk to the paper shop, and so on. We want to make certain where he is. Another thing, Keith.'

'Guv?'

'Some office furniture found its way to the top corridor. It was stored originally in the room we're using as our incident room. Georgina isn't happy about it. See if you can shift it somewhere else.'

'Right.'

'Don't look like that, Keith. It's priority, OK?'

'OK.'

'Directly we get back?'

'If you say so, guv.'

'And can you get the team together this afternoon, say around three? There's some news about to break that I want them to hear from me.'

They listened in silence to his prosaic, almost plodding account of the Mariner's murderous agenda. Officially it was news to them, but their faces didn't register much shock. Most, if not all, were familiar with the contents of the decrypted files. Only when he started telling them about the gas raid on the safe house did the interest quicken significantly. This was news to them, and it was pretty sensational. Yet no one interrupted. They were deeply curious to know where this was leading, how it affected them personally. Like the best storytellers, he kept them in suspense to the very end. 'Yesterday, after the snatching of Matthew Porter, I spent some time with the SIO on the case, DCI Jimmy Barneston. I think I've convinced him that the third of the Mariner's targets, Anna Walpurgis, isn't safe any more in a so-called safe house. A radical rethink is necessary, to take the initiative away from the Mariner. I suggested bringing Ms Walpurgis to Bath.'

He paused, letting this sink in. There was a nervous cough from someone. A couple of people shifted in their chairs. No one was ready to say that the boss had flipped, but doubt was in the air.

Halliwell was the first to speak. 'Do we have a safe house in Bath?'

'No – and that's the point, Keith, to do something he isn't expecting. It buys us a little time.'

'Don't you think he'll find out and follow her here?'

'I'm sure he will. That's OK by me. He'll be on our territory.'

'It's a hell of a risk, guv.'

He nodded. 'That's why I'm telling you. Any of you could get involved as well. The man is dangerous and single-minded. Stand in his way, and you risk being eliminated.'

'Where will she stay?' Leaman asked.

'Yet to be decided. She'll have a say in the decision.'

'She's a fireball, isn't she?'

'So I've heard.'

Ingeborg said, 'She could stay with me, if you like.' The first to volunteer again, so keen to make her mark.

'I'll keep it in mind.' At the back of my mind, he thought. 'I brought this to your attention because the main facts of the case are being made public at a press conference as we speak. The papers will be full of it tomorrow.'

'Anna Walpurgis included?' Leaman asked.

'No. For obvious reasons that's classified information. Don't discuss it with anyone. But the Mariner will make the headlines, which will please him no end.'

'Give him enough rope.'

'That's the general idea, John. Any other questions?'

'How does all this link up with Emma Tysoe?' Ingeborg asked.

'You put your finger on it. We don't know. She was working on a profile of the Mariner, so in a sense she was shoved into the firing line. That was my early assumption. Now I've veered in the other direction.'

'Because of Ken?' He was reminded of her sharp questioning in the days when she worked as a freelance journalist. She'd put him through the grinder more than once. Bright and keen as she was, he didn't want her dominating the case conferences.

'Not especially. We'll find out more about him tomorrow. No, I've come to think of the Mariner as the kind of murderer who plans his crime like an architect, every detail worked out, measured and costed. But the strangling of Emma Tysoe wasn't planned. Couldn't have been. She only made up her mind to go to the beach the evening before she visited Jimmy Barneston. And the murderer couldn't have known in advance which section of the beach she would choose, and if she used a windbreak and how close other people would be sitting. It had to be an opportunist killing. The variables would have horrified the Mariner.'

'So Emma wasn't killed because of the job she did,' Ingeborg tried to sum up.

'I didn't say that. I said it was opportunist. She could have been spotted by someone she'd fingered in the past.'

'Pretty unlikely.'

He eyed her sharply. 'Why?'

'They're all inside serving long sentences, aren't they?'

'That's something you can check for me.'

She'd walked into that one. There were smiles around the room.

Except from Ingeborg, who wouldn't shut up. 'But she hasn't been doing the profiling all that long. What is it – four or five years at most?'

'Yes, and some of the sentencing leaves a lot to be desired. See what you can dig up for me.'

'Personally, I think Ken is a better bet.'

'Personally, I think we've heard enough from you, constable. Bramshill gave me a list of all the cases she worked on. You'll find it on my desk.'

He brought the meeting to a close. Ingeborg, flicking her blond hair in a way that left no doubt as to her annoyance, stepped in the direction of his office. He ambled after her.

'Is this the way you run things?' she asked when he caught up with her. 'Anyone with a different opinion gets clobbered?'

'Don't try me,' he told her. 'You know where you went wrong in there. You've got a good brain, Ingeborg, or you wouldn't be on the team. Use it.'

'That's what I was trying to do.'

'You're not press any more. You're a very new member of CID. Have you heard any of them talk to me like you just did?'

She took a breath and hesitated. 'No, guv.'

'Getting along with them is just as important as keeping on the right side of me. At present they're giving you the benefit of the doubt. You're new and eager to impress, but you must learn to do it with more subtlety. Remember the pesky kids at school who sat at the front and were forever putting up their hands to answer questions?'

A little sigh escaped. 'That was me.'

He just about managed to conceal his amusement. 'Well, have the good sense to see it from other people's points of view. Theirs, and mine.'

She nodded. 'I'll try, guv. Thanks.' The blue eyes

flashed an appeal. 'Do you still want me to check that list?'

'You bet I do.'

After she'd gone, he reached for the phone and called Hen. He'd promised to let her know when Ken Bellman was being brought in for questioning. He didn't get that far.

'I was just about to call you,' she said. 'We've all been glued to the TV, watching the news breaking. Haven't you?'

'Jimmy Barneston's press conference?'

'That's what we expected to see. It's been overtaken. Petersfield police have found the body of a young white male on a golf course.'

'Matthew Porter?'

'Nobody is saying yet, but of course it's him. They haven't said what he died of, but they're treating it as murder.'

18

The body had been found by the greenkeeper, out early checking whether a fresh cut was necessary. After a warm summer's night there was barely a hint of moisture in the turf and he was thinking about mowing some of the fairways when he made the discovery. It was face up in one of the bunkers at the eighteenth, close to the clubhouse but hidden from view by the slope. Definitely male, definitely young and definitely Matthew Porter, a sensational fact confirmed by the early risers who came over for a look before the police erected a tent around the body. The corpse was fully clothed, in jeans and a polo shirt. There was a hole in the side of the head.

This was a local golf club, near Petersfield. Nobody of Matt Porter's eminence had ever played the course, so it was something of a coup to have an Open winner at the eighteenth, even in this inactive state. Everyone agreed that it was a dreadful tragedy, but there were strong undercurrents of excitement. There were no complaints that the day's playing arrangements were interrupted. Instead of teeing off for the final hole, players marched up the fairway to the clubhouse, passing as close as they were allowed to the crime scene. As the news spread, a number of members came in specially. The bar did good business.

The police and forensic officers went through their routines. Access to the scene was easy, this being the eighteenth and so close to the parking area around the clubhouse. Obviously the killer had been able to drive to within a short distance of the bunker. It was established soon that the body must have been killed elsewhere and dumped here.

The hole in the victim's head was a challenge to the pathologist who examined the body at the scene. Apparently it was not made by a bullet. His first thought was that some kind of stud gun may have been used, the sort used in the construction industry to fire steel pins into masonry. His other suggestion was an abbattoir gun, with a captive-pin mechanism. At this stage of the day the press conference announcing the crossbow shooting of Axel Summers had not taken place.

In fact, Jimmy Barneston's big occasion that afternoon turned out to be an embarrassment. He had spent the second half of the morning in the safe house with Anna Walpurgis – an experience on a par with lion-taming – and then arrived late and marched straight into the briefing room before anyone informed him what had been found at Petersfield. A short way into his opening statement one of the reporters asked him to confirm whether the body at the golf course was that of Matthew Porter.

Barneston stiffened like a cat that has wandered into a dog show. There was total disarray. One of his colleagues took his arm and steered him away from the cluster of microphones. He went into a huddle with other officers. Finally he returned red-faced and said, trying to sound as if he had always known about it, 'The body found this morning has not yet been formally identified. Until this formality is complete, I am not at liberty to comment. I shall continue with my statement about the murder of Mr Axel Summers.'

Of course the press didn't let him escape so lightly. He was hammered with questions about Porter and the identity of the third name on the Mariner's hit list. In the end he conceded that Porter was probably the dead man, but staunchly refused to name Anna Walpurgis. He reeled out of there, eyes bulging, and went looking for someone to jump all over.

Hen Mallin agreed with Diamond that the questioning of Ken Bellman had to take priority over what was happening in Petersfield. By now, Matt Porter's body would be at the mortuary and the forensic team would have searched the scene and picked up anything of interest. Best leave Jimmy Barneston to sift the evidence.

That evening she drove straight from work to the beach at Wightview Sands, partly because she wanted to refresh her memory of the scene, and also because a lone walk (and smoke) by the sea is as good a way as any of getting one's thoughts in order. This had been a pig of a case. There was still precious little evidence, and even that was circumstantial. Emma Tysoe's files had helped, but they weren't as telling as a fingerprint or a scrap of DNA. If Ken Bellman put his hand up to the crime, he'd deserve a pat on the head and a vote of thanks from his interrogators. More likely, he'd deny everything, and Peter Diamond – known to be tough in the interview room – would give him a roasting. Hen didn't care for confessions under duress.

She drove up to the car park gate just before seven. The man on duty asked for a pound and she said she was a police officer.

'How do I know that?' he asked.

'For God's sake, man. I'm investigating the murder. I've been here on and off for a couple of weeks.'

'I was on, you know,' he said.

'What?'

'The day when the woman was murdered. I was on

duty, but I can't tell you who did it. Can't see a thing from here.'

She was hearing an echo of a voice she seemed to know, an odd way of spacing the words, with almost no intonation. Familiar, too, was the self-importance, as if it mattered whether he had been on duty. She looked at him sitting in his cabin, and didn't recognise his brown eyes and black hair, brushed back and glossy. She normally had a good memory for faces.

'I'll show you my ID, if you insist,' she said, reaching behind for her bag.

He did insist. He waited until she produced it, and only then pressed the gate mechanism.

'And what's your name?' Hen asked, before driving through.

'I'm Garth. Don't be too long, will you? We close at eight thirty.'

It came to her as she was cruising up the narrow road that runs alongside the beach. She did know the voice. She'd only ever spoken to him on the phone. *Am I speaking to the person responsible for the murder? . . . Are you sure you're in charge?* He was the jobsworth who'd phoned in when Dr Shiena Wilkinson had turned up looking for her Range Rover. The reason she hadn't seen him was that she'd sent Stella to deal with it.

She thought of Garth, the strip-cartoon muscleman who'd gone on for years in the *Daily Mirror*. Parents little realise what their son will grow up into when they give him the same name as a super-hero. Maybe trying to live up to the name turned him funny.

After parking on the turf near the beach café she found the gap between beach huts that led to the lifeguard lookout post, above where Emma Tysoe's body had been found. You wouldn't have known it was a murder scene now. Children were busy in the sand where the body was

found, digging a system of waterways, ~~~~~~~~~~~~~~~~~~~~
in the evening sun. The tidal action clea~~~~~~~~~~~
If the strangling had happened higher up, o~~~~~~
the site would have been turned into a shrine, m~~~
with flowers and wreaths.

Most of the day's visitors had left. Nobody remained
at the lifeguard platform at this stage of the day, so she
stepped onto it herself to see how much they could
observe from there. It was a simple wooden structure that
needed repairing in places. A position well chosen for
views of most of the beach. Yet they wouldn't have been
high enough to see over a windbreak to the person lying
behind it.

She stepped off and moved down the shelf of stones
to the sand, trying to picture the scene on the day of the
murder. Emma Tysoe had spread out her towel and
erected her windbreak a short way in front of the Smiths.
The French family were to the right of the Smiths and
three teenage girls to the left. At some stage of the
morning, the man in the black T-shirt had come strolling
along the sand and tried to engage Emma in conversation, even offered to join her. She'd given him his
marching orders. This encounter – witnessed by Olga
Smith – was the one possible lead they had apart from
Emma's own files. T-shirt man was still the best bet, deeply
angered, perhaps, by the brush-off, and returning later
to kill the woman who rejected him. It would be an
extreme reaction, and a risky one to carry out, but rejec-
tion is a powerful motive.

Hen picked her way carefully over the children's digging
and out to a stretch of sand beyond the breakwaters, where
she could walk freely. She lit one of her small cigars and
let her thoughts turn to Peter Diamond. Up to now, he'd
proved less of an ogre than she'd expected. He was
brusque at times, but funny, too, and willing to listen. He

misery guts, like so many senior detectives. She couldn't fault the way he'd conducted the case so far, keeping her informed of each development. Mind, he was a risk-taker. This plan of his to take over the protection of Anna Walpurgis could so easily go wrong. It gave him what he'd wanted all along, a legitimate reason to be involved. But what resources did he have in Bath, and what guarantee that a spirited woman wouldn't upset everything? Hen could only hope he had a strategy. He'd talked of Walpurgis being 'bait' to the Mariner. He'd set his heart on catching this killer, but at what cost?

One of the problems with all this concentration on the Mariner was that there was a big incentive to wrap up the Emma Tysoe case as fast as possible. Hen wasn't going to allow Diamond to cut corners. The murder of Emma was a Bognor Regis case – hers. If Ken Bellman proved beyond doubt to be the killer, well and good. But if there were doubts, she wouldn't let Diamond ride roughshod over them.

So she liked the man, enjoyed his company, admired his independent ways, yet couldn't rest all of her confidence in him. The loss of his wife must have cast him adrift, even though he appeared strong. The shock was bound to have wounded him. She suspected he was hiding the pain.

She picked up a flat stone and skimmed it across the surface of the water, watching it bounce several times before meeting a wave and disappearing, a trick she'd tried many times but never before mastered. Typical, she thought, that I do it when no one is here to see. She continued her walk as far as the flagpole at East Head. If she walked any farther she'd be late getting back to her car, and she had no confidence Garth would let her out of the car park.

Georgina Dallymore, the Assistant Chief Constable, was

on her guard that morning. It wasn't like Peter Diamond to knock on her door and ask if she could spare a few minutes. He was the man who avoided her at all costs. He'd once nipped into the ladies' room and locked himself in a cubicle when he spotted her approaching along a corridor.

She folded her arms and rotated her chair a little. 'To what do we owe this, Peter?'

'I expect you noticed the furniture disappeared from the corridor, ma'am?'

'No,' she said with a faint flush of pink. 'I hadn't noticed. Do I have you to thank for that?'

'No problem.'

'It had to be sorted. It was a fire hazard.'

'You can enjoy your cruise now. When are you off?'

She relaxed a little. He was only there to get some credit for doing a good turn. 'Tomorrow, actually.'

'All set, then?'

'Pretty well.'

As if it was mere politeness, he asked, 'What's happening to the cat? That handsome white Persian?'

'Sultan. You know about Sultan?'

Everyone who'd been in her office knew about Sultan. There was a photo on her desk of this mound of fur with fierce blue eyes and a snub nose.

'Sultan, yes,' Diamond said.

'He has to go into a cattery, unfortunately. He doesn't care for it at all, but you can't let them run your life.'

'Shame. Quite a change in his routine.' He paused. 'I don't suppose he'll suffer.'

'*Suffer?*' A cloud of concern passed across Georgina's face. 'I should hope not. The place is well recommended, and very expensive.'

'He doesn't know that. Has he been there before?'

'No, this will be the first time.'

'Poor old Sultan.' Diamond picked up the photo in its gilt frame. 'I've got a cat myself, just a moggy, but a character. They hate their routine being messed about. Personally, I favour having a house sitter if I go away. They stay in your house and look after the place and feed the cat as well. It's nicer for your pet and you can relax knowing someone is there.'

'Ideally, that sounds a good solution,' Georgina agreed.

'Bit of a holiday for the sitter as well. In a city like Bath, house sitting is no hardship. You're convenient for everything in Bennett Street.'

Now she frowned. This was becoming a touch too personal. 'How do you know where I live?'

'You gave a party not long after you arrived. I came with Steph. Very good evening it was.'

She looked relieved to have her memory jogged. 'My "At Home". It slipped my mind.'

'A house sitter would jump at the chance.'

'It's a lovely idea, Peter. Unfortunately, it's too late for me to start looking for someone now.'

'I wouldn't say that.'

Georgina tried to appear unmoved, but he could see she was all attentiveness.

'If you'd like one, I may be able to help,' he offered. 'I know of a lady shortly coming to Bath who would gladly look after your home – and Sultan – for no charge at all.'

'No charge?'

'A chance to stay in Bennett Street would be reward enough.'

'Well, I don't know,' Georgina said. 'Who is she?'

He sidestepped the question, letting his sales pitch sink in. 'All you'd need to do is get in some tins of his favourite catmeat.'

'I bought those anyway,' she said, and there was something in her eyes she tried not to have there, a strong desire to clinch this deal and save herself some money.

'Then you're laughing. You may have heard of her – Anna Walpurgis.'

The eyes widened. 'The pop star?'

'As was. More a lady of leisure now. Very used to living in nice surroundings, until recently. Some maniac threatened her life and she's been stuck in a safe house being looked after by Special Branch for some time. It's Salman Rushdie all over again. She got so bored. It would do everyone a good turn if she could escape to Bath for a week.'

'Anna Walpurgis.' Georgina repeated the name, and there was a discernible note of awe. The idea of such a celebrity coming to stay in one's house had definite attraction. 'She wouldn't give parties?'

'Good Lord, no. She's keeping a low profile.'

'Is she under guard?'

'Not any more. It's a step towards a normal life. I can keep an eye on her, make sure she's able to cope.'

'Let me think about this.'

'Yes, of course, ma'am. It's a big decision, letting a stranger have the run of your home, but I've never heard a word of scandal about the lady. And I dare say Sultan would approve.' With a display of care, he replaced the photo on her desk.

At ten thirty, Ingeborg reported to Diamond that Ken Bellman was ready for interview.

'Did he give any problems?'

'He came like a lamb.'

'Say anything?'

'Just nodded and said, "All right."'

'Resigned to it, maybe. Has DCI Mallin arrived from Bognor yet?'

'Down in the canteen, guv, tucking into a fried breakfast.'

'Wise woman.' He went down to join her.

While Hen had a smoke, and Diamond a doughnut and coffee, they agreed on a strategy. Hen would ask the first questions, with Diamond chipping in when the moment was right. With so much experience between them, they didn't need the nice-cop–nasty-cop approach. They'd know how to pitch it.

Bellman had a paper cup of coffee in his hands. He slopped some on his jeans as his interrogators came in.

'Careful,' Hen said. 'You could ruin your prospects that way.'

'It's OK.' He didn't smile. He looked nervous. Sweatmarks showed around the armpits of his blue tanktop shirt. He placed the coffee well to one side.

'Finish your drink, love,' Hen said.

'I'm fine.' Yet he couldn't hide a ripple of tension across his cheek. The description they'd had from Olga Smith was spot on. Latin looks, definitely. Strong features. Broad shoulders, narrow hips, dark, curly hair that looked as if it never needed combing.

Hen and Diamond took their seats. Hen, unashamedly friendly, thanked him for coming in and apologised for the formality of asking his name and stating for the tape that he had been invited to attend of his own free will to assist with the enquiry into the death of Dr Emma Tysoe.

He blinked twice at the name.

'So may I call you Ken?' Hen asked after she'd identified herself and Diamond.

'Whatever you want.'

'You live locally, I gather. Do you work in Bath?'

'Batheaston. I'm an IT consultant.'

'Forgive my ignorance. What's that exactly?'

'I'm with a firm called Knowhow & Fix. Kind of

troubleshooters really. If a firm has a computer problem we do our best to sort it.'

'So people are always pleased to see you?'

'Usually.'

'Is it nine to five?'

'Not really. It can be any time. When they want help, they want help.'

'So you turn out in the evening sometimes?'

'I have done.'

'And – through the wonders of modern telecommunications – can you sometimes fix a problem from home?'

'Some of the work can be done on my own PC, yes.'

'Ken, this is beginning to sound like a job interview,' Hen said with a smile, 'but I'm getting a picture of how you spend your time. I suppose you need a car in this job.'

'That's essential.'

'What do you drive?'

'A BMW.'

'Nice.'

'It's quite old, actually, but it belongs to me.'

'Reliable?'

'I think so.'

'How long have you owned it?'

'Five or six years. I bought it secondhand.'

'Before you came to Bath?'

'Yes.'

'When *did* you come here?'

'Just before Christmas.'

'And where were you before that?'

'The job? SW1.'

'London?'

'Right. But I was living in Putney.'

'What sort of work? Similar?'

'Not quite the same. I was a techie – technical support programmer.'

'You've been doing this sort of work for some time, then?'

'Since university.'

'Where was that?'

'Liverpool.'

'Computer science, I suppose?'

'Pretty close. Electronic engineering. I picked up my computer skills later, when I was doing my MSc. In the end IT proved more marketable than pure electronics.'

Hen nodded. 'Seems to come into every job, doesn't it? Changing the subject, Ken, how long have you known Emma Tysoe?'

His hands felt for the arms of the chair and gripped them. 'About ten years.'

'As long as that?'

'I met her when we were students at Liverpool. She read psychology there. We went out a few times. I liked her.'

'And it developed into something?'

He shook his head. 'Not at the time. We were friendly, and that was all. After she left to continue her studies in the south, we lost touch. It was pure chance that brought us together again. I didn't know she was living in Bath until I met her one day in the library a few months ago. There was a lot to talk about, so we went for a drink together, caught up on old times, and what we'd each done since then. It blossomed into something stronger. Well, we weren't living together, but we got serious, if you know what I mean.'

'You slept with her?'

'Right.'

'And it lasted some time?' Hen asked with the implicit suggestion that the friendship came to an end.

'Some weeks.'

'Can you be more specific?'

He frowned. 'I didn't keep count, if that's what you

mean. Six or seven weeks, probably.'

'Was it a loving relationship?'

'I thought I loved her, yes.'

'You *thought*?'

'That's what I said.'

'Love is more about feelings than thoughts, isn't it?' Hen asked.

'I suppose you're right. I'm a scientist. I analyse things, including my feelings. My estimation was that I loved Emma. It's not easy, assessing your own emotions, trying to understand how genuine they are.'

'I'd say if you had to assess them, it's questionable whether you really were in love,' Hen said.

'And I say if you can't be honest with yourself how can you be honest with the person you're sleeping with?'

It was a neat riposte. Hen tried to make use of it. 'Was she honest with you?'

'I believe she was.'

'Did love come into it?'

'On her side? I don't know what was in her mind. She said she enjoyed being with me. We had Liverpool in common, our student life. Lots of good memories.'

'No more than that?'

'It was enough to be going on with.'

'So is it fair to say, Ken, that you were keener than she was?'

He frowned a little. 'Is that a trick question?'

'Why should it be?' Hen said.

'Let's face it. Emma was murdered. If I come across as the guy who pestered her for sex, it doesn't look good for me, does it? We were good friends, we slept together a few times because we wanted to.'

'I'm not trying to trick you, ducky. We just want to get the picture right. Did she have other friends? Did you go round in a group?'

'There were only the two of us. She wasn't the kind of person who enjoyed being in company.'

'I expect she had friends at work – in the university.'

'If she had, she didn't talk about them.'

'So you and she spent the time in each other's company – doing what?'

He shrugged. 'What people do. Pubs, the cinema, a meal out sometimes.'

'And at the end of an evening, would you go back to her flat in Great Pulteney Street?'

'A few times. Or else she'd come to my place.'

'Not long before her death, you took her for a meal at Popjoy's. Is that right?'

He gave a nod.

'Would it be true to say the evening didn't go according to plan?'

There was a delay before he responded. 'How do you know that?'

'We're detectives,' Hen said. 'It's our job. We'd like to hear your take on the evening.'

He stared into the palm of his left hand, as if he was reading the lines. More likely, Peter Diamond thought, watching him, he didn't want eye contact. 'It started well enough. It was a very good meal. Towards the end she complained of a headache and blamed the wine. There was nothing wrong with it. She said some wines had that effect on her, letting me know, in a way, that I should have let her see the list instead of going ahead and ordering. She asked the waiter for an Alka Seltzer, which I found deeply embarrassing in a smart restaurant. Then we had to wait a long time for a taxi. I thought we could walk home – it isn't far to her place – but she was wearing unsuitable shoes. I seemed to be saying the wrong thing at every turn.'

Diamond said, to keep the confidences coming, 'We've all had evenings like that.'

Bellman gave a shrug and a sigh. 'Well, it got no better. Back in her flat I made some coffee and asked if the headache was easing off and she said I was only asking because I wanted my money's worth, which was pretty hurtful. I think I told her so. She was in a black mood, for sure. I can't cope with women when they get like that. I left soon after.'

Hen asked, 'Was it a break-up?'

'I didn't think so at the time. I tried calling her next day to see if I was still in the doghouse. I had to leave a message on the answerphone, which wasn't easy. I think I just said I hoped she was feeling better and would she call me. But she didn't. When I eventually got through to her some time in the evening, she told me straight out that she didn't want to see me any more because she was seeing someone else. I was shattered. Gutted.' The pain of the memory showed in his face.

'Did she say who?' Hen asked.

'No. Just "someone". I reacted badly. I'm ashamed now. I called her some ugly names. A rush of blood, I guess. She slammed down the phone and I can't blame her for that.' He shook his head. 'Wish I could take back what I said. Death is so final.'

The self-recrimination didn't impress Diamond. With a glance towards Hen, he took up the questioning. 'Did you hear from her again?'

'Not on the phone.'

'You'd said these things – called her names – so did you regard the break as final?'

'No. I'd lost control. I wanted her back. Thinking about it after that phone call, I wondered if she was speaking the truth about going out with someone else. I'd got no hint of another man up to then. I wondered if she'd made it up – invented him, in other words – to hurt me in the heat of the moment. I didn't want our friendship to end.

I thought if I handled it right we could get back together again. This was the first serious row we'd had.'

'You said you'd lost control. What do you mean by that?'

'Control of myself, when I shot off at the mouth.'

'Ah, so you didn't mean you'd lost control of the relationship?'

'God, no! I was never in charge. Didn't wish to be.'

'OK. So did you do any more about patching it up?'

'Not immediately. As I said, I was slightly suspicious about this other man she'd met.'

'Only slightly?'

He coloured noticeably. 'More than slightly, then.' He shifted position in the chair. 'This doesn't reflect very well on me, but I'd better tell you. The next weekend I followed her, to try and find out. On Saturday morning she drove off in her sports car and I followed.'

'Didn't she know your car?'

'We'd never been out in it. She drove all the way to Horsham. There, she parked and bought herself a soft drink and a sandwich and sat for a while in a park. I was beginning to think I'd made a mistake and she was simply enjoying a day on her own. Then suddenly she returned to her car and drove south of the town until she came to a house near the river. It was fairly secluded, so I had to park some distance off or I'd have been far too obvious. I didn't actually see her go in, but her Lotus was parked outside. I watched and waited, not liking myself at all, but committed to finding out if she was visiting this other man. She could have been seeing her mother, or someone else in the family. The whole afternoon went by before they appeared. It was around six thirty when she came out.'

'Alone?'

'No, he was with her, a tall bloke, dark, in a suit, hair

brushed back. He opened the garage and backed out his car, a red Renault, I think. She got in and they drove off, leaving her car on the drive.'

'Confirming your worst fears?'

'Absolutely.'

'So what did you do?'

'This is going to sound daft. I didn't follow them. I guessed they were off for a meal somewhere, and I couldn't get back to my own car in time, so I waited for them to come back. I knew there was a man now, and I had to find out if she would spend the night with him.'

Hen said, 'Wasn't that torturing yourself?'

'It would have been worse not to have known. In my mind I was making up all kinds of scenarios to explain away this bloke.'

'But she'd told you she had another man.'

'And I wasn't willing to believe her. I still thought I had a chance.'

'So did they return that evening?' Diamond asked.

'About ten. And she went into the house with him and didn't come out again. I know because I slept in my own car that night. That's how single-minded I was.' He paused, looking shamefaced.

Diamond didn't press him and neither did Hen. The man couldn't have been more candid, and every detail chimed in with information they already had. This was beginning to have the force of a confession.

'But I had a surprise next morning,' he resumed, 'because the man left his house alone, dressed in his suit again, and drove off in his car. Hers was still outside. She came out half an hour later and drove away.'

'This was the Sunday – the day she died?'

'Yes. I got in my car and followed. She headed south and eventually ended up in Wightview Sands.'

'It must have been obvious you were behind her.'

'I don't know. She didn't attempt to lose me, or anything. I kept some distance back, often with another car between us. She may have noticed the car, but I was never close enough for her to recognise me.'

Hen commented to Diamond, 'Some drivers don't check their mirror that often.'

'And when we got closer to the beach, and everything slowed down, I made sure I was at least two cars behind,' Bellman added. 'As it happened, that almost threw me. There was a barrier system at the beach car park. You paid a chap in a kiosk. He was chatting to Emma and then she went through and drove off. All I could do was sit in the queue and watch her car disappear into the distance. It's a very large car park.'

'Large beach,' Diamond said.

'You're telling me. By the time I'd got up to the barrier and exchanged some words with this chatty car park man, I was resigned to having to walk along the beach looking for her.'

Hen said to Diamond, 'I know the car park guy who was on duty. Bit of a character. Wants a word with everyone.'

Diamond knew him, too, but wasn't being diverted. 'What did you intend when you found her?'

'By this time, I'd decided to try and talk her round.'

'Even after you knew she'd spent the night with someone else?' Hen said in disbelief.

'He'd walked out on her,' he explained. 'If there was any sort of romance between them, he wouldn't have allowed her to spend the day by herself on the beach.'

'He could have had a job to go to,' Diamond said, finding himself in the unlikely role of Jimmy Barneston's spokesman.

'On a Sunday?'

'Some of us work Sundays.'

Hen said without catching Diamond's eye, 'I'm with Ken on this. Any boyfriend worthy of the name would take the day off. So what did you do, my love? Park your car and go looking for her?'

'Yes. I knew she wasn't at the end closest to the barrier, so I drove halfway along, parked, and had a look at the beach, which was really crowded. All I could do was walk along the top looking for her. Fortunately she had this reddish hair which I thought would be easy to spot. So I set off slowly along the promenade bit above the beach, stopping at intervals to look for her. After about an hour of this, I had no success at all. It was really frustrating. I changed my mind and went through the car park looking for the car, figuring that she ought to be in one of the sections of beach closest to where she'd parked. I found the Lotus fairly quickly. It stood out. So then I put my theory to the test and made a more thorough search of the nearest bits of beach. This time I went right down on the sand, for a better view, and that was how I found her. She was lying down behind a windbreak. I'd never have spotted her from the top.'

'This was near the lifeguard post?'

'Yes.'

'Was she surprised?'

'Very.'

'How did you explain that you were there?'

'Coincidence. I wasn't going to admit I'd been following her for twenty-four hours. It would have seemed weird.'

Neither Hen nor Diamond chose to pursue this insight.

'If I remember right, I made a joke out of it. I was doing my best to put her at her ease. I thought if I could persuade her to let me sit with her on the beach, we could talk through our problem.'

Diamond said, 'What do you remember about her appearance?'

'She was sunbathing, in a bikini, lying on a towel.'

'Did she have a bag with her?'

'I expect so. I can't say for sure. Well, she must have put her car keys somewhere.'

'Sunglasses?'

'Yes.'

'OK, so you chatted to her.'

'I tried. She wasn't pleased to see me, and she made it very clear she didn't want me there. I offered to fetch her a drink, or an ice cream or something. Basically, she told me to piss off.'

'Bit of a blow.'

'Well, yes. I was upset.'

'Angry?'

His face tightened and he gave Diamond a defiant look. 'Not at all. I was unhappy, yes, but I couldn't blame her. I'd hurt her more than I realised when I called her those names. Give her time, I thought, and she may yet come round. So I walked off, just as she asked.'

'Are you sure about this? Sure you're not putting a different slant on the conversation?'

He looked up in surprise. 'Why should I?'

'Because a witness heard you swear at her. You were heard to say something like, "Suit yourself, then. I'll leave you to it. Oh, what the fuck?"'

He frowned. 'Someone was listening?'

'We have a witness statement.'

After some hesitation, Bellman said, 'If that's what I said – and it may be true – it doesn't mean I swore at *her*. I was disappointed. You say something like that when you're pissed off.'

'Then what?'

'I got myself something to eat at the beach café and returned to the car and drove back here to Bath.'

The point at which his version differed from the

expected one. He'd been so truthful up to now.

'Are you certain you didn't return to Emma at some point in the afternoon?'

He flushed deeply. 'No way. If this witness of yours told you that, they're lying.'

'And what were you wearing that day?' Diamond moved on smoothly.

'Oh, God, how would I know?' He sighed and looked up at the ceiling. 'Probably a T-shirt and jeans.'

'What colour?'

'The T-shirt? Black, I expect. Most of my T-shirts are black.'

'You were saying you drove straight back?'

'Yes.'

'Any idea what time this was?'

'Early afternoon, I suppose.'

'Try to be precise, Ken.'

'I can't say better than that, except I was home by four.'

'Can you prove this? Did you see anyone in Bath?'

'I told you I drove straight home. It was really warm on the road. I remember taking a shower when I got in. Then I crashed out for a few hours. I was short of sleep.'

'Did you stop for fuel on the way home?' Hen asked. 'Your tank must have been well down after so much driving.'

'What's that got to do with it?'

'The receipt. They usually show the time you paid. And the place, of course.'

His tone softened. He'd realised she was being helpful. 'Right. I follow you. I'm trying to think. I may have stopped for petrol, but I can't think where.'

'Which way did you come? Through Salisbury on the A36?'

'Yes, that was the route.'

'There are plenty of garages along there.'

'I keep the receipts in my car. I can check.'

'If you can find one that places you somewhere on the road to Bath that afternoon, it will save us all a lot of trouble.'

'OK.'

'But you don't remember stopping at a garage?' Diamond said. 'I would, if it was important.'

'You've got to understand I had other things on my mind.'

Diamond's frustration began to show. 'And you've got to understand we're investigating a murder, Mr Bellman. You were on that beach. By your own admission you'd been following Emma Tysoe for twenty-four hours or more. You confirmed your worst suspicion that she spent the night with another man. You trailed her all the way to Wightview Sands. You spent over an hour wandering the beach in search of her. When you found her and tried to engage her in conversation, she rejected you again. You were angry. In your own words, you were pissed off. And some time the same afternoon, she was strangled. Is it any wonder we're interested in you?'

Troubled, he raked his hand through his curls. 'You've got me all wrong. I'm cooperating, aren't I?'

'I hope so. You didn't come forward when we first appealed for information. It's been in all the papers and on TV.'

'In my position, would you have come forward?' he appealed to them. 'I didn't want all this hassle and being under suspicion. I was hoping you'd find the killer without involving me.'

'Any suggestions?'

'What – about her murderer? That's your job, not mine.'

'You were closer to her than anyone else.'

'You should speak to the guy she spent the night with. I can take you to the house if you like.'

'We've spoken to him.'

His eyes widened. He spread his hands. 'Then you know what I told you is true.'

'We've got your slant on what happened,' Diamond said. 'Yes, your account of your movements fits most of the facts. What I find unconvincing is what you say about your intentions. She dumped you after you'd taken her out for a special meal. You had every right to be angry. You tried calling and still she wouldn't see you. For most men, that would be enough. They'd swallow their pride and get on with their lives. You didn't. You stalked her.'

'That's not right,' he blurted out.

'It is by any normal understanding of the word. You followed her in your car. You spent a whole night waiting outside the house where she was in bed with another man. If that isn't stalking, I don't know what is.'

'I told you I wanted her back.'

'You were angry and jealous. You decided to kill her at the first opportunity.'

'No.'

'You followed her to the beach, just as you said, and tracked her down. She was lying on the sand, maybe face down, so you spoke to her, just to be sure you'd got the right woman. It was Emma, and you made out it was pure chance that you'd spotted her.' He said slowly, spacing the words, '"Of all the gin-joints in all the towns in all the world."'

Bellman jerked as if he'd touched a live cable. 'You know I said that?'

'I told you there was a witness. You masked your anger. You didn't let on that you'd stalked her. But this wasn't a suitable moment to kill. Too many people were about. They could see you in your black T-shirt talking to her. You went away – but not far. You waited for an opportunity, a time when the people around her left the beach or went for a swim. This is probably the time when you went looking for something to use as a ligature, something like a strap or piece of plastic tape or a bootlace. You may have found it lying along the pebbles where the tide throws up everything in its path.'

'This just isn't true,' Bellman said, white-faced.

'This time you crept up from behind. She was probably asleep. You slipped the ligature under her head and crossed it behind her neck and tightened.'

He slumped forward, his hands over his ears. 'No, no. Will you stop?'

Unmoved, Diamond said with a sharp note of accusation, 'Will you tell us the truth?'

19

'Can we speak outside?' Hen said to Diamond.
'Now?' So close to a result, he could think of no
reason to stop. Surely Hen, of all people, wanted to nail
this one?

'Yes, now.'

He was incensed by her interference at this critical
stage. If she'd been one of his own team, he'd have
brushed her aside. He listened, but only because she'd
won his respect in all their dealings up to now. They left
Ken Bellman, looking dazed, in the interview room in
the care of a uniformed officer.

Out in the corridor, Diamond felt and showed all the
symptoms of a dangerous surge of blood pressure.

Hen said, 'I have to say, Peter, I'm not happy where this
interview is leading. Are you trying to break him, or what?'

'You're not happy?' he said, shooting her a savage look.
'Hen, this is a police station, not the citizens' advice
bureau. He's a weirdo. He stalked the victim for twenty-
four hours before she was strangled.'

'He's been open with us.'

'He's had an easy ride.'

'That was easy, was it? You accused him of the crime.'

'At some point, you do. This was the right point.'

She said, 'I wouldn't mind if he was being obstructive.
He was talking freely in there. His story fitted the facts.'

'Up to when he met her on the beach and was given

287

his marching orders. Then it departs from what we know to be true.'

'Such as?'

'He said he couldn't blame her for telling him to move on – as if they shook hands and wished each other good luck. I had to remind him he said "What the fuck!" as he walked away.'

'He's not going to have perfect recall of every phrase he used.'

'He was angry, Hen. Didn't blame her? Of course he blamed her. He wasn't going to admit to us that he was in a strop. Fortunately Olga Smith overheard what was said. According to Bellman's version, he went tamely across to the café for a sandwich and then drove back to Bath. The man had stalked her since the morning of the day before. Do you really believe he gave up and went home?'

'I honestly don't know,' she admitted, swayed a little. 'But I think we should give him the chance to prove it before you roast him alive.'

'What – challenge him to produce a petrol receipt?'

'If he can, yes. If he can't, let's have another go at him.'

'I could crack him now.'

'I'm certain you could. He's brittle. They're the ones you treat with caution, Peter. They confess to anything. Only later, when you're writing it up for the CPS, or being cross-examined by some tricky lawyer, do you discover the flaws. Let's soft-pedal now.'

Diamond didn't want to soft-pedal. This was the first real difference of opinion with Hen. 'What if he does a runner?'

'We'll catch up with him. He isn't a danger to the public. This was a crime of passion if it was anything.'

He shook his head and vibrated his lips. 'I'm not happy with this.'

She said, 'I want a result as much as you. I've had a two-hour drive this morning and I'll have to come back

288

for another go, but it's worth it to get everything buttoned up – properly.'

There was a silence as heavy as cement. 'I can only agree to this if we take him home now and ask him to produce the petrol receipt.'

'And if he can't?'

He shrugged. 'We'll do it my way.'

They used Diamond's car, driving directly to the garage Ken Bellman rented on Bathwick Hill. Little more was said until he unlocked the up-and-over door and opened the car to look inside. His BMW, as he'd stated, had certainly seen better days. 'It passed the test,' he said, as if they might be interested.

'Where are those receipts?' Hen asked.

'I slot everything down the pocket in the door.' He scooped out a handful of scraps of paper. As well as receipts there were parking tickets with peel-off adhesive backing. Everything had stuck together. He handed a sticky bundle to Hen. Then he delved down and brought out another.

Hen started separating the petrol receipts and putting them in date order, arranging them in rows along the bonnet of the car. She pretty soon decided there were too many to be so methodical. They went back at least eighteen months. The date of the murder was June the twenty-seventh.

'Give me some,' Diamond offered.

Bellman was still retrieving fading, dog-eared slips from the depths of the car door. He made a point of handing them only to Hen. She passed a batch to Diamond. Expecting nothing, he went through them steadily and found nothing. He shook his head. Hen finished checking hers. She sighed.

'It's not looking good, Ken,' Diamond commented, as much for Hen's ears as Bellman's.

Bellman said, 'I'm not a hundred per cent sure I stopped for petrol on the way back.' He ran his hand down the pocket one more time and came up with nothing.

'How do you pay for your petrol?' Hen asked. 'With a credit card?'

'Cash, usually.'

'You paid cash at the restaurant, I noticed,' Diamond said. 'Don't you like using plastic?'

'Not much,' he answered. 'You hear so much about fraud.'

'Well, my friend, we're going to have to ask you to rack your brains for something else to confirm the story you gave us.'

'It's no story. It's true.'

Hen asked, 'Is it possible you put the receipt in your trouser pocket? Could it be somewhere in your flat?'

'I suppose.'

This wasn't merely prolonging the search. Diamond twigged at once that Hen's suggestion was a useful one. Without a search warrant, it would get them into Bellman's living quarters higher up the hill.

He accepted it for the lifeline it appeared to be. He closed the garage and they walked the short distance to the house.

He rented the upper floor of a brick-built Victorian villa, with his own entrance up an ironwork staircase at the side. Considering he hadn't been expecting visitors, it was tidy inside, as Diamond discovered when he began strolling through the rooms without invitation, saying benignly, 'Have a good look for that receipt. Don't mind me. I can find ways of passing the time.'

There were two computers, one in an office, the other in the living room. Any number of manuals with titles in IT jargon were lined up on shelves. He followed Bellman into the bedroom and watched him take several pairs of jeans from the wardrobe and sling them on the double bed, prior to searching the pockets.

'Did you furnish the place yourself?'

'It's part-furnished. The newer stuff is mine.'

There wasn't much newer stuff in the bedroom that Diamond could see. The pictures on the wall, faintly tinted engravings of sea scenes, looked as if they'd been there since the house was built. Perhaps he was referring to the clothes basket in the corner, a cheap buy from one of those Third World shops.

The search of the jeans' pockets produced a crumpled five pound note and some paper tissues, but no receipt.

'I can't think where else it's going to be,' Bellman said with a troubled look.

'Wait a bit,' Diamond pulled him up short. 'Not long ago you were doubting the existence of this poxy receipt. Now you make out it's waiting to be found. Is your memory coming back, or what?'

'What happens if I can't prove I was on the road that afternoon?'

'We go through it all again, asking more questions.'

'If you do,' Bellman said, 'I want a solicitor. I came in today to make a statement as a witness, not to be accused of the crime.' He was getting more confident here, on his own territory.

'Show me some proof that you aren't involved.'

'So I'm guilty, am I, unless I can prove I'm innocent?'

'In my book, you are, chummy. There isn't anyone else.'

Hen looked in from one of the other rooms. She'd obviously been listening, and not liking the drift. 'Peter, as the SIO on this case, I'm calling a halt for today.'

The eyebrows pricked up, but Diamond didn't argue. She had the right. It was, officially, her case.

On the drive back to the police station, he spoke his mind

to her. 'My team went to a load of trouble bringing this piece of pond life to the surface. I don't look forward to telling them I slung it back.'

'He's still there,' Hen said. 'It's up to you and me to make the case.'

'Ten minutes more in the interview room and he'd have put his hand up to the crime.'

'That's exactly what I objected to. Confessions don't impress the CPS. We need proof. Chains of evidence. A case that stands up in court.'

'You're asking for the moon,' he said. 'You know as well as I do that the tide washed over the body. There's no DNA. We've bust our guts making appeals for witnesses. It was hard enough finding Olga Smith. No one else is going to come forward now.'

'We've got Emma Tysoe's tapes.'

'Right – and who do they incriminate? Ken bloody Bellman.'

'"Incriminate" is a bit strong,' she said. 'She rejected him, yes, but she didn't say anything about violent tendencies. As a profiler, she should have been able to tell if he was dangerous.'

'We placed him at the scene on the day of the murder. He admits he was there. Freely admits it.'

'Not at the time she was killed.'

'You want a smoking gun,' he said, at the end of his patience.

Hen said, 'I'll tell you what I want, Peter. I want to know what happened to her car, the Lotus he says was in the car park. Emma didn't drive it out for sure, yet it wasn't there at the end of the day when I arrived on the scene.'

She'd scored a point. He'd given very little thought to the missing car. 'Stolen?'

'But who by?'

'Someone who knew she was dead.'

'And acquired the key, you mean?'

'There are ways of starting a car without a key.'

'Yes, but her bag was taken – the beachbag Olga Smith described, blue with a dolphin design. It's more likely, isn't it, that the person who drove away the car had picked up the bag and used her key?'

He weighed that, so deep in thought that he went through a light at the pedestrian crossing at the top of Manvers Street, fortunately without endangering anyone. 'That is relevant,' he finally said. 'Bellman couldn't have pinched her car if he drove his own. Why hasn't it turned up?'

'Not for want of searching,' Hen said. 'Every patrol in Sussex has orders to find it.' She was quiet for a moment, thinking. 'You know, there could be something in this. We've had cars taken from the beach car park before now. Nice cars usually, like this one. They're driven around and abandoned somewhere on the peninsula.'

'Joyriders.'

'Right. Teenagers, we assumed. I'd like to nick them, but they're clean away.'

'But they don't murder the owners?'

'Well, not up to now.'

'This wasn't a kid, Hen. You're certain it wasn't left in the car park that night?'

'Totally sure. I know the cars that were there.'

'How many?'

'Four. One of them belonged to the doctor, Shiena Wilkinson. That was a Range Rover. There was a Mitsubishi owned by another woman who came along in a rare old state when I was having it broken into.'

'She was on the beach?'

'In the car park, at a barbecue.'

'Unlikely to have pinched the Lotus, then. What about the others?'

'Another Mitsubishi and a Peugeot. The first was owned by a Portsmouth man. His name began with a "W". I can't bring it to mind. The other was traced to someone in London with an Asian name. Patel.'

'And they were abandoned?'

'Left overnight. The owners picked them up later.'

'Did you follow it up?'

'Oh, yes.' She remembered giving the job to George Flint, the complainer in her squad. 'The Portsmouth guy—'

'Mr "W"?'

'It was West,' she hit on the name triumphantly. 'He was called West. His story was that he ran out of fuel, so he got a lift home with a friend. He came back next day with a can of petrol and collected his car.'

'What about Patel?'

'Went for a sea trip with some friends, and they got back much later than they expected. Like West, he picked up his car the next day.'

'You see what I'm thinking?'

'I do,' she said. 'If one of those two was a car thief, they could have driven away the Lotus during the afternoon and returned for their own car the following day.'

'A bit obvious, leaving their own vehicle overnight,' Diamond reflected. 'A professional car thief wouldn't be so stupid.'

'Maybe this was an opportunist crime,' Hen said. 'They picked up her bag after she was dead.'

There was a flaw here, and Diamond was quick to pounce. 'But they wouldn't know which car the key fitted, unless they'd watched her drive in. Which brings us back to Bellman. He's the only one who knew she owned a Lotus. Could he have nicked it after killing her and acquiring the bag?'

Hen was equally unimpressed. 'And returned for his

own car before the car park closed? I can't think why he'd do it. If he's the killer, it was jealousy, or passion, or frustrated pride, not a wish to own a smart car.'

Stalemate.

Hen promised to follow up on West and Patel when she got back to Bognor. Either could turn out to be a car thief. People had murdered for less than a Lotus Esprit.

'We made some headway,' Diamond said as a conciliatory gesture after they'd parked behind the police station. 'It's not all disappointment.'

'Far from it,' she agreed.

There was a gap while each thought hard for some positive result from the morning. Displacement activity was easier. Hen lit up a cigar and Diamond checked the pressure of his car tyres by kicking them.

Inside the nick, a sergeant from uniform spotted Diamond and came over at once. 'Everyone's looking for you, sir. You're wanted at the Bath Spa Hotel.'

'Who by?'

'An inspector from Special Branch and a lady by the name of Val something.'

'Walpurgis?'

'That's it.'

'What the hell are they doing at the Bath Spa?' He turned to Hen.

She shook her head.

'Want to back me up?' he asked her.

'Why? Feeling nervous?'

They returned to the car.

The Bath Spa, on the east side of the city in Sydney Road, vies with the Royal Crescent for the title of Bath's most exclusive hotel. It is a restored nineteenth-century mansion in its own grounds, with facilities that include a solarium, indoor swimming pool and sauna. Diamond and Hen announced themselves at Reception and a call was put through to one of the guest suites. They weren't invited to go up.

'The gentleman said he's coming down, sir.'

'Special Branch being careful,' Hen murmured to Diamond. 'I'm going outside for a smoke.'

Diamond took a seat in the drawing room under an oil painting of one of the Stuart kings. He wasn't sure which.

The 'gentleman', when he arrived soon after, was in jeans and a black leather jacket, worn, without a doubt, to conceal a gun. He was chewing compulsively. 'Tony,' he said to Diamond. 'Special Branch.' Pale and red-eyed, he looked as if life in the security service was taking a heavy toll.

'My colleague smokes,' Diamond said. 'She'll join us presently.'

'I gave up,' Tony said, adding unnecessarily, 'I chew gum.'

'Whose decision was it to bring Walpurgis to this place?'

'Her own. She expects the best.'

'I'm against it,' Diamond said.

'So was I,' Tony said with a persecuted look. 'You haven't met her yet.'

'Isn't she aware of the risk?'

'I'm not sure if she's aware of anything except herself.'

Diamond said he would collect Hen. Tony decided he'd left Anna Walpurgis alone for long enough. He said he would see them upstairs on the top floor in the Beau Nash Suite.

Before going outside, Diamond phoned Manvers Street and spoke to Halliwell. It was agreed that Sergeant John Leaman should be assigned to guarding Walpurgis for the time being.

'Some buggers get all the luck,' Halliwell complained.

'Stuck in a posh hotel with a gorgeous bird like that.'

'I'm told it may not be so easy,' Diamond said.

He went into the grounds to find Hen.

Tony from Special Branch admitted them to the sitting-room section of the suite. There was no sign of the main guest.

'Taking a shower,' he explained. 'As soon as she's out, I'm off.'

'Anything we should know about her?' Diamond enquired.

'She'll tell you.'

'Does she have luggage?'

'Five cases and a garment bag.'

'*Five?*'

'Can't be seen in the same thing more than once.'

'Are you confident nobody knows she's here?'

'In a word, no. Fortunately that's not my problem any more. I'm told you volunteered to take her on.'

'I didn't have this place in mind.'

'She did, as soon as Bath was mentioned.'

'Wise woman,' Hen said, to take some heat out of the exchange.

A door opened and, almost on cue, the wise woman emerged from the bathroom wrapped in a white silk dressing gown and with nothing on her feet. She was stunningly pretty, with blue eyes and dead-straight blond hair. 'Is it a party?' she asked. 'Or maybe a wake, by the look of you.'

Before Diamond could introduce himself, Tony from Special Branch said, 'I'm off, then.' He was through the door and gone.

Anna Walpurgis delivered her opinion. 'Tosser. He shouldn't be in the job. Are you the replacements?'

Diamond gave their names and ranks. 'More of a

welcoming committee,' he explained. 'Someone else will be with you shortly.'

'Another kid, I suppose,' she said. 'I so prefer mature men. You're, like, over fifty, yah, approaching your prime? My husband – rest his soul – was well over sixty when I married him. And to save you asking, we were a perfect match and the sex was wicked. Do you like shopping?'

'Depends,' said Diamond.

'Don't be coy, big man. I'm addicted. I want to hit those Bath shops before they close tonight. Milsom Street first, and no prisoners.'

'That may not be such a good idea,' Diamond started to say.

'Why? You know a better place for shops? I'm thinking clothes at this point.'

'I'm thinking safety, ma'am,' he said. 'There's a man who means to murder you.'

She flapped her hand. 'Yeah, and like that's the only threat I ever received in my life?'

'We take it seriously, and so should you.'

'The only thing I'm taking is a taxi to the town centre,' she said, refusing to be sidetracked. 'After two weeks banged up, I'm suffering serious withdrawal from Harrods and Harvey Nicks. Don't look so glum. It's my AmEx Gold they'll be swiping, not yours. What's your first name anyway? Let me guess – something nice and codgery. Barnaby?'

'If we're going to get on, Miss Walpurgis—'

'Anna.'

'If we're going to get on, Anna, you've got to be serious about what's happening. It's not a good plan to go shopping. You'll be recognised. It'll get around that you're in Bath. He'll follow.'

She said as if she hadn't heard, 'Not Barnaby? How about Humphrey, then?'

'It may be necessary for you to stay here for the first night,' he explained. 'After that, we move you to a private address.'

'A private address,' she repeated with mock excitement. 'Would that be yours, by any chance? You're pretty confident for an old guy, huh?'

'You'll have the place to yourself.'

'There goes the last of my reputation, I guess.'

'With a guard outside.'

Blue eyes are not supposed to flash with such intensity. 'So it's another safe house? No way will I spend the rest of my life locked away with some gun-toting boy with a short haircut and no conversation. Pathetic is what it is.'

Hen said, 'It's not the rest of your life, Anna. It's just until this killer is caught.'

'And how long exactly is that?'

'This won't be anything like the regime in a safe house. If you're willing to help us, it can be over in a short time.'

'They all said that.' She turned to Hen. 'Is he married?'

Hen hesitated, then shook her head.

'Funny,' Anna said to Hen, 'but I'm quite attracted by the stiff upper lip. Sort of brings up all those old British movies on cable, Kenneth More and Jack Hawkins.' She flashed a look at Diamond. 'That you, is it? Cool in a crisis? The sort I could trust with my life?'

He said, 'This isn't about me. It's about you.'

'Yeah, you know all about me. Everyone knows about me, the gold-digger who married an elderly millionaire when her singing career was on the slide. The tabloids have done it to death. Nobody ever asks me if I loved Wally. That's not in the script. I shut my eyes to the wrinkles and went for the wedge, wrote off two years of my life for the legacy. It's in the papers, so it must be true.'

The bitterness was inescapable. Diamond had to

respond in some way. 'I never read that stuff. I've heard you sing. I respect you for that.'

'Perlease,' she said. 'You obviously know how to press all the right buttons. Why don't we do a deal, you and me, Humph? If I keep my head down until tomorrow, stay away from the shops and take all the meals in my room, will you come shopping with me tomorrow?'

'All right,' he said at once. It was the best trade he would get. 'And the name is Peter Diamond.'

'As in . . . ?'

He sighed. 'Yes – a girl's best friend.'

She flapped her hand in front of her face. 'Too much. Too, too, too, too much.'

20

Later in the afternoon, Georgina, the ACC, was tidying her desk, her thoughts on that Nile cruise, when Diamond knocked on her door.

'You sent for me, ma'am?'

'So I did, Peter. It was mainly about my house sitter, Ms Walpurgis. Is that a firm arrangement now?'

'Couldn't be firmer,' he said, beaming reassurance at her in case she was having second thoughts. 'She's already in Bath. She'll spend tonight at the Bath Spa Hotel, and move into your house tomorrow, after you've gone. You're still OK with it, I hope?'

'I'm depending on it. I've cancelled the cattery arrangement for Sultan.'

'Saved yourself some money then.'

'That's not a consideration,' Georgina told him curtly.

'Of course not. Sultan's well-being is the main thing.'

'I've been home,' she said, 'and written out some instructions about his routine. There's enough tinned food for the ten days, but he likes a little fresh fish, steamed. If Ms Walpurgis would be so good as to collect a fillet of lemon sole from Waitrose every two or three days and cook it between two plates over a saucepan of water he'll be her friend for life. I've left some money in an envelope.'

'You've thought of everything,' Diamond said, feeling a pang of guilt about Raffles, who hadn't had a sniff of fresh fish of any variety since Christmas. Actually he doubted whether Sultan had much prospect of his steamed lemon sole. Anna Walpurgis didn't seem the sort of person who cooked.

'I've also cleared a space at one end of my wardrobe and found a couple of spare hangers.'

With difficulty, he suppressed a smile. 'I can guarantee she'll make use of those, ma'am.'

'And be sure to ask her to sign the visitors' book. I've left it open on the table by the front door.'

The visitors' book. Georgina *would* have a visitors' book. And Anna Walpurgis's visit would be recorded and remembered for ever.

'Table by the front door. Sorted.'

With the important matters settled, Georgina leaned back in her chair. 'I understand you interviewed a man about the murder of Dr Tysoe.'

'This morning, ma'am.'

'A suspect?'

'Definitely, but it's early days. We're looking at his alibi – so-called.'

'So isn't he in custody?'

'No, ma'am. We let him go home. I don't rate him as dangerous to anyone else. He was the jilted lover.'

'A crime of passion, you think?'

'Yes, if he's the killer, it's all about jealousy and thwarted love. Don't worry. He won't be picking off the citizens of Bath.'

'God forbid. Are there any other suspects?'

'An Australian lifeguard we're still trying to trace. He went missing soon after the murder. And a couple of men who were at the beach that day and could have killed her for the car.'

'It must have been a good car.'

'A Lotus Esprit. It hasn't been traced.'

'Well, I suppose it's possible,' Georgina said. 'When I hear of things like this I'm glad I don't own a car myself.'

'People have been murdered for less,' Diamond said. 'Do you have a mobile phone?'

'Yes, I do.'

'Keep it out of sight, ma'am. Don't tempt them.'

'What's happening to our world, Peter?'

'Easy pickings, ma'am. The haves display their property and the have-nots relieve them of it.'

'Aren't the streets of Bath safe any more?'

'Never were. We'd be safer in the backstreets of Cairo.'

After that, Diamond wished Georgina a wonderful holiday in Egypt and she entrusted him with the spare key to her house in Bennett Street.

Hen had already driven back to Bognor – with some reluctance. She had enjoyed seeing the opening moves in the Diamond–Walpurgis game. She would have liked to remain for a sight of the shopping expedition. It was a pity there were important things to do in Sussex.

Back in the incident room, Halliwell told Diamond that Jimmy Barneston had been trying to reach him on the phone. Events had moved ahead so fast that Barneston seemed like part of a previous existence.

He returned the call. Barneston was under stress again.

'I've had Bramshill on to me demanding to know what the hell is going on. Special Branch told them you've taken over responsibility for Anna Walpurgis. They seem to think you've hijacked my investigation as well. I tried telling them it isn't like that, and we lost confidence in Special Branch after the fiasco with Matthew Porter, but they told me I made a mistake handing her over to you.'

'Pillocks.'

'I agree.'

'You're in no position to look after her yourself,' Diamond said. 'You've got your hands full investigating two murders.'

'Tell me about it!'

'She lost confidence in Special Branch, just as you and I did. She was about to jump ship. They should be grateful someone is willing to take her on board.'

'That's a neat way of putting it. I'll use it if they get on to me again.'

'I wouldn't bother,' Diamond said. 'They're probably listening to us, anyway.'

Barneston's voice registered alarm. 'Do you think so?'

He didn't go down that road. 'How's the Porter investigation going?'

'The PM results are in. Death was definitely caused by a missile the shape of a crossbow bolt. He was killed elsewhere some hours before and the body was transported to the golf course and dumped in the bunker.'

'Traces?'

'This time we got lucky. They found some fibres on the victim that could have come from whatever the killer was wearing. While he was manhandling the body he must have rubbed against the clothes. I wonder why he bothered moving it out to the golf course.'

'Making a point, Jimmy. The Mariner has an agenda, and he's carrying it out to the letter. Remember what Emma Tysoe wrote in her file: "methodical and cool under stress". She was spot on.'

'So are you taking good care of Anna Walpurgis?'

'Star treatment.'

'No problems, then?' he said, unable to hide his disappointment. He'd obviously been through purgatory with the lady.

'None that I noticed.'

'You want to watch out,' he said with a definite note

of relish. 'I don't mind betting the Mariner finds his way to Bath.'

If the threat from the Mariner was uppermost in Diamond's thinking, the matter of Emma Tysoe's murder was not to be shelved. He called Ingeborg to his office.

'Have you listened to the tape of the Ken Bellman interview?' he asked her.

'Yes, guv.'

'Don't say a thing,' he said, picking up the fault-finding note in the first word. 'I wasn't happy with it myself. We know a bit more now, but we don't have the full picture yet. He was on that bloody beach the day she was killed. He admits it. He'd been stalking her day and night. He claims he gave up and went home after she told him to take a hike, but I don't believe him. I want to put this bugger away, Ingeborg.'

'Are you going to have another go at him?'

'You bet. Only I need more to work with. Do some digging for me. Go right back to when he first met Emma as a student at Liverpool. He says there was nothing in it. Well, not exactly nothing—'

'They didn't have sex.'

'Right.'

Ingeborg said, level-eyed, 'You don't have to be coy with me, guv. I've been around the block a few times.'

'Right.' He was parroting 'right' to mask his unease. He *was* coy with her. She looked about fifteen. 'That's one thing to discover if we can. Did they or didn't they? What about the years since then? Did they stay in touch? He claims they didn't. He just met her in the library one day. Can that be true?'

'Not easy to find out without talking to him,' she said.

'I know. You may get nothing. The problem is that Emma Tysoe didn't share her confidences. The people

305

up at the university weren't much help when I talked to them. You might do better than me. There was a black woman called Helen Sparks who seemed to know her better than most.'

'They'll be off on vacation, most of them.'

Ignoring that, Diamond added, 'See if she knows anything at all about Bellman.'

'I'll get on to it right away.'

'I haven't finished. We didn't get much out of Bellman's employers, either. This lot who call themselves Knowhow & Fix. Have a session with them. We don't have to worry any more about alerting the fox. He knows we're on the scent. In particular find out where he worked previously. He mentioned somewhere in London.'

'SW1,' said Ingeborg. 'And he claimed he was living in Putney at the time.'

'See if that's true, then. I want the authentic life history.'

'Understood.'

'And Ingeborg . . .'

'Guv?'

'Got any plans for this evening?'

She blinked, uncertain what he was about to suggest. 'Not much – I think.'

'You *think*?'

She'd coloured deeply. 'There could be something in my diary I've forgotten.'

'Check it, then. You can do some overtime. Impress me with your efforts. You could swing this case yourself.'

She looked relieved. Eyes shining with so much responsibility, she returned to the incident room.

21

Shortly after ten next morning Diamond took the lift to the top floor of the Bath Spa Hotel. No news, he hoped, was good news – but he knew of course that policemen can't afford to rely on hope. John Leaman, looking tired but comfortable, was seated in an armchair outside the Beau Nash Suite with the *Daily Mirror* across his knees. Diamond approached unseen.

'Did the management provide this for you?'

Leaman rose like a startled pheasant. 'Morning, guv. What was that?'

'The chair?'

'That was Anna's idea. It comes from inside.'

'You're on first-name terms, then?'

'She suggested it.'

'How's it been? Quiet?'

'Remarkably.'

'She is still in there, I suppose?'

'Well, she hasn't come out, guv. The breakfast went in about nine fifteen.'

Diamond said in a taut voice, 'What do you mean – went in? You allowed someone to go in there?'

'Room service, guv.'

'And you didn't go in with him? Christ almighty, man. He could have been the Mariner. What do you think you're here for?' Diamond pressed the bell on the door.

There was an agonising delay before they heard

footsteps inside, and it was opened. Anna Walpurgis, triumphantly still of this world, looked out. 'My shopping escort! What a star!' she said. 'It doesn't get better than this. Five minutes to finish my face, guys. Come in, and wait.' Leaving the door ajar, she vanished inside.

Knowing every word would be repeated with relish in the Manvers Street canteen, Diamond said curtly to Leaman, 'You're in the clear, then. She survived. Go home and get some sleep.'

An order Leaman was only too pleased to obey.

Inside the main room, Diamond found more of the morning papers scattered about. A Flintstones cartoon was showing on the widescreen TV. A strong whiff of perfume wafted from the open door of the bathroom, more musky than the brand Hen used to mask her cigar smells. He helped himself to a banana from the fruit bowl and unpeeled it.

He'd assumed her five minutes would mean at least twenty, and that was an underestimate by ten. But he didn't complain. He was comfortable looking at the papers with half an eye on the TV.

When she did emerge from the bathroom she was in skintight black velvet trousers with vents showing portions of hip and thigh. Her small, sleeveless gipsy top announced to the world that she was not wearing a bra. To top it off, a black hat the size of a police helmet, but with the added feature of a vast floppy brim.

'What do you think?' she asked him.

Tact was wanted here, he thought. He got to his feet and gave her the full appraisal. 'Amazing.'

'Let's go, then. I'm in serious need of retail therapy.'

He cleared his throat. 'Allowing that we're trying to keep a low profile, maybe the hat is just a little too eye-catching.'

'A fashion statement,' she told him cheerfully, as if that

308

answered his objection. 'I'll be wearing my shades.'

He tried another tack. 'Before we do any shopping, we'll be moving you to your new address in Bennett Street.'

'You and whose army?'

Prickling, he reminded her, 'I told you about this yesterday.'

'Change of plan,' she said sweetly. 'This hotel will do for me.'

'Sorry. It's a security measure.'

'Another of these crap safe houses? You're not going to spoil my day before we even start on the shops?'

'Not a safe house.'

'Unsafe,' she said, with a mocking laugh.

He rephrased it. 'Safe, but not in the Special Branch sense. This will be your own pad, a beautiful Georgian house in Bennett Street, one of the most exclusive areas of the city. It links with the Circus. Saville Row, with its antique shops, is just across the street. The Assembly Rooms are—'

She butted in, 'What were you called again?'

'Diamond. Peter Diamond.'

She linked her arm under his. 'I know you mean well, Pete, but I'm comfortable here. The shower works and the waiters are good-looking. What else could I require? So let's you and me chill out a little and take a hike around the shops.'

'I don't like to spoil the fun,' he said, disentangling himself, 'but I've got to insist. The move has to be done before we see a single shop. Where are your cases?'

'Room Service took them away.'

He picked up a phone and dialled the front desk.

She said, 'This is getting to be a pain.'

'I'm having them sent up.'

'Masterful,' she said with irony.

'Only thinking of your safety.'

'Like I haven't heard that a zillion times in the past two weeks.'

'Why don't you start folding your clothes?' he said to her just as someone answered the phone. He explained that Miss Walpurgis would be checking out shortly and required her suitcases.

Tony from Special Branch had not exaggerated. Five large cases presently came up on a trolley. Their owner, uninterested, was sitting on the sofa watching Tom and Jerry. Diamond tipped the man himself.

Alone with her again, he eyed the luggage, wondering what she could find to fill it. 'I'll have a job getting all these in my car.'

'Don't bother, then,' Anna told him.

'Are you going to pack, or would you like me to do it?'

'"For you, Johnny, ze war is over."'

'I'm going to make a start.' He opened the hanging space behind the door and unhooked several coats.

She said, 'Do you blow fire as well?' Swinging her legs off the sofa, she got up and picked one of the empty cases off the trolley and carried it into the bedroom.

He'd won the first round.

The packing took a few minutes over the half-hour. Each bulging case had to be forced down before the zip-fastening would work.

'And you still want to buy more clothes?' he said in disbelief.

'Louis Vuitton expects . . . I can always get another suitcase,' she said.

They called the bell-captain and arranged for the laden trolley to be moved downstairs.

Down in the lobby, Anna insisted on paying for her

stay. 'This was my choice of hotel,' she said.

The receptionist checked for mail. 'There is a letter for you, Ms Walpurgis.'

'So soon?' She ripped open the envelope and took out a single sheet, unfolded it, went pale, and said, 'What sicko sent this?'

Diamond took it from her.

Six lines of verse, produced on a printer:

> Like one, that on a lonesome road
> Doth walk in fear and dread,
> And having once turned round walks on,
> And turns no more her head;
> Because she knows, a frightful fiend
> Doth close behind her tread.

He knew the lines. He'd read them recently in *The Rime of the Ancient Mariner*. Seeing them again, knowing who must have sent them, was chilling. They were picked to strike terror into Anna Walpurgis. Coleridge's words had been slightly altered to make the subject female. This time the message wasn't a prediction or a play on words, as the others had been. It was calculated to make the victim suffer before the kill.

'I'm afraid he knows you're here.'

'The killer?' She put her hand to her throat. 'How could he?'

'The point is, it's happened.'

'God! What can we do?'

He felt like saying, What I've been trying to do for the past hour – move you out of here. But he also felt sympathy. Seeing how shaken she was, he calmly told her they were doing the right thing. Mentally he was reeling himself, at a loss to understand how the Mariner could have penetrated the security.

He showed his ID and asked the desk staff if they recalled who brought the letter in, pointing out that it must have been delivered by hand, because there was no stamp.

Nobody had any memory of a letter being handed in. 'The night staff?'

They promised to make enquiries.

He took some rapid decisions. 'If you get anyone asking for Miss Walpurgis, tell them she's not in her room at the moment. Give the impression she's still a guest. Then contact Bath police at once. Do you understand? Next, is there a goods entrance? We'll use that for loading the car.'

Anna, ashen-faced and silent, was taken through a door marked 'Private – staff only'. Diamond moved his old Cortina to the rear of the hotel and the cases were stowed: three in the boot, one beside him at the front and the other on the back seat. After telling Anna to remove the hat he asked her to huddle up, head down, in the remaining space on the back. He covered her with the garment bag. Then he drove out, studying the mirrors for any sign of a vehicle following. He went twice around the perimeter roads of Sydney Gardens before deciding no one was in pursuit. Taking the Bathwick Street route, he crossed the Avon at Cleveland Bridge and turned south, past the Paragon, and joined Lansdown Road at the bottom. Satisfied he was still alone, he made his way up to the Bennett Street turn and came to a halt outside Georgina's house.

'How are you doing?' he asked.

Anna's muffled voice answered, 'Terrified. Are we there?'

'I'll open the front door first. Go straight inside when I give you the word. I'll bring the cases after.'

He took a long look up and down the street. There were parked cars in plenty, but not one appeared to be occupied. Taking Georgina's key from his pocket, he unlocked her front door and pushed it open.

Then he returned to the car and opened the rear door. 'OK. Go.'

Anna emerged with head bowed, like someone in custody going into court, and hurried across the pavement and inside.

Diamond allowed himself a sigh of relief.

Then she came straight out again, just as quickly, and got back into the car.

'For Christ's sake!' he said.

'There's a big white cat in there,' she said from the back seat. 'I can't stand cats.'

'Flaming hell! I'm trying to save you from a serial killer!'

'I'm not going in there.'

'Get your head down. I'll deal with it.'

He marched into Georgina's house and spotted Sultan reposing in a circular bed made of padded fabric. The cat heard him and fixed its blue eyes on him, ears pricked. Diamond scooped up the bed with the cat inside and carried it through the house to the patio door. 'Does she put you outside sometimes?' he said aloud. 'Calls of nature? I expect so.' He opened the door and set cat and bed on the paving.

Anna was persuaded into the house with extreme reluctance.

'What is it about you and cats – an allergy?' he asked.

'A phobia,' she said, her arms protectively across her chest. 'You'll have to find me some other place.'

A quick solution. His own house? No, she'd never agree to stay there. Another hotel? Too obvious. There was only one option. He said, 'I'll take the cat home with me.' The change of plan wouldn't please Georgina one bit if she found out, but it would have to suffice.

Anna still looked twitchy. 'Are you sure there isn't another one?'

'Another cat? No. There's only Sultan. I'm going to fetch your cases now. Why don't you go through to the kitchen and put the kettle on for a coffee?'

She said, 'Sod coffee. I need a tequila. Where's the cocktail cabinet?'

Leaving her to go exploring, he spent the next minutes struggling with the luggage. The cases all had to go upstairs.

He was short of breath when he finished. In the living room he grabbed the Scotch she'd poured him.

'Whose gaff is this?' Anna asked in a calmer voice. She'd settled into one of Georgina's armchairs, her legs dangling over one of the arms.

'One of my female colleagues.'

'Her taste in music sucks. Have you seen the CDs? It's all Gilbert and Sullivan and Verdi.'

It would be. He remembered Georgina telling him she sang in the Bath Camerata. 'It's a comfortable house,' he said, taking the chair opposite her.

'And I'm stuck in it,' Anna said. 'I was told if I came to Bath I'd be free to do those high-tone shops and restaurants. Now I discover this frigging killer is out there. How did he suss that I was in the hotel?'

'Not from me,' Diamond stated firmly. 'You're famous. Were you recognised when you registered?'

'Who knows? There were people around in the lobby. No one took a picture or asked for my autograph, but that doesn't mean they didn't spot me.'

'That's probably what happened, then.'

'And you think the killer got wise to it? How?'

'He's a very smart operator. He knew Matthew Porter was in a safe house and he found a way of getting inside and abducting him.'

She shuddered. 'He wouldn't know I've moved here . . . would he?'

He shook his head and tried to think of words that would reassure. His usually brusque manner wasn't going to work here. He could empathise with Anna's fears. He was starting to feel quite fatherly towards her. Under her glib exterior was a frightened young girl. 'Only you and I know where you are at this minute. You'll be safe if you don't go out.'

With a touch of spirit he admired, she said wistfully, 'No shopping today? I'll call AmEx, tell them to relax.'

'Some other time.'

'Pete,' she said, 'you're not the fascist pig I first took you for. You're doing a fine job.'

'And you can help me find him.'

'How?' she asked. 'I don't know the jerk.'

'Correction. You don't know who he is.'

'Come again.'

'But you may know him,' he pointed out. 'There's got to be a reason why he targeted you.'

She said, 'There are freaks out there who hate anyone who makes it big in the music industry.'

'The others weren't musicians.'

'They were celebs like me.'

'Did you ever meet Axel Summers?'

'No.'

'Matthew Porter?'

She swirled her drink in the glass and took a long swig. 'I don't even know what he looks like.'

'Not too good, the last I heard.' He glanced across the room. Anna had her back to the patio window, which was fortunate, because she couldn't see Sultan standing, front paws pressed to the glass, asking to be let in. 'Do you do any singing at all these days?'

'No, I called time on that. I don't need to work any more.'

'You're still a name everyone knows. Do you get asked to do charity work?'

'All the time. I cut the appearances right down after Wally, my husband, died. Financially I still have a big stake in British Metal and I wanted to contribute in the best way I could.'

'British Metal, you said?' He was on high alert now. He'd heard of British Metal in another context.

'Wally's empire, one of the top ten in the country. You knew that, didn't you? So I invented this role for myself, chairing a committee that looks at the public profile of the company. I know one hell of a lot about PR from my own career.'

'You don't get involved in the technical side?'

'Jesus, no. You work to your strengths. All my experience is in the music business.'

'Heavy metal, not British Metal.'

She managed to laugh. 'Yah. I leave the nuts and bolts stuff to the experts, the people Wally trusted.'

'So as well as deciding which good causes to support . . . ?'

'We sponsor events. And celebs, if they're big enough. The aim is to give us a higher profile in the media.'

'You make the decisions?'

'As chair of my committee, yes, it's my gig, basically. It was my idea to do this properly. When Wally was alive he dealt with it all himself when things came up. He was a sweetie and clever with it, but between you and me, Pete, it was anyone's guess who got lucky. He'd give thousands of pounds away without asking what the firm got back in publicity. A lot of it went on bursaries and sponsoring research that had nothing to do with British Metal. When I came in, I made sure the money was used for projects that put our name before the public.'

He was deeply intrigued, his brain racing. 'What sort?'

'Don't ask me about the nitty-gritty. My committee does all the hard work. I just use my eyes. I see the racing on TV and I'm not looking at the gee-gees. I'm checking the product placement. I go back to my committee and say I want to see British Metal in large letters along the finishing straight, and they see to it. I watch a new film on TV and I look out for the little commercial the sponsor gets in every break just before the show begins again.'

'So you moved into film sponsorship?' Diamond could scarcely contain his excitement at hearing things that promised at last to steer him to the origin of the mystery. 'You put a large amount of finance into the film about *The Ancient Mariner* that Axel Summers was making.'

'Did we? You've got me there,' she said, shaking her head. 'We put money into loads of film projects.'

'It's a fact. British Metal had a big stake,' he told her. He was sure she wasn't being obstructive. She genuinely didn't know.

'If you say so. Until the films are made, I wouldn't remember the titles or the directors. My committee could tell you. Janet is my movie and TV lady. She looks at the proposals and does the costing. If we had dealings with Mr Summers, Janet will have spoken to him.'

'You see the point, don't you? This is important, Anna.'

She raised the finely plucked eyebrows and said, 'I don't see what difference it makes, frankly. There's still a killer out there.'

'Yes – but you're going to lead me to him. Here's another question for you: do British Metal sponsor golf?'

'I guess,' she said vaguely. 'We do endorsements of sports people now. I encourage it. You only have to look at the logos a tennis player wears on his shirt. The sponsors win no matter who lifts the silverware.'

'Golf,' he said, trying not to get exasperated. 'I'm asking about golf.'

'Christ's sake, Pete, do I look like the sort of gal who gets off on watching some fat Spaniard poke a small ball into a tin cup? My sports person on the committee is Adrian,' she said. 'He clocks the players. We only endorse the best. Ade is an anorak, the sort of guy you'd cross the street to avoid, but ace at picking future champions.'

'If he picks the best, it's likely he picked Matt Porter.'

'You see?' Anna said. 'I have no idea.'

'But you could check with Adrian?'

'Any time.'

'Now.'

She still couldn't see the relevance of all this. Diamond couldn't entirely either, except that it would be more than a slight coincidence if Porter, too, had been sponsored by British Metal.

He picked up the cordless phone from the table in the corner and handed it to Anna. She pressed out the number.

'Don't tell him where you are,' Diamond warned. 'Just ask him if Porter was endorsed by British Metal.'

She got through. It soon became obvious from her end of the conversation that his guess was right.

Diamond prompted her, 'Ask him if it was a major sponsorship.'

It was: the largest amount they'd invested in any sports star.

'Has it been reported in the press?'

It had, widely.

The reason Diamond hadn't seen it was that he only ever looked at the rugby reports.

'Cheers, Ade,' Anna said. After she'd handed back the phone, she said to Diamond, 'There you go. We sponsored the two guys who were killed. Is that a help to you?'

'Enormous help.'

'But nobody sponsors me. Why am I on the hit list?'

He had no easy answer to that. He could concoct theories, and he would, but not for her to get alarmed about. The next step had to be an intensive process of deduction, the kind of mental exercise profilers took credit for, and detectives did as a matter of routine. Would Emma Tysoe, given these new facts, have seen immediately to the heart of the mystery? He doubted it. There was more to be unearthed. This, at least, was progress.

'Did your late husband have enemies?' he asked.

'Wally?' She shook her head. 'He was the sweetest guy in the world. Everyone loved him.'

'Rich men are envied.'

'Maybe.' She sounded dubious.

'He had the power to hire and fire.'

'That's business for you,' she said. 'Anyone who was laid off was given a fair settlement, and, take it from me, lay-offs were exceptional. Even when times were hard he'd bust a gut to keep people in work.'

'Did he lay off any in the year before he died?' Diamond persisted. The theory of the ex-employee seeking vengeance on the company was worth exploring.

'I doubt it.'

'Manufacturing industry is in decline. Even after the recession ended, unemployment continued.'

'Now you're losing me,' she said. 'I don't remember lay-offs.'

'OK, let's talk about something else. How did you two meet?'

She sighed and stretched her legs out. 'That's the question everyone asks. I always feel like saying something romantic – like he came to one of my gigs and sat in the front row and fell in love with me. What really happened is we both went for the same taxi one wet night in Dean Street, Manchester. I told him the cab was mine and slagged him off. Called him a waste of space and a bullyboy. He thought it was a great laugh. We ended up sharing the cab and telling each other old people jokes. Before getting out he gave me his card and said he'd like to take me to dinner.'

'When did you marry?'

'Six months after. His fourth marriage, my second.'

'He had family?'

'No children. A sister and three ex-wives, all getting handouts. Like I say, Wally wasn't mean to anyone.'

'After he died, did the payments continue?'

'Still do. It was written into the will. Those wives are on the gravy train as long as they live.' She suddenly became attentive. 'What's that noise?'

He listened. A rustling and scraping. For a moment, he thought the Mariner was breaking in somewhere. He got up from his chair, looked across the room and then breathed more easily.

'It's only the cat scratching on the patio door.'

She was not greatly reassured. 'You will get rid of him?'

'I'll take him with me when I go.' *Getting rid* of Sultan might be a step too far. 'You mentioned your husband's will.'

'Yah. Over a hundred million. The tax was unreal.'

'To your knowledge, was anyone upset by the will?'

'Only the pressboys. They gave me a predictable roasting. "His bride of six years, the former pop singer Anna Walpurgis, comes into a cool eighty-five million pounds. Not bad for a performer with maximum hype and minimal talent." Stuff like that can hurt. There was plenty like it.'

'You could afford to ignore them.'

'Sure, but I do have talent. I made it to the top before I met Wally.'

'No question,' Diamond said. 'I'm pig-ignorant about the pop scene, but I've heard you sing. You got there on merit.'

'Thanks.'

He chose his next words with care, not wanting to frighten her even more. 'The sad fact is that some people believe everything they read in the papers. The person behind all this could be someone who resents the power you wield through that committee. They've hit at two of the people you invested big money in, and now they're threatening you. I want you to cast your mind back and tell me if you received any kind of protest or complaint or threat about the decisions you made.'

She shook her head. 'I don't bother with that shit. I still get a sackful of fan mail I have to deal with. That's enough to be going on with.'

'So what happens if someone writes to you at British Metal?'

'About things we decide? Someone else deals with it. We have a publicity officer. She bins it, I hope.'

'I'll need to speak to her. It would speed things up if you made the call now, and put me through to her.'

'Be my guest.' She reached for the phone.

'You make it.'

He was right to insist. A call from Ms Walpurgis was given top priority at British Metal. No listening to canned music. She was put through to the publicity officer, a Mrs Poole.

Diamond was put on.

Yes, Mrs Poole told him, there was a small file of letters of complaint. Every business had to deal with them. Each one was answered, and in most cases the matter ended there. A few complainers prolonged the correspondence.

'Do you get any about sponsorships?' he asked. 'In particular the money given to Axel Summers, the film man, or the golfer, Matthew Porter?'

'I'll check, but I can't say I remember anything so specific,' Mrs Poole said. 'Each time a sponsorship is announced, it triggers some letters from people who feel they have a more worthy cause needing money. Some of the letters are heart-rending – when it's about someone needing medical attention, for example. I try to direct them to a charity who may be in a position to help.'

'That's different,' he said. 'I'm thinking of the sort of letter that carries bitterness with it, openly or between the lines. It's written by someone so angry that he'll carry out acts of violence.'

'I'm sure I'd notice a letter like that, and I'm glad to say I've never seen one.'

'You'll double-check for me?'

She sounded efficient and her memory was probably reliable. He didn't expect to hear any more. Another theory withered and died.

He told Anna he would arrange for someone to bring in lunch and keep her company during the afternoon.

'Do you have to go?' she said, flicking the blond hair and then pushing a hand through it. 'I was just getting to know you, and, like I told you, I still dig older men.'

He saw the funny side. 'I promised to deal with a pissed-off Persian cat. I wonder if there's a box somewhere in this house I can put him into.'

Keith Halliwell was the fall guy this time. He arrived with Anna's order for lunch, a Marks and Spencer salad, an apple and some mineral water. 'Doesn't look like a lunch to me, guv,' he confided to Diamond when they met at the door.

'This is what beautiful blondes are made of, Keith.'

'What's in the box?' Halliwell asked, eyeing the large carton Diamond was about to carry to his car.

'Top secret, I'm afraid.'

With fine timing, Sultan gave an aggrieved mew from the interior.

Diamond sighed. 'OK. Don't mention this to anyone else. Georgina's cat is coming home with me.'

'Are you fond of him, guv?'

'Not particularly. We hardly know each other. Anna will tell you about it. You've got plenty of time to talk. How many men do you have as a back-up?'

'Three. They're across the street in the unmarked Sierra.'

'That's not enough. I'll have more sent up. For God's sake be alert, Keith. The Mariner is in Bath already. He won't wait long.'

There was a problem still to be faced, and the problem was Raffles, his own cat, the official resident at the house in Weston. Raffles was not pure-bred like Sultan. He was a common tabby, frisky and combative. He'd never seen anything like Sultan. How Raffles would react to having this fluffy, blue-eyed lodger in his home was a cause of concern to Peter Diamond. It was essential that Sultan retained every tuft of his snow-white fur, and kept his two perfect ears intact and his pure-bred Persian face unscarred.

Raffles might have other ideas.

In the back of the car were the luxurious cat-bed, the tins of gourmet salmon and tuna, the special dishes with Sultan's name on them, the large plastic litter box with its modesty hood, the toys, the grooming comb and brush – and the box containing the user of all these products, who was yowling piteously.

Fortunately, when they arrived at Weston, Raffles wasn't at home. Having the freedom of the cat flap, he would be out hunting on the farmland at the end of the street.

Diamond gave Sultan a bedroom to himself, installing all his paraphernalia with him. Opened a tin of the gourmet food and found himself promising the steamed fillet of lemon sole if only the yowling ceased. Closed the door firmly before going out again.

Ingeborg Smith was alone at a computer in the incident room when Diamond looked in.

'Hi, guv.'

'Any progress on Ken Bellman?' he asked, forcing his mind back to the Emma Tysoe investigation.

'Quite a bit, actually. What he said about being at Liverpool University in the same year as Emma is true. He was reading electronic engineering and she was a psychologist. They both got firsts. He stayed on to do a higher degree and she transferred to University College, London, to do hers.'

'Good brains, then, both of them.'

'Yes. I'm trying to find someone from their year who would remember how friendly they were. No success so far. She lived in a hall of residence, so I may get something from the warden, or someone on the staff, if they stayed in the job that long. I'm waiting for a phone call about that.'

'Nice work.'

'I went up to Claverton this morning and talked to Helen Sparks, the woman lecturer you mentioned. According to her, Emma never spoke much about Liverpool. She says she was guarded about her private life as well. But she got the impression there was some man in the background. Emma didn't speak of him, but the confident way she dealt with the men on the psychology staff showed she wasn't in awe of any of them, even the ones who fancied their chances.'

'That's something she didn't tell me,' he said, slightly miffed.

'It's not a thing a woman would say to a man,' Ingeborg said. 'I asked if there were theories doing the rounds of the staff.'

'About Emma's murder?'

'Yes. The consensus seems to be that anyone who does offender profiling is taking a risk.'

'They think some villain was out to get her before she fingered him?'

'Almost as if it was her own fault, yes. Helen Sparks hinted that there was a certain amount of envy that Emma was the only one approached by the Home Office.'

'Envy, eh?' he said, putting a hand to the back of his neck and easing a finger around his collar.

'But not enough to be a motive for murder.'

'How would Helen Sparks know?'

'She's a pretty good judge, guv.'

'You're probably right. Is that it, then?'

'As far as I've got. I haven't yet talked to the people at Knowhow & Fix. That's next.'

'In short, we haven't come up with anything that conflicts with what he told us at the interview?'

'Not yet.'

'Keep at it,' he said. 'I'm putting more and more resources into the Mariner enquiry. If you can nail Ken Bellman by your own efforts, you'll do us all a good turn, Ingeborg.'

He went out to get lunch and buy some lemon sole.

On his return he was told there had been a call from Bognor CID. He got through to Hen. She asked if anything new had come up and he told her about the latest note from the Mariner.

She was shocked. 'So he's in Bath already?'

'Yes – sooner than I expected. Still ahead of the game.'

'Could he know where Anna Walpurgis is?'

'I don't see how.'

'If he wants to find out, all he has to do is follow you, Peter. He knows you'll lead him there at some point.'

'I hope I'm not so obvious as that,' he said with injured pride.

She switched to the matter she'd originally called about. 'Want to hear my news? We've found Emma's car.'

'The Lotus? Where?'

'Only a couple of miles from the beach, in a caravan park. The key was still in the ignition. It was parked beside an empty caravan and hidden under one of those fabric covers people put over cars. It's at the vehicle centre now, being examined for fingerprints and DNA. The forensic guys are confident.'

'A breakthrough at last.'

'We hope so. Have you fingerprinted Ken Bellman?'

'We will now, Hen. We will now.'

22

'So how was it for you?'

'If you're asking me is she still alive, the answer is yes.' After a night on watch outside Georgina Dallymore's house, Keith Halliwell was in no mood to trade humour with his boss. He'd come into the police station on sufferance, under instructions to report on the vigil.

'Have you actually spoken to her?' Diamond asked.

'Only on the mobile. The curtains were still drawn at nine, when John Leaman took over from me, so I checked. She wasn't thrilled to get a wake-up call, but she answered. At least she knows we care.'

'Any signs of suspicious behaviour in the street?'

Halliwell shook his head. 'It was dead quiet.'

'You checked the parked cars?'

'Made a list of all the numbers. I know a lot about Bennett Street I never knew before. It has more lace curtains per house than any other street in the city. And I can tell you how many chimney pots there are. The average is nine.'

Diamond said, 'What I really want to know is how the Mariner found out she was in Bath and staying at the Bath Spa. He's too well informed, Keith.'

'I can give you the answer to that.'

This straightforward statement in the same downbeat tone almost passed Diamond by. When it registered after a couple of seconds he grabbed the arms of his chair. 'Go on, then.'

Halliwell said, 'It was on Galaxy 101.'

'Come again.'

'A radio station. I was talking to one of the young guys on watch with me. He heard it the night she arrived.'

'On the *radio*?'

'Yes. Some DJ played one of her hits, saying he'd heard a rumour she'd been spotted in Bath. The next thing of course is that a listener calls in to say he saw her checking in to the Bath Spa Hotel.'

'And the Mariner happened to be tuned in.'

'Or heard of it from someone else.'

'As simple as that,' Diamond murmured as if he'd just been told the secret of a conjuring trick. 'Who'd have thought that kind of stuff would go out on radio?'

Halliwell looked too tired to enlighten his boss about the way broadcasting had changed since commercial radio came in. Some people never listened to anything except the BBC.

But Diamond wasn't blaming the DJ. 'It wouldn't have happened if Special Branch were doing their job,' he complained. 'They should have smuggled her in through the back entrance of the hotel instead of parading her at the check-in. My God, I've lost all respect.'

Halliwell's head was starting to sink from sheer fatigue.

'If I'm honest,' Diamond added, 'I didn't have much in the first place.' Still fretting over the security lapse, he sent Halliwell home to catch up on some sleep.

One mystery solved, then. And a little of the gloss rubbed off the Mariner's shining reputation. He'd heard it on the radio.

Ideally Diamond would have called a case conference this morning to bring everyone up to date on recent developments. Instead, information was being circulated through the bush telegraph. Bath's small murder squad was fully stretched to maintain this round-the-clock vigil.

John Leaman was now on watch in Bennett Street with four plain-clothes officers. After the lapse in the hotel, Diamond reckoned, he should be fully alert.

Towards the end of the morning he looked into the incident room. Soon the least experienced member of the squad would have to take a shift on the Bennett Street roster. He'd kept Ingeborg busy digging into Ken Bellman's past, shielding her from front-line duties. It wasn't good practice. In theory, she should face the same risks as anyone else. Knowing how sod's law worked, when she was on watch, the killer would make his move.

'Did you get out to Knowhow & Fix?' he asked her.

'Yes, guv. They look like a bunch of students to me, all shorts and T-shirts. Bellman is one of about ten consultants on their list. He's liable to be called out at any time, including weekends, but a lot of the work is done from home, so they don't keep track of his movements.'

'Doesn't matter,' he said. 'We know where he was in the hours leading up to the murder. That's on record, so he's got no alibi. What do they say about him as an employee?'

'No complaints. They're satisfied with his work. He seems to be up with the latest technology, which is what counts in IT.'

'Previous employment?'

'Like he said, he was with a London firm.'

'In SW1,' Diamond recalled.

'As a techie – a technical support programmer.'

This meant little to Diamond, but he knew London pretty well from his days in the Met. 'SW1. That's very central. Westminster, Downing Street, St James's. Scotland Yard is there. Not many computer firms, I would think. It's all government departments. Civil servants.'

'They use computers, guv.'

'I suppose they do. Why did he move to Bath? Do his bosses know?'

She shook her head. 'They say he came with good references. He's quiet. Doesn't talk about himself or anything personal.'

'They don't know what brought him here?'

'No.'

'Did *we* ask when we interviewed him? I don't believe we did. For a young man with a good job in IT in central London, a move to the provinces seems a strange career choice.'

'Did he move to be nearer to Emma?' Ingeborg asked.

'That wasn't the impression I got. If I remember right, he said they met by chance one day in the library – as if he didn't expect it.'

'I can believe *she* didn't.'

He was quick to pick up on the point. 'You're thinking he was lying – that he followed her here? Good point, Ingeborg. It crossed my mind, too. The way he told it, you'd believe they hadn't spoken since their student days at Liverpool.'

'That was my impression, listening to the tape,' Ingeborg agreed.

'I'd like to know more,' he said. 'We've only got his version of the way it happened.'

'A long-term stalker?'

'Possibly. He certainly pursued her for the last hours of her life. He admitted it. Could have been obsessed with her for much longer.'

'Does it make a difference?'

'What do you mean, does it make a difference?'

Ingeborg said with an embarrassed laugh, 'I mean, if he was the killer anyway, does it matter how long he knew her?'

'It strengthens the motive.' Slipping into his superintendent mode, he told her, 'Something you're going to have to learn, constable, is that we aren't here just to name the guilty man. We have to make the case to the CPS, and if it isn't rock solid they won't prosecute. If Bellman was fixated on this woman for years and finally got into the relationship he'd fantasised over, only to find she dropped him and started up with someone else, he'd take it badly. That's motivation. That's going to help the prosecution.'

'Is it worth questioning him again?'

'I wouldn't mind another go.'

The opportunity came sooner than either of them expected, in fact within twenty minutes. The desk sergeant called up to say a Mr Bellman had walked into the station and asked to speak to the officer in charge of the Emma Tysoe investigation.

Diamond asked Ingeborg to join him.

She was starry-eyed at the prospect. 'Do you think he's ready to cough, guv?'

'We can always hope.'

In the interview room, Bellman didn't have the look of a man about to confess. He sat completely still, studying his fingernails, apparently unimpressed when Diamond and Ingeborg entered the room and took their places. Last time, he'd slopped coffee onto his jeans. This morning, on Diamond's instructions, he'd already been brought coffee in a cup and saucer – not to prevent further spillage, but because china is a suitable surface for collecting fingerprints.

'You've already met DC Smith,' Diamond said by way of introduction. 'You don't mind if we tape this?'

'Whatever you want. It won't take long.'

Ingeborg spoke the formal preamble for a voluntary statement, and then Diamond said, 'You've got something to tell us, Ken?'

'To show you, more like,' he answered. 'When we were speaking before, there was some question about where I was on the afternoon Emma was killed. I told you I left Wightview Sands at the end of the morning and drove back here and you asked if I could prove it.'

'Right.'

'We looked in my car to see if there was a petrol receipt.'

'Correct. Have you found one?'

His mouth drew wide in a triumphant grin. 'Actually, yes.' He opened his right hand to show a slip of paper lying on his palm.

'Where did you find this?' Diamond asked as he took it, his voice betraying nothing of the plunging anticlimax he felt.

'Down in the slot where the handbrake is fitted. There are two sets of brushes, nylon, I would guess, and the brake moves between them. Sometimes I run my finger-tips along the gap when I'm waiting in traffic, and a small piece of paper could easily slip down there. It was stuck there, out of sight. I thought I'd have another search, on the off chance, and there it was.'

'Fortunate.'

'Very. Without it, I'd be getting worried.'

Diamond studied the data on the receipt. Beyond dispute, it showed someone had bought 35.46 litres of unleaded petrol from pump five at a cost of £25.50 at the Star service station, Trowbridge Road, Beckington, Bath BA3, at three forty-seven on the afternoon of the murder. A kick in the guts. Trying to salvage some respect, he said, 'Pity you didn't use a card for this transaction. It was a cash sale, evidently. There's nothing to link this receipt to you personally.'

Bellman was unmoved. 'What are you suggesting – that it's someone else's receipt?'

'Could be.'

'Knock it off, will you?' He was confident enough for sarcasm. 'Ah, I know what you're thinking. I suppose it stuck to the bottom of my shoe when I came along later and then a freak gust of wind blew it off the shoe and up to the handbrake? That's a long shot, isn't it?'

'We'll examine it, anyway,' Diamond said, passing the receipt to Ingeborg. 'Thanks for bringing it in.'

'By the way, I've photocopied it,' Bellman said, adding, in the same sarcastic vein, 'Just in case it goes astray.'

'Wise.'

'I'll be off, then.'

'Before you are,' Diamond said, 'I wonder if you'd clarify a couple of things you said at your previous interview. Only a matter of tidying up details. You said you worked in London prior to coming to Bath.'

'That's right.'

'In SW1. Did we have that right?'

'Yes.'

'But you didn't name your employer.'

'You didn't ask. Mitchkin Systems Limited.'

'Would you mind spelling that?'

Bellman did. 'I was a technical support programmer.'

'Yes, we got that first time around. Good job, I should think, based in central London.'

'They've got a good name.'

'I'm wondering why you left. What brought you to Bath?'

He answered smoothly, 'I'd had enough of London by then. I'm single. With my training I can work pretty well where I choose.'

'But why Bath, of all places?'

A shrug and a smile. He was confidence personified now. 'Nice city. Clean air. Less hassle.'

'Are you sure there wasn't another attraction – the fact that Emma Tysoe moved here.'

A touch of colour sprang to his cheek and he raised his hand as if to fend off a loose throw. 'Oh, no. No way.'

'Before you say any more,' Diamond came in, sensing a hit, 'we've done some digging, DC Smith and other detectives in my squad, and we know you contacted Emma quite soon after arriving here – very soon, in fact. That story about meeting her by chance in the library was a little misleading, wasn't it?'

Bellman frowned, back on the defensive. 'I don't think so.'

A note of caution that Diamond was quick to pick up on. This line of questioning had been a fishing expedition, no more, and now there was the promise of a catch. 'Let me put it this way. I'm willing to believe you met in the library, but I don't buy your story that it was pure chance. She was an old friend from your student days. You had every right to seek her out. Any one of us would have done the same.'

The man was silent.

Diamond continued in these uncharted waters. 'I'm not suggesting you harboured romantic feelings about her for all those years, checking what happened to her, where she lived, and so on. But I can't help wondering if you were reading your paper one day, and happened to see her name. She was rather well known in her professional life – as a psychological offender profiler, helping the police with their inquiries.'

He said firmly, 'I don't have time to read the papers. All my reading is technical. Computer magazines.'

'So you didn't know about the profiling?' Diamond paused, apparently to exercise his thoughts on this mistaken assumption. 'Maybe I was wrong, then. Maybe you *did* still carry a torch for her after all those years.'

Bellman's eyes flicked rapidly from side to side as if he

knew he'd been led into a trap. 'I don't know what you're on about.'

Keen, it would appear, to move on to things of more importance, Diamond said, 'It's simple enough and it doesn't really amount to anything. We know you were attracted to Emma. You had a relationship with her. You've just handed us the proof that you couldn't have killed her. All I'm asking is if you kept tabs on her ever since university.'

'And if I say yes?'

'Then I'll ask you again: did you get your job in Bath just to be nearer to Emma?'

After a pause worthy of a Pinter play, Bellman said, 'Yes.'

Diamond beamed, and sounded amiable. 'Even an IT consultant is allowed to be a romantic. Thanks for coming in, Ken. I'll show you out.'

Bellman was quickly out of his chair and through the door. Diamond got up to follow and had a sudden after-thought. He wheeled around and saw Ingeborg's hand reach helpfully towards the cup and saucer on Bellman's side of the table. Just in time, he made a sweeping gesture with his arms. Ingeborg, startled, drew back from the fingerprinted cup.

Diamond caught up with Bellman. 'You'll probably be interested,' he told him. 'We finally found her car.'

Bellman turned to look at him, nodded, and said nothing.

There was no denying the disappointment. It wasn't in Diamond's nature to make light of a setback so serious. They'd devoted many hours to Bellman that could have been put to better use.

Ingeborg tried to console him by pointing out that it wouldn't be all that difficult to forge a petrol receipt.

'He's a computer geek. He'd have no trouble reproducing the right font and printing it on the sort of paper they use. No way is this the alibi he claims it is.'

'It looks like the real thing to me.'

'Well, it would, guv. I could make another one just like it, no problem.'

'They ought to have a copy at the garage, didn't they?' he said, starting to function as a detective again.

'What's more,' Ingeborg chimed in, 'many garages have security videos running. If we tell them the date and the time, it shouldn't be any problem to check. We even know it was pump five.'

'Do it, then,' he told her. 'Get on to them now. Go out to Beckington and collect any video evidence the garage have for the time he claims to have been there. Let's call his bluff – if we can.'

'And the fingerprints?'

'I'll see to them.'

Hen Mallin had already sent through the fingerprints lifted from Emma Tysoe's car, an incomplete set, but enough, certainly, to make a comparison if the cup and saucer yielded good results. Diamond went in search of a SOCO.

Prints left on a china or porcelain surface and leaving no visible marks are known as 'latents'. They require dusting with a chemical. Any marks revealed in this way have to be sealed by exposure to superglue vapour for several hours.

Frustrating.

In truth, he wasn't optimistic. Ken Bellman had been on the defensive for sure, yet this didn't automatically indicate guilt. The man knew he was under suspicion. These days anyone picked up by the police was entitled to be apprehensive. There were too many stories, too many proven cases, of wrongful arrest and stitch-ups. He had been caught out in a lie about the circumstances of the reunion with Emma, but that could be put down to self-preservation. He *was* a weirdo and a stalker, but not necessarily a killer. They seldom are.

A call to John Leaman brought reassurance. Anna Walpurgis was still in the house in Bennett Street and had ordered the same lunch as yesterday and a long list of CDs and videos that Leaman had promised from the MVC shop in Seven Dials. 'So it sounds as if she's resigned to staying indoors, guv.'

'Make sure she does. Who's buying these things?'

'Uniform. I can't spare anyone.'

'I hope they don't know who they're for.'

'They think it's all for me. My street cred is sky high.'

'And what's happening in the street? All quiet?'

'So quiet I can see parking spaces.'

'Is there any way he could gain access from the back of the house?'

'I can't see how. The back gardens are enclosed. Sealed off.'

'Make quite sure, John. Have someone check.'

'Do you think he knows she's here, guv?'

'It's only a matter of time.'

Time that hung heavily for Diamond.

He called Hen and told her that Bellman seemed to be in the clear.

She said, 'In your shoes, darling, I'd have my suspicions about a bloke who produced his alibi as late as this. Where did he say the damned thing was hidden? Somewhere under the handbrake?'

He explained about the gap between the brushes.

'And it happened to be the one receipt he needed? Sounds dodgy to me.'

'We're checking. If it's a try-on, we'll know shortly.'

'You sound as if you're not expecting a good result.'

'He's laughing up his sleeve, Hen. I'm sure he was stringing me along. Probably had the sodding receipt all the time and just wanted to hit us with this at the last minute. That's the impression I get.'

'Dickhead. Do him for wasting police time.'

'Not worth it.'

'Don't the fingerprints match?'

'Don't know yet. They could be my last throw.'

'With *this* guy, perhaps,' she said, leaving no doubt that she had something up her sleeve. 'You haven't heard my latest. Remember the lifeguards, those two who called themselves Emerson and Laver? Stella has spent the past week trying to track them down. Finally, she found an ex-girlfriend, someone they each had a fling with, apparently, and now we know their real names, as well as their mobile numbers. They were travelling west, towards Dorset. Stella is confident of finding them today or tomorrow.'

'What are the names, then – Rosewall and Hoad?'

'I'm being serious, ducky. These two are my most wanted. Trevor Donald and Jim Leighton, both from Perth, Western Australia. Dorset police are on the case. Do you want to join in when we catch up with them?'

'I'd love to,' he said, 'but—'

'But you're hoping to catch an even bigger fish. Say no more.'

'You'll keep me informed?'

'Depend on it.'

As always, he felt buoyed up after speaking to Hen. Her hearty self-confidence didn't even contemplate failure. She deserved a result, and he wouldn't begrudge it in the least if one of those Australians turned out to be the beach murderer.

Ingeborg returned from the Star service station late in

the afternoon with the news that the cashier had found the duplicate receipt for the one Bellman had produced.

'Genuine, then,' Diamond said with disappointment he couldn't disguise. 'We can forget the clever forgery theory.'

Ingeborg said, 'But there's still no proof it was Bellman who bought the petrol. He may have come to the garage later and picked up a receipt someone else had thrown away. Easy to do.'

'Difficult to prove.'

'Not impossible,' Ingeborg said. 'They gave me the video for pump five.' She patted her shoulderbag.

They slotted the cassette into the machine in Georgina's office and sat on the leather sofa to watch the rather tedious images of cars moving up to the pump and drivers getting out to fill up. Fortunately a digital record of the time was displayed in the bottom left corner.

'What was the time on the receipt?'

'Three forty-seven.'

'He'll have filled up around three forty-five. Can you fast forward it?'

Ingeborg worked the remote control and the visuals became more entertaining as figures darted out of cars like Keystone Cops in an old movie.

'We must be getting close. Slow up.'

The pictures reverted to normal speed. The time was showing three forty-one. A grey Toyota was at the pump. The elderly driver filled up, went to pay, returned, and picked up a cloth to clean his windscreen.

'Get off, you old git,' Diamond said to the screen.

The man got in and drove away his Toyota and a blue BMW glided into its place.

'Oh, fuck a duck!' Diamond said – by his moderate standards, a cry of desperation, if not despair.

There could be no argument. The man who got out

to use the pump was in a black T-shirt and jeans. He had dark curly hair. There was no mistaking Ken Bellman.

Further proof followed at the end of the afternoon. When the fingerprints were compared, it was obvious that the last person to drive Emma Tysoe's stolen car was not Ken Bellman. They could forget him.

23

That same evening, Hen drove along the coast to Swanage. She'd had a call from Stella to say that the two Australian lifeguards, Trevor Donald and Jim Leighton, had been traced to a campsite a mile outside the town. She would meet Stella at Swanage police station at around seven thirty. It was that blissful time of year when daylight lasts until late and the low evening sun gives cut grass the lush look of velvet. There wasn't a cloud anywhere.

This time she felt the odds were in her favour. Other suspects had been eliminated, and the nature of the crime on Wightview Sands beach had undergone a reassessment. More and more it was becoming likely that the motive had no connection to Emma's work as a profiler and instead was casual and callous. The typical seaside crime is like that. Any detective working in a holiday resort knows there is something in the carefree attitude of visitors that gives the green light to criminals. At its most serious, the result is murder. The victims, usually women and usually alone, are unknown to the killers. Generally they are strangers to the town. They may be backpackers, campers, drifters, foreigners. But a minority of those attacked are affluent and invite trouble by flaunting their possessions: jewellery, handbags or sports cars.

It was likely Emma had been killed for no better reason

than that she owned a flash sports car. The killer had seen her park the gleaming Lotus Esprit, watched as she chose her spot on the beach, picked his moment and strangled her. Then he'd taken her bag with the car keys and stolen the car. The fact that it had been found on a caravan site – also used by campers – underlined the casual nature of the crime.

Hen's reliable assistant was waiting for her as she drove up. Stella had a glow about her, and it was more elation than sunburn. 'They're in a pub only five minutes away, guv. The local CID have had them under observation. How would you like to play this?'

Hen made some rapid decisions. 'I'm not interviewing them in a pub and certainly not together. Invite them here for questioning about the stolen car. We'll split them up. If they don't cooperate, we book them.'

'Both?'

'Which is the guy we haven't seen at all?'

'That's Jim Leighton.'

'We'll take him first. Yes, bring them both in and nick them if they won't play ball. See to it, Stella. I need a smoke first.'

She went in to make sure an interview room was available.

Jim Leighton certainly looked the part in a yellow singlet and faded denim shorts that set off the seaside tan. He was a handsome hunk of maleness, too, Hen didn't fail to notice: blue-eyed, with a swimmer's meaty shoulders and a thick blond ponytail. He had a single gold earring and around his neck was a chunky gold chain.

'For the record, this will be a voluntary statement,' Hen started to say for the tape.

'I said nothing about a statement, lady,' he said with the Aussie twang.

He turned his head away, and she got a sight of the profile. Why do most Australians have big noses, she wondered, and it made her wonder something else, indelicate and not easy to verify in the circumstances.

'You're here of your own free will?'

'You're joking. My own free will is to be in the pub. I came because I was asked, to let you know I didn't swipe anyone's car. I can smell cigars. Is someone smoking here?'

'*Was* smoking. Do you want one?' Hen offered.

'Christ, no, unless you have something sweeter on offer.'

Hen ignored that. 'How long were you in Bognor?'

'Three, maybe four weeks, doing the lifeguard bit with my mate Trevor. Piece of cake, that is, until you get an east wind.'

'Not much saving of lives?'

'None at all. Basically it's stopping stupid drongos from going out too far on airbeds. You get the occasional lost kid and minor injuries. Wasps and weever fish can be a problem.'

'Were you there on the day the woman was killed?'

'Sure.'

'But you didn't get interviewed.'

'Trevor did. He lifted her off the beach and into the hut. Look, you don't think I topped the poor lady? I was told this was about a car, for Christ's sake.'

'The car belonged to the woman who was killed,' Hen said. 'So where were you at the end of the afternoon when the body was found?'

'What time?'

'Say between four and five.'

'You really think I remember? It's a beach and I was there every day. Maybe I was chatting up crumpet. Or eating a burger. Or kicking a ball around.'

'You were on duty earlier?'

'Sure.'

'At the lifeguard station? What time did you go off duty?'

'Who can say? We're not the army. If I felt like a break at the end of the day, I'd take one. The job gets easier with the tide in. Trevor could manage without me.'

'Mid-afternoon?'

'I guess.'

'If you went for a burger, did you go through the car park?'

He grinned. 'Trick question. Everyone who goes to the café walks past some cars unless they cross the road where the toilets are. To save you the bother of asking, I didn't see the Lotus at all.'

'But you know it was a Lotus?'

'Trick question number two. Give me a break, will you? Everyone knows her car went missing and it was a Lotus Esprit.'

'It must have been parked quite close to where you were. She was on the same stretch of beach.'

'I know that,' Leighton said. 'I spoke to her.'

'You did?' Hen leaned forward. 'When was this?'

'"What time? When?"' Lady, I'm a beach bum. I don't look at my watch each time I speak to a woman.'

'After you went off duty, which you said was mid-afternoon?'

'If you say so.'

'So what was said?'

'One of my standard pick-up lines, I reckon. Like "Excuse me, is that a tattoo on your ass or a love-bite?"'

'I'm sure that goes down a treat. Did she have a tattoo?'

He flashed the teeth in a wide smile and shook his head. 'But they always check.'

'What was her response?'

'Told me to get lost, if I remember right.'

'And then?'

'I got lost, I guess. It's all a blur. One day is like another in the lifeguard profession.'

Hen was losing patience. 'Get a grip, will you, Mr Leighton? That day wasn't like any other. A woman was strangled. You were there, or somewhere nearby. What else can you tell me about her?'

'She was stretched out behind a windbreak. Bag. Big blue towel. White bikini. That's all.'

'We asked for witnesses. You didn't come forward.'

'Because Trevor told you everything. He's the bloke who was in on the action.'

'That doesn't wash,' Hen said. 'You *knew* she was on that beach. You spoke to her. Yet you didn't tell us until now. I think you know she was murdered. I think you saw an opportunity to take a joyride in a Lotus.'

He nodded. 'Now we're coming to it.'

'I'm giving you the chance to come clean over this. Joyriding isn't a major crime so long as no one gets hurt. Where were you staying in Wightview?'

'A field behind the village.'

'In what – a camper van?'

'Yeah. Pathetic, aren't we? Typical bloody ockers.'

'You moved out of there pretty fast after the murder. Trevor stayed on for a few days, but you were nowhere to be found.'

'Didn't he tell you? I was touring the British Isles in a Lotus Esprit.'

Hen stabbed her finger at him. 'Don't come it with me, sonny. I'll have you in the cells without your feet touching the ground. Where did you clear off to?'

'A sad place called Bournemouth. Trevor and me had a temporary falling out over some sheila.'

'Emma Tysoe?'

345

'Ease up, lady. This was a fifteen-year-old blonde from Amsterdam. I kicked around with her for a few days until it got boring. End of story.'

'So you deny ever taking the Lotus?'

'How the hell would I do that without the key?'

'Her bag was missing.'

'Nothing to do with me.'

'OK,' Hen said. 'Prove it. The car thief left his finger-prints behind. With your permission, we can take a set of your prints and compare them.'

He sneered at that. 'Oh, sure – and I'm in your records for ever more.'

'No. They'll be destroyed. You'll sign a consent form saying it was voluntary and I'll sign to say they're destroyed. You get a copy.'

'What's the alternative?'

'We carry on with the questions until I'm satisfied.'

Leighton went quiet, fingering the earring. Hen could almost track the process of his thoughts. He wanted to get back to the pub before closing time.

Finally he yawned and said, 'Looks like it's the prints, then.'

Hen glanced towards Stella, who nodded and told Leighton to follow her.

Never a man to shirk responsibility, Diamond took his turn that evening keeping watch over Anna Walpurgis. He relieved John Leaman soon after nine, when Bennett Street was as quiet as a turkey farm on Christmas Day. It's far enough above the hub of the city to escape the pubbers and clubbers. Leaman told him there was nothing untoward to report. The lady had remained inside all day.

'Did you speak to her?'

'A couple of times, guv. She's a frisky lass, isn't she?

Says some pretty outrageous things over the mobile, like she's partial to cops because we all have long things that spring out at a flick of the wrist.'

'You obviously got on well.'

'Want me to do another turn tomorrow?'

'Maybe. I've asked Ingeborg to relieve me in the morning.'

Leaman cleared his throat. 'Don't say stuff like that in front of Anna, boss. She won't let you forget it.'

He left to get a night's sleep and Diamond strolled across to speak to the officers with him on the night watch. They seemed incredibly young, but there were six of them, all eager to impress. If only Georgina knew, she'd be well satisfied with the house-sitting arrangements, he thought.

He looked up at the top-floor window of the house and saw that the light was on behind closed curtains. A phone call first, to let Anna know he was outside. Then, perhaps, a coffee with the lady herself.

She must have been close to the phone. 'Holloway Prison.'

He asked how she was doing.

'Dying from boredom,' she told him. 'You're the chief honcho, right? Sparkle?'

'Diamond, actually.'

'I know that, dumbo. I'm being playful. You coming to see me?'

'Yes, I thought I might call in, touch base.'

'Touch what?'

'It's an expression. I'll be right over.'

First, he detached his back-up team to their posts, warning them to watch for anything that moved in the street. Then he went over to the house and the door opened before he touched the bell. 'You want to be careful,' he said to Anna. 'I could be anyone.'

'The way I'm feeling, anyone will do.'

He didn't pursue it. She'd cooperated well up to now in a situation that was obviously a trial. She offered coffee and he followed her into Georgina's kitchen. What a mess since he'd seen it last. Unwashed dishes cluttered the table, with eggshells, spilt coffee and used tea bags. There was a cut loaf unwrapped and going dry and a slab of butter starting to sweat. And a pile of burnt toast.

'I don't go in for cordon bleu,' Anna said superfluously. 'I'd never manage in this poky kitchen. What happened to the kettle?'

'Did you take it to another room?'

'Sharp thinking, Sparkle.'

He winced. 'I'd rather you called me Peter.'

'Have it your way.' She fetched the kettle from the front room while he rinsed a couple of mugs above the murky-looking water in the sink. He didn't care to think what Georgina's bathroom looked like by this time.

Before Anna indulged in more games with his name, he asked about hers. 'I presume it's a showbiz touch, to add some interest.'

'Righty. I'm plain Ann Higgins in real life.'

'Why Walpurgis? Something to do with spooks, isn't it?'

'Witches,' she informed him. 'Walpurgis Night is the one before May Day, when all the witches are supposed to have a rave with the devil somewhere in the mountains in Germany. But before you say any more, Walpurgis herself was as pure as the driven snow. She was an English nun.'

'You named yourself after a *nun*?'

She pointed the kettle at him like a gun. 'Don't say another word. When I found out the nun part of the story, it was too late to do anything about it. And she just happens to have May the first as her day. Any connection

348

with Old Nick is a slander. Black or white?'

He realised she was asking about the coffee. 'Better be black as I'm on duty all night.'

She said, 'I could only find instant. This is your boss's house, right?'

'Right.'

'The high chief honcho?'

'One of them, anyway.'

'Tough lady, huh? She needs to be, lording it over all you hard-nosed cops. Shall I let you into a secret about your boss?'

'No thanks.' There were things he didn't sink to. He didn't want to be told that Georgina went in for black lace lingerie or Barbara Cartland romances. Her private life was her own and he wasn't taking any more advantage than this emergency required.

She said, 'You wouldn't believe what she keeps in the attic.'

'None of my business.'

'Ooh, listen to his holiness. All right, I'll keep it to myself. I guess I should be grateful to her for letting me stay here.' A more solemn note came into her voice. 'What I want to know from you, Pete, is how much longer this pantomime is going on. When are you going to catch this psycho?'

'Soon,' he said with all the confidence he could dredge up. 'I've got a team of trained officers on the street. All I want from you is the same cooperation you've given us up to now.'

'I'm only being good because I'm scared rigid. You know that?'

He gave a nod, and gave nothing away of his own apprehension, or the sympathy he felt. Instead, he took the opportunity while she was serious to clarify a couple of points. 'When we talked last time about British Metal, you said there weren't any lay-offs you could remember towards the end of your husband's connection with the company. I checked with your people, and your memory is right. The only redundancies in that time – and since – were by agreement. Some people took early retirement on generous pension arrangements.'

'We're a good firm to work for.' The kettle came to the boil and she poured water onto the grains of Nescafé in Georgina's Royal Doulton cups.

'Thanks.' Diamond picked his off the table. 'So I've got to look elsewhere for someone really embittered, someone who wants to get back at the company. You said before you took over the sponsorship committee, or whatever it's called, that the handing out of funds was all rather disorganised. Your husband didn't take much interest in the PR side. In your own words, it was anyone's guess who got lucky.'

'And it was,' she said.

'But your idea was to sponsor events and people that put the name of British Metal before the public, so you backed high-profile projects like the Coleridge film and top sportsmen like Matt Porter.'

'Darn right we did.'

'It obviously got up the Mariner's nose, because he set out to sabotage your programme in a vicious way.'

'I guess.'

'As he doesn't appear to have been a disgruntled employee, he could be one of the people who lost out through these changes you introduced. You said your husband gave thousands away without asking what the company got back in publicity, and you mentioned bursaries in particular. Pardon my ignorance. What's a bursary?'

'Don't you know?' she said – and then winked. 'I didn't, either. I had to ask. It's when money is given to people in colleges for research and stuff. We were giving big, big sums to support nerds studying the behaviour of ants, for Christ's sake, guys in their mid-thirties who should have been earning a crust in an honest job like you and me.'

'Ants?'

'And other stuff. Polymers. What are they – parrots? British Metal was getting nothing back from it.'

'So you axed the bursaries and switched the funds into media projects like films and sport?'

'You bet I did!'

'You know what I'm thinking?' he said. 'Some of these nerds, as you call them, are deeply entrenched in their universities. What if one of them was so angry about losing his bursary that he decided on revenge? Do British Metal have a list of the people who lost out?'

'We must have,' she said.

'Any idea how many?'

'About ten. Not many more.'

'I'll get that list in the morning. Who would I ask? Mrs Poole, the lady I spoke to before?'

'She's the one.'

He looked at the time. 'I must get back to the lads downstairs. You have our number in case of a problem?'

She said in a plaintive voice, 'Does being without a man count as a problem?'

He winked. 'Surely not to someone who named herself after a nun.'

Only a short time after he was back on Bennett Street, a call came through on his mobile. 'Is this the nunnery?' he said playfully.

'No, matey,' said Hen's husky voice, 'it's Bognor CID.'

'*You?* You're working late.'

'Wasting my precious time,' she told him. 'I thought

351

I'd pass on the bad news. Neither of those Australian boys matches the fingerprints in Emma's car. They're back in the pub now. What am I going to do?'

'That's tough.'

'And how. I really thought we were getting somewhere. I've run out of suspects.'

He tried to give it thought. Difficult, when he was focused on the Mariner. 'Do you still think she was killed for the car?'

'Ninety per cent sure. Did I tell you her key was still in the ignition?'

'Was it definitely her personal key?'

'The evidence is pretty strong. It had a Bath University keyring.'

'So it was taken from her on the beach. You said ninety per cent sure. What's your ten per cent theory?'

'That he killed her for some other reason and took the bag and drove away the car to make identification difficult.'

'That isn't bad, Hen. He *did* hold us up. I'd give it better than ten per cent. This guy abandoned the Lotus at some caravan site, you said, and covered it from view, right?'

'Yes.'

'If he was only interested in nicking the car, why would he abandon it so soon after?'

'Panic. He went for a joyride, used up all the petrol in the tank—'

'Is that a fact?'

'Yes. Empty tank. I mean really empty, Peter. The needle was well down in the red section. I think he was scared to fill up. And in case you're in doubt whether someone would kill for a car, just read the papers. Casual murder is the feature of our age. People are killed for their phones, their purses, their clothes. Some old lady was beaten to death the other day for her shopping bag containing a packet of bacon and two tins of beans.'

He needed no convincing. Six months ago he'd handled a case of murder for a mountain bike. 'I didn't know about the empty tank. That does alter things. Your joyrider theory looks the best. Can I get back to you tomorrow on this? There's something stirring in my brain and it's not going to surface right away.'

'I'll listen to anything from your upper storey, my old love, even your fantasies about nuns.'

Thinking time was a luxury in the modern police. It had been largely replaced by sophisticated, high-tech intelligence-gathering. The Sherlock Holmes school of detection had long since been superseded by computers and people in zip-suits looking for DNA samples. So this silent night was a rare opportunity to bring some connected thought to bear on the mysteries of the beach strangler and the Mariner. He sat in his car across the street from Georgina's house and mused on the problems. Sherlock would have smoked a pipe – or three. Diamond had a Thermos of coffee and five bars of KitKat.

He was fairly certain that the Mariner had declared a private war on British Metal and its beneficiaries. The key was to find the cause of the hostility. It looked increasingly as if this murderer could have been a loser in the changes Anna had introduced. The peculiar character of the crimes, the use of the crossbow and the taunts picked from *The Ancient Mariner*, suggested an obsessive, embittered personality willing to take risks to make his point. This was a killer with a monstrous grudge. Two hapless people had died in a bizarre way simply because they were sponsored by the company. To use a chilling but apt phrase, he'd made examples of them. He'd issued a challenge by naming his second and third victims – a calculated risk offset by what seemed the ability not only to predict each precaution the police would take, but to outfox them as well and penetrate their security. Was he an insider, a rogue policeman?

Difficult to reconcile with the link to British Metal.

Yet he'd spirited his way into the safe house to snatch Matt Porter. It must have required inside knowledge to pull that off.

Diamond thought back to Bramshill and his visit there, to the people in the know about the case: that supercilious twit, Haydn Cameron, and his coy superior, the Big White Chief. Was it conceivable that the Mariner had a line into the staff college? Or into Special Branch itself? What of the officers guarding Matt Porter? Were they as loyal as they should have been? Was Jimmy Barneston entirely reliable? These were all trusted, long-serving officers.

In the morning, he would obtain that list of academics who had been deprived of their bursaries under Anna's new regime. It looked the most promising avenue now.

He opened his flask and sipped some coffee. The light was still on in the bedroom. He liked Anna, but with a few caveats. Sparkle, she'd called him. He didn't care for that. The sort of name you'd give to a clown. And she was turning Georgina's house into a tip. But essentially she was an original, a lively, good-humoured woman. If anything happened to her, he would not forgive himself.

He looked at the clock on the dashboard. Almost midnight. Presently he would do the round of his team, seeing if anyone had anything to report.

Before that, he gave some thought to the Wightview Sands murder. The finding of Emma Tysoe's sports car, empty of petrol and with the key still in the ignition, certainly suggested a joyrider, but was it likely someone would kill for the gratification of a drive in a car? Personally he hated travelling at high speed, yet he knew the fascination cars exerted on some people. You couldn't park a car like a Lotus in certain parts of Bath and expect to find it when you returned. The attraction was almost sexual. They saw a special model and lusted to possess it. Advertisers had tapped into that for years. Every night on the television you were persuaded that if you had a powerful motor your sex life would go into overdrive as well.

On a beach, where nothing was the same from one day to the next, where different people and different cars come and go, the temptation was strong. It wasn't difficult to conceive of some oddball who saw an attractive woman step out of a smart car and made up his mind to joyride it. The killing of the woman was a prelude to stealing the car, and the driving of it was the climax.

Horrible, yet not impossible.

Again, he was conscious of some elusive memory, a connection with all this that he couldn't pinpoint. He knew better than to force it. Let the subconscious work on it, he told himself. When I'm busy with something else it will come to me.

He screwed the top back on the flask and got out of the car and looked at the stars. Two thousand miles away, on the Nile, Georgina would be asleep in her cabin, travelling at a civilised speed, unaware of all this interest in her house. Thank God.

He strolled towards the Assembly Rooms at the end of the street, where one of the team was stationed in a doorway just out of the lamplight.

'How's it going?'

'Nothing to report, sir. A couple of people across the street came home ten minutes ago. That's all.'

'Stay tuned, then.'

The man at the Saville Row turn gave him a similar response. Most of Bath was asleep.

The sum of the sightings so far was three couples and about six cars, not one of which had stopped in Bennett Street.

He returned to his car. Out of interest he tried to find Galaxy 101, the radio station that had let the cat out of the bag. Instead, he got some inane chat show about people's experiences after eating curry. 'What sad people listen to these things?' he said aloud, turning up the volume.

At ten past three, the intercom beeped.

'Yes?'

'A guy on his own, coming up Lansdown, sir. He's got a backpack with something in it. Looks heavy. Shall I stop him?'

'No. Stay out of sight. Just watch him and report.'

'He's made the turn into Bennett. Coming your way.'

'OK.'

Another of the team, at the corner of Russell Street, announced that he could now see the man. Diamond turned in his seat and he had him in sight, too. Average height, baseball cap, both hands at his chest under the straps of the backpack, as if to ease the weight from his shoulders.

'What's he carrying – a computer he's knocked off?' the man on Russell Street said.

'If it is,' Diamond said, 'we're not interested.' This was a focused operation. 'Just watch where he goes.'

The man remained on the side of the street opposite Georgina's. He didn't cross. Presently, he went down some steps to a basement flat and let himself in. If he had been out burgling, he would never know how lucky he was.

* * *

356

At seven thirty in the morning, for his peace of mind, Diamond gave Anna a wake-up call.

She said, 'Piss off, will you? I'm asleep.'

At eight, the new team arrived to take over. Ingeborg had thoughtfully brought a doughnut and a bottle of spring water for Diamond.

'Everything's under control,' he told her. 'But you know my number. Keep me informed.' He also handed her the spare key of Georgina's front door.

'Aren't you going for a kip, guv?'

'Keep me informed. Anything at all. And stay in regular touch with Anna. You can go in there for breakfast if you want. A word of advice. Don't ask her to cook for you.'

He left her in charge. He was tired, but there were crucial things to be done.

Back in his office in Manvers Street, he phoned Hen.

She said with heavy disapproval, 'Is the world coming to an end? Have the Martians landed in Bognor? No one calls me before nine. Don't you know that, whoever you are?'

'Hen, this is Peter.'

'Buster, if you were Saint Peter I still wouldn't want to come to the phone this early.'

'Will you listen to me, Hen? I've been up all night.'

'So?'

'So, I've been trying to get a grip on a vague idea about Wightview Sands that seemed to be hovering somewhere in my brain. It came to me a short while ago.'

'Can it wait?'

'No. I want to pass it on to you now, for what it's worth.'

'Be my guest,' she said with a sigh.

'This joyriding theory of yours. If it's true, the killer was more interested in the car than the victim, right? The motive was to steal that handsome car and belt the life out of the engine for a couple of hours.'

'That about sums it up.'

'You said it's not the first time at Wightview. Am I right? Other cars – nice cars – have been nicked and later found abandoned?'

'Over the past year, yes.'

'You thought kids were responsible?'

She yawned. 'We've been over this before, Peter.'

'So what if we're dealing with a serial joyrider, someone who makes a habit of pinching cars from the beach? Generally he follows the owner onto the beach and waits for them to go for a swim, leaving their bag or clothes unprotected. Then he helps himself to the car key and drives off in their nice car.'

'That's the pattern.'

'Now, on this occasion, the owner didn't go for a swim. By all accounts, Emma Tysoe remained where she was, stretched out on the sand. Our thief watches her and waits . . . and waits. He can't snatch the bag containing the car key because she's being careful with it, keeping the shoulder strap close to her hand. He's tantalised. He really covets that car. In the end he decides to go for the bag while she's still there. He moves in. There's a struggle. She hangs onto her bag. Trying to get it away from him, she passes the strap over her head. He grabs it, twists and strangles her. That would explain the ligature. Or the strap came away from its fixing and he twisted the free end around her neck. Are you with me?'

'Just about,' Hen said. 'Where does it get us?'

'Back to the killer.'

'Some kid, you mean?'

'Maybe someone slightly older, but still nuts about cars, the man in the perfect position to pick out the one he wants to joyride, someone who sees every car drive in.'

He waited, wanting her to make the connection.

Finally she said, 'The car park attendant?'

'We know he was on duty in the morning when she drove in, because Ken Bellman saw him chatting with her, holding up the queue.'

'That was Garth,' she said. 'A weird guy with slicked-back hair. But we didn't consider him because he was on duty.'

'All day?' Diamond said with more than just a query in the voice. 'I don't think so. They wouldn't have one man in the kiosk for the whole of the day. Someone will have taken over by the afternoon.'

She was so long reacting that he wondered if the line had gone.

Finally she said, 'You're right. I was told on the day of the murder. Someone else came on duty at two. When I spoke to Garth he tried to give the impression he didn't leave the kiosk all day.'

'Giving himself an alibi?'

'When actually he was free to stalk Emma and murder her. Oh my God!'

'Worth getting his prints, anyway.'

'Peter, you're not so dumb as I thought.'

There was one more call to make, and this time he had to wait for office hours, so he went down to the canteen and ordered a proper breakfast.

'You're early, Mr D,' Pandora, the doyenne of the double entendre, said, her ladle ready with the baked beans.

'Late,' he said. 'I've been on duty all night.'

'So was my husband, poor lamb. He was glad to get out of bed and back to work this morning.'

He managed a tired grin.

At nine fifteen, he succeeded in getting through to Mrs

Poole at British Metal. She promised to check for the names he needed.

At nine forty, thinking only of bed, he opened the front door of his house in Weston and Sultan streaked out and into the front garden, pursued by Raffles. There were tufts of white cat fur all over the carpet.

24

Hen and Stella were on the road by nine, heading for the caravan park at Bracklesham. They'd been informed that Garth (now revealed as Garth Trumpington, twenty-six, unmarried) had a mobile home there. He'd been described by his employers as reliable and friendly, if a bit slow in dealing with the public. He'd held the car park job for just over a year. He drove an old Renault 5.

'The funny thing about mobile homes is that most of them aren't mobile at all. They're static,' Hen said as they drove into the park. 'The owners have no intention of moving them anywhere.'

Caravans and tents occupied most of the field. The more permanent homes were lined up on the far side. Hen steered a bumpy route around the edge and came to a stop near a woman who was hanging up washing behind her van, and asked if Garth was about.

'Third one from the end, if he's in,' the woman said. 'He works at the beach, you know, on the car park.'

'It's his late morning,' Hen said. 'We got that from the estate office. Do you know him?'

'He's all right,' she said. 'Bit of a loner, but that's up to him. He's paid for his bit of ground, hasn't he?'

They drove the short way to Garth's residence, a medium-sized cream-coloured trailer secured to the ground at each end. Some of the paint was peeling off the sides. A red Renault was parked close by.

'Velvet glove, at least to start off with,' Hen said to Stella.

The man was at home. He answered Hen's knock right away, opening the door a fraction to look out. From what Hen could see through the narrow space he was in khaki shorts and a white T-shirt. He hadn't shaved and his breath smelt.

'Garth, we've met at the beach,' Hen reminded him. 'DCI Mallin, Bognor CID, and this is DS Gregson.' They showed their IDs.

'What's up?' he said in a shocked tone.

'A few simple questions. May we come in?'

His brown eyes widened in alarm. 'No. It's not convenient.'

'Untidy, is it? Don't worry, Garth. We're used to that.'

'You can talk to me here.'

'Certainly we can talk to you here, but it's going to be overheard by some of your neighbours.'

Garth opened the door a little wider to look about him. As if on cue, a couple of small girls stepped in close to hear what was going on.

'If you prefer,' Hen said, raising her voice a fraction, 'we can do this at Bognor police station, but I don't suppose you want to make a big deal of it.'

'No, I don't,' he said.

'So may we come inside?' she asked, becoming curious as to what he wanted to hide from them. Was someone in there with him? Or was it evidence he didn't wish them to see?

'Can we do it in your car?'

This was a battle of wills, however gently it was being contested.

'No,' Hen said. 'We can't. What's your problem, Garth? Something to hide?'

He folded his arms as if to ward off the cold, even though it was a fine, warm morning. 'No.'

'Stolen goods?'

He shook his head.

'You see, you're making me suspicious before we start,' Hen said. She held out her hands in appeal. 'OK, if you're going to insist, we'll take you down to the nick.'

'I don't want that.'

Hen turned to Stella. 'Give the young man his official caution.'

Stella spoke the approved words at the speed of a tobacco auctioneer.

'Right,' Hen said. 'Step this way, Mr Trumpington.'

'I've got something cooking,' he said on an inspiration.

'Better see to it, then,' Hen said, putting her foot on the retractable step.

He tried shutting the door, and she said, 'Naughty,' and slammed the flat of her hand against it. Stella gave the door a kick and so it was that they gained admittance, forcing him back inside.

Of course there wasn't anything cooking, except possibly an alibi. They found themselves in the kitchen area, and there wasn't even a tap running. Hen stepped through to the living section and said, 'Now isn't this something? What do you make of the decor, Stell?'

Every portion of wall space was taken up with colour photos of cars. The ceiling was covered with them, too. And there were model cars on every surface: shelves, table, top of the TV set. A large stack of motoring magazines stood in one corner.

'Talk about bringing your work home . . .' Hen murmured.

'It's none of your business,' Garth was bold enough to say.

'We'll find that out,' Hen responded. 'Let's all sit down.'

Stella brought a stool from the kitchen and they started, Hen seated in the only armchair, Garth tense on the edge of a put-you-up.

'Cars are obviously your thing,' Hen commented. 'Is that your Renault outside?'

He nodded.

'I'd have thought a man like yourself would have gone in for something more flash, but I guess it's what you can afford. You see some really smart motors drive past your kiosk at Wightview Sands, I reckon. Do you ever get the urge to drive one of them?'

'No.' He was watchful, and his conversational knack had temporarily deserted him.

'The reason I ask is that we've had a spate of joyriding over recent months – from your car park, so I'm sure you know all about it. Nothing too serious. The cars are recovered later. Not much damage, if any. The doors aren't forced, because the joyrider goes to the trouble of borrowing the key, usually from clothes or handbags left on the beach. The owners are so pleased to get their cars back that they don't press charges. So it's one of those minor problems. Annoying, but not high priority for us. Would you know anything about it?'

'No.'

'Pity. Your advice would be taken seriously. You're well-placed to see what goes on.'

'I'm too busy issuing tickets,' he said, finding something to say in his defence.

'All day long?'

'While I'm there.'

'How long is that? A couple of hours at a time?'

'Longer,' Garth said. 'Four, five hours.'

'That's a long stint.'

'I do mine back to back for preference.'

'Then what do you do? Rush to the loo, I should think.'

He didn't smile. 'If I want to go during my duty hours, there are people I can ask.'

'OK,' Hen said. 'So you knock off after four or five hours. Is that your working day over?'

'Could be, unless I've promised to do another turn later.'

'Coming back to my question, how do you spend your time off?'

'I don't know,' he said. 'I might get something to eat. If it's nice, I could go on the beach.'

'And match up the drivers to the cars you fancy?'

'No.'

It was said a shade too fast. Hen paused, letting him squirm mentally. She was playing a tactical game here. Nothing had been said about the murder. The aim was to manoeuvre him first into admitting the joyriding episodes.

'You know a lot about cars. That's obvious. You must be an expert, Garth. A connoisseur.'

He didn't respond.

'You could probably tell me the makes of cars that were taken for joyrides in recent weeks. An MG. A Lancia. A Porsche.'

'No,' he said. 'You're wrong.'

'Wrong?'

'There was never a Porsche. That's wrong.'

'I believe you. You'd remember, I'm sure of that. It must have been something else in the sports-car line. But you confirm the MG and the Lancia, do you?'

'I didn't say I took them.'

'Borrowed them, Garth. Joyriding is only borrowing really, isn't it? What do you say, Stella? It's hardly a crime if the cars aren't damaged.'

Stella said, 'Kids' stuff.'

Hen said, 'We issue an unofficial warning usually. It's too much trouble to take them to court.'

Garth wiped some sweat from his forehead.

'We're inclined to be lenient if they admit to the joyriding, and haven't been caught before,' Hen continued. 'Mind you, if they deny it, we don't have much difficulty proving their guilt. They leave their fingerprints all over the cars, and those surfaces pick up the prints really well. Remind me, Stella, did we find prints in the MG?'

'And the Lancia,' Stella said, nodding.

'And the Porsche?'

'There wasn't a Porsche,' Garth blurted out.

'I keep forgetting,' Hen said. 'You should know. You're better placed to know than anyone else, aren't you? Did you go for a spin in the MG, Garth?'

'No.'

'The Lancia?'

He shook his head.

'So you're in the clear. You won't mind letting us take your fingerprints down at the nick just to remove all suspicion?'

She watched his hands clench, as if to press the telltale ridges out of shape. He was trapped. He said the only thing he could, knowing in his heart that it was hopeless.

'What if I said I took those cars for a ride?'

'Admitted it?'

'Yes.' His face had gone white.

'Admitted you were the joyrider?'

'Yes. Would you let me off with a warning, like you said? I wouldn't do it again, ever.'

Hen said, 'Let's get this clear, then. You've been taking cars from the car park without the owners' consent and driving them just for the pleasure of being at the wheel?'

'That's it,' Garth said, nodding vigorously. 'Just the pleasure. I wasn't stealing them.'

'But you stole the keys first. Tell us about that.'

'Borrowed them.'

'Borrowed them, then. How, exactly?'

He was forced to explain. 'I remembered who the owners were.'

'So what's the system? You chat to them from your kiosk, just to get a good look at them?'

'Usually, yes.'

'Go on, then.'

'When I go off duty, I go looking to see where the car I fancy is parked. Then I make a search for the owner. They nearly always pick a place on the beach near the car. I observe them. I might watch from the sea wall, or go down on the beach myself. I wait for them to go for a swim. Then I choose my moment to pick up a bag or some clothes with the keys.'

'What about the people around? Don't they say anything?'

He shook his head. 'Not if you do it with confidence. I know what I want and I go directly to it. The stuff goes into a beachbag and then I'm away and straight to the car. I find the key and drive off.'

Stella said, 'What about when you go past the barrier to get out? Aren't you afraid of one of the other attendants spotting you in a smart car?'

'They're facing the other way, checking the incoming cars.'

'You've got it all worked out,' Hen said. 'You're a smooth operator.'

'I'll stop now,' he said, desperate to draw a line under this. 'I knew it was wrong. It was getting to be a habit. I'm sorry. It was stupid of me.'

'I wouldn't mind if that's all it was,' Hen said.

'Unfortunately, Garth, we all know it's far more serious than you make out. The last time it happened, things went wrong, didn't they? There was a struggle for the bag containing the key. You killed the woman.'

'No,' he said vehemently. 'No, no – I didn't do that!'

'This joyriding was more than a habit. It was a compulsion. You had to get that key from her, and she didn't leave her bag unattended for one second. So you snatched it.'

'That isn't true.'

'And she wasn't asleep, as you thought. She was awake, and she tried to hang onto her bag, which was very unwise of her, because you panicked, thinking she would scream and make a scene, and you killed her.'

'No,' he said, his eyes stretched wide.

'OK,' Hen said calmly. 'We've got the fingerprints on the car – the dark green Lotus Esprit – and we'll check them against yours. You're under arrest, Garth. We're taking you for fingerprinting now.'

He gave a sob and sank his face into his hands. Any uncertainty was resolved in that moment.

25

Diamond finally got to bed at ten fifteen that morning, later than he wished, and with a Band-Aid on his right hand. He'd had to get out the ladder to collect Sultan from one of the high branches of the hawthorn in the front garden. Reluctant to be dislodged from this place of safety, Georgina's pet had let Diamond know with a couple of swift, efficient paw movements, almost causing him to tip backwards. Only with the greatest difficulty had he brought the terrified cat down the ladder. All of this had been observed from the front-room window by Raffles with an expression of supreme contempt.

The exhausted man sank immediately into a deep sleep, blanking out everything. So when Ingeborg phoned him from Bennett Street twenty minutes later, he slept through the sound. After an hour the phone beeped again, this time with more success, because he happened to be turning over. He groaned, swore and reached for it.

'Guv, are you there?'

All he could manage was another groan.

'Guv? This is Keith Halliwell. It's an emergency.'

'Mm?'

'We just heard from one of the lads on watch in Bennett Street.'

Bennett Street. Bennett Street, Bennett Street. The conscious mind groped for a connection. He forced himself to pay attention.

'Ingeborg put in a routine call about ten thirty to make sure Anna Walpurgis was all right and got no answer. She tried several more times. Nothing. She tried calling you as well, and you didn't answer. In the end she acted on her own and used the key to let herself in.'

'Oh, Christ.' He was fully awake.

'And now we can't raise her, either.'

He felt as if the floor caved in and he dropped a hundred levels. 'Tell them to go in after her – all of them. I'm coming at once. Get everyone there you can. This is it, Keith!'

Recharged and ready to go, he threw on some clothes, dashed out to the car and drove to Bennett Street at a speed he would normally condemn as suicidal.

Two response vehicles had got there before him. Halliwell was also there, ashen-faced, standing in the open doorway.

'Well?'

'Come and look at this, guv.'

In the hallway of Georgina's house someone had used a red marker pen to write on the wall in large letters:

The game is done! I've won, I've won!

Diamond stood blankly before it, shaking his head. He felt a throbbing sensation in his legs. Not the shakes. Not now. He didn't want to get the shakes.

He knew the line, and he was certain who'd written it. There was a scene in *The Rime of the Ancient Mariner* when Death was dicing with Life-in-Death for the ship's crew and everyone except the Mariner himself dropped dead.

Halliwell said, 'We've been right through the building. There's no one in there, guv.'

'There won't be.' Still staring at the wall, Diamond crossed his arms over his chest to control his hands. They *were* starting to shake. 'What's written here is the truth. He's beaten us. I don't know how, but he's done it. He's got to Anna, and he's got Ingeborg as well.'

One of the team on duty said in his own defence, 'We've had round-the-clock surveillance, sir. No one went in except DC Smith.'

'You *saw* no one go in,' Diamond said without even turning his head to look at the speaker.

'But the place is empty. He got out as well, with the two women. It's a bloody impossibility.'

'Shut up, will you?' He looked to his right. 'Keith.'

'Guv?'

'The roof. These are terraced houses. The roof is the only way I can think of.'

Together they ran upstairs, up two storeys to the attic, a surprisingly spacious room with surprising contents – the secret Anna had wanted to impart to Diamond. Eccentric, weird even, but harmless and of small consequence now. Georgina's attic was occupied by a family of people-sized teddy bears dressed in knitted garments and seated around a table laid for tea with real cups and saucers and a plate of biscuits. 'Try the window,' Diamond said, blotting out the rest of the scene.

It was a small double-sash, and Halliwell made an effort to shift it, but with no success. 'I don't think this has been opened, guv.'

Diamond had a go, and felt the resistance. The thing wouldn't budge a fraction.

'Look, it's been painted over at some time,' Halliwell said, pointing to where the bottom rail of the window met the sill. An unbroken coat of paint connected them. 'He didn't go this way.'

'Bloody hell. How did he do it, then? The back of the house?'

'I don't think so. Every door and window is still locked

from the inside. She had locks on all the ground-floor windows and fingerbolts on the door.'

Diamond pressed his hands to his forehead and shut his eyes, desperate to make the mental leap that was required. It wasn't for want of trying that he didn't succeed. But there was another way to approach this problem, and he had the vision to recognise it. All he'd done so far in this emergency was what the Mariner would have predicted, reacting to events by trying to understand them, charging up the stairs in the hope of finding which way the Mariner had escaped with the two women. Truly there wasn't time for that. Ingeborg and Anna had been missing for an hour already. Not much could be gained from discovering how it had been done.

He said to Halliwell, 'Where has he taken them? That's the priority. That's what we've got to work out.'

Halliwell didn't say a word. The answer was beyond him.

Beyond Diamond, too, it seemed. He shook his head and sighed heavily. After a long interval, he started to talk, more to himself than Halliwell. 'This man has a sense of the dramatic. He went to all the trouble and risk of leaving Porter's body on the eighteenth hole of a golf course – just for the effect. The act of murder wasn't enough. It had to be done in the most symbolic way. He'll have worked out something for Anna, some place of disposal that he considers fitting. But where?'

Where? His body strained to *do* something, to race off in some direction with sirens blaring and stop the killing. But until his brain supplied the answer, any action would be futile. While he floundered like this, apparently indecisive but actually groping for the truth, two lives were on the line, for nothing was more certain than that the Mariner would kill again.

Georgina's giant teddies, immobile in their chairs, reinforced the inertia in his brain. He couldn't stay in the room any longer. 'No use standing here,' he told Halliwell. He led the way downstairs, still trying to animate his tired, shocked brain. But the physical action of moving about the house was no help. It solved nothing. Down on ground level again, he was still without an explanation or a plan.

Forcing himself to face the worst outcome, he tried once again to work out the Mariner's strategy. In all probability, he'd have killed Ingeborg first. Inge, poor kid, was extraneous to the plot. She'd walked into the crossfire because of inexperience and blind courage and the stupid overconfidence of her boss. I should never have left her in charge, he told himself. I could have stopped her if I hadn't slept through the call they say she made to me. God knows I've made mistakes before, but this is the worst ever.

And I failed Anna, the Mariner's target, the last name on the death list, that free spirit, railing against all the constrictions in her witty, boisterous way, yet actually resting her trust in me. Arrogantly, I assumed I could protect her. How wrong we both were!

Self-recrimination wasn't going to help.

Instead, he forced his thinking back to the Mariner and his embittered plot. He visualised the execution of Anna, first tied up, or drugged senseless, then despatched, almost certainly by a crossbow bolt to the head. The body would be driven to whichever location the Mariner had selected as appropriate.

The game is done! I've won, I've won!

Think ahead, he urged himself. It's the only chance I've got now. I have to out-think him, anticipate him for once. He's already picked the place where her body will be discovered, somewhere fitting, or symbolic, like that eighteenth hole. He wants the world to know how clever he is. Where is it?

Somewhere appropriate to Anna. Her pop music career? Some place that links with a song title. Or her name?

No, he told himself. The Mariner isn't interested in her career. He's entirely taken up with the part of her life that affected him. If I'm right, and he was one of those academics whose bursaries were taken away, he blames her personally for that. This is the climax of his killing spree. He'll have thought of something that makes the point. He's been hitting back at British Metal by killing the people they sponsor, but Anna is different from Summers or Porter. She hurt him. He'll turn her death into some emblem of his anger.

Now something was beginning to stir in his memory. Faint and tenuous, just out of reach, it tantalised him for what seemed an intolerable interval before vanishing again.

He felt certain it was significant, and it derived from personal experience, an observation he'd made some time ago, not in the last twenty-four hours, or even the last week. Surely, he reasoned with himself, if it's of any significance, it must have a connection with British Metal.

And now the image surfaced. Concorde taking off.

Because it's British Metal.

He gave a cry that was part triumph, part self-reproach. He'd got there at last. That mechanical billboard he'd driven past on Wellsway with the rotating images. The slogan perfectly summed up the Mariner's twisted rationale. All the bitterness, his justification for the killing, was encapsulated in those four words.

He explained his reasoning to Halliwell. 'And as far as I know,' he added, 'it's the only one of its kind in the city. Have you seen another?'

'No, guv. I know the sign you mean. Shall we go?'

He thought for a moment and shook his head. 'I'd bet anything that's where he means to leave the body, but not in broad daylight. It's too busy up there. He'll go tonight, when it's dark.'

'And then we ambush him?'

'Too late, Keith. He'll have killed them both already. Remember he killed Matt Porter first and transported the body to the golf course. We've got to find him before tonight.'

The disappointment in both men was palpable, although nothing was said. Even when you achieved the aim of anticipating this killer's movements, it wasn't enough.

Halliwell started stating the obvious just to fill the silence. 'Nobody saw them leave. He'd need transport. Every car in the street has been checked.'

'Then they're still here.'

'No, guv. I promise you, I went through every room myself.'

'Including the basement?'

Halliwell nodded. 'It's filled with cartons and packing material for the boss's electrical appliances, and, believe me, we looked in every box.'

'Was it locked?'

'The basement?'

'*Yes*. Was it locked?'

'The door to the street was. And bolted. As I told you, all the external doors in the house were locked, and none of them show any sign of being tampered with.'

'I'm going to take a look myself. The stairs down?'

'The internal staircase? Next to the kitchen.'

Diamond stepped out of the front room into the hall. An internal door was fitted at the top of the basement stairs. The lock had obviously been forced, the strike plate ripped from the woodwork. 'Who did this?'

'We did. She keeps it locked. There wasn't time to go looking for the key.'

'What if the key was in the lock and the Mariner locked it himself and took the key with him?'

Halliwell stared back with a slight frown, failing to see what difference it would make.

Without adding to his question, Diamond pulled open the door, switched on the light and went down into the basement. Just as it had been described to him, the back room, the largest, was in use as a box room, each box labelled.

'They were stacked tidily when we came in,' Halliwell said.

Diamond rapidly checked the other rooms. In the front room was a second door. 'What's this – a cupboard?'

'Sort of,' Halliwell said. 'It's more storage space, but she doesn't use it. Actually it's a kind of cellar. Goes right under the street. All these old houses have them. There's no one in there. Just some wood and a heap of coal left by a previous owner.'

Diamond opened the door. 'Someone get me a torch.'

One was handed to him and he probed the interior with the beam. He'd have called this a vault. Basically it was a single arch constructed of Bath stone, and tall enough to drive a bus through, except that a wall blocked off the end. Yet it was obvious no living creature larger than a spider was lurking there.

Halliwell said, 'It's not connected to any other house, if that's what you were thinking, guv. They used them as wine cellars two hundred years ago. There's been a lot of concern about them because they weren't built to support the modern traffic going over them.'

Diamond stepped around a dust-covered heap of coal that had probably been there since the Clean Air Act came in, and moved towards the back wall. He swung the torch beam over the stonework and bent down to look at some chips of broken mortar he'd noticed among the coal. 'This is recent.'

Halliwell came closer.

Diamond shone the torch close to the wall itself. 'You see where this comes from? Some of these blocks of stone have been drilled out and moved. They're not attached to anything. The wall isn't surface-bearing here. It's just a screen to separate this side of the street from the house opposite. Someone has broken through and replaced everything later.'

Halliwell crouched down to look. 'Sonofabitch!'

Now it was Diamond who felt the need to speak the obvious. 'He must have got in from the house across the street, down into their basement. He got to work on some stones in the wall and cut his way through. And that's the way he got out with his prisoners. When they were through he shoved the blocks back into position from the other side.'

'But the door to the basement was locked,' Halliwell said.

'From the inside. He locked it when he left, and took the key with him. I don't believe it was locked when he came in the first time. It was in the lock, but he was able to open the door and get into the house.'

'Cunning bastard,' Halliwell said. 'And none of us spotted this.'

'You were looking for people, not means of entry.' Diamond's mind was on the next decision, not past mistakes.

'I can shift this lot, no trouble,' Halliwell said.

'Not yet. We'll go in from upstairs. Get some men down here, but have them in radio contact, ready to go when I say, and not before.'

'Armed Response are waiting in the street.'

'Good. But I don't want a shoot-out in a confined space. He's got his hostages and he'll have his crossbow with him. We don't know what we'll find when we go in.'

He ran upstairs and out to the street. It was already closed to traffic. He briefed the inspector in charge of the ARU, telling him how he proposed to handle the situation. Men were posted at strategic points. Diamond was fitted with a radio.

Exactly as he expected, there were signs of a break-in when he went down the basement steps of the house across the street from Georgina's. The door had been forced with some kind of jemmy. Like several of the basements along the street, this one was unoccupied, though the flats on the upper floors were all in use.

With two armed officers close behind him, Diamond entered as silently as possible, stood in the passageway and listened. The place was ominously quiet. He felt the cool air on his skin. He waited a moment, letting his eyes adjust to the restricted light. Then he reached for the handle of the door to the front room, the one with access to the vault below the street.

Nobody was in this unfurnished room, so he crossed to the door to the vault and cautiously opened it. One glance confirmed that no one was inside. However, there were tools lying against the wall, including a power drill, hammer and chisels. Any lingering doubt was removed that the Mariner had been here.

Turning away, he indicated to the marksmen that he would check the other rooms. He returned to the passageway and looked into a small room once used as a kitchen. Nothing was in there except some bottled water.

There remained the back room, presumably used as a

bedroom when the flat was occupied. He looked towards the back-up men and gestured to them with a downward movement of his hand. He wasn't going to rush in. The door was slightly ajar, so he put his foot against it and gently pushed it fully open.

A crossbow was targeted at his chest. The Mariner, in baseball cap and leather jacket, stood against the wall. Beside him, on the floor, were two motionless bodies.

Diamond's heart raced and a thousand pinpricks erupted all over his skin. For this was a triple shock. There was the sight of the dead-still women; there was the threat from the crossbow; and there was the hammer blow of who the Mariner was. With a huge effort to keep control he managed to say, 'It's all over, Ken. I wouldn't shoot if I were you. Killing me isn't in the script.'

But Ken Bellman kept the crossbow firmly on target.

Ken – boring old Ken, the lover Emma Tysoe had dumped without ever realising he was the killer she'd been asked to profile. Ken, the man Diamond and Hen had put through the wringer, or so they believed. Ken – the wrongly accused, the man who'd proved beyond doubt that he didn't carry out the murder on the beach.

Ken Bellman was the Mariner.

Diamond's best – his only – option was to talk, steadily and as calmly as he could manage, as if he'd fully expected to be facing this. 'You're not going to shoot that thing. You've settled the score, several times over. If you take me out – as you could – you'll be gunned down yourself. The men behind me are armed.'

'Hold it there,' Bellman said, his eyes never shifting from Diamond. They looked dead eyes. He, too, was in deep shock. This was a petrifying humiliation for him and he was dangerous. He'd believed himself invincible.

'The game is done, just as you wrote on the wall,' Diamond said with a huge effort to keep the same impassive tone, 'and if you say you won, well who am I to argue? You outwitted the best brains in the Met and you had me on a string until a few minutes ago. I watched you arrive last night with your rucksack full of tools, and still I wasn't smart enough to twig who you were, or what you were up to. OK, you didn't get to your last location. That advertising board on Wellsway, wasn't it? "Because it's British Metal". Give me credit for working that out for myself. I don't take much out of this. And now I'm asking you to call it quits.' He took a step towards the crossbow.

Bellman warned in an agitated cry, 'Don't move!'

But Diamond took another step, spreading his palms to show he was unarmed. This had become a contest of will power. 'I'm going to ask you to hand me the crossbow, Ken. Then we'll have a civilised talk, and you can tell me how you managed to achieve so much.'

'I won't say it again!'

Diamond had taken three or four short steps and was almost level with the feet of one of the bodies. He said, 'You know you're not going to shoot now.'

Then the unexpected happened. There was a moan from one of the women and Bellman reacted. He swung the crossbow downwards and released the bolt.

In the same split second, Diamond threw himself forward and grabbed at the bow with both hands. The bolt missed Anna Walpurgis's head by a fraction and hit the floor with a metallic sound, skidded towards the nearest corner and ricocheted off a couple of walls. Bellman let go of the bow and lurched backwards. The two ARU men hurled themselves on him.

Suddenly the room was full of noise and people. Hands gripped Diamond's arms and hauled him upright. 'Get to the women,' he said. 'Are they all right?'

They were both alive. Their arms and legs were bound.

Anna vomited when the straps came off her. Ingeborg said, 'It's the chloroform. He used it on both of us, several times.'

'But you're OK?'

Anna said in a croak, 'Thanks to you, Sparkle. Man oh man, that was bloody heroic!'

26

Ken Bellman was forced to wait twenty-four hours before having the satisfaction of telling his story to the chief investigating officers. Diamond needed to catch up on his sleep. Hen Mallin wanted to tie up another case before leaving Bognor. And Jimmy Barneston had been called urgently to the staff college at Bramshill.

A lot more happened in that twenty-four hours.

Anna Walpurgis, quickly and fully restored, moved out of Bennett Street and back into the Bath Spa Hotel. From there, she made a series of shopping trips, contributing handsomely to the economy of the city. As well as buying five new outfits for herself, she treated Ingeborg to a stunning red leather suit. And there was a present for Diamond: a widescreen TV and DVD player combined, with a disc of herself in concert. 'Just so you don't ever forget the broad whose life you saved, Pete.'

Red-faced, he thanked her.

Keith Halliwell's skills as a home decorator were put to good use in Georgina's house, repapering the wall the Mariner had defaced with the red marker. A team of professional cleaners went through the building, tidying up and restoring the place to inspection order.

In Bognor, Garth Trumpington was charged with the murder of Dr Emma Tysoe. His fingerprints matched those on the stolen car. A check with the duty roster at Wightview Sands car park showed he'd been in the kiosk when Emma arrived on the day of the murder and off duty at the time she was killed. He asked if he would get a lighter sentence if the court was told he hadn't meant to strangle her. He claimed that the shoulder strap of her bag got entangled around her neck and tightened while he was struggling with her. No one would venture an opinion on that one.

So it was early on Thursday afternoon when Ken Bellman and his solicitor were ushered into interview room two at Manvers Street, where Diamond, Hen and Barneston were already seated. The solicitor's presence was only a formality. One glance at Bellman told them he was as eager as the Ancient Mariner himself to tell his story, all they wanted to know, and much they didn't. He'd been caught with the murder weapon in his hands and made no attempt to conceal his guilt. He intended to justify his actions now. Nothing would stop him. The glittering eye was all too apparent. *The Mariner hath his will.*

'None of this would have happened if British Metal hadn't pulled the rug from under my research project,' he said with control, taking his time. 'The work I was doing up at Liverpool won't mean much to anyone who isn't in electronics, but it was the culmination of years of study. All I wanted was the chance to get on with my project. It was my purpose in life. I got up every day eager to do more.' He paused to register the impact of the outrage against him. 'Imagine how I felt when I was told by the head of department that I'd lost my funding through no fault of my own. There was no appeal, and no other possibility of finding another sponsor. I was out. Overnight. Later, I was told about this woman Anna Walpurgis being the new broom at British Metal and wanting to make sure the sponsorship money brought a return for the company. Sickening.'

'Did you try for some funding from anywhere else?' Hen asked.

'Wasted a month and a hell of a lot of energy writing to other firms. *"We're fully committed for the next eighteen months." "We regret to say we're cutting back on sponsorship because of the economic downturn in our industry."* Blah, blah, blah. I gave up and came south and got a job in London. What a comedown.'

'In electronics?'

'A security firm installing anti-theft systems.'

'This was in central London?' Diamond put in, understanding how it tied in.

'The head office is. They're very big. I worked all over the south.'

'And I suppose they had the contract for Special Branch?'

He said with a superior smile, 'You're catching on. We won the contract to upgrade the security on all their properties. I designed the circuits. I had to be vetted, of course. They're very sensitive about who they employ. But I'm cleaner than clean. I was given the top security rating.'

Jimmy Barneston muttered, 'Bloody hell.' Special Branch had blamed him for their failings. He'd come here straight from a roasting by the Bramshill overlords.

'And that's how I got to know the codes for all the latest safe houses. They came in useful when I wanted to spring Matthew Porter.'

Barneston's eyes flickered keenly. 'So you had all this planned from way back?'

'No, I only decided to get my revenge on British Metal when I saw an item on TV about them putting a huge amount of money into a film, something about upgrading an arthouse film into a blockbuster movie. That really got to me. I mean, my bursary was peanuts to what Summers was given for this crap film about a two-hundred-year-old *poem.* How does mankind benefit from that? These ponces who make films are burning up millions on things that add nothing to people's knowledge. My work was important, and real, and I'm not bullshitting when I tell you it would have been a notable contribution to computer science. A few days later I saw in the paper that this kid Porter had been handed a fortune by British Metal just because he can roll a small white ball into a hole. I flipped. I've never been so angry in my life.'

'But you didn't kill in anger,' Diamond said.

A new quality came into Bellman's voice, a distinct note of pride. 'That isn't my style at all. I approached it as a scientist should, starting by assembling all the information I had at my disposal and then deciding how to maximise its potential. The objective was to damage British Metal and its sponsorship programme.'

Hen said, 'Couldn't you have done that without resorting to murder?'

He gave her a surprised look. 'How? I needed to make an impact with newspaper headlines. Letters to the editor won't do that. Protest vigils? What do they achieve? Sudden death is the only thing that gets through to people in these violent times. Listen to the news any day and you'll see that I'm right. I needed a campaign that guaranteed those headlines. I'm not squeamish. I can do what's necessary to get attention.'

'Taking life?' Hen said, making clear her revulsion.

'How about *my* life?' he said, his voice rising. 'My research was trashed, my academic reputation, my hopes and dreams and all the work I'd already put in. Nobody gave a damn about me. My future, my career, was tossed aside to give even bigger handouts to these fat cats. I saw no problem in putting them down. As I was telling you, I worked from my strengths. First, my inside knowledge of the security arrangements in the latest safe houses.

Second, I'd seen a former university friend on TV.'

'Emma Tysoe.'

'Emma, yes.' He grinned at Diamond and there was total contempt in the way he said, 'You tried to pin the wrong murder on me, didn't you? Got it all wrong. I didn't kill Emma. She was far too useful to me. But I mustn't jump ahead. One evening I happened to watch this programme about psychological offender profilers and there was a face I knew, a girlfriend from my student days, being called out to all the most difficult cases of serial murder. She was now a star in the profiling world. Based at Bath University. Quite a celebrity. I decided to renew the friendship.'

'You moved to Bath just to get friendly with her again?'

'The timing couldn't have been better. Once I'd decided to make use of my inside knowledge of safe houses it was sensible to get out of the security systems job as soon as possible, and I have no family arrangements. I can live anywhere I can find a job, so I applied for the IT post with Knowhow & Fix. Easy little number for me, low profile and flexible hours. And just as you were saying, I started going out with Emma. I knew she was likely to be brought into the investigation once they began to see how complex it was, and even if they used someone else, Emma was close enough to the police to feed me some inside knowledge.'

'Luckily for you, she *was* assigned to the case,' Diamond said. He wanted to encourage this frank talking. 'So you were firing on all cylinders.'

But Bellman didn't want anything to sound easy. 'Luck didn't come into it. Haven't you been listening? I calculated that she would be of use to me. I went to no end of trouble to revive that friendship.'

'I follow you,' Diamond said, indulging him. 'It was deliberate.'

Hen said, 'As cold-blooded as that?'

He didn't rise to the comment. Clearly he saw no problem in cynically exploiting a relationship. 'Well, I got my plan under way. I put down Summers, the first of the fat cats. And seeing how everything comes down to presentation these days, I decided to dress up the action with an Ancient Mariner theme. Remarkable, isn't it? A lot of that poem could have been written with me in mind.'

Jimmy Barneston made a sound of displeasure deep in his throat. He was a restless presence, locked into his own disappointment.

'The crossbow?' Diamond prompted Bellman. 'Where did you get that?'

'A man in Leeds who works in the Royal Armouries Museum and makes replicas as a hobby. I heard of him through the internet. You've seen the bow, haven't you?'

'Pointing at my chest, thank you.'

He nodded. 'It's a beautiful weapon, easy to use, quick and efficient. I guess it will end up in the Black Museum. It deserves no less.'

'So you murdered Axel Summers . . .'

'. . . and set the whole thing in motion.' Bellman smoothly completed the statement. The memory of the killing didn't appear to trouble him at all. 'The blueprint was there from the beginning, as you know, because I shared it with you. I gave you people the names of the second and third victims. Has that ever been done before in the history of crime? I don't think so. The whole point was to force you to send Porter and Walpurgis to the high-security safe houses I could break into, and it worked. I knew a lot about the thinking of Special Branch.'

'Through Emma?'

'She was brought in very soon, as I calculated. She wasn't all that keen to talk to me about the case, but she confided her thoughts to her computer – which, naturally,

I updated and made secure for her – so, knowing her password, I could hack in when I wanted and read her latest findings. Highly instructive, even down to the progress of our relationship. I have to admit I'm not the world's most expert lover, and it wasn't all complimentary. In fact, my plans began to go adrift when that oversexed detective on the case started his own relationship with her.'

Barneston blinked and sat forward, jerked out of his introspection. 'What did you say?'

Bellman continued with the narrative. 'Emma did her best to dump me, as you know. That's how I nearly got my fingers burnt, trailing after her, trying to cling onto her. She wasn't indispensable to the project, but she was my window on you people, so I didn't intend to lose her.'

A phrase Emma had used of the Mariner came back to Diamond: 'emotionally disconnected'. Much of what she had deduced about him was accurate.

'You followed her to the beach and tried to talk her round,' Hen said.

Bellman said with his self-admiring grin, 'And so became your number one suspect. I had to keep my nerve then. Have you found the actual killer yet? I'm sure it was an opportunist murder. Poor Emma! She didn't deserve that, even though she was stupid enough to give me the brush-off.'

'You had your alibi, the petrol receipt,' Diamond said. 'All that stuff about losing it under your handbrake wasn't true, was it? You were stringing me along.'

'Dead right, Mr Diamond, and do you know why?'

'Because it distracted me from your real crimes.'

'Come on now.' He curled his fingers in a sarcastic beckoning gesture. 'You can do better than that. Thanks to your interest in me, I was on the inside again, getting a sense of what was going on here, in the police station.

I knew Walpurgis was in Bath at that hotel, and I guessed you would move her to some other house when you discovered I was on the scent.'

'It was on the radio about her being in Bath,' Diamond said to make clear he hadn't been entirely taken in.

'Right. And give me my due. I played fair. I let you know I was up with the news. I sent a little message to Walpurgis at the hotel. I hope they passed it on.'

'" . . . a frightful fiend doth close behind her tread."'

'She got it then. Excellent. As I was saying, I was perfectly willing to spend time at your nick listening out for the gossip. When I was first brought in, the news was just going around that the ACC was going on holiday. When I came back to show you the receipt, I had a nice chat with the desk sergeant, a bit of a joke about the boss being away. He got very cagey when I mentioned her. It didn't require rocket science to find out where you were holding Walpurgis.'

'Where did you get her address? She's ex-directory.'

'She's the only female ACC, and her name is often in the local press. She isn't in the phone book, as you say, but she votes in elections. She's in the electoral register. People forget how simple it is to check up on them. I went to the library and asked to see the register. It's all in the public domain.'

'We know you got into the house opposite during the night. You'll admit you were lucky the basement wasn't lived in?'

'No,' he said, affronted by the suggestion. 'Empty basements are the norm if you walk along Bennett Street. Either that, or they're in use as store places. Let's be frank. Your so-called security was seriously at fault, Mr Diamond. It was rubbish.'

'We caught you, didn't we? Where did you get your chloroform?'

'My old university. They kept a row of bottles in one of the labs. Chloroform has gone out of fashion for anaesthetics, but it's still widely used as a solvent.' He smiled. 'The effect of inhaling the stuff is rather enjoyable before the victim goes under. Ask Ingeborg. She might remember.'

'I told you all this was on tape,' Diamond said.

'I heard you.'

'You've admitted to everything.'

'I'm not ashamed of it, either. I look forward to my day in court, when I shall repeat it all for a wider audience.'

Such self-congratulation was hard to stomach. The entire performance had been repellent. Murderers of Ken Bellman's type, seeing themselves as the maltreated victims, are the most unrepentant. True, he had a genuine grievance at the beginning. But the vengeance he took was out of all proportion. He had expressed not a word of remorse for the killing of people who had done nothing to damage him. As he said it himself, they were 'put down'. It was as callous as that.

Diamond walked to the car park with Barneston and Hen.

'I feel as if I need a shower after that,' Hen said.

'I practically thumped him for one thing he said,' Barneston said.

Neither of the others asked what.

'And he still thinks he's the bee's knees,' Hen said.

'But none of that came out when we interviewed him for the beach murder,' Diamond said. 'I thought he was a weak character at the time.'

'A piece of pond life, you called him.'

'He's that, for sure. But I didn't see him as the Mariner. He fooled us, Hen, and I blame myself. I was doing the interview.'

'And I was asking you to soft-pedal,' she said. 'Don't knock yourself, Peter. You got everything else right. The British Metal connection and the fact that he was a pissed-off academic. Did you ever get that list of the people who lost their bursaries?'

'On my desk.'

'And was his name on it?'

'Yes. I just didn't get a chance to see it on the morning we nicked him.'

'But you would have got there,' Hen insisted. 'You did all right. And I hate to say that you solved my murder for me, by fingering Garth, but let's face it, you did. I was up a gum-tree with those Aussie lads.' She opened her car door and then held out her hand to him. 'But don't let it go to your head. You're still a pushy bastard.'

On the day Georgina Dallymore returned from her Nile cruise and let herself into the house in Bennett Street, Sultan was curled up as usual in his basket in the hall. The big ball of fur opened both eyes briefly but didn't get out to greet her.

'Exhausted, are you, my darling?' she said. 'That makes two of us. But the difference is, I've got every right to be tired. I've had such an exciting time.'

The place looked immaculate, maybe even better than she'd left it. You wouldn't know anyone had stayed here. Yet when she opened the visitors' book, there was the name of Anna Walpurgis with the date and the comment, 'I'll always remember my visit here.' How good it was to come home to a tidy house and a famous name in the visitors' book and a contented cat, she thought. The house sitter had been one of Peter Diamond's better suggestions.

Other bestselling Time Warner Books titles available by mail:

☐ The Last Detective	Peter Lovesey	£6.99
☐ Bloodhounds	Peter Lovesey	£6.99
☐ Upon a Dark Night	Peter Lovesey	£6.99
☐ The Vault	Peter Lovesey	£6.99
☐ The Reaper	Peter Lovesey	£6.99
☐ Diamond Dust	Peter Lovesey	£5.99
☐ Dead Gorgeous	Peter Lovesey	£5.99

The prices shown above are correct at time of going to press. However, the publishers reserve the right to increase prices on covers from those previously advertised without further notice.

TIME WARNER
BOOKS

TIME WARNER BOOKS
PO Box 121, Kettering, Northants NN14 4ZQ
Tel: 01832 737525, Fax: 01832 733076
Email: aspenhouse@FSBDial.co.uk

POST AND PACKING:
Payments can be made as follows: cheque, postal order (payable to Time Warner Books), credit card or Switch Card. Do not send cash or currency.

All UK Orders	**FREE OF CHARGE**
EC & Overseas	25% of order value

Name (BLOCK LETTERS) . . . .

Address . . . .

. . . .

Post/zip code: . . . .

☐ Please keep me in touch with future Time Warner publications

☐ I enclose my remittance £ . . . .

☐ I wish to pay by Visa/Access/Mastercard/Eurocard/Switch Card

Card Expiry Date ☐☐☐☐   Switch Issue No. ☐☐